# SNOW SPIRITS

*Children of the Wild*

by

## MARCI BAUN

**Wild Child Publishing**
*Culver City, California*

Editor: S.R. Howen

ISBN: 978-1-61798-199-9, print
978-1-61798-198-2, eBook

If you are interested in purchasing more works of this
nature, please stop by www.marcibaun.com.

Wild Child Publishing.com
Culver City, CA 90231

Printed in The United States of America

# Acknowledgements

I'd like to thank my husband Charlie, my child, and my mother for all of their love, support, and encouragement, my Area 42 beta crit read group (Shawn Howen, Steve Anderson, Julie Duncan, Kayelle Allen, and Jackie Leigh Allen) who helped me kill my darlings and write a better book, Lin Morel for her continued support and guidance, Lizzie Dunlap for the amazing cover art, Wei-Lin for her help with the Mandarin, Jenn Nixon for her marketing savvy and friendship, and, again, my friend Shawn Howen for the hours of phone discussions, talking me off ledges, and just being there when I needed a sympathetic ear (or a kick in the pants, whichever was most appropriate at the time).

# Mandarin Glossary

àikòu—love button, clitoris
báijiǔ—Chinese rice liquor
bakkwa—a dried meat similar to jerky
bàoyú—abalone, but also an implied way to say pussy
bharal—Himalayan blue sheep/mountain sheep
chiru—antelope on the Tibetan steppes
chǔnlǘ—idiot. Literally, stupid donkey and term of abuse.
dìyù—the Chinese version of hell. It's based on the Buddhism concept of Naraka and has 18 layers
gōnglǐ—a Chinese distance equivalent to 1 kilometer or .62 miles
hàntǎ—marmot
jījī—literally means "thingy" only when it means cock
jūnshì zhǎng—master sergeant
làmèi—spice girls. This can be considered flirtatious or derogatory, depending on the context.
láng—wolves
lǎoshǔ—mouse
liàn rén—beloved, lover, sweetheart
luòtuó—camel
nǐ hǎo—hello
nián—year
māo—cat
mǐ—this is a Chinese measurement and equivalent to 3.28 feet, or the same length as a meter; also can mean rice.
nián—year
nǚ'ér—daughter
pán yáng—mountain goat; argali
qīn›ài de—darling
qípáo—a close-fitting woman's dress with high neck and slit skirt; cheongsam; mandarin gown; a popular Chinese wedding dress in the 1920s
tánggǔ—traditional Chinese drum
shàngwèi—captain; guard, imperial bodyguard

*shānshàng de guǐ*—ghost of the mountains; how the Chinese sometimes refer to snow leopards
*shi*—yes
*sǐ*—die
*tā mā de*—fuck, shit, damn it, but literally means "his mother's." Do not say this to people. It can literally start fights.
*wǒ ài nǐ*—I love you.
*xiāng zhāng zi*—Himalayan musk deer
*xiānshēng*—sir
*xiǎo gūnián*—little girl
*xiǎoshí*—hours
*xièxiè*—thank you
*xīn'ài de*—beloved
*xíng*—okay
*xīngān*—this literally means heart and liver, but it is a way to say darling, dear, sweetheart, honey..
*xióng*—bear
*xué*—snow. It is common for Chinese name for their children.
*xuébào*—snow leopard
*yardang*—ridge
*yīndào*—vagina
*zhōngwèi*—first lieutenant

## Japanese Glossary

*gojû ni*—52
*maruta*—log/logs
*taii*—lieutenant
*taisho*—general
*yukihyō*—snow leopard

## Uyghur Glossary

*Siki*—fuck

# Tibetan Glossary

*Bsang*—to clean (Note: there were 11 entries for this word. I'm unsure as to whether this is the correct one to use at this point. https://www.freelang.net/online/tibetan.php?lg=gb) *Tujay-chay*—thank you.

# The Logs

*A Secret Division of Unit 731, Yumen, Northern China*
*Early April 1945*

The cold seeped into five-year-old Gojû Ni's bare feet and up her ankles. A shiver shimmied down her spine, and she shifted her weight to the outer edges of her feet, trying to find a way to lessen the pain of standing on the icy stone floor without bringing attention to herself. Her *yukihyō* chuffed, wanting out, but she couldn't shift. Not in front of these people. The last child who'd shifted without permission had disappeared. She glanced at the boy next to her. Their gazes connected. Her eyes widened. He had silver eyes, too. Was his animal-self the same as hers? She wanted to ask him, but feared speaking.

The sound of footsteps ricocheted down the hall. A door opened behind them and slammed shut. The click, click, click of shoes continued until a tall, austere man stood in front of them. He ignored them.

The lieutenant and doctor in charge of the children bowed and said, "Taisho Ishii."

"Taii Yoshimata." The general bowed, towering over his subordinate.

His voice sent a frisson of unease rippling through the room. A different kind of cold than the one that had chilled Gojû Ni moments before sank into the marrow of her bones. Her lower lip trembled for a second before she smothered the reaction. Any show of emotion resulted in punishment.

"Japan will lose the war. Tojo refused Operation Cherry Blossoms at Night. It was our last hope to stop the United States. If they win, they'll want our records. I will hand them over, but only as a bargaining tool." He turned to the gathered children. Piercing black eyes behind wire-rimmed glasses studied them with detachment. "But we won't give them *this* knowledge. These experiments," he gestured to the children standing silently in front of him, "will remain our secret alone."

Every cell in Gojû Ni's body screamed at her to shrink away from his inspection. Instead, she thrust her chin out in defiance, but he ignored her.

"Then what will we do with these *maruta*?" the lieutenant asked.

The doctors and soldiers who worked at the facility always referred to them as logs, as if they weren't human and couldn't hear or understand what they said.

"How many do we have total? A few hundred?"

The lieutenant raised the clipboard he held in his hand and flipped through the papers. "One hundred and forty-two survived birth, Taisho. These fifty-six are the ones who shape-shift."

The general shrugged. "They appear healthy and look human. Leave them at the Buddhist temple. I'm sure they'll find them homes with childless families."

"Taisho?" Taii Yoshimata frowned. "I don't understand."

He smiled and the temperature in the room dropped a few more degrees. "We let them live."

"But . . . why?"

"Imagine the havoc they will cause. It will be our present to our enemies. They are too stupid to know what to do with them, so they will fear them. Understood?"

"Hai." The lieutenant bowed.

Taisho Ishii bowed and turned on his heel. The sound of his footsteps stopped at the door. "And, lieutenant?"

"Yes, Taisho?"

"Give them names to match their race and make sure no one knows what they are."

Gojû Ni stood in the same concrete room as the day before, but, this time, five tables lined the front. At each table, a man sat with papers in front of him. Every few seconds, one of them called out a number, a child walked up to the table, and the man gave them a new name. She stood in silence with the other children, waiting.

"Gojû Ni." At the front of the room, the man sitting at the center table didn't look up from his paper until she stood in front of him. "You will be called Xuě. It means snow in Chinese." His attention returned to the papers, and he drew a line through some characters.

*Xuě*. No longer the number 52, she had a name. A real name. She lifted her chin, her shoulders back.

When she didn't move, he looked up. Impatience flashed across his face, and he motioned toward the other children. "Go stand with the other *maruta* over there."

The group of children already assigned names were lined up to the left of the tables. They stood as trained, eyes straight ahead, mouths closed, no movement.

Xuě walked over and lined up with the named children.

"Come, *maruta*. Time to go to your rooms."

One by one, the children in front of her filed out of the room. She marched behind them through the halls. Within a few minutes, they reached the section where the human "patients" were housed. Careful to keep her gaze straight ahead, she tried to tune out the moans of the patients in rows upon rows of cages. The smell of open wounds and rotting, disease-ridden flesh assaulted her senses. She swallowed the bile that rose in her throat, and her gut churned.

"Please . . ." someone begged, followed by an agonized scream.

The children in front of her picked up their pace. Xuě hurried on their heels, looking neither right nor left until she escaped through another door out into the weak winter sunshine. The door clanged shut behind the last child and cut off the horrors of that ward.

She continued across a courtyard and to another rectangular concrete building that housed their ward. With a sigh of relief, she settled into her small, metal, square cage and wrapped her thin, woolen blanket around her shoulders. As she relaxed, leaning against the crosshatched bars, an officer came by, shut the door to her cage, and locked it.

Soon, she would leave this place. Her palms grew clammy, and her heart raced. Cold and brutal, the doctors cared little for their charges, but, if she behaved as expected, they fed and clothed her. She lived. Only those who disobeyed disappeared.

What were the rules of the outside world? How would she survive out there?

*Two days later, Yumen, China*

The lieutenant crowded the children into the back of several trucks. Xuě rode with the other children across the city huddled together against the biting wind. The truck jolted to a stop in front of a large, beautiful building. Blood red pillars supported elaborately decorated eaves topped by a black roof. Blue, green, and red clashed with one another. A black sign with gold figures hung over the steps leading to the steps and the door. It was the most beautiful building Xuě had ever seen.

She stared at the giant building and chanted her new name, Xuě, in her head. Her pulse leaped, and she started to shake and slouched low in her spot on the bed of the truck, wrapping her arms around her knees. What would happen to her now? A cold hand touched her arm. She jumped and dropped her arms to her sides. Her gaze met that of the boy who'd stood next to her in the room a few days ago. He sat next to her.

"It'll be okay," he whispered.

"How do you know?" she asked.

His gaze turned to the building in front of them. "I don't. I just hope."

He slid his hand down her arm and clasped hers. A strange sensation shimmied down her spine, and she sat up straight. Her *yukihyō* chuffed. She stared at the temple once more, hope burgeoning in her heart.

She leaned closer to him. "What is your name?"

"I am called Bao. And you?"

Before she could answer, a man in a uniform said, "You there, no talking. Everybody up. Get in line."

Xuě dropped her gaze but kept hold of Bao for a brief second more. He squeezed her hand, and she smiled. Then, she stood and silently followed the others to the temple.

# Chapter One

*Qílián Shān Mountains, China*
*January 1960*

"It's time for you to marry," Lin Hui said, grabbing her daughter Xuě's hand.

"But, Mama, you need me—"

"No. It's past time. We cannot keep you here any longer. You must start your own life. He comes tomorrow. You marry New Year's Day."

"We should wait for spring when there's more game, and we can catch fish."

"There's no time for that. Fish for luck is an old wives' tale. You must marry soon and start your own family."

Xuě's throat threatened to close and suffocate her. In four days, she'd join with a man she'd never met and leave the only home she'd ever known to go live with an unknown family. Cold sweat trickled down her back. She drew in a deep breath and shook her head, stepping away from her too frail mother. Over the past two years, only her hunting ability had provided meat for the village. Before Chairman Mao's Great Leap Forward program, life had been a struggle, but they'd survived. After Mao's soldiers came and took their village's livestock, many had died or left in search of food despite her best efforts.

With each death or disappearance, the villagers grew colder toward her, as if she were somehow to blame. The women hurried away when she approached; the men tolerated her for her hunting abilities. Only her parents treated her as a regular human being.

How could they send her away when they needed her more now than ever? And marriage . . . Marriage meant children and exposing the truth about herself to someone not in her village. Her village barely tolerated her. What would these new people do if they found out what she was? She shuddered.

Her mother stepped forward. "It will be good. You'll see. He's a good man."

Panic clawed at Xuě's insides. "No." The word erupted from her. She retreated another step, shaking her head in denial. Even with years separating her and Unit 731, the horrors had never truly left her.

"Enough." Despite his wasted frame, her father still commanded her obedience. His voice brooked no argument. "It was arranged years ago. We must honor our agreement. You knew this day would come."

She did, but she'd never agreed to it. They'd arranged it before they knew what she was. As the years passed, it had loomed in the back of her mind. Hoping everything she'd done for the village would convince her parents to break the arrangement, she'd ignored it. Now, the time had arrived. Nothing she said would change their minds, not even the knowledge of certain death if she left would change it.

Her mother approached. Love shone in her eyes. Reaching up, she cupped Xuě's cheek. "We won't be around much longer. You have done much for us, repaid us for taking you in a hundred times over. You are the daughter of my heart if not my body. It's time for you to live your life, have a family of your own. *Wǒ ài nǐ*."

The cherished words so seldom spoken pierced her heart, and she whispered, "I love you, too, Mama."

Tears stung her eyes. The snow leopard in her chuffed in protest and twitched its tail. It itched to shift and escape. Instead, she bowed her head and slipped outside without a word.

Snowflakes swirled in a beautiful dance, gently landing on her eyelashes and blanketing the world. A gust of wind whooshed past her parents' mud hut, chasing the flakes through the village. She watched the maelstrom of snow pass by. The wind tugged at her, and her *yukihyō* shuddered again.

"Xuě," her mother's voice called over the rising wind.

"*Shi*, Mama?"

15

"Bring home some meat so we can celebrate."

"I will."

A heavy weight settled on her. If she could find any. The starving masses had invaded their mountains in search of food. Many died, ill-equipped to survive the harsh environment. Perhaps the mountains would be quiet due to the storm, but desperation drove people to do desperate things—like brave snowstorms in search of food. With winter upon them, prey was scarce.

She jogged across the dirt road, past a few huts with smoke curling out of the center of their thatched roofs, to the edge of the village. Snow-covered conifers towered over her. A hushed silence shrouded the forest. Not even rodents dared the oncoming storm.

Her navy-blue liberation shoes sank knee-deep into the undisturbed snow that had fallen overnight. The cold penetrated the canvas-topped, rubber-soled shoes. Snow clung to her rag wool, loose-fitting trousers and shoes with each step she took. By the time she reached her destination, she panted from the exertion. Normally, she'd spend more time covering her tracks, but the storm would erase them soon enough. No one would be traveling today.

Kneeling behind a large tree, she swept snow off a wooden box and sat down. She untied her damp shoes and slipped out of them. Resting her feet on the top of her shoes to prevent her wool socks from getting sodden, she removed them and stuffed them in her pocket. She stood barefoot in the snow, opened the box, and slapped the shoes together to dislodge as much snow as possible before setting them in the box to the side. She took the socks from her pocket and stuffed them inside her shoes. The snow stung where it touched her feet. She wiggled her toes, yearning for the days before Mao and the Cultural Revolution had swept the country—and for her heavy, sheepskin boots that had kept her feet toasty warm.

With a sigh, she continued disrobing. It didn't do to worry about things she couldn't change. Unbuttoning her drab gray, high-collared, cadre wool jacket, she shook it out as well, folded it, and carefully placed it on top of her shoes. The pants quickly followed. Just as gently, she shut the box and covered it back up.

Delicate snowflakes landed on her skin in increasing succession, melting as they hit. Soon, there'd be a whiteout. She needed to move quickly. Shivers rippled over her. Each breath created a puff of white fog in front of her.

She stood naked for a moment longer, staring into the trees, searching for any sign of life before turning her focus within to the waiting animal. Her skin undulated and stretched. Bones popped and expanded. Thick, luxurious fur sprang up, replacing her pale human skin. She dropped down onto all fours. Her wide, furry feet acting as snowshoes, she only sank a few inches into the fresh snow. Her ears flicked back and forth, alert for sound of any kind, but only the soft shushing of falling snow greeted her.

After one quick glance back toward the quiet village, she trotted deeper into the woods toward her usual winter hunting ground. The turmoil of the discussion with her parents dissipated with each step, and her mind cleared. Up the mountain she climbed. The trees grew smaller until the forest disappeared, replaced by loose rocks and scraggly, tough grass interspersed with patches of snow. She settled under an overhang and watched the scree below.

A few hours passed with no sign of life. Her heart heavy, she stood, leaped down from her perch, and turned toward home when a dark shadow shifted ahead of her. She stopped in midstride and zeroed in on the movement. A large *pán yáng* munched on some grass 15 *mǐ* ahead of her. A layer of snow covering its brown back, it inched forward from tuft to tuft, occasionally stopping to dig into the snow with its hoof to uncover more food.

Xuě paused, her tail twitching, and then climbed above the spiral-horned animal, accelerating as she closed in on her prey. Its head jerked up, and the brown sheep scrambled in a zigzag down the steep hillside. She leaped after it, gaining ground with each stride. With a lunge, she swiped the back legs out from under the animal and pounced on top of it. It kicked out and bleated, but she crushed the top shank and sank her claws into its back. She dragged the struggling *pán yáng* back toward her, careful of its horns. With a powerful swipe, she ripped out its throat. Its legs thrashed one last time, and it stilled.

She crouched, panting next to her kill. Adrenaline rushed through her. Her heart pounded a rapid tattoo. The scent of fresh blood filled her, and she battled the instinct to eat a portion. Her stomach growled, but she ignored the ever-present gnawing sensation. Her village would have meat for the wedding. If she stopped to eat, she wouldn't make it in time and there wouldn't be enough for everyone.

She clamped onto the haunch and dragged the carcass slowly down the hillside. Every few feet, she stopped, listened, and scanned the rocky face, alert for danger. Snow swirled around her, obliterating her trail. Chuffing in satisfaction, she ignored the snow and continued on until she crossed the tree line. She kept moving until the trees grew taller and closer together. Once under a thick canopy of the trees, she dropped her burden and hunkered down to rest. Her muscles burned, and she puffed from the exertion.

The village lay a few *gōnglǐ* away. The *pán yáng* would grow heavier the farther she carried it, but if she kept a steady pace, she'd make it back before dark. She'd promised her mother meat for the celebration dinner, and meat they would have. Standing, she bent, latched onto the haunch again, and repeated the routine she'd started on the scree.

A few hours later, with dusk falling, she tucked the carcass against a tree, covered it, and padded over to her chest. Dragging that full-grown ram through the deepening snow had sucked at her strength. Her muscles screamed in protest, but she was almost done. She dug the chest out of the snow and shifted. Lifting the lid, she shivered and donned her clothes and shoes as quickly as possible. She shut the chest and buried it once more.

Only a little bit farther, and she'd be done. Eager to escape the elements, she trudged toward the village, but her steps slowed near the edge of the trees. Her *yukihyō* growled a warning, twitching her tail. Strangers.

He had arrived early. Despite the storm.

Her shoulders hunched forward. The elation of the hunt and bringing home a large ram disappeared completely, and the reality of her impending marriage loomed. Soon, she'd live among strangers and have to obey her husband's mother. She'd become a servant. Perhaps her husband's mother would be kind. Perhaps she'd beat her.

She turned toward the beckoning forest. The thought of escape tempted her. She could disappear, and no one would be able to find her. She didn't need anyone to survive. Her *yukihyō* would see her through. Her mind roiled in turmoil. That would dishonor her parents. They'd taken her in, loved her despite her differences, and stood by her through all the years the village struggled to accept her. Even now, some of them referred to her as *shānshàng de guǐ*. If only she could turn into the ghost of the mountains they named her and disappear. She could live out of the cave she retreated to when the ostracism stung too much, and she needed solitude. The idea appealed to her.

Lifting her chin, she stepped away from the protection of the trees and strode toward her parents' hut. Smoke curled above the occupied huts she passed, writhing like dark snakes amidst the falling snow. She shivered and increased her pace. As she approached her home, laughter reached her ears. Despite her worries, she pasted a smile on her face, strode up the two steps, and opened the door. Snow chased her inside, and she shut the door quickly behind her.

Conversation stopped, and five faces turned toward her. Her gaze skimmed the group and stopped at her parents' faces. For the first time since their sheep were confiscated, joy twinkled in their eyes.

"Come, Xuě," her mother said, taking her hand and pulling her farther into the warm room, "you must meet your new family."

She looked down at the ground and gathered her courage. "Kwan Sheng, Wang Shi, this is my daughter Lin Xuě."

Xuě bowed to the older couple.

"And this is Wang Bao, your betrothed."

Without raising her eyes, she turned and bowed to the man who'd soon be her husband.

"It's a pleasure to meet you at last."

The softly spoken words teased at her senses, and she glanced up at his face. Her breath caught her in throat. A distant memory stirred. She stood in front of a temple and held the hand of a boy with the same color eyes as hers. The memory of his hopeful words had seen her through the dark times before the monks had placed her with her parents.

"Bao?" she whispered.

He nodded.

A sob caught in her throat. Could it be . . . ? Was he . . . ? "Are you . . . ?"

Again, he nodded. She wobbled and reached out to steady herself. He grabbed her arm. A tingling began where his hand held her elbow and spread to the rest of her body. She leaned toward him, her gaze zeroing in on his lips. What would they feel like against hers?

"Xuě?"

Her father's voice brought her back to her senses, and she moved away from Bao. "*Shi*, Father?"

"Were you able to . . . " Her father waved his hand.

She glanced at their guests. Did Bao have an animal, too? Not all children created by medical experimentation at Unit 731 shifted, although those that couldn't ended up in the "patients" ward. Distracted by the man in front of her, she didn't immediately respond to her father's question. She itched to brush the thick, black bangs that tumbled down across his broad forehead out of his eyes and trace high cheekbones that flanked a straight nose. The kindness in his eyes drew her as much as his looks.

A memory from long ago rose in her mind.

Shaking off the urge, she clenched her hands and moved

toward the door. "Oh, *shi* . . . *shi*, I did. I will get Shi Sheng to help me," she said. "I meant to do this before I came home, but I heard you laughing and—"

"No, I'll go with you."

Bao's voice shimmied up her spine and danced along her nerve endings. He rested his hand on her shoulder. Goose bumps raced across her skin. Heat rushed to her face. Bowing her head, she hid her reaction to his touch. The image of his handsome face remained before her even though she stared at the floor.

He took liberties not usually allowed, but, soon, they'd be married. Surely, it was okay. The sound of their parents' voices behind them continued unabated. She closed her eyes and relaxed her shoulders.

For the first time since stepping into the hut, she inhaled deeply. His musky scent awakened her *yukihyō*. It twitched and chuffed. Her eyes opened wide. A smile curved her lips, and her heart beat faster. She glanced over her shoulder into his eyes. He knew.

"I'll go with you," he repeated.

Unable to find her voice through her emotions, she nodded.

He slid his hand down her arm and laced his fingers through hers. She gazed for a moment at their hands, warmth spreading through her. Her parents were right. This man was her future.

Hand in hand, she stepped out with him into the deepening gloom.

# Chapter Two

"I remember you," she said.

"I remember you, too."

She smiled at his words, leading him toward an empty hut.

"Where are we going?" he asked.

"To get the . . . "

She glanced at him. Had she misread him? Was her *yuki-hyō* wrong? She searched his face for any hint of his thoughts. Even with the last daylight fading, she could see the indecision clouding his eyes.

"I thought you were . . . that you . . . I . . . " she stuttered and stopped in her tracks. "Are you not the Bao I met many years ago?"

"*Shi.*"

"Then surely you know—"

"What you are?"

She nodded.

"Yes, but why are we going this way?"

"Because the *pán yáng* I hunted earlier today is in the forest where I left it."

"Why didn't you bring it to your parents' hut?"

She cocked her head to the side and considered him for a moment. "Because the villagers haven't seen me in my, you know, as a—"

"Snow leopard?"

"*Shi*, since I was very young. I always leave my kill a distance from the village and have one of the village men help me bring it here in human form."

He studied her, his eyes full of sadness. "Do they not accept you?"

She stared at her shoes growing damper and colder the longer they stood there and shook her head.

"Oh, Xuě," he murmured and clasped her hand.

Warmth infused her, and tingles shot up her arm. Heat bloomed in her cheeks. She looked away from him but squeezed his hand. For the first time, someone other than her parents understood. Their future held promise. She smiled and lifted her chin, her heart lightening at the prospect of life with another shifter.

"We must pick up the stretcher first. We keep it in an empty hut."

"You've lost villagers as well?" he asked.

With a nod, she said, "They either starved, were taken by the People's Liberation Army, or left thinking food could be found elsewhere."

Snow crunched under their feet as she led him to the hut that had become storage.

"There isn't any."

"I know, but, even with the meat I bring in, it isn't enough. I would do more—"

His grip tightened around her fingers, halting her steps and her words. "We do what we can. It's no different in my village. You cannot blame yourself," he said, his voice gruff.

Easy to say, not so easy to do. Gazing up at him, she studied his face, the high cheekbones, the generous lips, the slash of dark eyebrows over intense silver eyes, strong chin, and broad forehead. Again, the urge to brush the straight black fringe that fell into his eyes seized her. She clenched her fingers. He may soon be her husband, but she couldn't bring herself to commit such an intimate act.

She turned and stepped into the dark hut. Her eyes adjusted quickly in the near darkness. The stretcher leaned against the wall next to the door. Retrieving it, she turned and ran into a hard chest. Warm hands steadied her.

"Xuě," he murmured before his mouth brushed hers in a feather light kiss.

The pressure disappeared so quickly she flicked her tongue out as if unsure it had even happened. His eyes narrowed then widened, and a light fired in their depths that sent shivers coursing through her and a dampness at her core. Her nostrils flared, and she inhaled the scent of their arousal as it swirled around them in the dark hut. Wide eyed, she gazed up at him. The stretcher clattered to the floor, and she jumped away from him.

Bending, she picked it up.

"Let me help you," he said and reached for the stretcher.

His husky voice raked over her raw nerves, and she shivered, but she didn't let go. "We can carry it together. It's easier that way."

"Okay."

He stepped into the open and moved out of her way. She smiled and followed him outside. He picked up one end, and they retraced her earlier route into the trees. Each step left a knee-deep impression in the snow. They walked in companionable silence to the spot where she'd left the *pán yáng*. Her breath hung in the gathering gloom in front of her. Ignoring the ever-present cold, she set the stretcher down and dug at the snow covering the ram. Bao knelt beside her and helped. The storm had added to her original pile of snow. A few minutes passed with only the sound of digging and their breathing marring the quiet of the woods.

When the last of the snow fell away, they stood.

"You caught this ram?" he asked

She glanced at him. "*Shi*. It was a good hunt today. I was lucky."

"Where did you find it?"

She motioned to the west. "Up on the scree above the tree line a few *gōnglǐ* on the north slope."

"You dragged it all the way here?" Disbelief colored his voice.

She shrugged and bent down, grabbing a hold of the sheep's back feet. "It was the only way. They don't like the woods in this area. I usually bring it closer to the village, but I was tired today."

He stepped to the front of the ram and reached for the forelegs. "I'm not surprised. It's a big ram."

Her skin prickled at his praise. One did what one had to do. Rather than respond, she nodded. They hefted the ram onto the stretcher, lifted it, and started back toward the village.

"How often do you hunt?"

She glanced over her shoulder at him and said, "Every three days or so. You?"

"Every couple days. Why not more?"

"We have intruders coming to the mountains looking for food. The numbers of wild *pán yáng* have decreased. I try to take only as much as we need and no more."

"We are lucky, living deeper in the mountains. They find it harder to reach our area."

"*Shi*, you are."

To live somewhere without fear of starving hunters appealed to Xuě. Leaving behind days of gnawing hunger did, too. But it meant leaving her parents behind. Uncertainty clawed at her. The cold bit at her fingers, and they threatened to cramp. Without a word, she increased her pace, careful to step in the path they'd made on their way out to conserve energy.

In the silence that had fallen between them, she said, "I worry that, if I leave, my parents will die."

"I—"

"They will insist I go with you. They've already done so. I can't stay, but—" She bent her head, focusing on each footstep unable to finish her sentence.

The stretcher jolted to a halt, nearly pulling her off her feet and forcing her to stop. She turned to look at him. He bent and set the stretcher down, and she followed suit lest the ram slip off. Stepping around the dead animal, he walked over to her and gently grabbed her shoulders. Warmth shot through his hands and into her arms. Tingling spread through her body. A yearning to press her body against his burgeoned inside of her. She suppressed it.

"You don't have to marry me right now. I understand. I can return when this famine has passed."

Warmth spread through her at his words, reaching all the

way to her toes that curled in her shoes. She searched his earnest face. Did he truly mean it? Did it matter? No. Her parents insisted they marry now. Staying would bring them dishonor. She shook her head. "No. We can visit them, though, and bring them food, if that's okay with you."

"Of course. We'll visit at least once a month."

The tension that had built inside of her released, and her shoulders sagged in relief. She stared at his chest and nodded. The trek would be difficult, but she would be able to take care of her parents and the village.

"*Xièxiè.*"

"*Xuě?*"

Their gazes met. Her breath caught in her throat at the intensity and tenderness in his eyes.

"I only want this if you do. Do you?"

Did she? She didn't know. Given a choice, would she marry him? Or not? He understood her, or, at least, her condition, and accepted it. To him, she was no different than any other woman. Well, perhaps, that was untrue. Perhaps, he wanted her *because of* her difference. She'd never had that before. Even the men who'd watched her grow up hadn't fully accepted her, and his touch . . . His touch intoxicated her, like the rice liquor *baijiu* she'd sipped once as a child during a time of plenty. It had tickled her nose, burned her throat, and heated her insides. Except she wanted more of his touch.

"There will be no dishonor if you don't."

There would be no matter what he said. If he made it his fault, the villagers would find fault with her. If she refused, her parents would never forgive her. She couldn't stay in the village and wouldn't be able to help them survive. Whether she wanted this or not mattered little. His thoughtfulness harkened well for their marriage, but it did little to calm her nerves.

"*Shi,* I think I want this," she lied. She didn't know what she wanted. A chill crept down her spine, and she retreated. "We should take the *pán yáng* to the village."

"Of course," he said, releasing her.

They picked up the stretcher and continued to the village in silence, but his words continued to echo in her mind. She led him to the empty hut where they set the stretcher down. Moving farther into the darkness, she fetched a bucket and rope. With anyone else, she would've lit the lantern, but their abilities made it unnecessary.

"If you tie the back feet together, we can hang the ram for draining. We weren't expecting you to arrive until tomorrow. We would've been ready for you then. I'm sorry we won't have fresh meat for you this evening," she said.

He smiled, taking the rope and did as she'd instructed. "I was anxious to meet you."

"I—" As much as custom demanded she respond in kind, a second lie wouldn't come out. Instead, she blurted, "I was scared to meet you."

He frowned and said nothing as they raised the *pán yáng* and hung it on a hook in the roof. She placed the bucket under it and headed to the door.

She avoided looking at him. His offer to break the contract had shaken her. Even though she'd dreaded the upcoming marriage, while hunting, she'd come to accept that it had to take place. Now that he'd offered her what appeared to be a choice, her emotions warred between screaming in rage, weeping with relief, or retreating into indifference. Yet hope surfaced. If he proved to be as kind to her as he was right now, married life might prove to be happier than her current one. Perhaps she could even come to love him.

His muted footsteps followed her, and a whisper soft touch caressed her back. She stopped just inside the door and braced herself. A frisson of longing snaked down her spine. The musk of his arousal wrapped around her, captivating her, and his body heat penetrated her clothes. Her nipples peaked.

He turned her to face him. "I meant what I said."

She averted her face. "I know, but it's not that simple."

He trailed his fingers down her cheek. Goose bumps followed in their wake. He lifted her chin. When she still refused to raise her gaze to his, he said, "Xuě."

Something in his voice compelled her to look at him.

"I will be a good husband. We can make this work."

At the thought of leaving, a pit opened in her stomach. "My whole world is changing. Everything I've known since we escaped the Japanese will be gone. What will happen to me if something happens to you?"

"What will happen to you when your parents die?" he asked, his face all harsh lines and angles.

The barb hit her in the gut. She gasped and recoiled from his touch.

"I don't mean to be cruel, but, even in the best of times, all of us must face death. They're growing older. Your village tolerates you. Mine accepts me."

"*Shi*, I'm not accepted. It can be lonely, but I know my place here. In your village, I don't know what will happen to me. Perhaps I'd be alone for the rest of my life if I stay here, but I'd do what had to be done. I could survive." Her words evoked a vision of an empty life. Her eyes stung with the threat of tears at what a barren future with no family would mean, but bringing children into the world with her abilities frightened her more. Being alone was better. "A husband means children. What will happen to them?"

"We may not be able to have any. We don't know."

One tear escaped and slipped down her cheek. He caught it on his fingertip. His intense expression softened.

"Whether we have children or not, I want someone I can grow old with, someone with whom I can share my abilities. I want you. I want to be with you. I want a life with you," he said. "Do you want me?"

His words washed over her, settled inside, and slipped through a crack in the wall she'd built around herself. Words failing her, she nodded. She wanted him, but would it be enough? If his parents were as kind as he, she'd be more fortunate than most women in their marriages.

Her stomach grumbled, and he stepped away.

"We should go to your parents' and eat."

Cold air swirled in his place. She stared at her clenched

hands, fighting the urge to grab him, gather him to her, and never let go. Instead, she nodded and turned toward her parents' hut.

# Chapter Three

*Three days later*

"You look beautiful, *xiǎo* Lin," her mother said.

Xuě bowed her head. Heat stung her cheeks from the uncustomary compliment. "I'm no longer little, Mama."

Her mother patted her hand, her eyes glistening with unshed tears. "You will always be my *xiǎo gūnián*."

Xuě's eyes burned, and she blinked several times in an attempt to stop her own tears from falling. "Mama—"

"Shh . . . It is a time of rejoicing." She stepped away and cocked her head to the side. "My wedding dress fits you well, although a little short." She bent and tugged on the hem before standing and running her hand lovingly over the *qipao* with the embroidered phoenix. "You should wear red more. It brings color to your cheeks."

"Only for today. I should be wearing my uniform as everyone else does. If someone were to see me in this besides Bao and his parents . . . well, we haven't survived this long to be taken by the authorities."

Her mother grimaced. "Pshaw! That drab uniform isn't meant for a wedding, no matter what the young ladies are doing. You can wear it to the banquet later, but, for now, in our home, you'll humor me. Chairman Mao can—"

"Mama!" Even in the privacy of one's hut, saying anything against Chairman Mao was dangerous.

Snorting and waving her hand as if brushing away an annoying gnat, her mother crossed to the door. "It's time."

A covey of blue grouse took flight in her stomach, and she hesitated, shrinking into the darkest corner of the hut. Once she married Bao, her current life would end. Her pulse beat in her throat, and she licked her dry lips.

"Xuě!"

The sharp tone in her mother's voice snapped her out of her frozen state. Staring at the ragged woven mat that covered the packed dirt floor, she focused on taking one step at a time to the center of the hut where a fresh mat waited for the ceremony. Her red skirt swirled around her feet in a maelstrom of bright color.

Her mother opened the door. "She's ready."

Suddenly, Bao stood before Xuě. He'd shed his uniform, too, in favor of the black silk traditional robe decorated with a gold dragon.

"Did anyone see you?" she asked, her stomach in knots. Their feudal clothing could bring the authorities down on them.

At least, her parents had agreed to skip the traditional Chinese customs. They were frowned upon by the new communist government. The old ways would have brought much celebration, but also censure. No one celebrated them anymore. The firecrackers, drums, and loud gongs of the bridegroom procession, the bridesmaid games, where friends of the bride—of which she had none, so they would've had to skip that part anyway—required the groom to perform stunts or "tricks" until he paid them with red packets full of money, and the bride riding in a rickshaw back to the groom's house in another procession. She'd step on a red mat instead of the earth and then over a saddle or a lit stove to chase away evil spirits.

These pre-wedding ceremonies were much more elaborate than the wedding, which consisted of only the bride and groom's families. In her case, her parents and his.

He shook his head. "Everyone's inside celebrating the new year. Even though the sun has melted much of the snow from the storm, it's still cold out there."

In short, no one cared about her marriage . . . at least, not until the wedding feast. The price of being different. Did the villagers see her as less than human? Was she no more than a *maruta* to them, too? Would his village be the same? Perhaps their acceptance only extended to him.

Their gazes met, and he smiled. She swallowed and nodded, a smile refusing to form, but a little bit of the tension that had wound around her since waking loosened. In silence, the ceremony began. He joined her at a shelf that had once been their family altar until Mao cracked down on the old ways. Everything had disappeared years ago, until today.

A small brass bowl with three lit incense sticks burned. To the right, her mother had placed the ancestral tablets. In the center, a pot of water and a bowl waited for later. She bowed her head.

*Thank you, Heaven and Earth, for giving me this life and this man. Thank you for providing everything needed in this life. May this union be blessed and may we find happiness and health. And please take care of my parents after I leave.*

He reached for her hand, and, as tradition dictated, she kneeled next to him, heads bowed, to the ancestral tablets before turning and kneeling to their parents who watched them with expectant looks. Finally, she faced him, and she kneeled, even as he did, to show her respect for him.

Rising, she crossed to where the pot of water and bowl waited on the family altar. Hands trembling, she picked them up and carried them to her mother- and father-in-law. Placing the bowl on the floor between them, she poured the water over first her father-in-law's hands and then her mother-in-law's to cleanse them. She returned the pot and bowl to their place and retrieved a tray of tea. She brought this back to her in-laws and served them.

No one said anything until she completed the ritual.

"Welcome, *nǚ'ér*," Kwan Sheng said, addressing her as a daughter. A kind, gap-toothed smile creased his lined cheeks.

Xuě bowed her head. It was done. Tomorrow, she'd leave for his village and say goodbye to her parents. Her new life would begin.

Her stomach clenched. A new life. What would it hold? Would her parents survive? Would she?

Her mother grabbed her elbow. "It is time. Let us go to the banquet."

Lightheaded, Xuě stumbled and fell into Bao. His hands came up and steadied her.

"Is everything all right?" he asked.

She nodded. Panic clawed at her insides. She had to change. "I must change into my uniform. No one can see me in this. They'll report it to the authorities. We'll be taken away, and then they'll know—"

"It's okay. People—"

"No," she said, looking into his concerned eyes, "you don't understand. Our village isn't like yours. If they see us dressed like this, they'll think we don't support our leader. They tolerate me. I bring in food, but give them one reason not to . . ." She motioned with her arm toward the door, her heart beating a frantic tattoo. "You see our empty village? It isn't just from the famine."

Shock flitted across his face.

Pulling away from him, she rushed to the curtained off area and stripped off the beautiful red *qipao* as if changing clothes could alter the course of her life. It already had. That gown signaled she was now married. Married. Her breath caught, her heart raced like a panicked *pán yáng* charging down the mountain, and her hands trembled. She had to calm herself. She refused to start her new life in this state.

"Xuě?"

Bao's voice broke into her scattered thoughts. The chill air caressed her bare skin. It whispered of a frozen land and death. A tremor ran down her spine. Goose bumps sprouted all over her body.

"I'm fine. I'm almost done," she said, shivering. She grabbed her pants and pulled them on, quickly following it with her shirt. She slipped her feet into her shoes and slid the curtain open. "Your turn."

Bao frowned at her. "My turn?"

"Yes, you must change your clothes."

"I'm not changing my clothes. Surely, they're not that bad."

Her father stepped up next to them. "She is right. Some of the villagers are very zealous about throwing away our old beliefs." Sadness filled his rheumy eyes. "Families have gone away never to return."

Her new husband looked from her to her father and back again. He nodded his head. "I'll change."

The tension slipped out of Xuě's body, and she drew in a deep breath. "*Xièxiè*."

Their gazes met. Something shifted. Passion swirled and danced between them. The scent of their arousal teased her senses, awakening her *yukihyō*. His nostrils flared, and his pupils dilated. He leaned toward her until his breath mingled with hers. She licked her lips.

"Xuě . . ."

His voice shimmied over her skin, and she quivered with longing.

The click of the door shutting echoed through the hut like a gunshot. They jumped apart. Her cheeks burned with heat, and she averted her gaze. What kind of woman felt this way—even for her husband? It must be the animal in her. Her cheeks burned hotter with the realization of what being a shifter did to her sexual drive.

"We must go," she said again, her voice coming out in a husky growl.

"Xuě," he breathed and raised her chin so that their gazes collided.

But she glanced away, refusing look at him.

"Xuě," he said again.

This time, she lifted her gaze and looked into his eyes. They glinted with a desire that evoked an answering need within her. Such a beautiful man, and he was hers. Hers . . .

"We must . . ."

The words died in her throat as their lips connected. Her eyelids fluttered close, and fire shot through her, igniting all of her nerve endings. She moaned and pressed her body to his, slipping her arms around his waist to draw him closer still. The muscles of his back rippled under her hands, and her nipples peaked. The silk of his robe rubbed against the oversensitive buds, intensifying the sensation. Liquid trickled between her legs, and she squirmed, rubbing against him.

This was wrong. She knew it was wrong. Women weren't meant to enjoy this animalistic act, but, instead of protesting and pushing away, she pulled him closer and said, "Please."

He groaned and stroked her back before sliding his hands down to grab her hips and thrust himself against her. His hard *jījī* pressed against her stomach. Her insides clenched in response. Ancestors forgive her, but she craved to have him inside of her *bàoyú*. She would do anything to get him there.

He lifted his head, breaking the kiss, and she opened her eyes in question. She didn't want him to stop.

"I would . . . do you . . . "

His question trailed off. Words had failed him as they did her. It didn't matter. She knew what he was asking. With a nod, she pulled his head back down to kiss him because she couldn't stop herself, no matter how much she tried. He groaned into her mouth, his passion stoking the inferno that already threatened to consume her even higher.

She ached to be bare chest to bare chest. No, more than that. Only his bare body pressed to her bare body would quench the need raging inside of her, but the silk robe stood in the way. It had to go. Shoving the little voice admonishing her for being immodest deep into the back of her brain, she stepped back and set her attention to untying the knot securing his robe. When it fell open, she moaned, his pale skin so beautiful in the dim light of the hut. Goose bumps raced down his chest, disappearing into his black silk pants, and she itched to follow their path. She reached out and lightly touched his skin, tracing the well-defined muscles that danced under her fingertips from his collarbone all the way to the top of his trousers. His *jījī* jumped in response, and she drew back. He grabbed her hand and laid it on his engorged *jījī*. Tingles shot up her arm, and she wrapped her fingers around it, marveling at its hardness. He covered her fingers with his and pumped up and down slowly.

Her breath stalled in her throat and came out in a huff. She flicked her tongue out and moistened her dry lips, searching his face. His eyes were screwed shut, and his mouth turned down. His reaction awoke the voice again.

*"You're a wanton, Xuě, for responding to his touch this way. No better than an animal,"* it whispered. *"Only a prostitute would enjoy his touch and kisses the way you do. You dishonor your family."*

She gasped and pulled away. This was wrong. She must submit to him, pliant and unresponsive, not enjoy it, and, now, her wanton nature had hurt him. She must not touch him again. She must be a good wife and woman.

"Bao?" she said. "Did I hurt you?"

He opened his eyes and looked at her. "No. It feels good. More than good. Let me show you." He reached a hand between them and touched her *àikòu* between her legs.

A jolt of electricity shot through her, her head rolled back, and her legs buckled. She grabbed his arms, holding on for dear life, as she slid toward the floor. "Oh . . . "

Bao caught her before she hit the ground and swung her up into his arms. Her head nestled against his bare chest, she wrapped her arms around his neck and breathed his musky scent deep into her lungs. Her *yukihyō* shuddered in ecstasy. With long, purposeful strides, he carried her to her mat behind the curtain in the corner. He laid her down with the reverence of a priest handling a sacred relic. His eyes shone with a fervor that sent her pulse careening even farther out of control.

He knelt beside her and unbuttoned the top button of her shirt. The shirt parted, and cool air kissed her overheated skin. Hands shaking, he stopped, leaned over her, and nuzzled the hollow of her neck. She moaned, arched toward him, and stilled. She shouldn't be responding this way. It was wicked and immoral, but his breath sent chills shimmying through her body until her entire body sang. The sensations overwhelmed that voice in the back of her head until only silence and need remained.

"Please," she whispered.

Another button opened, exposing more skin to his touch,

and then another and another until the shirt lay open, and she felt vulnerable. She reached to cover herself, but he caught her hands.

"No, don't. You're beautiful," he said and kissed the skin between her small breasts.

Tingles shot across her skin. She opened her mouth to protest, but he closed his lips over a nipple and sucked. A quiver of need wracked her body. She curled her fingers into the blanket under her and clenched them tightly.

"Touch me," he said.

She shook her head. She couldn't touch him again, or she'd be lost.

"Touch me . . . please . . . "

His plea dissolved the last of her resistance, and she reached out and brushed the muscles outlined on his stomach with her fingertips. She followed the ridge of the muscles down to the edge of the top of his pants and paused. His lips found her other nipple. She surged upward, running her hands up his back and into his thick, coarse hair, and held his head in place. Another moan slipped from her lips. The sound of their panting echoed in the silent hut.

He released her nipple and trailed kisses down to the edge of her trousers. Here, he paused for a moment before he unbuttoned them. She lifted her hips, and he slid them down her legs. Her heart fluttered, and her breath caught. Their gazes met. A fierce need glowed in his eyes. He bent down until his head was nearly even with her stomach and inhaled. He bumped her legs apart, kneeled between them, and kissed her hipbone. She jumped and squeezed her legs together, but, when he found her *yīndào*, she gasped and pressed herself against his mouth. Lightning raced along her nerve endings. Her body shook with an unknown need, as if it prepared to shatter in a million pieces.

What was he doing to her? She struggled to break the mind fog that had overcome her, but the more he licked and sucked, the more her body, and the sensations coursing through it, overrode any thought processes that attempted to seep through. All of her focus centered on what he was doing with his mouth on her *àikòu*. Like the fury of a snowstorm in the mountains, an orgasm broke over her. An involuntary scream rushed through her lips, and her entire body convulsed in ecstasy.

Limbs loose, she lay on her back and stared at the ceiling. What had just happened? She opened her mouth to ask, but he entered her slowly, and her thoughts scattered once again. Her inner walls stretched around his *jījī*. She battled the urge to push him away and stop the intrusion, but this was the part she must endure as a wife.

He stopped his forward motion, and their gazes met. "Are you okay?" he asked.

She nodded, not sure what he was asking. Then he thrust into her, and pain ripped through her. She whimpered and bit her lip. He stilled. The muscles on his arms and neck bulged, his breath coming in great gasps. He stayed embedded in her, unmoving, for a few moments. Anxiety trickled out of her as her *yīndào* stretched to accommodate him and the pain eased.

Tentatively, he pulled out a little bit and slowly slid back in. He repeated this motion a few times, and the need that had taken hold of her only moments before came roaring back to life. She wanted him to thrust deeper and faster. Flexing her hips, she met his next thrust. The movement intensified the sensations, and she gasped. How could it possibly get better?

But it did. The whirlpool of sensation that had rushed through her earlier paled in comparison to the avalanche crashing over her this time. A rumbling filled her ears, and the earth shook beneath them as the orgasm exploded over her. He thrust again and spilled his seed inside her. Her eyes rolled back in her head, and she collapsed against the mat beneath them, panting. He rolled off of her and pulled her into his arms.

She stared at the ceiling, unable to comprehend what had just happened. A tiny seed of hope unfurled inside of her and fear. What did Bao think of her now? He'd brought her pleasure, but maybe he'd only been testing her to see if she was a wanton or a normal woman.

"Bao? How did you know to do what you did? And am I," her heart pounded in her ears, and she struggled to find the courage to continue, "am I a bad woman for enjoying this between us?"

Her question floated on the cool air between them.

A sigh escaped him, and he tightened his arms around her. The heat of his body seeped into her. She snuggled closer.

"No. There's nothing wrong with you. I wanted to give you pleasure. Women should experience as much pleasure as men."

"But that's not—"

"I know. It's not our custom, but . . . " He trailed off.

Xuě's insecurities taunted her in the silence. "But?"

"But I believe the custom's wrong." He propped himself up on an elbow and looked down at her, his earnest face already growing dear to her. "Why should pleasure be only the domain of a man?"

"Because men were made for pleasure and women were made to submit to them," she said.

He shook his head. "No. No, that's not true."

"But—"

"We can talk about it later. There will be plenty of time . . . Our whole lives. I want you to enjoy this as much as I do." He brushed the hair away from her forehead and kissed it. "Now, we're expected at the banquet."

Heat burned her cheeks at the thought of facing everyone after what they'd just done. People would know, but Bao was right. Their families and the village expected them. But what would everyone think?

He stood and pulled her up beside him. "Let's get dressed and celebrate."

Nodding, she tucked her chin to her chest and dressed.

# Chapter Four

They stepped outside into brilliant sunshine, and all of the hairs on her body stood on end. Something wasn't right. Loud, angry voices filtered back to them from the direction of the banquet. She recognized her father's voice, but not the other male.

Xuě looked to Bao. His entire body tense, he grabbed her arm. Their gazes met. Without a word, she motioned for him to follow her. They circled around the back of her parents' hut and slipped into the forest.

Retreating farther into the trees, they sneaked around the village until the banquet area came into view. A truck with eight to ten soldiers of the People's Liberation Army with rifles at the ready stood next to the vehicle. An officer stood at the front of the soldiers and looked around the village as if searching for something. Her heart raced, and she shrank back. Slipping her hand into Bao's, she pulled them behind a tree and crouched down in the melting snow. A pit opened in her stomach.

Why were they in her village? Soldiers only arrived to take something, or someone, away.

Even from the distance, their conversation echoed loud and clear in her ears.

"Where is she? Where is your daughter?" the officer asked.

She peeked around the tree.

Her father bowed his head and said, "I don't know."

The man stepped closer to her father, towering over him, and scowled. "I don't believe you. Tell me where she is, and you won't be punished."

Her father stared at the other man, his expression giving nothing away. "I don't know."

The officer glared at her father. "I will only ask one more

time: Where is your daughter?"

"I don't know. She went for a walk early this morning with her new husband, and she hasn't returned yet."

"You lie. This is their banquet feast. They wouldn't miss this." He turned to two of his soldiers. "Check their hut."

"No," her father protested. "They're not there. I told you they left early this morning for a walk."

The officer raised his arm and struck her father, who reeled and crumpled to the ground.

She gasped and rose, almost giving away their position, but Bao pulled her back, whispering in her ear, "No. They're protecting us. The best thing we can do is leave."

"But—"

"If we're gone, then your father isn't lying. The officer may not punish him. We must leave before the soldiers find our wedding clothes."

Fear rocketed through her. "The clothes will prove Father has lied."

"No, they will prove we were married, but not when." He pulled on her arm, and she turned to face him. "We must leave now."

"We can't—"

"Xuě, we must. What do you think will happen when they confront you?"

Xuě paused. She would freeze. Her *yukihyō* instincts ensured that. All of her life, she'd battled those instincts. Not once had she won, but maybe this time . . . "We can save them."

"No, we can't." He grabbed her shoulders and captured her gaze. "Why do you think they're looking for you?"

Her heart stuttered in her chest. Somehow, Mao knew. They knew about her. If they knew about her, then they knew about Bao, too, and possibly all of the others. Mao's government had proven to be no more kind than the Japanese. Mao might kill them, but he might also do as the Japanese had done and experiment on them. He was right. They had to leave.

Behind them, someone said, "*Zhōngwèi*, the old man is telling the truth. They aren't in the hut."

"Then they are somewhere in this village. Search all of the huts," the lieutenant ordered.

When they didn't find them in the huts, they would search the forest. At least, the snow had melted enough to hide their tracks. And she knew this forest better than anyone.

"Come." Bao's whisper, a breath on the air, tickled her ear.

Xuě bowed her head and nodded. With one last glance at her parents and the village, she sprinted after him into the trees. He surged ahead of her. She picked up her pace. Their footfalls barely a murmur above the silence. Some minutes later, he stopped and turned to her, his eyebrows raised. This territory belonged to her. He could only lead them so far.

With a nod, she ran ahead through the trees, heading toward her hunting ground and the cave she used to get away from everyone to think.

A few *gōnglǐ* away, the cave would be a perfect hiding place. Above the scree, in a rock outcropping, it nestled between two large boulders. From a distance, it looked like the other rock formations around it. Not even an experienced tracker would find them let alone regular soldiers. They would disappear into the mountains, like ghosts.

In a few days, still unable to find their quarry, the soldiers would give up and move on. Then they could return to the village and check on their parents.

Her spirits lifted, and she smiled. Plans of returning home and then continuing on to Bao's village spun in her head. The comforting sound of her husband's light rasping breath urged her forward.

They'd covered about a quarter of the distance to the cave when a shot rang out. Its echo ricocheted through the silent forest. A second shot followed by a third and a fourth then multiple shots reverberated in her ears. Xuě stumbled. Bao caught her and pulled her into his arms, turning her to press her face into his chest. She clung to him.

"Bao?"

The unasked question hung between them.

She looked up into his face. All color had drained from it.

He nodded. She didn't need to witness what had happened. In her heart, she knew. Her entire village was dead because of her and what she was—what the Japanese had made her and her new husband. Because their family had protected them, their blood now seeped into the earth, their lives but a memory.

Her knees buckled. Bao clasped her to his chest, supporting her.

"We can't stay here. We must leave," he said, but he didn't move. Instead, his arms tightened around her. His chest expanded and shuddered under her cheek.

She closed her eyes. "I know."

Her whispered words caught on a sob, but she couldn't cry. She didn't have time to cry. Once they reached the cave and they were safe, she would let her emotions take hold, but not now. Now, they had to escape.

Stepping away from him, she raised her chin and narrowed her eyes. Mao wouldn't win. They'd escape the soldiers and live as their parents had wanted them to live. And if they had children . . . She couldn't think about that now. That would happen, or it wouldn't.

"Let's go," she said and turned her back on her village. She knew they'd never return.

A chill wind blew past them. Above them, dark clouds scudded across the sky, threatening to wrap the sun in their cold embrace and blanket the world in another onslaught of snow.

By the time they reached the cave, the storm had closed in on them completely, turning the world into a white prison. Only her knowledge of the mountains and their enhanced eyesight allowed them to find it. They stumbled inside.

Xuě rubbed her arms and shivered. They'd either need to change into their animal form or build a fire. A stack of wood lined one wall. She frowned. They wouldn't be using it tonight.

A fire would draw attention. Not while snowing, but, once it stopped, the smoke would seep out of the cave and alert anyone looking in their direction. With a sigh, she crossed to the mat covered by a blanket she kept in the corner and rubbed her hands together in an attempt to warm them. Next to it was a rucksack she kept packed with a few supplies for the days she stayed in the cave when the village closed in on her. Although she could sleep in animal form, she chose not to most of the time.

"You come prepared."

Bao's voice interrupted her thoughts.

"I like to get away from the village from time to time."

"Your parents don't mind?"

She shook her head. "They seem to understand . . . "

Her words caught in her throat, and tears welled up. Grief and anger lanced through her. She crumpled to the mat, wrapped her arms around her knees, and rocked back and forth. Her parents were dead. Killed by the officer and his men. Killed because of them, but more because of Mao. Senseless deaths. All of them.

Bao encircled her with his arms from behind and pulled her against his chest.

"There's nothing we could've done . . . even in snow leopard form." His voice hitched, he paused. "There were too many of them with guns. You know that, right?"

Was he trying to convince her or himself?

"Right?" he repeated more forcefully.

She nodded, but, inside of herself, she couldn't help but wonder. "Perhaps if we'd come forward and turned ourselves in—"

A bitter laugh echoed against the rock walls. It grated on her ears and cut across her shredded nerves. Xuě looked up into his face. Tears streamed down his cheeks, and a flush stained his pale cheeks a bright red.

"Do you really think he'd've let anyone live once he found us? First, it would've meant your father had lied to him. Second, do you really think they want anyone to know about us and what we are? I doubt the officer even knows, but I bet his orders included capturing us and killing anyone who knew about us anyway. What's a few more deaths amidst the famine?"

She widened her eyes. He was right. Had she not just been thinking how little Mao cared about the people of China? How the government had come and taken their animals a few years ago? How cold she was? How much better it was before the Cultural Revolution? Treasonous thoughts. Thoughts she'd never have dared to speak aloud, even whisper, for fear someone in the village would report her and her family. Perhaps someone in the village had reported her because of what she was. She'd done everything she could to prevent giving them any excuse to do so. But the famine had changed people, and she'd never know how the government found out. Whether it was another villager, or the government had found records, or . . . it didn't really matter how now.

"We can never return to my village," she said. Pain lacerated her already shredded emotions, but she swallowed it, raised her head, and straightened her spine. Her life had never been easy, but she'd survive. Her parents had sacrificed themselves for her. She wouldn't disappoint them. She lifted her gaze to Bao's. "Nor can we go to yours." She closed her eyes and took a deep breath before opening them to regard him solemnly and saying, "Nor can we stay here. It's not safe."

His face a stoic mask, he nodded. Icy determination glinted in his eyes. "Do you keep any food here?"

"I have some *bakkwa*. Most of what I catch I take," she stopped, the pain resurfacing, and corrected herself, "took to the village. We always dry a portion of it in case I'm unable to bring home fresh meat. The rucksack keeps vermin out of my clothes when I'm in snow leopard form."

"We can carry our clothes in it when we shift."

A shiver ran down her spine. "I'm freezing. I either need to shift or build a fire."

"We need to plan our escape. We can't do that in cat form."

She nodded. A fire . . . the thought scared her. The smoke

. . .

"A small fire will help heat the cave," he said. "We can smother it as soon as we have our plan set out and shift when we go to sleep."

"Okay."

They gathered some wood and tinder in silence. While Bao stacked the wood, she found the matches wrapped in a waterproof skin she kept in the rucksack. There weren't very many, but they should see them through this night and maybe a few more. With the scarcity of supplies, these would be the last they'd have for a very long time.

Tears threatened to fall. She swallowed them again. Her throat burned with the effort, but, once they started falling, they'd never stop. They had to escape Mao and the People's Liberation Army. Tears wouldn't help them do that. She stuffed the pain deeper and turned her attention to building the fire.

A few minutes later, a small fire kindled to life. Its faint heat pushed back the darkness that loomed on the edges of her consciousness.

Without a word, Bao pulled the mat closer to the fire and sat down. She joined him, and they wrapped the blanket around their shoulders and huddled together, sharing warmth. She took a piece of *bakkwa* from the rucksack, tore it in two, and handed him half.

"*Xièxiè,*" he said and took a bite.

She nibbled at her piece, savoring each tiny bite. The flavor popped in her mouth, and her stomach growled.

He finished his jerky and held his hands out to the small fire. "We'll need to hunt and avoid other snow leopards. They won't take kindly to us in their range."

"I know, but we can leave what we don't eat behind for them to find . . . if humans don't find it first."

He shrugged. "We can't control that."

She bowed her head, acknowledging the truth. They could only do so much. "Which way?"

"To Tibet and on to India. We'll never be safe here."

Her heart plummeted. Leaving China? The land that had given her life? It hadn't been kind, but she'd survived. Not only had they taken her parents, but now her homeland. He was right. They'd never be safe in China. They couldn't stay.

He wrapped an arm around her and drew her close, kissing the top of her head. She stiffened then relaxed against his side. The warmth from the fire and his body eased some of the fear that coiled tight around her heart.

"We'll escape. You'll see. We can outwit them."

She didn't respond. Whether they eluded the People's Liberation Army or not remained to be seen. They had many *gōnglĭ* to travel to get to India. And, even then, the Indian people may not welcome them.

Gritty-eyed, she stared at the fire and clung to her new husband.

# Chapter Five

Xuě startled awake. She lay on her side facing the dying fire. Only the embers were left, and they glowed red in the gloom. Bao spooned her from behind, his arm draped over her waist. His chest rose and fell in the steady rhythm of sleep. Outside, nothing stirred except the gently falling snow. How long had she slept?

Her stomach growled, and her thoughts wandered to the events earlier that day. She closed her eyes, but the image of the officer hitting her father played over and over in her mind's eye. The shots rang in her ears again, and pain knifed through her.

A tear slipped out and trickled down her cheek. Another one escaped and followed the first one's path. Soon, a torrent of tears erupted, and she gasped for air.

Bao's arm tightened around her. "Xuě?"

The gentleness of his voice increased the flood of tears, and sobs wracked her body.

"Shh . . . it will be all right."

"They're gone."

"I know," he whispered into her hair.

"Mama will never call me her *xiǎo gūnián* anymore. And Papa—" The words caught in her throat. She would never hear him call her his *xiǎo māo*. If only she'd been a little cat instead of a shape shifter, things would've been different.

"I know." His voice hitched on the two words, reminding her of his loss.

Turning, she gazed into his face. Such a strong face and so handsome. Tears stained his cheeks, and a gentleness lurked in his eyes that was missing from so many other men she'd known in her village. Certainly, she'd never seen it from the Japanese doctors. She shuddered and pushed the memories of that place away. They haunted her still, but they deserved no place in this moment of grief.

She curled into him and allowed the pain out. He clasped her to him. She found comfort in their combined grief. The sounds of their sobs mingled in the quiet. Slowly, the pain ebbed to a quiet, dull ache. She sniffled and sighed, her head resting against his chest. The steady beat of his heart reassured her of his solidity. She snuggled in and kissed his chest.

The action sent a tingle rippling through her, and she stilled. He ran his hands down her back and cupped her butt. She thrust her pelvis against him, the need to connect to another living being sweeping through her. She looked up, and he swooped down, capturing her lips with his. Desire exploded over her, and she pressed herself against him.

He lifted his mouth from hers and trailed kisses down her neck. Raising her chin, she allowed her head to fall back and give him better access as she slid her hands down and under the waistband of his pants. He groaned and ground his *jījī* against her. A mewling sound escaped her.

"Please," she begged. "I need you inside of me."

He pulled away and kneeled next to her. With shaking hands, he stripped. Goose bumps dotted his skin where the cool air came in contact with it.

Unable to stop herself, she reached out and ran her hand down his smooth chest over his stomach down to his rigid *jījī*. His muscles contracted under her touch. His hand covered hers and closed her fingers around it. She licked her suddenly dry lips, her gaze finding his. He nodded and pushed his hips toward her mouth. A pearl of liquid hung suspended on the tip.

"Taste me."

Her eyes widened. "I—"

"Please, Xuě."

Closing her eyes, she leaned forward and tentatively licked his *jījī*. It was smooth, but hard, like silk encasing a bamboo staff.

He moaned and cupped her head, holding it in place. She

glanced up at his face. A grimace pulled the skin taut. She tried to move away, but he tightened his grip and looked down at her.

"Do you want to taste me?"

Words stuck in her throat, and she moistened her lips again and nodded. She wanted to take him in her mouth and . . . She wasn't sure what she'd do next, but she wanted to give him pleasure as he'd given her in her parents' hut. That thought shot arrows of desire zipping through her. She squirmed, and her *yīndào* contracted. Was that wrong of her? Why did she want this? But the desire to please him and experience the bliss of orgasm again erased her misgivings.

"Open your mouth."

Without a word, she obeyed, and he slipped his *jījī* inside with a moan. Not sure what to do, she closed her mouth around him. He held her head there and moved slowly in and out. Just when she thought he'd gone too far, he'd pull back and slide out to the tip before gliding back in. His movements evoked images of their lovemaking, and the need to have him pumping inside of her swelled to an agonizing yearning that consumed all of her thoughts.

He pulled out and fumbled at the buttons on her clothes, until he succeeded in slipping her shirt and pants off. Pressing her back against the blanket, he positioned himself between her legs and thrust into her.

She cried out and rushed up to meet him. His pelvis pressed against her *àikòu*, and a shower of sparks flew behind her eyelids, sending her over the precipice on a wave of pleasure. She collapsed against the blanket, panting, thinking she could find no more pleasure.

He continued to stroke in and out. Each stroke kindled a new fire within her. She opened her eyes in surprise as the pressure mounted once more. It built into a raging inferno, burning through her fears and misgivings. It burned through her carefully constructed barriers and expanded her consciousness into him, until his breath became her breath, his senses became her senses, and they exploded into a million, tiny particles of light and their souls kissed.

Bit by bit, the world came into focus. She lay staring at the ceiling of the cave, her heartbeat returning to normal, but the beauty she'd just experienced overwhelmed her. How was this possible? How could enjoying this be wrong? What they shared transcended the animal aspects of sex. If she believed in a god, this would confirm its existence.

"I've dreamed of sharing a bond like this for . . . ever. Although the villagers are kind, they'll never know what it's like to be half man, half animal." Bao pulled her close and trailed the tips of his fingers up and down her arm in a lazy pattern. "I watched other men in my village marry and wanted that for myself—someone who'd be mine, and I'd be theirs. When my parents described you to me last year, I hoped it'd be you, the girl who sat beside me in that truck, the girl I felt a connection to all those years ago."

His husky voice caressed her exposed soul. She shivered and pressed herself closer. His kindness that day in the truck had stayed with her the entire time she'd lived at the monastery until her parents adopted her. She'd never seen him again. The monks had kept the boys separated from the girls at all times. The monks were kind but strict, certainly better than the Japanese.

"What if I wasn't that girl you'd met in the back of the truck so long ago?"

"I prayed every night to Buddha that you were, but, in the end, my parents had chosen you and I'd obey them, and I'd finally have the wife I'd always yearned for." Their gazes met, his shone silver in the dying light of the fire. "It's my great fortune that you and she are one and the same."

She rested her head against his chest, a smile pulling up the corners of her mouth. Happiness wrapped itself around her for a moment, blocking out the world and the pain of loss.

A contented silence surrounded them. His chest rose and fell with his relaxed breathing. His heart beat a comforting tattoo under her ear. She yawned and blinked, staring at the dim outline of the cave entrance. Beyond the opening, the wind howled, and the snow fell, protecting them from the reality that awaited them.

Later, when night fell, they'd leave the safety of this cave and begin their long trek to India. But she didn't want to think about that right now. She wanted to enjoy this moment of peace, where fear and loneliness didn't exist. Only his heart beating, his arms around her, this feeling of connection and belonging mattered.

She blinked again and allowed her eyes to close, drifting into an untroubled sleep.

"Xuě . . . Xuě . . . "

A man's voice dragged her from a deep sleep. Cracking open her eyes, she looked into Bao's face, and all of the memories flooded into her. She closed her eyes and pushed the pain away. She didn't have time to cry.

He cupped her face, his gaze full of understanding. "I know."

She glanced away to gather her composure.

"It's time to leave. The snow has stopped, and night has fallen."

She nodded and sat up. Cold air whirled around her bare shoulders, and she shivered. Grabbing her clothes, she folded them and put them in the rucksack. She folded and carefully placed the blanket, followed by the mat, in the rucksack along with her shoes. Shivers ran down her bare skin. One last shiver, and her skin rippled. Fur sprouted, bones popped, and she stood on all fours.

Bao's eyes widened. A grin broke out on his face, and he rubbed his hand down her side, ruffling her pelt. She leaned into his touch and chuffed.

"You're beautiful."

The corners of his mouth tipped up in another smile. He stripped, put his clothes and shoes in the rucksack with hers, and closed it. She chuffed at him and lifted a paw. He slipped it over her paw and shoulders. She lifted her other paw, and he finished putting it on. He tightened the straps to prevent it from sliding.

They'd discussed this earlier. They'd travel at night in their cat form, taking turns carrying her rucksack full of their belongings, even hunting at night when necessary as most snow leopards did. During the day, they'd find somewhere to rest as humans.

She sat and stared at him unblinking, her long tail swishing against the stone. A tremor overtook his body, and the sounds of his bones cracking as they adjusted to his cat form echoed in her ears. Fur sprouted, covering his skin. He jerked, a grimace flashing across his face, and then he dropped down onto all fours.

Xuě padded forward and rubbed her head against him before turning toward the entrance and stepping out into the cloudless night. Nothing stirred. Moonlight glinted off the snow. She crouched lower to the ground and slunk up the mountain. Even though she'd known when they left the village she'd never return, this solidified that fact. Turning her back on the village she'd called home and crossing these hills meant goodbye forever. She blinked and pushed those thoughts away. Her new life awaited her outside of China. She had to focus on surviving the trek.

They crested the mountain above her cave with relative ease. Descending the other side proved tricky with the shifting snow and loose shale underneath it, but they reached the bottom. They crossed a frozen over stream and stopped. What appeared to be an abandoned village lay nestled against the mountainside just beyond the stream. The moon had long since set.

Xuě lifted her head and sniffed the air. Her tail twitched. Although they had traveled several *gōnglǐ* of difficult terrain, she feared they'd be caught. She looked at Bao. Their gazes connected. In silent agreement, they skirted the perimeter and continued through the snow farther up the next mountain. The trees dropped away the higher they ascended. Finally, she spotted a rocky outcropping. In its shadow, where no one could see her, she collapsed, resting her head on her front paws, and closed her eyes.

The pack pulled at her aching shoulders.

Bao padded up next to her and shifted. "Let me take that off of you."

She pushed herself up to a sitting position and allowed him to remove the uncomfortable bag. He set it next to her. She lay back down and sighed.

"I'm going to hunt for food. Rest for a bit. I'll be back." He shifted and disappeared into the darkness.

It seemed like her eyes had just drifted closed when he returned and head butted her awake. Early morning light cast shadows on the ground at the front of the outcropping. The scent of a fresh kill tickled her nose. Her stomach grumbled. Standing, she rubbed against him before walking over to the young *pán yáng* he'd killed and dragged to just inside their hideout. He joined her. Her cat purred with excitement and twitched her tail, but her human side recoiled at the thought of eating raw meat, even in her cat form. Necessity took precedence. Cooking required a fire, and fire would give away their location to others. At least, they wouldn't go hungry.

She bent and forced herself to eat as much as her stomach and mind allowed. When done, she walked over to the end of the overhang and looked out to the east, back toward her village. The sun peeked over the edge of the mountains, its rays streaking across the pale, blue sky and casting a fiery glow to the tips of the peaks.

Behind her, Bao chuffed. She turned. Their gazes connected. He broke the eye contact and retreated to the back of their hideout. With a sigh, he lay down, blinking his eyes lazily at her as if inviting her to join him, but the nap had refreshed her. Later, she would sleep. For now, the quiet serenity of the dawn soothed her aching spirit.

# Chapter Six

Stars winked in the velvety black sky. Each breath she took created a white puff. The moon had long set, fatigue haunted her every step, but the urgency to escape pushed her onward.

She missed her human form. For the past three days, they'd traveled as cats, avoiding all contact with other humans. They'd traversed their mountain range and had crossed into another one. The further they traveled from her home range, the fewer plants she recognized. The land became more arid the farther south they traveled. Soon, nothing looked familiar, but some of the animals. They caught another *pán yáng*, leaving behind what they couldn't eat. Only when they needed to remove the rucksack did they shift. Today, when they stopped and found a place to hide, she would shift to help him with the rucksack. Perhaps she would stay in human form and wear clothes for a few hours just to feel normal again.

She padded ahead of him downhill into a larger canyon. If they kept the same pace, they'd reach the floor before night gave way to dawn. Perhaps they'd have time to hunt before finding a place to hide.

The sound of a solo gunshot echoed through the night air. Xuě froze before crouching as close to the ground as possible and racing across the frozen ground for a large boulder up ahead to slip behind it. Bao scrambled after her. No sooner did he settle next to her than the area below them erupted in gunfire. Stray bullets whizzed over their heads. She flinched and hunkered closer to the ground, wrapping her tail around her body and pressing herself against the stone. Bao pushed up against her.

She closed her eyes but quickly opened them. Staying alert and using all of her senses could save her life. She twitched her tail back and forth, searching for any small sound over the firefight below.

She stayed in this position for what seemed like hours. Her legs cramped, but the continued gunfire kept her affixed to the spot. The cries of dying men drifted up to them. Each cry burned into her memory. A sound she doubted she'd ever forget.

Dawn broke, and the gunfire petered out until it stopped completely. Voices filtered up to them, but the distance combined with the slight echo prevented her from understanding what they were saying. Eventually, the voices moved away. A lone shot reverberated in the canyon, and an eerie silence descended.

Crows and kites circled overhead. Only when they swooped down toward the ground did she inch forward and look around the rock down to the canyon floor.

Bodies littered a snow-covered ground stained red. Other than the crows and kites feasting on the grisly aftermath, nothing stirred.

Her stomach churned, and bile rose in her mouth. She retreated behind the rock, shaking. They couldn't stay here. They had to leave, but, even with their coats to camouflage them against the rocks, a soldier could spot them. Did they continue and find a better place to hide or stay where they were until nightfall?

Bao nudged her, licking her ear. Their gazes met. He stood and stared at her expectantly. Her instincts screamed in protest, but she followed his lead.

He stepped out from behind the rock and trotted down toward an indentation that concealed him from below. She waited until he slipped into it before she sprinted across to join him. They repeated this process until the canyon floor lay a few feet below them.

Even though the birds appeared to be the only living things besides the two of them in the canyon, her skin itched as if something or someone watched them. She searched the area for any other sign of life, her tail twitching behind her.

Nothing moved. Had everyone left? They should be running the opposite direction. Why was Bao leading them down here?

Once again, he rose to move closer, but she stopped him with a paw. He swung around to look at her. Their gazes met, but then a flicker of movement beyond him drew her attention. A soldier in a PLA uniform stepped out from behind a rock and stared in their direction, his rifle at the ready.

Her breath caught in her throat. Had he seen them?

As if in answer to her question, he moved toward them. The sound of his rifle cocking echoed in her ears.

"Chin, what are you doing?" someone barked from beyond the soldier.

"I thought I saw something move, *xiānshēng*. Maybe a snow leopard," the soldier said.

The officer shrugged. "Let it have the dead. We're leaving. Get in the truck."

"Yes, *xiānshēng*." The soldier pointed his rifle at the ground, turned away from them, and walked around the rock, disappearing from view.

An engine rumbled to life. The ground vibrated as the truck drove away.

When the sound finally faded into the distance, Xuě slipped out from behind their cover. The Chinese troops had left behind a scene of horror. Her stomach churned from the sights and smells, but she forced herself to walk amongst the bodies, blood staining her paws. She chuffed at Bao. He glanced in her direction. With a flick of her tail, she turned, trotted behind a boulder, and shifted. She rubbed her feet in the snow, trying to remove the blood. He came up next to her.

"We cannot leave them like this," she said and removed the pack from his back. She opened it and pulled out her clothes. "They must be buried."

He chuffed and shifted. "We don't have time." But even as he said this, he reached for the pack and his clothes.

"We'd be resting now anyway."

"We can't—"

"Please . . . " Tears welled up and threatened to spill over. "I

hope that, if someone found our parents, they'd do the same."
She swiped at the tears and swallowed the pain. "Please . . .
Bao, let's help their spirits rest and hope that our parents can
cross to the other side even if they aren't buried."

He bowed his head and drew in a deep breath. His shoulders slumping, he nodded. He donned his clothes, slipping
the pack back on his shoulders, and they returned to the death
scene, chasing the birds away.

As they had no way to dig holes for each corpse, they piled
rocks until no part of the person could be seen. With each finished grave, they stopped and wished the dead peace. Anger at
the senseless death billowed up until she wanted to scream in
rage. Instead, she continued to pile one rock at a time side by
side with her new husband, silent tears of rage trickling down
her cheeks.

She glanced in his direction. He'd stopped and stood over
a man. He nudged him with his foot. The man moaned and
opened his eyes. They widened. The smell of his fear reached
through the stench and tickled her nose.

Bao squatted next to him and said, "Please don't be afraid.
We're here to help."

The man's eyes widened even farther. When he spoke, it
was in halting Chinese. "You not soldiers?"

She walked over to Bao and knelt next to him. Blood oozed
from his side. "No."

"We must stop the bleeding," Bao said.

She nodded. They needed water and a clean cloth to wrap
him in. But nothing was clean.

He strode to another man, lying on his back, eyes staring
wide into the distance, seeing a land only the dead could see,
and pulled at his jacket.

"What are you doing?" she asked.

"He doesn't need this anymore. We can tear it into strips
and use it to bind his comrade's wounds. When we're done,
we'll bury him. Come. Help me."

Her stomach roiled in protest, but she suppressed her reaction and helped him. The threadbare jacket tore easily once

removed. She closed the dead man's eyes and crossed his arms over his bare chest. Turning her back on him, she returned to the man moaning on the ground. While Bao opened the wounded man's shirt, she climbed the hill and gathered a bit of snow. It burned her hands, but they would be able to use it to clean the wound. She trotted down to join them and knelt.

"It looks as if the bullet only grazed you," Bao said, his voice full of suspicion.

"I was scout." He waved an arm toward the mountain they'd hid on for hours, exposing a sunken stomach and protruding ribs that matched his gaunt face. "When I heard shots, I came running, but I was too late. All dead." He stared at the sky, his nearly black eyes full of anger and sadness. "They shot me and shoved me to ground. I hit head. I don't remember after."

Xuě looked up at the mountain. Even over the gunfire, they would've heard him. Bao glanced at her. His expression strengthened her suspicions. He lied. She narrowed her eyes and stared at him. What was he hiding?

The melting ice stung her fingers. She handed it to Bao, who placed it on the wound. The man flinched and cried out.

For the first time, she noticed his clothes. "Why are you dressed differently than the others?" she asked.

His gaze darted to the left and then the right. "We're Tibetan rebels. We don't have a uniform."

The more he spoke, his Chinese increased in fluency. Instinct told her to run, but she ignored it. Simple humanity required they help him. Once done, they'd leave him behind.

Bao wrapped the man's wound and stood. He didn't say anything.

"Let's finish burying the dead," she said. "We must leave."

She turned away from the man and went back to stacking stones. Only two more to go. Bao joined her. Her arms ached, and her eyes stung from lack of sleep, but she wouldn't rest until they'd buried all of the dead and found a safe place to stay for the remainder of the day.

Rocks clacked together behind them, and all of the hair

on her body stood on end. Her *yukihyō* yowled a warning. She spun. The man they'd saved swung a rock at her head. Her *yukihyō* cowered and froze, but her human will to survive fought against her animal's incapacitating fear. She ducked and shoved him away from her. He toppled to the ground. A crazed look lit his eyes.

"You can't have them. They're mine. I waited out the battle for them. If that bullet hadn't ricocheted and hit me, I'd be fine," the man said in perfect Chinese. Spittle dripped from his mouth. He licked at it. "All of them are mine."

She shivered and backed away from him. "We don't want them. We're honoring them so their spirits can go to the afterlife."

The man crawled toward her. She continued to back away.

"Honoring them? They're nothing but Tibetan rebels, no better than animals, but their flesh is sweet."

A shudder ran down her spine when she realized what all of his babbling meant. He planned on eating the dead men.

"Bao?" she called.

The man stood and advanced on her.

"Bao?" Panic threaded its way into her voice. She could kill a *pán yáng* without a thought—they were food, but a man? Her *yukihyō* cowered. Snow leopards froze at confrontation with humans, but they also avoided each other to prevent unnecessary fights unless they were mating or a mother was caring for her cubs. Her cat would be of no use as she viewed this man as kin to her human side. Xuě steeled herself for the upcoming fight, struggling to subdue the snow leopard's instinctive paralysis and refusal to fight. Where was he?

Bao streaked in front of her and tackled the man. They thudded to the ground, and the man went limp, his eyes open wide. Bao kept him pinned, but the cannibal didn't move. Blood seeped from under his head. Leaning closer, her husband sniffed at him.

"Is he . . . ?" She couldn't finish the sentence.

"*Shi.*"

Her shoulders drooped, and a sigh escaped her. Bao had

saved her. He battled his instincts and beat them, but death had struck again. The man would have to be buried as well.

"Why would he—"

"He was starving. Starvation makes people do things they'd never consider doing," Bao said and stood.

"We should've waited for dark. Maybe he'd still be alive. Maybe this wouldn't have happened." Guilt gnawed at her.

"He attacked you. He would've killed you and eaten you without a thought. He lost his humanity because of—"

"Mao," she said. "Because of this famine." She stood staring at the ground, her mind back in her village. "Do you think our village would've resorted to the same without us?"

He shrugged. "Maybe, but we didn't live in the valleys where they depend solely on rice and their livestock. We could hunt the animals in the mountains if necessary. Our villages could have done that without us."

She gasped as the truth hit her.

# Chapter Seven

They covered the man they'd tried to save with rocks before leaving the canyon in search of a place to rest and spend the remainder of the day. Despite his attack, she couldn't leave him to the animals. He'd suffered enough. If she couldn't shift, would she do the same? She hoped not.

She trudged behind Bao for what seemed like hours, lifting her feet inches above the ground. The overnight travel, the ordeal of the firefight, burying the dead, and the shock of being attacked had drained her. Luckily, picking up her feet and placing one foot in front of the other required all of her focus. It prevented her from agonizing over her realization about her life in the village and her questions for Bao.

Bao stopped, and she ran into him. He stumbled forward. She sank to her knees.

"Xuě . . ."

She looked up at him and swayed.

"There is a cave a little bit away."

Nodding, she placed her hands on the ground, pushed herself up to her feet with a groan, and followed him. As soon as the cool dark surrounded her, she sank to her knees again and shivered.

"Are you okay?"

Bao's concerned voice came from a distance. She nodded, but she couldn't stop her teeth from chattering. Her mind careened out of control with the earlier revelations, and they beat at her understanding of her function in the village.

They hadn't needed her. She'd thought she'd contributed to the village, but they hadn't really needed her. They'd used her just like the Japanese and treated her no better than a *maruta*. She'd created that fantasy in her head so she felt like she belonged, but she'd never belonged. Not there. She'd never belonged there. Maybe, she didn't belong anywhere.

She wrapped her arms around her knees and rocked back and forth. Her eyes dry, her heart numb, she stared into the darkness, riding the storm that raged within her.

Had it all been an illusion? Wishful thinking on her part?

"Xuě?"

Their gazes met. His pale face stood out against the inky gloom of the cave.

He knelt beside her, reached out, and cupped her cheek. She leaned into him. The heat from his hand seeped into her, unfurling its tendrils. Peace slipped into her bloodstream and along her nerve endings. She closed her eyes, her breathing slowed, and the shivering stopped.

This man's gentle touch was quickly becoming as necessary to her survival as her beating heart. It would scare her if she weren't so tired.

Opening her eyes, she stared into his and said, "*Xièxiè.*"

He smiled and stood, removing the backpack and setting it on the floor. "I think I will hunt. You can rest here. I should return soon. I imagine I'll find a marmot or two."

She grabbed his hand and pulled him down. "Don't go. Stay. Hold me. We can hunt together tonight before we leave."

He hesitated. Indecision shone in his eyes. Would he stay?

"Please . . ."

"If you wish," he said. Sitting down and sliding his arms around her, he gathered her close to his chest.

She snuggled against him and breathed in his scent. It filled her and stirred a deep need for connection. Over the past few days, her life had been turned upside down. Without Bao, she didn't know how she'd have continued on. She tightened her arms around him. Her parents' insistence she marry this man had saved her life, even if they'd lost theirs.

A single tear trickled down her cheek before she shored up the dam that threatened to burst. No more tears. The past couldn't be changed. Only the present mattered . . . and the future that lay ahead of her.

He brushed her hair back from her forehead and kissed it.

"It really would be better if I hunted now so that we can leave tonight. We aren't that far from the canyon floor. We'd be safer away from here."

He was right, but all of her yearned to be a part of him, to be bonded to him with a life-affirming act.

"Stay. Love me." She raised her head and kissed him.

His mouth opened to her tongue, and he moaned. With a jagged groan, he pulled away. She reached for him, but he shook his head.

"It's too dangerous, and we must eat. Rest," he said. "I'll be back soon."

He stood, stripped, and shifted, disappearing into the late afternoon sun. Even after that one kiss, her body ached for completion, but he was right. Later, *gōnglǐ* away from this cursed place, they could make love.

Without the distraction, unwanted thoughts bombarded her defenses. She shoved them away and reached for the backpack to retrieve the blanket, a spare piece of cloth, and a pan to collect snow for melting in.

Pan in hand, she stood with a grunt, wrapping the blanket around her shoulders, and plodded to the opening. Off to the side in the shade, clean snow sparkled in the weak light. She piled a few handfuls in the pan and set it on a rock in the sun. She crouched down beside it, closed her eyes for a brief moment, and lifted her face to sun. What little warmth its weak light shed soothed her battered senses. She opened her eyes and jiggled the pan back and forth to create more friction and speed up the process of melting the snow.

As she waited for the snow to melt, she huddled in the blanket and stared out across the canyon. They'd traversed enough ground and gone around a large rock outcrop that blocked her view of the battle site. Only the large number of carrion birds circling alerted her to its location.

She turned her gaze and mind away from the horrors resting under the soaring birds and focused on the task at hand. Once the snow melted into water, she drank her fill and added more. This would be for bathing. She hadn't bathed for days.

Of course, she'd been in animal form for most of them, so it wasn't as noticeable. In human form, it felt as if layers of dirt had caked onto her skin, especially after moving so many rocks.

Bao padded up and dropped a *hàntă* at her feet before shifting.

"*Xièxiè.*"

He trotted into the cave and emerged a few minutes later in human form and dressed. "There isn't much game around here," he said.

Which was obvious if all he could bring back was the large rodent, one of her least favorite meals.

"Did you see any other signs of life?"

He shook his head. "It's quiet out there."

The thought of starting a fire and cooking the food tempted her, but they couldn't chance it. With a sigh, she stripped and shifted. Someday, when they were safe, she'd never eat in her cat form again.

Compared to so many others, they at least had food. An image of the crazed cannibal wavered in her mind's eye. She pushed it away.

Smothering her ingratitude, she bent and ate only enough to sate the gnawing hunger. She moved away, giving Bao room to come in and finish it. As he ate, she shifted and dressed.

With nothing left to occupy her, she stared sightlessly at the rock walls in front of her. Her mind circled the epiphanies about her village in a never ending loop. Despair pushed against the carefully constructed walls that she'd built to protect her from the overwhelming pain of reality.

How could she've been so blind? So stupid?

She huddled into herself and squeezed her eyes shut, trying to stop the voices telling her she was useless, that no one cared about her anymore now that her parents were dead.

*Bao cares for you.*

She raised her head and focused on her husband. He crouched in his *yukihyō* form over the remains of the marmot. He sat back on his haunches and cleaned himself. His pelt thick and luxurious beckoned to her. Tentatively, she reached out and slid her hands through his coat, fascinated with how her fingers disappeared into his soft fur. He paused, and his silver gaze captured hers. Something flickered within them—something that called to her. Her *yukihyō* chuffed, and her breath caught.

He head butted her, leaning hard against her until she laid back. The air filled with electricity as pops and snaps lit the darkness around them. Seconds later, a naked Bao leaned over her, his lips finding hers.

Desire heating her blood, she pulled him close and allowed the sensations to chase her sorrow away.

Days passed in a blur of monotony. The terrain under her feet had long since shifted from the rocky scree of home to hard packed dirt on steep, slick mountainsides. Every night, she rose, shifted, and joined Bao to continue their journey. The stars winked silently above them. In the light of the day, she slept replete in his arms in caves or under overhangs. Sometimes, he hunted; sometimes, she did. Often, she melted snow in the pan for water. On the sixth night of travel, as the stars receded into the soft, gray light of dawn, she nearly bumped into Bao's tail at the edge of a vast valley. A rolling grassy plain extended out to the horizon. In the distance, large rock outcroppings rose from the valley floor like giants reaching for the sky. A cold, dry wind whooshed up the steep slope and ruffled her fur, carrying a scent they'd avoided up to this point. Bao stilled and turned to her. Her gaze met his in silent understanding.

*Láng.*

# Chapter Eight

Xuě crouched low to the ground and scanned the valley floor. Her body screamed to shift and sleep, but the need to eat, secure a safe resting place, and steer clear of the newest threat superseded everything else.

Bao leaned into her, and she glanced at him. He stared into the distance. She followed his gaze. Two—no three—*láng* trotted straight through the grass toward them. Their coats would have provided excellent camouflage amidst the grass if they'd stayed still. Either they didn't see her and Bao, or they didn't care.

Her instincts urged her to bolt, but the barren landscape behind them offered few, if any, hiding places. They could slip into the grass, but, crouched low, they'd be unable to see where they were. If she moved, the *láng* would certainly see them. Perhaps the group would turn and move off in another direction. But, as the seconds ticked by, the trio continued their course straight for them.

Xuě's heart pounded an uneasy tattoo. Her muscles wound tighter and tighter. Bao's tail twitched against hers, echoing the tension that roiled with her.

About ten paces out, the *láng* stopped advancing. The largest sat down, cocked its head, and stared at them, its thick fur ruff the color of the sandy stone beneath its paws. Golden eyes regarded them with intelligence. The other two paced behind it as if unsure what to do. The leader barked, and the two sat, flanking it.

Dawn stretched pink tendrils across the sky, the dark of the night giving way to the new day, and Xuě shifted her weight and narrowed her eyes. Usually, the two species avoided each other. What did they want?

Bao rose and slinked backward up the slope. The middle

wolf stood and stepped toward them. The other two joined the first. Xuě tensed, her tired muscles aching, and followed her husband one tentative step at a time. Running would activate their hunt instinct. As exhausted as she was, she couldn't outrun them.

The *láng* backed them up the mountain several feet. With each step, the fatigue settled deeper into her bones, and her nerves wound tighter. Sleep knocked at her eyelids, dragging them down. With a chuff, she sat and refused to retreat any farther. Their path lay across the plain ahead of them, not over the mountains behind them. She'd rather die by wolves than suffer under Mao.

Anger and fear pulsed through her. She would live.

A shiver rippled across her skin, and, with a flash of light and a popping noise as her bones readjusted themselves, she shifted from cat to human. The wolves didn't even flinch. Anxiety snaked through her. All the wolves she'd encountered feared humans. Were they . . . ?

The alpha smiled, revealing sharp canines. His pelt rippled and stretched, bones popped, and a light flashed. A man with golden eyes, fair skin, and hair the color of the sand arose before her. She smothered a gasp. Years had passed since she'd seen someone of his heritage. Not since . . . She blocked the thought. A chill snaked up her ankles as if reminding her of that last day facing Taisho Ishii.

*Maruta* whispered over her soul.

With a blink, she came back to the present and the man in front of her. He didn't try to hide his nakedness. Instead, he stood, chin raised, as if daring her to run.

Prickles of heat streaked up her neck and into her cheeks, chasing away the goose bumps rising on her bare skin from the sudden assault of cold air. She averted her eyes, glancing back at Bao, even as she tried to cover herself. He padded up to her and sat between her and the naked man. He wrapped his tail around her feet, as if to claim her. Why didn't he shift, too?

She frowned and bent down. Reaching for the backpack

Bao carried, she pulled out her clothes and quickly donned them.

"What do you want?" she asked, wriggling her toes in the fine powdered dirt. She kept her focus on the puffs of fine dust disturbed by her actions.

"Why are you here?"

The chill tone added an edge to the heavily accented Chinese. The harshness drew her gaze up to meet his. Steel and suspicion glinted in his eyes.

"I'm just passing through."

"Passing through?" He raised a tawny eyebrow at her.

She nodded. "*Shi*."

He studied her in silence. Unease trickled down her spine. Bao's muscles tensed. She buried her hand in his ruff and squeezed gently.

"Where are you going?"

"India."

"Why?"

She looked to the horizon. Echoes of gunshots filled her ears, and the memories she'd buried deep crept closer. A quiver threatened to overtake her. She clenched her hand in Bao's fur. He chuffed. With a shake of her head, she loosened her grip and banished the unwanted visions before meeting the alpha's steady regard.

"The famine has stretched into our mountains. There isn't enough food to keep us alive."

It wasn't a lie, per se, but it wasn't the whole truth.

He didn't say anything, just continued to stare at her. A shiver of apprehension shot through her under his probing gaze. Only years of concealing her emotions kept her silent and expressionless. Any sign of weakness could give away her lie.

"Many have come through here to escape the famine. Most do not make it."

She swallowed the unexpected sob that rose in her throat. Tears burned at the back of her eyes. Her nostrils flared. She raised her chin, determined not to cry, and blurted, "My family is dead."

Something flickered in the shifter's eyes. "I'm sorry," he said.

She nodded. "*Xièxiè.*"

He turned to the *láng* behind him and said something in a language she didn't understand. In humanlike fashion, they nodded, confirming her suspicions. Wolf shifters. What had she done? Had her actions betrayed them? Were these *men* in league with Mao? Narrowing her eyes, she reached for the buttons on her shirt and unbuttoned them. She would shift and be killed before she'd become a medical experiment again.

When he faced them, he raised his eyebrows at her near nakedness.

"Shift and follow me," he said.

Xuě resisted the command in his voice. Instead, she held her ground. "Who are you? And why should I follow you?"

"I am Aynur, the alpha of this small pack." He cocked his head and grinned. It didn't reach his eyes. "You're right to be careful, but the PLA is out there looking for you. We've also been looking for you. You can't travel as a pair of snow leopards. It's how we knew who you were. Two full-grown snow leopards traveling together out of breeding season . . ."

He let his words trail off. She flushed. He was right, but they hadn't had any other options and had hoped that the PLA would give up once they disappeared. They'd assumed they were safe traveling at night. This new information changed their plans.

"They want you," he pointed at her and then motioned to Bao, "and your husband. If you wish to get away from them, you'll need our help. This valley is wide. We can get you to India, but you'll have to follow us."

She stared at him. Could she trust him? Did she have a choice? And why hadn't Bao shifted yet?

"We don't have much time." Aynur's voice interrupted her thoughts. "The patrols are headed this way. Are you coming with us or not?"

Her cat strained to run the opposite direction—wolves were

their enemy, but she squelched it. Their options were limited. Neither had the energy nor the stamina to outrun them. In the end, she shifted and fell in line. Seeing a bushy tail not belonging to Bao in front of her further agitated her cat, but it eventually quieted when no attack came. Bao padded behind her, a silent, reassuring presence. Only the shushing sound of the brittle grass parting around the quintet disturbed the hushed countryside.

By the time they reached the *láng* den, hidden behind some brush, the adrenaline had long since worn off, and she struggled to hold her head up. A dark corner in the back of the cave beckoned. She padded toward it and lay down, wrapping her tail around her body until it covered her nose. She closed her eyes, not caring what happened to them.

A warm body pressed against her, and Bao's scent surrounded her. With a sigh, she allowed herself to relax into sleep.

The sound of her name being repeated reached into her subconscious, drawing her from a deep sleep. She cracked her eyes open. Amidst the darkness of the cave, a fully dressed Bao knelt next to her. Her eyes widened. When had he shifted? Then, the scent of cooked meat tickled her nostrils. Her stomach grumbled, and she licked her lips.

"*Nǐ hǎo*," Bao said, a soft smile curling his lips up.

Warmth bloomed in Xuě's chest. It rippled through her, and she averted her gaze, unable to look him in the face. Would her body always respond to him this way?

"They have food for us, and we can eat as humans. Here's the backpack." He set it next to her and stroked her fur.

She leaned into his touch, her cat purring. A man's voice broke the spell, reminding her they weren't alone. Groaning, she stretched from the tip of her toes to her tail and sighed. Eat as a human. It seemed so long ago that she'd had cooked meat.

In the middle of the large cavern, Aynur and a woman and another man with the same heritage as Aynur sat around a small fire, relaxing and eating. The woman's long, brown braid hung down her back. Their conversation and occasional muted laughter carried in the quiet cave. They spoke the same language Aynur had used earlier.

Bao stood and stepped in front of her, blocking her from the others, as she shifted and dressed. She peeked over his shoulder and whispered, "Have you talked to them?"

Before he could respond, the three looked their way. Aynur stood and approached them. They'd heard her. They understood Chinese, but she and Bao didn't know their language. How could she have private conversations with her husband? What if they needed to flee? What if . . . ?

"You're awake finally." Aynur's words interrupted her runaway thoughts. "We roasted a bharal we caught while you slept. Would you like some?"

Her stomach growled. They laughed. She bowed her head, blood rushing to her cheeks.

"Aren't you worried about being caught?" The words rushed out of her with more force than she'd intended. She looked up and found him staring at her, a pensive look on his face.

He glanced at his companions before turning back to her. "There are only so many meals I can eat in my wolf form. Your presence gave us an excuse to cook."

His words echoed her thoughts from a few days before.

The tension in her shoulders released a tiny fraction. "I'm grateful for your kindness. *Xièxiè.*"

"Come." He motioned to where the other two sat around the fire. "Join us."

She looked to Bao. The wariness that lurked in his eyes mirrored her own doubts. She nodded and approached the others. They adjusted, making room for the two of them.

"You can wash your hands with water from the bowl over in the corner." Aynur pointed to the other side.

A metal bowl much like the one she carried in her backpack sat on small natural rock shelf.

She crossed and washed her hands. The cold water stung her skin, but she scrubbed at the days' old dirt until her hands were raw. She closed her eyes for a moment and drew in a deep breath. The fluttering in her stomach subsided. Her nerves calmed. Facing the others seemed possible for the moment.

She joined them at the fire and squatted. Aynur handed her a wooden plate with a large piece of cooked bharal. Her stomach rumbled again, and she dug into the meat. Her eyelids fluttered closed as the flavor of the cooked sheep exploded across her taste buds. Its juices dripped down her chin onto the plate, but she didn't care.

When had she last eaten cooked meat of any kind? The day before her wedding.

Tears burned her eyes. A little more than a week had passed, yet it felt like a lifetime.

"Xuě?"

Bao touched her shoulder, and she blinked, emerging from her dark reverie.

"Aynur believes they can help us escape."

For the first time in days, hope surged in her breast. She turned to Aynur. "You do? How is this possible?"

"We can if you do as we say." He gestured to the others who sat silent. "Nur, Zuhre, and I are members of the Tibetan liberation movement. Others will help us, but you'll have to trust us and them." Determination and satisfaction glinted in his narrowed eyes. "Mao is determined to capture all of us. If he does—"

Zuhre snarled. Aynur glanced her way. They stared at each other for a moment before she looked away and continued eating in silence.

Xuě didn't need him to finish that sentence. Years had passed since the time before her parents, but the memories haunted her, surfacing unexpectedly to torment her.

"The valley is full of the PLA. You're lucky we found you first. You'll need to stay here for a few days, perhaps a week, before we can move you. We'll give you new clothes, but you must look only at the ground, unless we say otherwise."

Xuě frowned and glanced at Bao. Their gazes met, and her eyes widened. Their eye color would give them away.

"You can't go out, until I say so. Take this time to rest. Unless there's a snowstorm, we'll be traveling in human form at night."

Unable to stay silent, she said, "Why human?"

"Snow leopards are rare in this valley. Two snow leopards—"

"Would never happen here," Bao said, nodding.

Aynur's nostrils flared, and his lips turned down. The two wolf shifters stopped what they were doing and looked from Aynur to Bao and back, their gazes alert and wary. A tense silence engulfed the group.

"We don't interrupt each other," Aynur said.

Bao bowed his head, his jaw clenched. Xuě touched his arm. The muscles undulated under her fingers. She squeezed gently. Their gazes met, and she gave a slight shake of her head. He relaxed.

"I'm sorry. We've been traveling for days. Our parents died so that we could escape. But the PLA didn't stop with our parents. They killed Xuě's entire village on our wedding day. It has been . . . difficult."

Aynur inclined his head, rocked back on his heels, and stared into the fire. When he finally spoke, his voice grated in the silence. "I'm sorry. This has happened to many we've met. Even when the villages would've turned them over, they've killed everyone not a shifter."

"You've helped many escape?" Xuě asked.

"A number of them. More are coming, but so is the PLA. Which is why we've covered your scent with ours, and you'll need to stay away from the front of the cave until it's time to leave. One of us will stay here with you at all times."

# Chapter Nine

Two days trudged by. She slept most of the first day, exhaustion having caught up with her. By the second, her *yukihyō* twitched at the confinement, and she paced the interior of the cave, the walls closing in on her with each pass. In the village, there'd always been something to do, whether it was hunting or chores. If she needed release, she could disappear into the woods. Their escape from the village, while exhausting, had kept them in constant motion. There'd been very little time to think beyond eating, sleeping, and running. Even her conversations with Bao consisted of the bare minimum. Often, both were too tired to talk at the end of the night.

Now that they were idle, the desire to voice her concerns, ask questions, and see if her worries matched his beat at the back of her throat. But the presence of one of Aynur's pack keeping a constant vigil over them stilled her tongue and intensified the sensation of being trapped.

She glanced over at Bao. He sat in lotus position on the floor, his eyes closed, hands relaxed with palms facing upward like the Buddhist monks did during their daily meditation when they lived at the monastery. How long had he lived there with them before joining his parents? Had they taught him to meditate? Was that why he was so different from the men in her village? This inactivity . . .

"It's only for a short time," she mumbled under her breath.

"It's . . . hard, *shi?*"

Broken Chinese in a soft, female voice interrupted her manic thoughts.

Zuhre motioned to her. "Sit with me?" Understanding gleamed in her dark greenish gold eyes.

Something about the wolf shifter made Xuě want to share all of her deep dark secrets.

"I . . . "

"My Chinese is—how do you say?—bad, but I understand .
. . better. I'm . . . learning more. We . . . talk?"

Zuhre's gentle suggestion soothed the ragged edges of
Xuě's nerves. Up to that moment, the woman had said very
little to her. She'd seemed content to remain silent and leave
them alone. Now that the other woman revealed how little
Chinese she spoke, warmth burgeoned in Xuě's chest. Zuhre
was making an effort. Few had ever expressed any interest in
her. The villagers, while not unkind, had left her alone. The
village women her age had gathered in groups but never included her. And the young men had helped her bring in the
animals after the hunt, but their conversations had consisted
of only what was necessary to get the job done.

Her heart thumped hard in her chest. Only now did she
acknowledge how lonely her life had been. Denial hadn't
changed the years of isolation and loneliness, but it had kept
her going.

Xuě walked over and sat down on a rock in front of the fire
across from the female wolf shifter. She had always wondered
what other shifters experienced. Strangers didn't share per-
sonal information with each other. Since leaving Yumen, and
until Bao, she'd never met, much less talked to, another shifter. If she had, she wouldn't dare ask them anything.

Now, she could.

"Do you mind . . . " She hesitated. Courtesy dictated she
allow Zuhre to lead the conversation, but curiosity and excitement warred with her natural reticence.

Zuhre laughed softly and shook her head. The smile lit up
her face and softened the strong lines of her high cheekbones.
Strands of amber glistened in her dark brown hair in the fire-
light. "No, you speak first."

Xuě stared into the fire, her thoughts swirling. She'd
dreamed of this for so long she didn't know what to ask first.

"Should I . . . try?"

Xuě glanced over at Bao. He sat in the same position as
before. With a nod, she said, "*Xíng.*"

"When did you get . . . parents?"

The memories flooded back. She shivered. "I don't really know, but I'd say I was around six. Old enough to remember . . . that place."

Their gazes met in mutual understanding.

"And you?" Xuě asked.

She shrugged. "I don't know. Maybe . . . " She held up three fingers. "I have wake at night from," she frowned and paused, "bad dreams?"

"Nightmares."

"*Shi*. Nightmares." Zuhre motioned with her hands. "Long halls, smelly . . . dead flesh, evil men..."

"*Maruta*," Xuě whispered.

Zuhre's face blanched. "What?"

"*Maruta*. It means 'log'. We weren't human to them. They called me 'Gojû Ni'." Xuě raised her chin. Heat rushed to her cheeks, and she bit her lip. The urge to hide how this affected her nearly overpowered her desire to learn more about the woman sitting across the fire from her. Her *yukihyō* chuffed its support. She unclenched her hands and breathed deep, slowly releasing it. Being different had controlled her life in so many ways. It separated her from the others, never knowing acceptance. Now, it had made her a wanted person running from a madman.

Her cat twitched in distress.

*It's not your fault. I'm grateful to you.* Xuě didn't resent her animal. She resented being different.

"I hear *maruta* in my dreams. You remember. I'm sorry."

"Me, too. I try to forget."

She stared at the other woman. Her gaze met with Zuhre's in understanding. Neither said a word. Seconds ticked by swallowed in silence and the sound of the crackling fire. The cold of the rock seeped through her thin pants, and Xuě leaned closer to the fire.

"You're not Tibetan," she said

Zuhre shook her head, a faint smile tipping up the corners of her mouth. "No. I'm Uyghur . . . or half . . . or part . . . or whatever it is. All three of us are."

"Where did you learn to speak Chinese? Do the Uyghur speak it?"

The smile disappeared. "No. I . . . it's long story. Not very nice."

"Bao was lucky. His parents and village accepted him, but I--" The words caught in her throat, and Xuě swallowed.

"My parents wanted me to marry an Uyghur man at sixteen."

"Did you?"

She nodded. "It's common among my people. I hadn't . . . ." She paused and looked into the depths of the cavern over Xuě's head before focusing on the fire. "I didn't know my... *börä* . . . um . . . *láng*."

Xuě frowned. "What do you mean?"

Zuhre smiled, but pain filled her eyes. "No shift."

Xuě gasped. "You'd never shifted?"

"No. She hid until that day."

"But . . . " How was that possible? Children who didn't shift disappeared. She thought the Japanese had killed them. "How old are you?"

"Twenty, I think." She sighed. "To me, I was human. Then Alim, my husband, said I with another man to our village."

Xuě sat quietly, unsure how to respond. In Chinese society, it varied on one's social status whether infidelity mattered or not. For the wealthy, cheating was common, expected even among the men and not uncommon among the women. But, in her small village, infidelity resulted in shame on the family honor and ostracism.

Zuhre drew a deep breath, her gaze moving from her clasped hands to meet Xuě's.

Xuě leaned forward but remained silent, allowing Zuhre to speak uninterrupted.

"Women die for this."

Xuě gasped. Ostracism was bad enough, but death? She couldn't imagine such a fate.

Zuhre clasped and unclasped her hands in front of her.

"My family . . . they believed him, spit on me, turned their back on me." Anger flickered in her eyes, but no emotion showed on her face. "The village threw stones. They rained on my head. My family," she slashed her hand downward, "helped. They not my family now. I snapped." She shook her head. "I don't remember. I woke alone with no," she motioned to her clothes, "tired, scared with bad dreams—nightmares." She raised her chin and grinned. It resembled more a baring of her teeth than a show of happiness. "Not a dream."

Breath whooshed out of her, and her expression softened. "Honestly, I thank Alim. His lie gave me Aynur. My mate. My *true* mate." She smiled. It lit her eyes and brought a glow to her face. "I am lucky."

Lucky. Zuhre had lost her family, but considered herself lucky. Of course, she'd lost them in a different way than Xuě. She'd never be able to return to her family, though, just like Xuě. Xuě wanted to reach out and touch her, but more than the fire divided them.

"Do you wish to ever go home?"

Zuhre's eyes narrowed, and she pursed her lips. "No. I miss when I was child, but," she shook her head and looked around the cave, "this . . . is home. Aynur is home. He teach me Chinese, and much more, *and* we save others like us—like you and Bao. I like it . . . better than village."

A rustling in the back of the cave drew Xuě's attention. Bao stood and walked toward them. Each step spoke of coiled energy and power. Memories of their matings rose in her mind. If only they were alone . . .

A knowing smile spread across his face. She flushed and looked away. His hand captured hers, and he gave it a gentle squeeze. She glanced up through her eyelashes. Desire glowed in his eyes. A shiver rippled down her spine, sending goose bumps rushing across her skin in its wake.

Zuhre cleared her throat. "Come . . . I show you a place to be alone."

Heat prickles burned up Xuě's chest, up her neck, and into her cheeks. She stared down at their clasped hands. Oh, how she'd love to lose herself in the pleasure Bao brought her, but the thought of Zuhre knowing . . . She shook her head.

"No, *xièxiè*."

"Xuě," Bao said. He turned to their hostess. "We—"

"No, it *xing*." She picked up something next to her and stuck it in the fire. A torch flared to life. She stood and gestured for them to follow her. "I show you where it is. Perhaps you sleep there tonight. I talk to Aynur about it. You can . . . love there."

How could they be talking about this? If her body flushed anymore, she'd burst into flames. Instead of protesting, she nodded and studied the floor.

Bao stood and tugged on her hand. She rose and followed Zuhre past their backpack and sleeping roll at the back of the cave. Zuhre stepped to the left and continued farther into the gloom, disappearing into the stone. Light illuminated the edge of the opening. Xuě paused, glancing up at Bao. He shook his head. Zuhre reappeared and laughed.

"Come," she said, beckoning.

With Bao before her, Xuě slipped in behind him and followed them into the crevice hidden by the rugged walls. They walked several steps before the narrow tunnel opened into another large room. Shadows danced along the walls. The ceiling soared into the darkness. Three rucksacks sat against the back wall. Next to them were canteens. The sound of gurgling water echoed in the silent chamber.

The thought of cool, fresh water slipping down her throat pushed her forward, her mouth suddenly dry. She walked toward the sound. As she approached the back, a break in the wall appeared. She stopped and looked over her shoulder.

Zuhre watched her, her eyes alight with some indecipherable emotion. "*Shi*, we have pond around corner. We fill our," she waved her free hand, "I don't know what it called. We stop here for water and rest."

"May I?" Xuě licked her lips. It had been a while since she'd drunk directly from a stream.

The other woman nodded.

Xuě stepped around the corner, her eyes adjusting to the dim light. A pool shimmered in the darkness. Its smooth surface disturbed by the water that flowed into it at the far end. Where did the water go?

Light filled the chamber as Zuhre and Bao joined her. Torches lined the closest walls. Zuhre walked up to one and lit it with hers. The water was so clear the bottom was visible. It deepened closer to its source. Xuě itched to remove her clothes and scrub the dirt off. She turned and looked at her companions.

Before she could open her mouth, Zuhre said, "We bathe here. You want?"

Xuě nodded.

"Water is very cold. It's hard to bathe." She pointed to a small opening to the right of them. "The water goes out that way." She walked along the edge of the pool to its source. "Here, we fill up." She motioned to them. "Come."

Xuě hurried forward and cupped her hands under the water. Prickles of cold stabbed at her fingers and palms, but she ignored the pain. Raising them to her lips, she drank. The cold water slid down her throat, leaving a trail of refreshing cool in its wake. She shivered, but reached out for more. After the second drink, she stepped back to give Bao room.

"I'd love to bathe, but . . . " She shuddered at the thought of immersing herself in the frigid water. Perhaps a sponge bath would be enough.

"I'll warm you afterward if you want to."

Bao's voice washed over her. His breath fluttered across her neck. She shuddered. Heat pooled in her *bàoyú*. Lust, hot and needy, raced through her.

Zuhre cleared her throat. "I . . . um . . . go. Okay?"

Unable to bring herself to look at her new friend, Xuě nodded. The light dimmed as the other woman retreated into the front chamber.

Her husband stroked her arms, pressing his erection against her back. "Xuě . . . "

His whisper tickled her ear, stirring a few wisps of her

hair. She shivered, leaned back into him, and twined her arms around his neck, turning her head to the side and exposing her neck.

He trailed kisses from her collarbone up to her earlobe.

"Bao," she murmured, grinding her hips into his.

He spun her around, desire glinting in his eyes. She lifted her head in invitation, and he bent and kissed her. A sigh of longing escaped her. She yearned for more. Pressing herself closer to him, she rubbed against him. He licked her bottom lip. With a moan, she opened to his sensual request. The taste of him fanned the raging fire. Her entire body burned with the need to feel him moving inside of her.

Suddenly, there were too many clothes separating them. She fumbled with the buttons on his shirt, desperate to touch his bare skin. He nudged her hands away and unbuttoned his shirt, slipping it over his broad shoulders and letting it drop to the floor.

The torchlight flickered off his pale skin, gilding it and accentuating his hewn muscles. She licked her dry lips and traced the line defining his abdomen muscles from the bottom of his ribcage to the top of his pants. His muscles rippled under her touch. Her breath stuttered in her chest, and her *bàoyú* clenched. This man's beauty left her breathless and aching for him. His gentleness warmed the cold, empty places in her heart.

She looked at his face. Her gaze collided with his. A desire that matched hers roiled in their silvery depths. His eyelids drooped to half-mast, and the corner of his lips turned up in a seductive smile. She shivered and slid her fingers to his pant buttons teasingly before slipping her hands down to cup him. He groaned and thrust his hips into her hands.

She gasped and couldn't wait any longer. With eager movements, she pushed his pants down to his ankles. His *jījī*, hard and ready, jutted out from his body. Before she could wrap her hands around it, he pushed them away, kicked his shoes and his pants off, before divesting her of her clothes.

"I can't wait."

The raw tone of his voice rasped against her nerve endings. Her nipples peaked, and goose bumps chased along her skin.

They moved together at the same time. He grasped her hips and lifted her. She wrapped her legs around his waist and thrust down onto his *jījī*, clinging to his shoulders. He rocked his hips forward, thrusting deeper into her. She gasped as pleasure, centered in her *àikòu*, expanded in a wave of pure ecstasy to encompass her entire being. Her body shook with the intensity and unexpectedness of the release. It overwhelmed her, and she collapsed against him, her eyes fluttering shut.

He tightened his grip on her hips and pumped faster, his breath coming in short pants. His muscles tensed under her, and he groaned in her ear, coming inside her.

A feeling of contentment washed over her. She feathered kisses across his cheek before untwining her legs from around his waist and sliding down to the floor to stand.

Wrapping her arms around his waist, she rested her cheek against his chest. The solid sound of his heartbeat comforted her, and she smiled.

He kissed the top of her head and held her tight.

# Chapter Ten

Later, after dinner, Xuě lay staring into the darkness, unable to sleep. Bao snuggled around her, his arm draped across her waist, his breathing even. In the quiet of the night with nothing to distract her, questions and worry haunted her. Despite Aynur and Zuhre's assurances they were safe in the cave, the fear of capture increased with each passing moment. Somewhere, out there, Mao's army searched for them. According to Aynur, the hunt had intensified, and yet another shifter had been brought to the cave, her story similar to theirs. Remembered terror and sadness lurked in her eyes, stirring up Xuě's own fear.

The weight of the mountain pressed down on her. The stench of unwashed bodies evoked the memories of long ago and the tiny cage she'd called home. With a shudder, she pushed them away, but panic circled, tightening its noose until she gasped. She needed to breathe fresh air, to see the stars overhead, to feel the wind ruffling through her fur. She needed out.

Inching forward, she lifted Bao's arm. He murmured something indecipherable into her hair, and his arm tightened around her. The feeling of being trapped overwhelmed her yet again. Her *yukihyō* chuffed. It needed out, to run, but they were stuck in the cave.

She pushed against his arm, slid out from under it, and crouched, stilling when she heard the rustling of their blanket.

"Xuě?" he whispered sleepily.

She froze, hoping he'd fall back to sleep if she didn't respond.

He sat up, his shadow a dark blob against the rest of the cave. "Xuě," he whispered again, "what is wrong?"

With a sigh, she sat down. "I can't stay here any longer."

He reached for her. "Come here."

She shook her head. "No. I need to go outside. I can't stay here any longer."

"We can't. We'll be caught."

"I'd rather be caught than trapped here."

He grabbed both her arms. "Xuĕ, listen to me."

She shuddered and struggled to get away from him. Panic rose up again, clawing at her. She panted. "No."

He shook her. "Look at me. We will leave soon. They wait for a safe time—"

"How do you know? Maybe they're waiting for them to come get us. Maybe they're—"

"They're *helping* us."

She pushed at his shoulders. "You don't know that. Have you seen any of the soldiers? Have you heard them? We only know what they've told us, nothing more."

"We have to—"

"No." She shoved at him.

Fear ate at her insides, and the strain since the death of her parents rushed over her.

Why did he insist they stay? Why didn't he shift when she did? Why did he lead them down into that valley where the dead were rather than wait to make sure no one remained? Could she trust him?

"If they had intended to turn us over, don't you think they would've done so by now?" he asked.

A light flared, and she flinched. Aynur walked over to them and crouched next to them. Behind him, three pairs of eyes glowed in the dark, staring at her.

"She's right to question," he said. "There are many out there who'd turn you over to Mao for a bowl of rice. The famine has grown so fierce."

"Even here?" she asked.

"Even here. Not everyone is for Tibetan freedom. We are, but not everyone. We have the means to hunt."

"So, why haven't we left yet? What are we waiting for?" Bao asked.

Aynur swiped a hand over his face. "Because we've had reports that more shifters are fleeing and headed our way and we thought the soldiers' presence would lessen with time, but it hasn't. Our network is stretched thin. We must find them before the PLA does."

She frowned. "How do you know about these shifters?"

"Because we do. We don't talk about that. The less you know, the better. If we separate and you're captured . . . "

She nodded in understanding. "*Xing*. But traveling in a large group . . . "

"We won't be. We'll be splitting up. We'll be leaving in two more days. This is all I will tell you. Can you manage that?" His golden gaze bored into her as if trying to probe her mind.

Two more days. The tide of panic slowly ebbed, and she nodded.

"Good because going outside now could put everyone in danger."

She wavered. He steadied her with a hand to her elbow, but her mind spun with how close she'd come to bringing the soldiers to their cave. Had Bao not stopped her, they would've been caught. She bowed her head, and her shoulders slumped.

"Try to sleep. It won't be much longer," Aynur said.

With a nod, she returned to their bedroll and slid in beside Bao. Aynur padded over to where the others sat watching. The light snuffed out, and the cave descended back into darkness.

She wrapped her arms around herself and curled into a fetal position. What was she doing? She was a menace to all of these people. As thoughtless and useless as a *maruta*. Perhaps, when they left, she should slip off by herself and go it alone. That way her fears wouldn't potentially put them in danger again.

Tears trickled down her cheeks. Her shoulders quaked with silent sobs. They were better off without her.

"Sshh . . . " Bao whispered against her head and drew her to him. "It's okay. I'm scared, too. We're surrounded by enemies, we've lost our families and our homes, but we're lucky. Together, we can make it . . . if we don't give into our fears.

Fear will defeat us."

She turned in his arms and tried to search his face in the dark. A question that had burned in her for the past several days slipped out. She no longer cared if the others heard them. "Why did you go down into the valley after the firefight? Why didn't you wait? We could've died. That soldier saw us, was prepared to shoot us, if not for his superior officer stopping him."

He sighed and tightened his arms around her. "I—I don't know. I thought it was safer . . . safer than being up on the mountain. I thought all of the trucks were gone with the soldiers. Had I realized they weren't, I would've waited." He pulled her close, resting his head on top of hers, and sighed again. "It was fear."

"What?" She leaned back and gaze at him.

"My fear nearly killed us."

"Just like mine could have tonight. We were lucky it didn't." She hugged him and kissed his cheek. "You're right, together, we are stronger."

Together, they *were* stronger. They had to be. Together, they would escape and survive.

At breakfast the following morning, the newest shifter sat next to Xuě. Her black hair rested over her shoulder in a braid that reached her waist. Keen, dark brown eyes regarded Xuě solemnly from out of a kind face. Her swarthy complexion and broad features proclaimed her Tibetan heritage.

The young woman leaned in and said, "I am called Pema."

Xuě smiled. "I'm Xuě."

Pema nodded. "*Shi*, I know. The cave is small, and I have good ears." Her twinkling eyes took the sting out of her remark.

"I'm sorry about last night. I didn't mean to . . . " Xuě stopped talking. Of course, she hadn't meant to wake everyone, but she had.

"It's all right. I understand. I'm scared, too."

"You speak Chinese?"

Pema nodded. "My village was close to China. We learn Chinese to protect ourselves from them. I'm good with languages and have often crossed deep into China as a *láng* to spy. It was helpful."

Zuhre walked over and joined them by the fire. "I'm scared, too. Aynur likes it, thinks it's fun. Not me, but I like saving," she pointed to them, "I feel good doing that."

"We're grateful to you," Xuě said.

Zuhre bowed her head. "It's nothing. It's our duty. In Uyghur we say, *God will be happy with you once you serve His servants well.*"

Xuě bit her tongue. She didn't believe in a god. "How long will you do this?"

The other woman shrugged. "As long as we can. I pray Mao die every day."

"I do, too," Pema said. "Mao has chased the Dalai Lama out of his home. Now I'm forced to leave mine, too, because of him." She turned to Zuhre, anger in her voice. "I'd stay and help you. The fewer like us in Mao's evil hands, the better."

"You talk to Aynur when he return. We need more help."

Xuě bowed her head and glanced to where Bao sat in the back of the cave. Could he hear their conversation? Would he want to stay and help Aynur and his pack, too? She didn't know if she had the courage to do it. Not once had she experienced a desire to save others as they ran from the PLA. Fear, anger, and anxiety, yes, and the need to get as far as possible from China and its reach. Her thoughts had centered on escape even after meeting up with their rescuers. They still did.

The alpha and his second had gone out. To where, Xuě didn't know. Perhaps they were looking for the other shifters fleeing Mao.

Pema and Zuhre's words washed over her, but her mind was far away. Xuě stood and excused herself. The two women nodded to her. She crossed to where Bao sat in the back of the cave. He smiled up at her and motioned for her to sit.

"Did you hear our conversation?" she asked.

He nodded.

"What do you think?"

"I don't know. We can't help in this place."

"Would you?"

His intense gaze pierced through her. "I don't know. Would you?"

She stared down at her hands. "I . . . " She peeked up at him before averting her gaze. Prickles of shame-induced heat fanned up her face, and she squirmed under his scrutiny. "I don't think I'm that type of person."

He stroked her hand. "It's all right. I would help as I can, but not here. Not now."

Selfish. She was selfish. She didn't want to stay here and help others escape, even if she could have. In truth, she desired a quiet life, the end of constant fear, the end of the famine, and vengeance against Mao for ordering the death of her parents and village. That last would never happen. The famine would only end when Mao dictated, and that could continue for decades. But a quiet life without fear could be attainable . . . if they could escape.

# Chapter Eleven

Late in the afternoon, Aynur and Nur trudged into the cave followed by two large, black *xióng* and a cream-colored *láng*. A blanket of white covered their fur. Aynur shook the snow off and disappeared into the back, returning a few minutes later as a man and dressed in thick fur boots, leather pants, and a heavy coat. The others didn't shift, but, instead, they padded over to the fire and joined Xuě, Bao, Zuhre, and Pema who crouched in human form around it, collapsing in the empty spaces next to it. Wind howled past the entrance. Despite the bushes blocking the entrance, the cold penetrated into the depths of the cave.

Xuě huddled next to Bao and shivered, their blanket spread over their shoulders, hands outstretched to catch any of the fire's warmth. Sporadic conversation interrupted the silence that held everyone in its thrall.

"We'll leave tonight, an hour after sunset," Aynur announced. "We'll travel as animals during the storm. If we travel at a good pace, we can make it to the next shelter before dawn. Any questions?"

No one said anything.

He nodded. "Get some rest. It will be a long night." Turning to Zuhre, he said, "Fill the canteens and get the packs together. We won't be coming back for a while."

His mate lit a torch and strode to the back of the cave without a word, disappearing into the crack that led to the back room. Xuě stood and followed her. With only a few more hours to wait, she itched to be on her way. Rest would elude her. Sitting around would make the time pass more slowly.

"Do you need any help?" she asked.

Zuhre glanced over her shoulder and smiled. "*Shi*. If you like. *Xièxiè*." She handed her the canteens by the straps. "We fill these—how do you say," she motioned to the containers.

"Canteens."

"Canteens with the water and take these," she pointed to the backpacks on the floor, "up to front."

Xuě crossed to the waterfall, set the canteens down, and unscrewed the top of the first one. She held it under the water. Her skin burned where the water spilled over, but she continued filling the containers until each had water to the top. She hefted them, slung them over her shoulder, and carried them back to where Zuhre finished up with the bags, setting them down next to her.

"I'm almost done. You go back to fire if you want." She folded down a flap and fastened the buckles of one of them before doing the same for the next one.

"No, I can wait." Xuě stamped her feet to keep them warm and tucked her hands under her armpits, the chill transferring from her hands to her body. "What about the clothes you're wearing now?"

"They go in this last one. Here," she handed her the empty one, "take this one and the," she paused for a moment before smiling and saying, "canteens. I carry these." Again, she pointed to the packs on the ground.

"Packs," Xuě said, smiling.

The other woman nodded and returned Xuě's smile. "Packs. *Xièxiè.* I want to speak better Chinese. You're helping."

Warmth blossomed in Xuě's chest and inched outward to encompass her entire body. It was unlike what she felt with Bao. Could it be what it felt like to have a friend? Other than her parents, no one had ever thanked her for helping. Perhaps her new life would be better than her old.

Zuhre slung one pack onto her back and picked up the other one. She grabbed the torch and started back through the passageway. Xuě followed her. They stopped next to the area where Zuhre and Aynur usually slept and set everything down.

Bao sat by the fire where she'd left him, quietly talking to Nur. He looked up and held open the blanket when she approached. She slipped in beside him and snuggled up to his side. His heat seeped into her, and she sighed. Leaning into him, she closed her eyes and relaxed.

When she opened them again, everyone sat around the fire. A slender woman with a long, golden braid and pale skin sat next to Pema, their heads bent in quiet conversation. Xuě had never seen someone so fair. The woman caught Xuě staring at her, the expression in her keen, ice blue eyes friendly. Xuě smiled shyly and blushed at being caught gawking before turning her attention away from the beautiful, exotic woman to study the other newcomers.

From their stature, she assumed they were the *xióng*. The burly Chinese man sat close to a Chinese woman similar in build. Their khaki green liberation suits matched Xuě's and Bao's. Like so many of the women in Xuě's village, his companion had cropped her straight black hair in a popular bob that ended just below her ears. Aynur still hadn't given them any new clothes. Perhaps it would happen before they left. Or maybe he didn't have any.

"We're splitting into groups of three."

Aynur's voice interrupted her musings. She turned to look at him.

"Xuě and Bao," Aynur pointed to them, "you'll be going with me. We leave first. Pema and Akilina, you go with Zuhre. You'll leave second about ten minutes behind us. Chang and Huan, you're with Nur. You'll be the last group to leave. Nur will tell you when. This prevents all of us from being captured in the event that something goes wrong." He looked at each person around the fire. "Stay close to your leader. In this weather, it will be easy to lose each other. If all goes well, we'll meet again at our next stop."

He motioned to Zuhre who stood and produced some yak jerky. She handed out a few pieces to everyone.

"Eat the jerky before we leave and be sure to drink some water," he said. "There is water over in the corner. Then get your stuff together. It's going to be a long night."

Xuě headed to where they'd left their stuff and prepared

to leave. Bao joined her. Silence stretched between them. She had little to say, but fear and excitement welled up with each passing moment.

The time had come. Soon, they'd be gone from the cave. She bit into the jerky and chewed. Its salty, gamey taste exploded in her mouth. Her stomach rumbled. The jerky wouldn't satiate the hunger, but it would keep her going. She had packed everything except their clothes. These she saved to put in the bag last.

Bao sat and held a hand out to her. She took it and allowed him to pull her down next to him. He wrapped an arm around her shoulders. Warmth spread through her, and she smiled. Her *yukihyō* chuffed in contentment. When Aynur gave the signal, they would shift and begin the long trek to the next stop on their quest for freedom. Now that only minutes remained before they left, she could enjoy the man next to her in peace.

The quiet conversations of the others whispered around the cave.

"Are you ready to go?" Bao's deep voice rumbled in his chest vibrating against her ear.

"*Shi.*" Part of her couldn't wait to get out of the cave. Another part worried about what awaited them out there. Would all of them make it to the next place?

He tightened his arms around her. "Me, too. Perhaps we should shift now. We need to be ready. I will shift first so that I can carry the rucksack."

With a sigh, she nodded and stood, looking around at the others. The cave left little room for modesty, but no one paid any attention to them. She tried not to think about it. Bao stood and stripped. He handed her his clothes and, with a flash of light, shifted.

She glanced around the cave. No one seemed to have noticed, or, if they had, they chose to ignore them. She quickly rolled the clothes up and placed his shoes at the bottom of the rucksack. Gathering her courage, she removed her shoes and put them on top of Bao's then placed his clothes on top of the shoes. She removed her pants first rolling them up and put them in the bag. Her shirt hung to the tops of her thighs. She paused to survey the cave yet again.

No one even glanced their way. Some were starting to shift like she and Bao.

She slipped off her shirt, rolled it up, put it in with the rest of their clothes, and stuffed the blanket on top. The cold air nipped at her skin. She shivered and hurried to secure the rucksack on Bao. Then, with a stretching of bones and muscle, she shifted.

They padded over to Aynur, who waited in wolf form. He inclined his head and turned to the entrance of the cave. Xuĕ and Bao dropped into line behind him, and they trotted out into a world of darkness and snow flurries.

❧ ❧ ❧ ❧

She trotted behind Aynur for hours, the snowstorm raging around them. Wind howled past her, driving the snow sideways into her face. Even with her heightened senses, she had to keep her nose nearly on Aynur's tail and keep pace with him to prevent losing him. Bao's shoulder brushed against her hip every step they took. Her ears flicked back and forth listening for any sound above the storm.

Aynur stopped abruptly. She raised her head and peered around him. Two faint lights approached them. Aynur veered off to the right at a loping run. With a chuff, she took off after him, Bao close on her heels. Her mind spun. Despite the heavy snowfall, the light would reveal their prints. Whoever held that light could follow them.

Her adrenaline spiked, coursing through her muscles, propelling her forward. The ground sloped upward. She bounded up it after the *láng*. A dark shadow loomed above them. He disappeared into it. She skidded under an overhang behind him. Bao bumped into her, knocking her forward.

Aynur shifted and crouched before them. "Stay here. I will distract them long enough for the snow to cover our tracks and return for you."

With a flash of light, he shifted again and ran off into the blizzard. Minutes passed. The wind died down, and a howl, along with men shouting and a shot, followed by a yelp echoed through the night. She looked to Bao. They couldn't leave him to whoever was out there. Her *yukihyō* balked, but she overrode its fear.

With Bao beside her, she sprang back into the darkness, tracking Aynur's prints. A faint light appeared ahead. The sound of two men shouting rose over the storm. She slowed and looked to Bao, inclining her head. She would go right; he'd go left. He nodded and turned left. They would circle the men and take them down.

Again, her *yukihyō* tried to pull back. *Think of the man as a pán yáng. He is not human. He's not our kin. He is maruta.* She shuddered at the thought but crept forward, turning her ears back and forth, listening for any other sounds. Why were these two men out in the snow alone? There must be more, but, other than the wind, the falling snow, Aynur growling, and the shouting men, nothing disturbed the night.

She came up behind one of the PLA soldiers. His rifle pointed at Aynur. Blood trickled down the wolf's shoulder. The other soldier stood across from him, his rifle also pointed at the wolf.

"We should kill it. It attacked us," one of the soldiers said. "It is nothing but a mangy wolf."

"What if it's," his companion paused as if afraid to voice it aloud before continuing, "one of those. Our commander will want it. We take it back with us to the truck."

"And do what with it? The truck won't start, and I don't know where it is. Do you?"

The first soldier shook his head.

"It could kill us if we try to take it alive. No, we should just kill it. *Zhōngwèi* Lee doesn't need to know. Fuck him for sending us out here in this storm."

Behind him, Bao lurked beyond the circle of light. Aynur snarled at the soldiers. The soldier facing Bao raised his gun and tightened it to his shoulder.

Her muscles coiled, and she leapt, swiping her claws down the soldier's back, tearing through his clothing and skin. He cried out and collapsed under her, face first in the snow. The scent of his blood smelled different from the animals she hunted, and it curdled both her cat and her human stomach. Her attention shifted to the other soldier. What would he do? He stared at her, his eyes wide with fear. He babbled something and pointed his rifle at her. Where was Bao? Fighting her instincts to freeze, she prepared to leap at the man.

Then, out of the darkness, Bao struck. The wind picked up and howled past them, swallowing the soldier's bloodcurdling scream as he toppled into the snow, falling silent. The soldier beneath her moaned again. He wasn't dead. Eyes wide, Xuě backed away from him, her cat's instinct to flee instead of fight rushing back in. Aynur stepped forward and silenced him.

Blood pooled around the downed men, spreading wider and wider, staining the white snow crimson. Their lanterns lay next to them, flickering.

She shuddered. They had now killed three men. All were prepared to kill them, but did that matter? She bowed her head and closed her eyes. Something bumped up against her. She jumped and looked around.

Bao stared at her in concern and rubbed against her. She sighed and leaned into him. Behind him, Aynur dragged one of the soldiers away from the bloody mess. A few minutes later, he returned and did the same with the other soldier. When he joined them again, he dug in the snow, covering the bloody patches with fresh, white snow. Xuě and Bao copied his movements until every red patch disappeared.

Aynur turned and limped back down to their original path. The other groups had since passed by, leaving a large trail in their wake. Would the snow fall thick enough to cover their tracks? She could only hope.

They continued in silence for what seemed like several more hours. Their pace slowed. Aynur's limp grew more pronounced with each *gōnglǐ* they traveled. At last, Aynur disappeared between some bushes. Bao and Xuě followed him into a large cavern. In the center, a small, smokeless fire burned, beckoning to them. The others gathered around it, some in human form, some as their animals. All conversation stopped as they entered.

Zuhre jumped to her feet and rushed forward, Nur on her heels. "Aynur!"

He took a few halting steps toward the fire and collapsed.

She turned to them. "What happened?"

Bao chuffed and stepped up to him, licking Aynur's shoulder where the blood had matted.

Zuhre bent closer, inspecting him. "We must get him to the fire."

Nur and Zuhre picked him up and carried him to where the others waited.

"Pema, bring me my backpack, water, and blankets. He's shot." She placed his head in her lap and said something in their language.

He woofed.

Xuě trotted with Bao to a corner. They shifted and donned their clothes as quickly as possible, rejoining the group.

Aynur lay in human form, eyes closed, an angry shallow wound on his shoulder. Zuhre cleaned it with a wet cloth. She didn't look up when they approached.

"How did this happen?"

Xuě and Bao exchanged a glance before he spoke, telling the story of their narrow escape.

"You saved his life." Zuhre's voice shook with emotion.

"He saved ours," Xuě said. "Had he not gone back, they would've found us."

"Had *you* not gone back, he die." Tears shimmered in her eyes. "*Xièxiè.*"

"How did you miss us?" Bao asked.

Aynur's weak voice filled the cave. "I drew them far enough off the path to allow the others to pass. Hopefully, they won't be found until spring, and we'll be long gone."

"We stay here for few days," Zuhre said.

Aynur opened his mouth, but Zuhre's words stopped him.

"No. We stay here. You lead us. They will search for those men, and it give us a chance to rest. Nur and I hunt in the morning."

Again, Aynur opened his mouth, but she shook her head.

"It is for the best." She looked around the circle. "Everyone rest. We take turns and keep watch. I stay up for a while with Aynur. Pema, you next." She assigned watch duty to each shifter before everyone dispersed to their bedrolls around the fire.

Xuě watched the flames dance for hours until her eyes finally closed, the screams of the dying men echoing in her ears.

# Chapter Twelve

Aynur healed quickly. The days blended into each other as the storm raged on. Only Zuhre, Nur, and Aynur left to hunt because of the increased patrols. They returned with food and told of numerous narrow misses with different groups of soldiers. With nine adult shifters to feed, whatever they brought in disappeared quickly.

Xuĕ balked at the inactivity. With nothing to do during the day, her mind created frightening scenarios of them being caught and returned to the medical facility of her early childhood. At night, the dying soldier's cries shattered her dreams. Their ghosts chased her across the barren, snow-covered basin, cursing her. No matter how fast she ran, she couldn't escape. When she finally collapsed in exhaustion, the ghosts turned into her parents. Their angry faces snarling, they pointed accusing fingers at her for leaving them to die. She awoke panting and shivering.

On the third night, she jerked into wakefulness and lay gasping for air, staring at the ceiling. The ghosts danced on the edge of her consciousness.

Bao stirred next to her.

"Sh . . . it's all right."

His whispered words wrapped around her, soothing her a little. He drew her closer and spooned her. His hard *jījī* pressed against her buttocks. He slid his hands under her shirt and cupped her breasts. Her nipples peaked. Liquid fire skittered along her nerve endings. Goose bumps zipped along her skin in its path. The ghosts evaporated with the haze of desire settling over her.

Involuntarily, she wiggled against him, seeking a deeper connection.

Heat flushed her cheeks. What if someone heard or saw

them?

She pushed at his hands, but he lightly pinched her nipples. She arched into his hands. He tugged on the tight peaks. A moan rose at the back of her throat that she quickly swallowed, and she thrust her pelvis back into him. Her cat purred.

"That's it. Let me love you. Let me take away this fear."

He breathed the words into her ear. She shivered and nodded, closing her eyes.

One hand abandoned her nipple to trail a path of fire down her stomach and into her pants. His hand hovered just above her *àikòu*, teasing her.

She wiggled against him and whispered, "Please."

His dexterous fingers played with her *àikòu*. Desire jolted through her, and she jumped at its intensity. Too many days had passed since their last time. All the pent up fear, anger, and desperation coalesced into a fierce hunger that threatened to consume her.

A moan escaped through her lips, and she froze.

Had anyone noticed?

Bao slipped a finger into her *bàoyú*, and her thoughts scattered into tiny fragments. She clenched her fists and gritted her teeth, screwing her eyes tightly shut as she struggled to contain the sounds that writhed at the back of her throat. His finger slid out before dipping back in. With one hand, he built a slow rhythm, swirling around her *àikòu* first before plunging his finger into her and pulling out again only to repeat the process. With the other, he held her immobile hips pressed against his. Her instincts urged her to move with his rhythm. She squirmed, trying to break his hold so she could match his strokes.

But he withdrew both hands, leaving her gasping on the precipice of an orgasm. Her cat yowled in protest. She echoed it with a silent, frustrated scream. His hands returned and pushed her pants down her legs. He lifted one of her legs and his *jījī* brushed her opening.

All of her attention zeroed in on where he moved within her. An electrical charge cracked through her, and she stiffened, her whole body clenching as a sensation after sensation crashed over her. She shuddered. He drew back and plunged back in, sending her back into the maelstrom.

The tension mounted within her. His breath grew labored, accelerating, and he spilled his seed inside of her. She barreled to a second orgasm, her consciousness shattering into darkness.

The cave slowly came back into focus. She felt boneless and content. Slipping her pants back on, she snuggled into Bao's embrace and closed her eyes, but sleep escaped her. She stared into the darkness. Guilt pricked at her conscience. She could only hope this would fade with time.

\*\*\*\*

One afternoon, she sat in front of the fire, staring at the dancing flames. Her shoulders drooped, and she fought the urge to fall asleep, her head nodding.

Zuhre sat down next to her and touched her arm lightly. "You *xing*?"

Xuě wanted to say, "*Shi*," but couldn't conjure up the strength to lie. "Those men . . . I . . . Have you ever killed anyone?"

The other woman nodded, her eyes haunted with memories.

"How do you . . . "

"Not remember?"

Xuě bowed her head and stared at her hands. "*Shi*," she whispered. "How do you forget?"

"I haven't, but it was them or me. You saved Aynur." She reached over and touched Xuě's arm. "They would . . . kill us. Remember that. To live or . . . die. We choose."

"I don't like that choice." She clenched her hands and stared up at her friend, her eyes burning with unshed tears. "To kill him, I had to tell myself he was an animal. An animal. And, yet, here I am. *I* am the animal. They were looking for me because *I'm an animal.*"

101

"No. They look for . . . us. We not wrong. I'm not an animal. You are not. We are not *maruta*. Bad men made us animals. Mao is a bad man. He kills with no care. If they get us," she motioned to the other shifters in the cave, "what they do to us?"

She dropped her gaze down to her hands, unable to meet Zuhre's fierce look. "They'll take us to Mao."

"You want that?"

"No, but I don't want to be like them."

Zuhre squeezed Xuě's arm. She didn't say anything until their gazes met. "You not like them. You had to kill to live. We do the same. Do Mao and his army do that?"

Xuě said nothing and turned her attention back to the fire. Leaning forward, she rested her head on her knees. Light footsteps approached her. Bao's scent surrounded her right before his arm encircled her shoulders. She sighed and relaxed into him.

"We can't focus on the past. We can only move forward," he said.

"You're fine with having killed a man?" she asked him.

His arm tightened around her shoulders, and his breath hitched. "No, but he was going to shoot you and Aynur." He pulled away and studied her. Their gazes collided. "Should I have let him?"

She looked down at the dirt and shook her head. He'd saved her life. Did she think less of him because he killed a man to do so? No. She'd had to attack the soldier. There'd been no choice—at least, not one that wouldn't have ended up with them caught or dead. If they'd let them live, the army would have them by now. Just as she'd protected herself against the cannibal and fled the village. Would her parents still be alive if they'd turned her and Bao over to the officer and his men? In her heart, Xuě knew those men would've killed the villagers anyway. Could she kill again if she had to?

She shuddered. Better to avoid the soldiers all together.

Looking around the cave, she wondered how their large group would manage. Even broken up into smaller groups, they'd run into them . . . in a snowstorm where they shouldn't have been. Who would send men out on a night like that? If they'd been captured, how would they have brought them in? None of it made sense.

A commotion at the entrance of the cave drew her attention. Aynur and his second dragged a blue sheep between them. Chang and Huan, the two bear shifters, joined them and carried the kill to the back where they would skin and prepare the meat. The two *láng* trotted into the darkness, returning a few minutes later in human form.

Xuě's stomach grumbled. It would be several hours yet before they would eat. She stood. Perhaps she could help them prepare the sheep.

"Are you all right?" Bao asked.

She looked down at him and shrugged. "I will be." She paused. "I have to be."

Concern etched a line in his forehead and darkened the silver of his eyes into pewter.

"I'm going to see if Chang and Huan need my help," she said, ending the conversation.

"Okay."

She turned.

"Xuě?"

Without facing him, she stopped.

"We'll survive this and find peace. I promise."

Nodding, she walked away. He'd made a promise he couldn't keep, thinking she'd feel better. She didn't. Only escaping Mao's long reach and setting up their own place far from danger would she feel safe enough to believe his lie. Even then, she didn't know if peace would ever find her. Not now.

The following morning, four of the group gathered around the fire, eating the sheep from the night before. Having finished her breakfast, Xuě paced the perimeter of the cave, anxious to be on the way. Zuhre stood watch at the entrance in tense silence. When would Aynur, Nur, and Pema return? They'd left earlier to scout the safest route in preparation for their next leg of the journey. What if they didn't come back? She shivered. The patrols had increased, and, over the past few days, the sound of rapid gunfire had echoed multiple times through the basin.

Everyone was on edge and ready to go. It seemed only a matter of time before they were discovered if they stayed where they were. Aynur agreed. Today, they would travel as humans in one large group rather than animals with Aynur and his pack acting as their guides. Xuě hoped they'd escape the notice of the PLA.

"Xuě," Bao called to her.

She turned to face him.

He motioned to the spot beside him. "Come sit with me. Save your energy for the trek."

Her *yukihyō* protested, but he was right. She wasted energy best saved for later. If they covered as much distance as their leader wanted, they'd be exhausted by the end of the night. She crossed the cave and joined him by the fire.

"Focus on escaping," he said. He grabbed her hand and squeezed it gently.

"I'm ready to go. How much longer do you think they'll be?"

"Soon," Zuhre said.

Xuě stood and joined her at the entrance. Zuhre held a branch to the side, her attention fixed outside. Xuě followed her gaze. In the darkness of predawn, three figures raced toward them across the hard-packed dirt of the desert. She met her friend's gaze.

Zuhre released the branch and turned to face the group, tension in every line of her body. "Kill the fire. Get your . . . backpacks. They come. We leave when they're ready."

In silence, the group gathered their belongings, donned their packs, and put out the fire. They assembled by the entrance and waited. The sound of running footsteps grew louder until it stopped right outside the cave. Xuě tensed and backed away with the group just in time for the wolves to push through the bushes. No one said anything as the duo trotted past them and disappeared into the back of the cavern.

A few minutes later, Aynur appeared, face flushed, clothed, and his pack on his shoulders.

"The PLA is just over the ridge. The sentries didn't see us, but we must hurry before the rest of the camp rises," he said. "Follow me in single file. Nur and Zuhre, take the rear." He turned and slipped through the bushes.

One by one, the group fell in line behind him. Xuě hung back, wanting to be near Zuhre. Chang looked at her, a question in her eyes. Xuě shook her head and motioned for the bear shifter to go ahead of her. The other woman smiled, her teeth glinting in the darkness, before stepping outside. Her partner, Huan, slipped in behind her.

"Are you going?" Bao asked.

"*Shi*, but you go ahead of me," she said, matching his hushed tone. "I'd like to walk with Zuhre."

"You like her?" He held a branch out of her way, and she ducked under it.

She smiled. "I do. For the first time in my life, I have a friend."

Someone tapped her arm. She looked back. Zuhre was smiling but held a finger up to her lips.

"No talking for hour or so. No sound to bring them to us," she whispered. "Dangerous."

Xuě sighed, disappointed, but, then, she turned and followed behind Bao, jogging to keep up. At least, they were moving again. Every step took them farther away from China and Mao and closer to freedom.

Freedom. What would that look like? Would it mean she no longer had to fear others knowing what she was? Or would it still mean hiding her true self as she did in the village? Everyone knew, but pretended otherwise and shunned her unless they needed something. Only her parents . . .

She caught her breath and stumbled, bumping into Bao's back. He glanced at her. She straightened her shoulders and focused on keeping up with the others.

Aynur had set a brisk pace that didn't allow for conversation and didn't slow down until the sun crested the horizon. One of the many towers of rock loomed ahead of them. He headed straight for it. They stopped in its shadow. He removed his pack and pulled out a container. The smell of jerky teased Xuě's nose. Her stomach clenched. He took a piece and passed it around. Following his lead, each person withdrew one piece.

Xuě bit into the jerky and closed her eyes in pleasure.

When he finished eating, Aynur drank from a canteen and handed it to Pema.

"Only take a swallow or two. We've a long walk before we reach the next source of water."

Both Nur and Zuhre followed suit. Zuhre passed hers to Xuě.

"*Xièxiè*," Xuě said and swallowed a gulp of water. It trickled down her throat, snaking a cold path to her stomach. She clamped down on the urge to drink all of it and, instead, passed it to Bao.

He smiled at her before tipping the canteen and drinking. Warmth spread through her. How lucky she was to have married this man.

"What?" he asked.

Heat rushed into her cheeks. She glanced away and peeked back up at him. Even after all they'd been through, she found it hard to share her feelings with him. What were her feelings for him? She didn't know. "I . . . I was thinking—"

"How much farther is it?"

Xuě turned at Huan's question. Relieved at the interruption, she hoped it would distract Bao enough that he'd forget and wouldn't push her to answer.

"See the *yardang* in the distance?" Aynur pointed to a ridge that towered over the basin floor several *gōnglǐ* away. "We'll stop at its base for the night. Now, if everyone's ready, we'll continue on."

The alpha hefted his pack, slipped it over his shoulders,

and strode off. The group quietly fell in line behind him.

"What were you going to tell me?" Bao looked over his shoulder and asked her.

Xuě stared at his back. She didn't want to tell him. Zuhre walked behind her and would hear. Yes, they'd grown close in the short time they'd known each other. In a dangerous situation, she could count on him to be there for her, as she would be for him, but Xuě questioned what she felt for her husband. Did she love him? Or did she only want him? She cared for him. He righted her world when things fell off kilter. He brought her peace and made her laugh. But love? In a marriage, to have what she had with him and for him to be a kind man was more than she had a right to ask for.

"Xuě?" he asked.

Her breath caught. "I . . . Nothing. It wasn't important."

She wasn't ready to share how she felt about him because she didn't really know. And doing it where someone would witness it? She shook her head. No. Hopefully, with more time, that would change.

# Chapter Thirteen

The sun had reached its zenith when the ground vibrated under her feet and a dark shadow appeared far off in the distance. The dark shadow grew larger as it bore down on them, morphing into two large military trucks filled with men. The rumbling increased, and the ground trembled. Xuě watched them. Her heartbeat accelerated, and her breath caught in her throat. What would Aynur do?

As if to answer her question, he broke out in a run, veering left toward a rock tower a few hundred feet away. The group sprinted behind him. He crouched down next to the base of the tower, blending into the desert, and motioned for everyone to follow suit. The ground shook under their feet. The loud rumble of trucks ricocheted from rock tower to rock tower.

The convoy rolled past them and stopped. A door opened and a soldier stepped out. A man of obviously higher rank walked up to him.

"Here, *zhōngwèi*," a voice shouted over the din.

"Are you sure?" the lieutenant asked, his gaze scouring the area around them. "I don't see anything. Perhaps you imagined them."

"I tell you, *xiānshēng*, I saw a group running toward this tower."

Xuě shrank back, deeper into the brush. Bao squeezed her hand. It didn't stop her heart from racing.

"This way," Aynur whispered. "Stay low."

Still crouched, they wove their way through the brush, placing the tower between them and the soldiers. A shot rang out. Someone yelled. Another shot echoed through the basin. Another yell. The sound of gunfire erupted on the other side of the tower.

Xuě curled into the smallest ball she could make and put

her arms over her head. Bao leaned into her, wrapping his arms around her.

"We must leave *now*," Aynur said over the noise. "This way." He sprinted through the shrubs, zigzagging away from the firefight raging behind them, keeping the rock formation between them and the battle.

They raced through the brush to the next outcrop of rock. The farther removed they were from the fighting, the more muffled it became.

Fear held her in its grip. Would it last as long as the firefight in the canyon? The thought spurred her forward, despite her protesting muscles.

In front of her, Bao slowed. Like her, his body was reacting to the sustained pace. Snow leopards weren't designed for long sprints. She could travel many *gōnglǐ* in a day, but she wouldn't be able to maintain a sprint for much longer. Her muscles burned. Would they leave Bao and her behind if they couldn't keep up? They couldn't be caught because of this. She'd die before she'd let Mao's soldiers take her.

With renewed determination, her entire focus zeroed in on staying close to her husband. Everything else fell away. Time slipped by in a blur of pain.

The sound of shooting had long since faded when the group slowed to a trot. How much ground they'd covered she didn't know. At that point, she didn't care.

Relief washed over her when they stopped. Her legs wobbled underneath her, and she bumped into Bao. He stumbled into Chang, the bear shifter in front of him. Chang took a few steps forward and bumped Huan. The pattern repeated until the last person knocked into Aynur.

The alpha caught himself against a rock tower before turning to the shifters behind him. His concerned gaze scanned the group.

"Is everyone okay?" His low voice carried to the back.

Only the *láng* answered aloud. The rest responded with a nod, their pants loud to Xuě's ears. That she and Bao weren't the only ones struggling to keep up eased her worries. They wouldn't be left behind.

"We will rest here for a few minutes," he said. "Do not sit or your muscles will cramp."

Xuě trudged to a rock overhang and leaned against it. She stared at the ground, her breaths coming in deep gasps. Even in the cold, sweat stung her eyes. Bao came up beside her. He smoothed a long strand of black hair out of her face and tucked it behind her ear. Cupping her face with his hand, he tilted it up until their gazes met.

"How are you?" he asked between pants. He searched her face.

She attempted a smile, but it felt more like her cheeks were cracking open to bare her teeth. "I'm—" Air scratched over her vocal chords, and she coughed.

"Here." Zuhre seemed to materialize beside her and handed her a canteen. "Drink."

Xuě nodded gratefully. The cool water eased the dry burning of her parched throat. She passed the water to Bao.

He nodded his thanks and drank.

"Come," the she wolf said. "Aynur wants to . . . talk to us." She walked to the where the rest of the group had gathered.

Too tired to answer, Xuě pushed off the rock and straightened. Bao clasped her hand. Her heart lightening at his simple gesture, she glanced up at him. Some of the tension abated. They'd escaped the soldiers this time. They would do it as many times as they needed to be free.

She stepped toward where the others had gathered around Aynur with her husband by her side.

"Our flight has taken us off course. We're heading to a different location for tonight. Considering how close we came to being captured, we're lucky. If the Tibetan Resistance hadn't attacked, we'd be in the custody of PLA."

"The Tibetan Resistance? Are they friends? Or enemies?" Huan asked.

"Friends. China has claimed Tibet as theirs. They've chased the Dalai Lama out of his land. Their sacred relics have been destroyed. Anyone who opposes China is a friend to the resistance. Tibetans want no part of China and their chairman." Aynur nearly spit out the last part, his jaw clenched. "Nor do we."

Murmurs of agreement circulated the group.

"Aynur." Zuhre's voice brought everyone's attention to her. "We must . . . slow down. We go too fast."

"They will have—"

"She's right," Bao said. "Xuě and I barely made it here. I don't know how much farther I can maintain that speed before my legs stop."

Chang stepped forward. "Huan and I feel the same."

"Then we'll slow down, but we must make the *yardang* by tonight," Aynur said. "It's too dangerous not to."

Silence greeted his statement, and Xuě joined the line just ahead of Zuhre again. The alpha led the shifters across the empty basin toward the ridge at a fast walk.

Xuě plodded at the back, with Zuhre bringing up the rear, in silence for hours, only stopping for short breaks. Night blanketed the land before the *yardang* rose above them. Xuě was struggling to put one foot in front of the other without falling when Aynur led them into a cave. Unlike the others they'd stayed in, no bushes concealed the entrance. It opened into a large space, the area extending to either side of the mouth and several feet back. The darkness of the cavern closed around them when Xuě bumped into Bao. She leaned against his back.

He turned and wrapped his arms around her. "Let's find a place to sit with the others."

She raised her head, her consciousness expanding beyond the sore muscles. The other shifters had broken off into smaller groups. They passed around the canteens, drinking sparingly, and sat on the floor. Tonight, there would be no fire, no melting of snow for water. She nodded.

Without a word, he led her to an empty spot, and Xuě collapsed on the floor, her back against a rock. Bao dropped down next to her and handed her a canteen. She rested her head on his shoulder.

"There'll be no hunting tonight," Aynur said. "We'll leave

after midnight and continue on in the dark. If we keep the pace of the past several hours, we'll make it to the outer reaches of the *changtang*, where we should have been by now, before dawn. It's unlikely the army will follow us there. We'll rest there with some friends and travel at night."

He pulled his pack off, set it on the ground, and opened it, retrieving a bag. When he opened the bag, the smell of meat tickled Xuě's nose, and her stomach grumbled.

"Zuhre? Nur?" he said. "Make sure everyone gets two pieces. This will have to do until tomorrow night. We should be beyond this basin and into safer territory."

The two wolf shifters removed their packs and dug around, pulling out matching bags. They passed out jerky to the waiting group and settled down with their own.

Xuě nibbled at the first piece, savoring the tangy flavor of the yak jerky. The constant battle with hunger was nothing new to her. She'd lived with hunger pangs in the village since Mao's Great Leap Forward. If it meant escaping him and his policies, she could survive a few days without food.

They shared water from the canteens one more time before quiet settled over the company. Xuě snuggled back against Bao and closed her eyes.

Xuě woke with a start. Goose bumps raced from the top of her head down to her toes. Something was wrong. Bao slept peacefully beside her. Scanning the stygian blackness, her gaze settled on Zuhre who crouched at the entrance, her shoulders rigid. Rising, Xuě walked over to her.

Zuhre pushed her back. "Get down."

Xuě immediately hunkered down and searched the darkness outside. About a quarter of a *gōnglǐ* away, four soldiers patrolled the basin floor. Every few feet, they stopped, and one of them studied their surroundings before continuing on.

"How can they see in the dark?" Xuě asked.

"I don't know... unless they're like us. If they're . . . "

Xuě caught her breath and drew back deeper into the cave. What would make a shifter work for Mao's regime? Were they following their trail? What if they found them? "Our trail . . . "

"Aynur and Nur . . . um . . . covered it? I think that's what you say. You slept," Zuhre said.

"What's going on?"

Aynur spoke behind them. Xuě jumped.

Without turning, Zuhre responded in Uyghur. He frowned and snarled.

Bao slipped in beside her. "What do we do?"

"We wait and watch," the alpha said. "And stay low . . . And hope they follow the false trail Nur and I made."

Xuě turned to him. "You knew this would happen?"

He shook his head. "No, but it's better to be prepared."

"Are they shifters?"

The muscles in his jaw clenched and unclenched. He narrowed his eyes. "They could be, but the PLA is known for moving well at night."

The rest of the group gathered behind them in silence.

"If they take the false trail, we wait until they're out of sight and leave."

"And if they don't?" someone asked from behind them.

"We prepare to fight."

Xuě gasped. A pit opened in her stomach. Fight. Fighting meant killing. Someone, maybe all of them, would die this night if the soldiers didn't turn off soon. Could she kill another person again? Every fiber of her being shrank from the idea. She could only hope she wouldn't have to make that choice.

Next to her, Bao brushed her arm. She looked over at him. Wide, concerned eyes stared at her. She tried to smile, but she couldn't quite make it happen. Without a word, she returned her attention to the soldiers who tracked them.

Several tense moments passed. The soldiers inched closer and closer to their location. They stopped, studied the ground, retreated the way they had come a few steps, and studied the ground again. They repeated this process multiple times. One of them pointed away from them. Two of the soldiers headed in that direction. The other two continued their slow progress toward the shifters' hiding place.

The echo of a faint yell floated up toward them. The two soldiers turned toward where their compatriots had headed. Neither made a move to go and investigate. Instead, one of them scanned the ridge. Its gaze coming to a halt at the cave where the shifters watched in silence. Xuě shrank back against the others who pressed in around her. Did the soldier see them there?

"*Siki*," Aynur muttered.

Xuě's eyes widened. She didn't understand the word, but his sentiment was obvious. In the days she'd know Aynur, she'd never heard him swear, not even when he'd been shot.

"Everyone spread out. We must take them should they find the cave," he said. "I will stay on this side of the mouth. Nur," his second in command inched forward, "you take the position on the other side. The rest of you hide where you can. If that soldier isn't a shifter, he's a better tracker than I've ever seen."

A shifter ... working for Mao. Rage burned in Xuě's breast. She could understand a human working for the chairman, but a shifter? She backed farther into the cave to be stopped by Zuhre's voice.

"No," Zuhre said. "Only men should hide. Let them find us women. We pretend we flee the famine and band together for safety. They believe us. They see us as helpless. You men hide in the dark."

"Zuhre—"

"She's right," Pema said, "but it must be only me, Chang, and Xuě visible. I can pose as their guide. Zuhre, you and Akilina must hide with the men."

"But—"

"We're the most believable. I can pretend to be their guide," Pema said.

Aynur looked to Xuě and Chang. Xuě nodded. Pema was right. The three of them were the only ones who could do it. The others could hide in the darkness and wait.

"They're almost upon us. Hurry," Aynur said as he disappeared into the gloom with the rest of the shifters.

Xuĕ laid down several feet back from the entrance next to the other two women facing the entrance, feigning sleep. She closed her eyes. Should they come in and discover them, she had to remember to not look at the soldiers. Her eyes would give them away.

She suppressed a shiver of fear and breathed deeply. Panicking wouldn't help them. She must remain calm. Her cat urged flight, but she did her best to soothe her. This journey had taken its toll on her *yukihyō*. She'd forced it to do many things it never would've done in normal circumstances. Once more, it had to act other than its natural inclinations.

But these weren't normal circumstances. Together, they'd do what they needed to do in order to survive.

The crunch of gravel along the path alerted her to their presence. Pema and Chang stirred beside her, but neither sat up. Taking a cue from their actions, Xuĕ stayed as she was.

"It's just an empty cave," one of the soldiers whispered and coughed. "It stinks of animals, though."

Xuĕ swallowed the hysterical giggle that threatened to burst forth. If he only knew.

"Shut up and go in," another soldier said.

"I'm not going in there. If you don't believe me, you can go in. I'm telling you, it's empty."

"*Tā mā de*," the other soldier swore.

The sound of footsteps echoed in the cave. They were coming in. Xuĕ tensed.

"You're a fool, Chung. Empty, you say? Look what I found." The soldier now stood over them.

"I'm staying out here," Chung said.

Xuĕ sat up, scooted closer to Pema and Chang, and held their hands. As he didn't have a light with him, he had to be a shifter. No way could he see them otherwise. Xuĕ kept her gaze planted firmly on the ground.

"What brings *làmèi* to the Qaidam Basin?"

The tone of his voice and the way he said *làmèi* hinted at

both a cruel nature and trouble. Xuě had known men like him in the village. They pretended to be kind in public but beat their wives and children over imagined slights in private.

"We're heading to India," Chang said.

"Three women? Alone? You expect me to believe that?" He stepped closer, towering over them.

Instead of shrinking away, the women sat up taller. Anger stiffened Xuě's spine. Oh, *shi*, he was one of *those* men. No wonder he worked for Mao.

"Where are your men?" he asked. "Certainly such pretty young women as yourselves have men to protect them."

Chang moved as if to attack, but Xuě squeezed her hand in warning. Although she couldn't see above his knees, the traitor still had his rifle trained on them.

"We haven't needed any so far," Pema said. "No one has bothered us."

"I don't believe you," the solder said and leaned in. "You know why I don't believe you? Because you aren't just women. But you know who I am, don't you, Pema? I knew you were a *láng* the moment I came to your village."

Pema stiffened next to Xuě. "If only I'd known what you were, Gang. I'd've killed you then and saved ourselves the trouble now."

"You think you can kill me?" He laughed with malicious intent. "I don't think so. We didn't catch you then, but I have you now. You think I'm the only shifter who supports Mao? Who knows? You might even have one in your group now."

Xuě's heart raced at the thought. A traitor in their group? Who could it be? One of the women with her? Surely, not Pema, but Chang? She didn't really know Chang. The bear shifter kept to herself most of the time or with Huan. She forced herself not to look around and give away the others who waited to attack.

"But I will be the one who takes you in. When I return with you to Mao, I'll ask him to give you to me for breeding as my reward. We'll start a superior race of shifters." He licked his lips and turned his attention to Chang. "And you? You're a filthy bear, but you might produce strong babies for our new army. But what are you?" He stepped closer to Xuě and sniffed.

Xuě held her breath.

"Aw . . . isn't that cute? A useless snow leopard." He stepped back. "A snow leopard . . . That means—" He spun around, searching the depths of the cave.

With his back to them, Xuě leaped forward. The other two women must've been thinking the same thing as they all went at once, knocking him down. The rifle hit the ground. He opened his mouth to say something, but a knife materialized in Pema's hand. She held it to his throat, kicking his rifle out of his reach. Xuě pressed her knee deeper into his back, Chang held his legs down, and Pema kept the knife at his throat.

"One word more and I'll cut your throat," she said. "Not that it'd be a great loss. Such a big, strong man who thinks he's so smart, and yet so stupid to turn your back on shifters."

Gang growled.

Xuě glanced at Pema. They had him down, but under her fingers, his muscles bunched with tension as if readying to strike.

Pema leaned in closer and sniffed. "Not such a big, strong man now, are you?" She spat in the dirt next to his face.

He snarled.

"Gang?" Chung, the soldier who'd stayed outside, said. His voice rose timorously as he stepped into the cave. The whites of his eyes shone stark in the darkness.

The smell of his fear permeated the air. Xuě tensed and prepared to attack. Her nails dug into their prisoner, piercing Gang's skin. He grunted.

Chung swung his attention toward them and pointed his rifle in their direction. "Gang?"

Xuě pressed against Gang.

No one answered. A rock skittered across the floor, echoing in the silence. The scared soldier spun toward the sound and right into Aynur's fist. He lurched sideways into the arms of a waiting Nur. Nur wrenched the rifle away from him and pointed it at the stunned man. His eyes wide, Chung babbled something and backed away. Aynur grabbed him and forced him to the ground.

"What now?" someone asked from the darkness.

What would Aynur do? What were they going to do? Did they kill them? Bring them with them? But, judging from Gang's response, he'd cause trouble at every opportunity. If they left him behind, he'd continue to hunt them.

Gang's muscles rippled under her fingers. Xuě tightened her grip on him, her claws extending, digging into him deeper. The sharp tang of blood tickled her nostrils. He stilled. She looked at Pema who smiled grimly.

"How does it feel to have a 'harmless' snow leopard hold you down? You're lucky I don't kill you now, *Mao lover*, but don't push me," she said, leaning in closer.

"We tie them up," Aynur said, "and get information."

Zuhre appeared out of the darkness with some rope. They tied up Chung and dragged him over to where Xuě, Pema, and Chang held the enemy shifter down. They tied his hands and legs together none too gently. He snarled at them, but said nothing.

"How many are tracking us?" Aynur asked them.

"Two—"

"Say nothing to these *scum*," Gang interrupted Chung and glared at the shifters in front of him. "These ropes won't hold me. When I get loose, I'll start with your women." He turned to stare at Xuě, his yellow eyes full of malevolence. "The little snow leopard will be my—"

Aynur struck him across the face. "Gag him."

Blood trickled from Gang's lip, and he barred his teeth in a gruesome replica of a smile.

"Gladly," Pema said and stepped forward to do it.

Gang struggled against the gag, and it took both her and Huan to secure it. When they were finished, he glowered at them.

Bao picked up Gang's discarded rifle and slipped in beside Xuě. He put his arm around her.

She leaned against him for a moment, taking comfort in

his presence, her gaze never leaving Gang. She retreated several feet from the man. Bao let her go. Even with the gag and the rope, she didn't trust she was safe.

"Chung?" Aynur said.

The soldier bowed his head.

"How many track us?"

Chung glanced at Gang and back at Aynur, refusing to answer.

Gang growled, his eyes glowing red in the darkness of the cave.

Chung's eyes widened at the threat. His Adam's apple bobbed as he swallowed, but he still didn't respond. Clearly his fear of Gang surpassed his fear of them.

Aynur sighed. Turning to Pema, he held out his hand. "Pema?"

She stepped forward.

"May I borrow your knife?"

Without a word, she handed it to him.

"I didn't want to . . . " Aynur drew closer to Chung.

"Two squads. We're the scouts. Gang is the best tracker because he's a—"

A flash of light blinded her, and a roar echoed through the cavern, followed by a bloodcurdling scream. When the light cleared, a leopard stood over the dead Chung. Only shredded ropes and torn clothing remained where Gang had once been. Snarling, its fangs bloodied and tail twitching, the leopard spun and leapt at Xuě.

Her cat chuffed and froze. Her mind screamed for her to shift, to move, to run, but she stood glued in place.

The retort of a rifle filled the chamber, and Gang jerked, falling to the ground a few feet from her. Released from the paralytic fear, she retreated farther away from him. Light caught the glow in his eyes, and his gaze followed her. With a grunt, he dragged himself up, blood oozing from a hole in his chest. He took a step toward her, dragging each paw across the ground. Another shot echoed in her ears, and Gang dropped, a hole through the center of his forehead. His body shimmered, slowly shifting back to his human state.

Pema walked up to him and nudged his body with her foot. "He's dead. Good. One more Mao lover gone."

Xuě sagged in relief. Bao gathered her in his arms, and she leaned into him, tucking her head against his chest.

"Why me?" she asked without raising her head. But she knew why. Compared to the other shifters, she was weak.

"Why any of us?" Pema responded. "He was a bastard. He saw us as easy prey."

Aynur stepped forward. "How do you know him?"

The intensity of his voice drew Xuě's gaze to his face. A muscle ticked in his jaw. Had Pema lied? Was she a spy? Xuě glanced at Pema. How would she respond?

Pema scowled. "Gang came to my village, pretending to be a refugee fleeing Mao's regime in need of help."

Xuě drew closer to Pema. "Did you know he was a shifter?"

"I—" She dropped her gaze to the ground. Her voice dwindled to a whisper. "He smelled different . . . animalistic. I was excited. What if he was a shifter like me?" She paused and looked at everyone. "I'd never met another shifter . . . well, not since . . . " She raised her chin. "I'd never smelled another shifter since then either. It had been years. Had I known his purpose, I'd've killed him, or chased him from our village, or left and let him track me." Her voice caught. "But I didn't know. I returned from a hunt to find my entire village dead. The PLA walked through the dead. Gang was among them. He must've left to bring the troop with him."

"So he was hunting you?" Aynur asked.

"Not just her," Bao said, his arm tightening around her shoulder. "When he realized that Xuě was a snow leopard, he was looking for me."

# Chapter Fourteen

"What do we do with them?" Huan voiced Xuě's own thoughts.

Something in the way he said it drew her attention. Was there a tremor in his voice? Did he know Gang? Was Huan a spy?

"We take their guns and leave them."

Aynur's matter of fact answer distracted Xuě, and she flinched at the thought of leaving the dead without ceremony. She had forced Bao to help her bury the soldiers a few days ago. Now, they would leave these two to the animals. As if Chung and Gang meant little now that they were dead. While Gang had intended to harm them, Chung had just seemed frightened. That she could understand. Fear lived with her every moment of every day. It preyed upon her, chased away her ability to sleep, and paralyzed her in the face of her own physical danger. How was it that she could fight for others and not for herself?

"We need to take care of the other two," Aynur said. "They've come too close to us. They will search for their comrades and report what they find. Do we have any volunteers?"

Xuě shrunk away. She did not trust herself should they come under attack.

*Maruta*, a voice whispered in her head. She shoved it away.

Huan, the bear shifter, stepped forward. "I will."

Pema brushed past Xuě. "And me."

Aynur frowned and opened his mouth, but she raised her chin and said, "Let me. If this is the same group of filthy Mao lovers who came to my village, I want to make them pay."

"You cannot let your anger guide your actions."

Pema's body quivered with a suppressed emotion that had a metallic odor attached to it. "Anger?" She snorted. "Anger is a tame emotion compared to what I feel, but, no, it will not control me."

"Nur," he nodded to his second in command, "go with them. Catch up to us or meet us at our next stop. We cannot wait for you."

"We don't need a third person. Pema and I can take care of them," Huan said.

Aynur stared at the bear shifter for a moment. "It'll be safer with three than two." He turned to Nur and said something in Uyghur. Nur nodded.

Without a word, Nur motioned to Huan and Pema, and they disappeared into the night.

A longing to be more like Pema swept over Xuě, and she blinked back tears of frustration. But her *yukihyō* was as much a part of her as her human half. She could no more have the fierceness of a *láng* than a *lǎoshǔ* did when facing a cat.

"You should leave me here," she said to Aynur. "I will only bring you trouble and am no good to you in a fight."

Bao grabbed her arm and turned her to face him. "Xuě, no."

When she shook her head, he wrapped his arm around her and said, "Then I stay with her."

"We are leaving no one behind. Is that clear?" Aynur's tone brooked no argument.

A murmur of ascent rose through the air. Xuě bowed her head and said nothing. They didn't understand, but they would see it soon enough.

He stepped closer to her. "Is that clear?"

The gentleness in his voice startled her, and she looked up at him.

"Do you forget that you saved my life back there? We are in this together." He smiled.

He was right. She had saved him despite her *yukihyō* . . . and because of her. Next time, if there was a next time, she wouldn't fail them as she had this afternoon with Gang.

His gaze traveled back to the weary group. "Now, pack your stuff. We leave as soon as everyone is ready."

Tears threatened, but she refused to let them fall. Too many tears had fallen already. They had many *gōnglǐ* ahead of them and two squads behind them armed and prepared to kill. It only took one squad to kill her entire village.

Bao stepped up next to her and took her hand. "I have our stuff. Are you ready to go?"

"*Shi.*" She squeezed his hand. "*Xièxiè.*"

He cocked his head and stared at her. "For what?"

"For—"

"If everyone is ready, we will leave," Aynur said.

Xuě held Bao back until everyone else filed in front of them. "For saving me."

And he had saved her in so many ways. His support, his loyalty, his quiet strength, all of it in the face of all that came at them, and their marriage had yet to see three weeks. Surely, if they survived this intact, they could weather anything together.

He cupped her face. "You don't need to thank me. I—"

"Xuě? Bao? We leave." Zuhre's voice interrupted them.

"*Shi*, of course." Xuě searched his face for one more second before joining the others.

What had he been about to say? Did it matter? Would she ever have the confidence to admit to her feelings? What *did* she feel about him? She shook her head and trudged behind Chang along a game trail.

Her muscles had stiffened up during their brief time in the cave and protested with each step she took. The dry, cold air sucked the moisture from her mouth.

Ahead, the mountain rose steadily higher, its sides getting steeper and steeper. Despite the sharp incline, Aynur's pace didn't falter for what seemed like hours. The line came to a halt in front of her, and she stopped.

Gray, jagged rocky peaks blanketed with snow reached for the sky on either side of the narrow path that angled down instead of up and curved off to the left, disappearing from view. A bitter wind rushed through the gap, piercing her thin jacket. She raised her hands to her lips and blew on them, stamping her feet to keep the circulation going.

Chang passed her a canteen. Xuě nodded her thanks and clasped it tightly. Although the water was welcome, she longed for some hot tea and fresh meat. She took a few sips and handed the canteen to Bao.

After the canteens made their rounds, Aynur pulled a piece of rope from his pack and tied it to his belt. He turned to Akilina looped it through her belt and pack before continuing down the line. "I stopped here not just for a break, but because, for this next section, it's safer for us to be tied together. Part of the path has crumbled away. It is still passable, but it's very dangerous. We will take it slow. Do not place full weight on your foot until you are certain the trail will hold it."

Xuě tied the rope around her waist, leaving four to five feet between her and Chang, and handed the rest to Bao. He followed suit as did Zuhre. She walked slowly behind Chang. As she rounded the corner, she gasped. The mountain fell away, and the pace slowed to a crawl as she inched along the narrow path covered in snow, hugging the sheer rocky face. In her *yukihyō* form, she'd bound across it in a few strides. The sure-footedness of her animal would aid her, and the rest of them, but fatigue dogged her footsteps, her muscles ached, and her eyelids threatened to close even with the adrenalin pumping through her. It would require all of her concentration to maneuver the last twenty or so feet.

A muffled cry sounded ahead of her, and the rope tightened around her waist. She grabbed the rocky face and hung on. The line came to an abrupt halt. Her heart beat a rapid tattoo. The pressure eased, but still no one moved.

"Is everyone *xing*?"

Aynur's voice echoed back to her. Murmurs of assent slid over her, urging her to add her own even if her legs threatened to collapse under her. She wouldn't be the one to slow them down.

She rested her head against the jagged rock face in relief and waited. Her body quivered with tension. Several minutes passed before the line moved forward again, stopping and starting every few steps.

Then Chang stopped and turned her head to face Xuě. "There is a part of the trail that has completely crumbled away. I am going to jump across the gap. You'll need to inch as close as you can to the edge once I've crossed and do the same."

Xuě nodded before relaying the information to Bao. He nodded and slid closer to her. The rope went slack then tightened as Chang leapt across the small gap. When she landed, her left food slipped off the edge, and a chunk tumbled down the mountain. Xuě gasped, but Aynur grabbed Chang's hand and steadied her.

Now, it was Xuě's turn. The others gathered on the other side where the trail had widened to a few feet across. With a nimble leap, she sailed over the empty space and landed safely on the other side. She moved to one side and turned to wait for the others. Bao and Zuhre quickly followed suit.

Aynur made quick work of untying the rope. "We can take this off now as it's no longer necessary. The rest of the trail should be clear."

"What about Nur, Pema, and Huan?" Akilina asked. The blonde *láng* had been quiet most of the trip.

"Aynur, Nur, and I all carry ropes in our packs," Aynur said. "Nur is familiar with the path. He will know what to do."

Zuhre returned the coiled rope to Aynur who stored it in his pack and continued down the trail.

"It's not much farther now."

No one responded. A miasma of exhaustion hung over Xuě. Even the thought of being close to the end of their journey didn't increase her energy. The hours of sprinting, then walking combined with minimal water and food had eroded what little reserves she had. As more time slid away and the sky turned from the dusky gray of predawn to the palest of pink and yellow with the sun's slow climb over the horizon, she dragged her feet, her muscles protesting every step. Just as the sun's rays shot golden light over the peaks, chasing away the last of the night's darkness and bathing the world in pearlescent light, Aynur led them into the darkness of a cave.

"We will rest here until tomorrow evening, if all goes well, and wait for Nur, Huan, and Pema to join us." Exhaustion laced Aynur's voice. He propped the rifle he'd had slung over his shoulder against the wall of the cave and dropped his pack down next to it. "Zuhre, pass around the canteens. Is anyone up for hunting with me before we settle in?"

Bao stepped forward. "I don't know how we'll hunt as a team, but I'm game."

Aynur smiled.

"I'll come, too. I think we'll have a better chance with more of us working together," Akilina said.

Aynur motioned to the back wall of the cave. "There is dried yak dung if anyone wishes to start a fire. It could be a few hours before we return."

Xuě waited her turn to drink. She drank her fill. Grateful for the opportunity to build a fire and put snow on to melt. A few minutes later, her husband left with the other two shifters, and silence filled the cave. Chang, Zuhre, and Xuě were alone. Zuhre's shoulders drooped, and Chang rubbed her eyes. No one moved to get the fire going.

Although everything in her wanted to lie down and sleep, Xuě pushed forward, crossing to the stack of droppings and picking up a number of pieces of dung and bits of dried grass. Next to them, someone had placed some flat granite rocks. Blackened around the edges and covered in rust-colored stains, they told a story of being used for cooking meat. Saliva pooled in her mouth with visions of cooked *bharal* or *pán yáng*. Her stomach gurgled. Ignoring the hunger pangs, she trudged to the center of the cave where someone had set up a fire pit and placed the dung on the floor next to it. With a shrug of her shoulders, she removed her backpack and dug around until she found the package with her few remaining matches and set them aside. She took a couple handfuls of grass and set them in the center of the pit. Then she piled the dried yak dropping strategically, ensuring there were openings for oxygen to fuel the fire. Her hands shook with weariness when she struck the match and lit the grass. With a whoosh, the fire caught hold.

Silently, Zuhre handed her dung patties one at a time until the fire gave off a cheery warmth. Chang settled on Xuě's other side with a tired smile, adding a few more patties to the pile they'd accumulated to feed the fire. The smell of burning grass wafted up into the cave.

So much dung. When did they have time to to stock the cave with it?

"You have time to gather this?" Xuě motioned toward the pile.

Zuhre shook her head. "Local tribes on," she motioned toward the steppe below, "help us. They hate Mao. We're thankful."

"I thought you've only saved a few shifters." Xuě leaned forward, stretching her hands out to capture some of the fire's heat.

The two other women did the same.

She shrugged. "We have. Aynur is good at making . . . "

"Allies?" Xuě said.

"What mean allies?" Zuhre asked.

"Not really friends, but we help one another as they're on the same side."

Zuhre nodded. "*Shi*. Allies. We're on the same side."

Xuě smiled. Yes, being on the same side usually made a difference. "Well, I'm grateful to them . . . and to you."

Zuhre returned her smile, but didn't say anything.

Chang stood. "I think I'll shift and try to sleep."

Zuhre followed suit. "I'll keep first watch, if you'd like to sleep." She nodded to Xuě.

Chang stopped what she was doing. "Do you think we're safe here? You don't think they'll find us, do you?"

"No, but," Zuhre sighed, "I . . . it's hard to say. They came close. They don't do that. I feel better with one of us on watch." She glanced at the entrance. "I hope Nur, Pema, and Huan are good."

Chang nodded and retreated to the back of the cave. Her companion Huan had joined Nur and Pema. Had Bao chosen to go with them, Xuě would be consumed with fear for him right now. Chang's face had given away none of her emotions.

"Chang?" Xuě called.

The woman padded forward in her bear form.

"Are you okay?"

Chang nodded, laid down next to the fire, and rested her head on her front paws. Her eyes closed.

Xuě turned to Zuhre. "*Xièxiè.* If you don't mind, I'll shift, too, and get some sleep while I can. Wake me in a bit. I'll take the next watch."

Zuhre smiled before crossing to the cave entrance.

Xuě stripped off her clothes, folded them, and stored them in her pack. With a crack of bones, stretching of skin, and sprouting of fur, she shifted. Her thick coat protected her from the bitter cold. She lowered herself to the dirt floor by the fire and closed her eyes.

Slowly, the cold receded with the rest of the world.

Bao, Aynur, and Akilina returned on Xuě's watch. They stumbled past her into the cave carrying a large *chiru, t*he Tibetan antelope's long, black, spiraled horns positioned away from the three hunters. They dragged it to the back of the cave and dropped it on the floor.

All of them needed to rest. Even Xuě, who'd napped for an hour or so, battled the lure of sleep. Every time she moved, pain shot through her muscles. Her *yukihyō* could easily travel many *gōnglǐ* in a night with no repercussions, but, in her human form, with little rest, little water, little food, and the continual fear of capture, the journey was breaking her down. At this point, no matter the promises made by Aynur and his pack, hope of crossing into India and eluding the Mao regime dwindled with each passing day.

But she did what she had to. Despite the Japanese, despite her village, despite Gang, despite everything, she'd survived this long. Whether she'd ever find a peaceful existence remained to be seen, but she'd continue as long as it was necessary.

While the three hunters settled next to the fire to sleep, Zuhre and Chang brought out the granite rocks and placed them next to the fire before getting to work on the *chiru*. Xuě sat just inside the entrance of the cave, watching and listening for any kind of threat.

With only the sounds of the crackling fire and the quiet talking of the two women behind her for company, she stared out of the cave and into the distant valley. She pushed herself to a standing position and stretched her legs before returning to the squat. The weak winter sun had reached its zenith, offering little warmth when the sound of running footsteps brought her to her feet. Her heartbeat accelerated, and beads of cold sweat dotted her brow.

"Zuhre," she said softly. "Someone is coming."

The wolf shifter raced over to her and grabbed the rifle that leaned against the wall behind Xuě. She pointed it at the opening and waited.

The footsteps pounded closer along with the scent of fear and *láng*.

Xuě glanced at Zuhre who lowered her weapon. Pema raced past the entrance.

"Pema!"

Xuě's voice stopped the she wolf midstride. Wild-eyed, Pema spun and ran toward them. Her breaths came in great gasps.

"Come. Nur is hurt and cannot cross the gap in the path. He sent me ahead. I don't know how long, or if, he's still standing."

Pema's words brought the rest of the shifters to the front of the cave.

"What happened?" Chang asked.

"We killed the scouts, but not before one of them got a shot off. Nur didn't say anything about being injured until we crested the summit of the pass where he collapsed. Chang and I have been carrying him most of the way since that point, but we can't get him past the tight ledge and over the gap."

"You couldn't smell the blood?" Aynur asked.

Pema opened her arms wide. "Look at me." Blood stains dotted the front of her shirt. "We moved the soldiers to the cave so they wouldn't be found out in the open. All of us have a certain amount of blood on our clothes."

He nodded.

Pema continued. "I don't know how much time he has. We need to get back and help him."

"Bao, grab my backpack," Aynur said. "Zuhre, you come with us. Akilina, you stay here and help Chang with the antelope. Pema, you stay here and rest."

Pema scowled. "But I—"

Aynur shook his head. "No, we've had some time to rest. You've done your part. Stay and get some rest. Bao, Zuhre, and I can take care of this."

"And me?" Xuĕ asked.

"Keep watch," he said.

Useless. Aynur viewed her as useless. Well, good enough to keep watch, but not much else. Maybe he was right. Maybe she was no better than a *maruta*. She batted her eyes to stop the tears. She hated tears.

As if reading her mind, Bao walked over to her, placed his hands on her shoulders, and kissed her forehead before leaning back. Their gazes met. "We will return. You need to rest, too. You can do that here."

She shook her head. "What about you? You went hunting. I'm not some weakling."

"He doesn't think you're a weakling—"

"Bao," Aynur called, "are you coming?"

"*Shi*," Bao said. "I'll be back. He's trusting you to watch over everyone. If he thought you were weak, he wouldn't ask you to do it."

Before Xuĕ could respond, Bao spun on his heels and followed Aynur and Zuhre back up the path, disappearing from view.

Xuĕ sighed. His words made sense, but the memory of

her freezing when first that man attacked her and then Gang rushed to the fore.

Aynur was right. Leaving her behind in the cave protected everyone from her weakness, including her.

She slouched down next to the cave entrance and continued her vigil, counting the minutes until the others returned.

# Chapter Fifteen

Stars winked in the sky when the absent shifters trudged into the cave with Nur. Strips of *chiru* sizzled on the granite rocks next to the fire. The aroma filled the cave and tickled Xuě's nose. Her stomach growled. Next to the fire, Akilina and Chang turned the meat every so often to prevent it from burning. After the meat cooked, they placed it on another rock farther from the fire to keep warm and allow it to cool. The shifters lined up to get their dinner.

Xuě glanced over her shoulder. Her stomach protested again, and her mouth watered.

Pema approached her. "Go eat. I'll take watch."

Xuě shook her head. "You haven't eaten yet. At least get some food. You can come relieve me when you've done that."

Pema nodded and retreated to the fire.

Between the successful hunt and Akilina finding a source of drinkable water and filling their canteens with fresh water that didn't taste like smoke, for the first time in many nights, they would eat and drink their fill. Perhaps the meat would last a few days. Xuě hoped so.

Pema dropped down next to her, a piece of *chiru* between her fingers. "Eat. I've got it."

With a nod, Xuě hurried over to the fire. Bao handed her a strip of meat. The juices dripped down her fingers, and she bit into it. It tasted different than the *pán yáng*. Its bold and tangy flavor awakened her *yukihyō*, but she fought the urge to gobble it down. Instead, she savored every bite before reaching for another strip. By the fourth strip, her shrunken stomach protested.

She sat back and sighed. Bao wrapped his arm around her, and she rested her head on his shoulder. The yellow and orange flames of the fire gyrated in a hypnotic dance. A meditative calm settled upon her. The tension of the last couple of days oozed out of her. She slid her arms around him, his warmth seeping through her clothes.

He kissed the top of her head, and she snuggled closer. For the moment, the worries and fears slipped away and hope burgeoned. The border of India drew closer with every day they managed to elude the PLA. If . . . no, when they crossed the border into India, she'd spend the rest of her life honoring her parents' decision to arrange this marriage.

She tightened her arms around him. He squeezed her shoulders.

"Do you ever wonder what India will be like when we get there?"

He shook his head. "I haven't thought that far ahead."

"Me either, but we are closer. It seems like it could be real. We might escape the PLA and be able to live free. Can you imagine it?" She leaned away from him, searching his face.

His gaze met hers. Worry darkened the beautiful silver to pewter. "I . . . I don't think too far ahead. I focus on each day and getting through it."

She nodded. "You know what I hope for—if we make it to India?"

"No. What?"

"I hope to have friends, like Zuhre and Akilina." She glanced down. "I've never had people to talk to, other than my parents, like I've had these past couple of weeks. It's been nice. I don't want that to end, but I don't want to be caught."

She looked up.

He was frowning. "Xuě—"

"Shhh . . . It's okay. I was used to being alone, but, now, I don't want to be." She nestled against him, resting her head on his chest.

"You'll never be alone again. I won't let you be."

She smiled. He was a good man.

A comfortable silence descended. It stretched for several minutes. His heart beat steadily in her ear.

"Will we be accepted? China and India are enemies."

"Mao is our enemy, too. We are not the only Chinese flee-ing his government."

"That doesn't mean they'll welcome us. Perhaps there are too many Chinese flooding India already." A sudden thought hit Xuě. Her stomach clenched. "What if they turn us away? What if they turn us over to Mao?"

Bao stroked her short hair. "Aynur wouldn't lead us some-where if he thought that would happen. He has already helped others escape. We must trust him."

Trust. She'd trusted few people before meeting Bao and the other shifters. Someone in the village had betrayed them. People she'd known most of her life. In doing so, they'd en-sured that everyone died. She swallowed a snarl. They were dead now. All of them, including the one person she suspected of turning her in. After all Mao and his soldiers had done to her village, how could he have believed that would help?

She could forgive the cannibal. He was a product of the famine, but she'd never forgive the man who killed her par-ents. She hoped his soul never found peace. If *Diyu* existed, they'd drag him into the room with the cauldron of oil and boil him. He deserved no less. Let him boil forever.

"Xuě?"

Bao's whisper drew her out of her musings.

"What's wrong? You're shaking."

She released a shuddering breath, ashamed of her thoughts. Her thoughts could land her in one of the many rooms of *Diyu*. Her parents hadn't raised her to be vengeful nor cruel. Even in the face of great adversity, she must live up to their expec-tations. Doing anything else would bring dishonor upon their memory.

"Xuě?"

"I . . . I'm ashamed of my thoughts." She glanced at him, her gaze meeting his. "I . . . I don't wish to tell you. They're not kind."

"It might help you if you do."

Pulling away, she wrapped her arms around her body and scooted closer to the fire, its cheerful dance in direct conflict with her dark thoughts.

"I wished the man responsible for the death of my parents to boil in the oils of *Diyu*."

He chuckled.

A bright flame of anger flared within her. "You think this is funny?"

"No . . . I mean, *shi* . . . I mean . . . "

He turned her body towards him. She averted her gaze. His laughter stung.

"Look at me."

She shook her head.

"Xuě."

The plea in his voice breached her defenses, and she gave in. Their gazes met. The understanding in his eased the anger and fear raging inside of her.

"I laugh because you voiced my thoughts. Every day, in silence, I've cursed Mao and his government. Even after my years at the temple, I find it hard to forgive him. In some ways, he's like the monkey king, Xuanzang, except he's human and evil. He knows what he does and should be able to control himself. Xuanzang . . . "

He didn't need to finish. Xuě nodded. Mao was as capricious, intelligent, and ruthless as the monkey king of the Chinese fairytales. She used to laugh when her mother told them to her. Xuanzang always caused trouble for the other gods. No one could control him. No one but Buddha. But Buddha was another fairytale, and Mao was not. No one could control Mao. Not in China. They had to escape. They had no other options.

"So, I'm not alone?" she asked.

"No. Haven't you heard Pema? She hates Mao. She wants revenge. Most of us do. Like you, Pema lost her village. I don't know Huan's or Chang's stories, nor any of the others', but I would bet they're like ours. Why would any of us leave our homes—our families—unless we had to?"

Why would they? Zuhre's family had chased her from their village. Who knew what brought the others to this point. All of them had lost something. Whether their families had died or survived, they were lost to them now.

She looked at the people gathered around the fire. Worry, fatigue, fear, hunger, and anger had left their mark. Dark circles under their eyes and haunted expressions hinted of the tragedies that'd caused them. With the ever-present exhaustion eating at her, doubts eroded her confidence in their ability to escape and survive. But closing her eyes didn't bring her rest. Instead, sleep ushered in the screams of dying soldiers as they chased her through the snow and her parents reaching out skeletal hands, their eyes full of accusations.

"Do you dream of the dead?" she asked Bao.

"*Shi.*" Pain snaked through the timbre of his voice.

"I can't forget the faces of those I've killed or those who've died because of me." She scooted to the side, pulling out of his embrace. Cool air filled the space between them, and she huddled closer to the fire.

"I know. They haunt me, too, and I don't know if I want to forget them. If I do, will I become like Mao?"

He spoke the question she feared. Part of her wanted to forget them. Not her parents, but the men. But if she forgot them, what would it say about her as a person? How did one find peace with killing another person no matter the reasons behind it? How did one justify it even if the killing had been a choice between her life and theirs? But, if she didn't, it'd drive her crazy.

"Xuě?"

Akilina's voice startled her out of her dark musings. The woman rarely spoke, at least not to her. Her accent hinted that she grew up in the borderlands of China.

The blonde-haired wolf shifter moved closer and spoke in low tones. "I'm haunted by them, too. Good people are, but," anguish settled over her features, "given the chance, I'd kill Mao and not mourn his loss. He's an evil man who should die before he kills more. And he *will* kill more in his desire to rule everyone." She clenched her fists. "His soldiers are evil. They killed your entire village. I don't know about mine, but—" She paused and gazed off into the distance before blinking and returning to the present. "In the dark hours of the night, I'd shift and prowl the countryside in search of anything to eat. Then, one morning, I came home to find . . . " Her voice caught, and she swallowed, blinking a few times. Tears trickled down her cheeks. "My village was starving. Everyone. From the smallest child to the oldest grandparent. One of the children had died. Rather than bury the child, they were preparing it to eat." She turned haunted eyes on Xuě. "Eat. When my parents died, despite everything I did to try to save them, I smuggled them out of the village and buried them before they could become food, too. That's when I left."

Akilina's hands twisted in her lap. Anger flashed across her face. "This famine didn't have to happen. It's Mao's fault. Mao and the dirty, greedy bastards who follow his orders.

"No, we'll never be like them." Loathing laced her words. "*They* shot Nur. *They* shot Aynur. Gang would've killed you and enjoyed it if he hadn't been stopped. Such people, if you can call them that, don't deserve to live. We don't kill innocents. They do."

Akilina's words brought Xuě little comfort. The expression of the soldier who'd accompanied Gang rose in her mind. That one had been scared, like them. What if Mao forced him to serve as he did so many others? What if the fear of his family being captured and imprisoned pushed him to join the army? Would serving mean their families would be fed? That they wouldn't have to turn to cannibalism? Perhaps he'd believed in the beginning that the Cultural Revolution would change the lives of all their people for the better, like so many of them had. Only after the Mao regime was running at full speed and the famine struck did its ugly underbelly reveal itself.

She could hate Mao but kill him? Only if he threatened the people she cared about.

Heat rushed through her body as the fire of anger burned in her belly. She owed it to her parents to make it out of Tibet and out of Mao's grasp. If she didn't, their deaths would mean nothing. And she wanted to live.

Aynur walked up to the fire. "We'll be staying the night. Nur needs rest." He looked around the group. "We all do. Chang, are you up to taking the next watch?"

The bear shifter nodded.

"Good. We'll rotate every hour. Everyone should have plenty of rest before we start the next leg of our journey across the steppes tomorrow morning. Once we start, there'll be little rest."

"No, Aynur. Nur needs more rest," Zuhre said from where she sat tending to Nur.

Aynur crossed to crouch down beside his mate. Although he lowered his voice, his words traveled across the distance from the back of the cave to where Xuě huddled by the fire.

"We're not safe here. Huan said they covered their tracks, but the squads weren't too far behind the scouts. They could follow us over the mountains."

"And onto the steppes?" Zuhre asked.

"He's right." Nur sat up.

Zuhre pushed him back down. "Lay down. You must rest."

"We can't stay here. We need more distance. I can travel."

"Nur—"

"No, we must leave. Tonight is all we can give up. They'll find us, Zuhre. I can feel it." The sound of a grumbling stomach echoed in the cave. "If one of you could bring me some *chiru* . . ."

Zuhre motioned to Aynur who stood and crossed to the fire where more strips of *chiru* roasted. He took a few and carried them back to Nur.

Pushed beyond their limits but with little choice but to move forward. Xuě turned back to the fire. The quiet conversations between the other shifters swirled around her, but her thoughts bounced from one nightmare scenario to the next. They had to escape.

The light in the cave faded with the setting of the sun. Chang traded places with Pema, who curled up next to the fire and closed her eyes. Night and day no longer mattered. Sleep came when they could. The soft breathing of the others told Xuě that only she and Chang remained awake. Gritty-eyed, she lay with Bao spooned around her and stared at the fire. Hours slipped by. Each time her eyes closed, something woke her.

Sometime in the middle of the night, just as her eyes shut, a faint scream tickled her ears. Xuě cocked her head, listening intently. At first, only the wind howling past the cave entrance greeted her, but then another muted cry infused the blizzard with a terrified wail. The volume would increase before fading away. The pattern repeated several times. Looking around the cave, she searched for anything that could create the sound, but nothing stood out. Only the sight of the other shifters sleeping greeted her. Perhaps the wind had found a hollow in the rocks outside.

She laid down again. Her breath caught in her throat as the wailing resumed. What could it be?

Disengaging herself from Bao, she sat and strained to hear more. At the entrance of the cave, Chang sat unmoving. Didn't she hear them, too? Or were they echoes of her own memories?

The sorrow she'd buried for the past several days rose to the surface in a groundswell of emotion. Tears sprouted in her eyes, and sobs burned in her chest. Bao stirred behind her. Unwilling to wake him, she drew in deep breaths until the feelings subsided then she wiggled out of their blanket and crossed to Chang.

"Did you see or hear anything?" she asked her.

Chang shook her head.

"Are you sure? I thought I heard screaming."

Tired eyes stared back at her. The woman shook her head again. "It is just the wind."

*Just the wind.* Her instincts disagreed. Still chafing from being left behind earlier to keep watch, Xuě said, "I'm going to check it out, just to be sure."

"I don't think Aynur would like that. It'd be better to wait," Chang said.

Fear crept along her spine, but she pushed it away. "He may not, but I must do something more than wonder." She raised her chin. "I may not be good in a fight, but Bao and I can move more silently than everyone else, and I am used to hunting in this weather."

"Xuě?"

She jumped and spun. Aynur stood behind her.

"What are you doing?"

"I . . . I heard wailing."

"It's the wind," he said.

She jutted her chin out. "No, it wasn't."

He drew in a deep breath and released it. "It can wait until morning. No person, or animal, can travel in this storm. It isn't safe. All of us will stay in this cave and rest. Understood?"

She burned with the desire to be useful, to prove she could do more than sit watch, that she wasn't imagining things, but, rather than argue, she nodded.

At her agreement, he turned away and padded back to the fire.

A slow burn built inside of her. She itched to venture out into the storm and discover the truth. Instead, she was stuck inside. Trapped. She stared out into the world of white, her thoughts as turbulent as the swirling snow.

The specter of the men she'd killed wavered in her mind's eyes, morphing into one person. Xuě banished the unsettling image.

"Are you *xíng*?" Change asked.

With a shrug, she said, "I'm fine, but I won't be able to sleep. I'll take the rest of your watch if you want."

"*Xièxiè.*" Chang handed her the blanket she had draped around her shoulders.

Xuě accepted it with a nod. She sat, slipped it over her shoulders, and wrapped her arms around her knees. Resting her chin on top of her knees, she stared out into a world of white. Snowflakes gyrated in an uncontrollable orgy even her enhanced sight strained to penetrate. The wind howled past the opening, carrying with it the eerie wailing. It whooshed by again, chasing snow in front of it, and then everything went silent. Nothing moved. Behind her, the dung fire crackled cheerfully. Outside, the storm quieted. The snow stopped falling. Clouds parted, and the stars twinkled. The dark of the night enveloped her in its embrace.

She stayed that way until Akilina relieved her some time later.

Long, pink tendrils of dawn streaked across the awakening sky when Xuě opened her eyes. Most everyone else was already awake and quietly talking as they sat eating around the fire. Bao sat next to her with food. He handed her a piece. Without a word, she smiled her thanks and dug in. A few minutes later, Aynur trotted past them, continuing to the back where he shifted and dressed before joining everyone at the fire.

He stood quietly until everyone stopped talking. "It's safe to remain here for a few days." He turned to Nur, who rested against a rock in obvious pain. "You can rest. The squads won't be catching up to us today or tomorrow." His gaze swept the room until it landed on Xuě.

About to take a bite, she froze, her stomach churned. She lowered the food in her hand. "What happened?"

His scrutiny pinned her to her spot as he focused on her. "You were right. It may not have been the wind you heard last night. They tried to cross the gap in the storm. I found the remains of their equipment. It appears they didn't see it in the snowstorm and fell to their deaths."

Everyone but Xuě cheered. This was good news, but a chill crept down her spine, sending goose bumps racing across her skin. The faint, haunting cries heralded more senseless deaths in Mao's pursuit of them. She grabbed Bao's hand and squeezed. He looked at her.

"I heard them . . . last night while everyone slept. I heard their death cries. They woke me."

"Oh, Xuě." He pulled her into his embrace and kissed her temple.

She released a shuddering breath and clung to him. The need to feel alive, to connect to another human washed over her. She nuzzled his neck.

He drew back and stared down at her, a question in his eyes. Without a word, she drew his head down to hers. Their lips met, and tendrils of desire unfurled. It zipped along her nerve endings and woke her entire body. Her *yukihyō* purred. Everything became about him, and only him. No one else existed. She pulled him closer, but he broke the kiss and rested his forehead on hers.

"We're not alone," he whispered, and reality rushed back in.

Heat flared in her cheeks, cooling the desire, but not the need.

"Tonight, I promise, *xing?*"

She nodded and snuggled closer. This was a promise she'd make sure he'd keep.

# Chapter Sixteen

On the third day, with Nur recovered enough to travel, Aynur announced, "We'll leave after the sun sets. Zuhre, Nur, and I will only be going as far as the village. Our contact, and your guide, will be a wolf shifter named Bantowa."

Zuhre frowned and said something in Uyghur.

He responded and gave her a look. She flattened her lips in a straight line and shook her head, but said nothing.

He faced them again. "Bantowa has guided many out of Mao's reach. He will do the same for all of you. We," he motioned to his small pack, "will go back for more shifters. Everyone rest while you can. Crossing the steppes will be as taxing as the last few weeks."

The alpha crossed to the fire, lay down next to it, and closed his eyes. The others followed suit, but Xuě hung back with Zuhre.

Zuhre shook her head.

"What is it?" Xuě asked.

The wolf shifter glanced at her mate. "I don't . . . like Bantowa."

"Zuhre—" Aynur's voice held a warning.

"No, I tell her. She should know."

Her mate shook his head and settled back down.

Zuhre grabbed her arm and drew Xuě closer to the entrance. "Don't be by self with Bantowa. Tell the other women."

Xuě widened her eyes.

"He is—how do you say?—like that small animal with a," she motioned with her hands in an arc, "cover. It eats green . . ." She huffed.

"A snail?" Xuě asked.

Zuhre's eyes lit up. "*Shi*. The trail it puts on the ground."

"Slimy."

"*Shi. Shi.* Bantowa is slimy to women."

"But he's a good guide, Zuhre," Aynur said. "You don't have to like him for him to get you to safety." He sat up. "Come. Join me. It's time to rest."

Zuhre nodded. "I said what I wanted. I join you now."

Amusement filled Aynur's eyes, and he lay down again.

Before Zuhre could go to Aynur, Xuě touched her arm. "*Xiéxié.* I will be careful."

The other woman smiled and crossed to her mate.

Xuě padded out with the others onto the trail and turned down the mountain toward the valley. Dark spots marred the white surface. The last couple of days of rest had helped her even if she slept in fits and starts. The atmosphere in the cave changed from tense to relaxed, but each person took a watch shift, switching every couple of hours.

Throughout the day, more snow fell, blanketing the world in white. As they exited the cave, the full moon glinted off the clouds gathering on the horizon threatening another storm. Even in her *yukihyō* form, the biting cold stung. Xuě hoped it held off until they reached their destination.

Somehow, regular humans survived this terrain. According to Aynur, they'd be staying in tents at a Tibetan camp, that supported the resistance. Although China had conquered Tibet in the 50s, there were still pockets of resistance against Mao's regime.

Her nerves fluttered at the thought of being surrounded by humans. Despite Aynur's assurances that these people were their allies, she feared what they'd do to them.

Hours, and many *gōnglǐ*, later, the pace slowed. Predawn light crept up the horizon, and the stars faded against the graying sky. Xuě padded up to stand abreast of Huan and the other shifters. Bao stopped next to her.

Before them, four or five large, black tents sprung out of the snow. Smoke drifted out of the top of each of them. She raised her head and inhaled. Her *yukihyō* chuffed at the mouth-watering smell of cooked meat. Her stomach grumbled.

"We'll need to hunt first."

Xuě jumped at the sound of Aynur's voice. She'd been so focused on the village and food she hadn't noticed he'd shifted.

"Mao has brought the famine here, too, with his war on Tibet. The people are generous to allow us to stay and will offer us what little food they have. We'll repay them with a *chiru*. It won't feed the entire village, but it will help. Once we've caught one, we'll shift and walk into the village in our human forms, carrying our gift."

Her body protested the thought of chasing down an animal after such a long trek, but Aynur was right. They couldn't stay without a gift.

"There is a herd of *chiru* in the distance. We'll break up into two groups. Zuhre, Nur, Akilina, Pema, and I will separate the weakest from the herd and drive it toward the four of you. Be prepared to take it down."

Her cat swished her tail. She hadn't hunted for a number of days now and itched to be in on the action, but she was an ambush predator. Waiting for the *chiru* to come to her worked to her strengths.

She trotted behind the *láng* until Aynur signaled for them to stop. In the distance, a herd of long legged animals huddled against the cold. The *láng* crouched and circled the beasts.

A large male with long horns bleated a warning and took off across the steppes. The herd startled and raced after the leader, a writhing dark mass against the white snow in the pale dawn light.

The *láng* darted back and forth until one of the *chiru* peeled off from the group. They herded it toward where Xuě and the others waited. Its long legs ate the distance between it and Xuě.

As the animal thundered toward her, she crouched, doing her best to blend in with the ground, her muscles tense, ready to spring.

At the last moment, it saw them, bleated, and veered off.

Xuě sprang into action, but Bao beat her to it. He leaped, claws extended, and hit the animal in the side. They rolled together. The *chiru*'s legs flailed. Blood stained the snow.

Her breath caught in her throat, and she froze. Whose was it? Was Bao okay?

The *chiru* struggled to its feet, but deep gouges ran from its back down its belly. It wobbled, trying to get its legs under it to flee.

Bao stood and shook his head.

Assured he was okay and roused from her trance, Xuě pounced and knocked the injured animal to the ground. It bleated weakly one last time.

She backed away from the *chiru*. Her *yukihyō* growled in protest, wanting to rip the animal apart, but this was for their hosts. They'd have dinner soon enough.

Turning away from the corpse, she chuffed at Bao. He trotted up to her and head butted her. She licked his face and purred.

Snaps, pops, and flashes of light broke out around them. Others were already shifting. She proceeded to do the same, her days of modesty giving way to the need to shift from animal to human and back frequently. No one paid attention to anyone else. Even now, naked and shivering, she helped Bao take the pack off before hurrying into her clothes and shoes.

"We'll take turns carrying the *chiru* to the village," Aynur said. "Huan, Chang, do you mind starting?"

The bear shifters lifted the carcass and fell into line behind Aynur.

Xuě allowed the others to go ahead of her, waiting for Zuhre, wanting her company, not caring if it meant being the last in line. Fatigue dug grooves bracketing Zuhre's eyes and mouth, but she smiled at Xuě, coaxing an answering one from Xuě. Too tired to talk, Xuě walked in companionable silence next to the wolf shifter she'd come to consider her friend.

Aynur pushed through the snow, blazing a trail for those behind him. By the time they reached the village, the cold had seeped into Xuě's bones and soaked her shoes, and she longed for her *yukihyō* shape once again.

Halfway to the village, Bao and Nur traded places with the bear shifters. Xuě trudged behind them.

Their leader stopped in front of a black, rectangular wool tent. Long, black ropes attached around the edge of the top at regular intervals stretched several feet away from the sides of the tent to a stake in the ground. On the rope in front of the door, several small, square flags with images and symbols hung along the entire length. Blue, white, red, green, and yellow, they fluttered gaily in the wind.

"Those are sutra streamers," Pema said softly. "They're to honor our river and mountain gods. They represent the blue sky, white cloud, red flame, green water, and yellow earth—the five elements. See how all the tents have them? They always hang them at their door or on their roof." She scowled. "The PLA trampled on every single one in our village, ripping through the tents, dishonoring our ancestors."

A flap swung open, and Xuě jumped. A wizened man stood in the doorway. He stuck his tongue out at Aynur. Just as quickly, his tongue disappeared.

Xuě frowned and turned to Pema. "Why'd he do that?"

"What?" Pema asked.

"Stick his tongue out?"

"Oh, it's how Tibetans greet each other and a sign of respect. It shows you come in peace."

Aynur spoke in a language Xuě didn't understand and stepped back, motioning for Bao and Nur to come forward.

The old man's eyes widened, and he stuck his tongue out at the them like he'd done with Aynur before his face split into a smile. He turned around and called to someone in the tent. A frail, older woman appeared from behind him. When she saw the *chiru*, she clapped her hands, showed her tongue, and spoke rapidly to Aynur.

Aynur nodded and turned to the group. "Follow me."

Welcome heat washed over Xuě as the warmth from the large earthy fireplace that dominated the middle of the floor reached her. Weak light filtered through the hole at the top where the smoke escaped.

To the left, a shrine with images of their ancestors and the Dalai Lama sat in one corner. To the right were utensils and what looked like containers of some sort to hold food. A younger woman with two thin, young children sat off to the right side of the fireplace on a few of the bright patterned cushions scattered across a square carpet. Two different sized, red diamond shapes broke up the olive green background, alternating in rows. On either side of the tent were piles of rectangular carpets with blankets and sheepskin neatly folded on top. What were they for? One large, rusty red-colored carpet took up the area in front of the fireplace.

The older man motioned for them to come in, greeting each of them in kind. Self-consciously, Xuě stuck her tongue out at him. His eyes lit with happiness, and he babbled something to her in Tibetan. Xuě smiled, bowed her head, and followed the others into the tent. As the last shifter slipped inside, he swung the flap shut.

A younger woman stood at the fireplace, stirring a pot. She smiled, set the spoon aside, and wiped her hands before coming forward to greet them. Her face glowed with pleasure. She gave them the traditional Tibetan greeting and gestured for them to use the water to wash their hands. Her calf-length yellow tunic hung loosely around her body. With its high neck and long, cup-shaped sleeves, it covered every part of her body to just below the tops of her boots. At the hem, a flash of sheepskin hinted at a warmth Xuě only dreamed about. The woman's brown leather boots with upturned toes and leather appliqués at the top would keep the woman's feet toasty.

What Xuě wouldn't give to have her beautiful sheepskin-lined boots again.

She sighed, washed her hands in the cold water, and joined the others around the large fireplace.

Four more children of varying ages smiled at them, their nearly black eyes brimming with curiosity and welcome. All were dressed in the same manner as the adults. They had a gauntness about their cheeks reminiscent of her village. Sadly, these people hadn't escaped the famine either.

Which meant they were well within Mao's reach. Her shoulders drooped. Would it never end?

Once they crossed the border into India, she'd believe they were free.

The older woman, carrying a tray of dumplings, came up to Xuě, handed her a wooden plate, and motioned for her to take one. Xuě hesitated. She didn't want to take food away from these people, but the woman pushed the bowl into Xuě's hands. To refuse would insult the woman, so she accepted it and bowed in thanks with a smile.

The skin around the woman's dark brown eyes crinkled as she smiled. She tapped her chest and said, "Bayarmaa."

Xuě repeated, "Bayarmaa," then pointed at herself and said, "Xuě."

Bayarmaa beamed. "Xuě?"

Again, Xuě nodded.

The woman smiled and moved to Bao who sat next to Xuě. She treated each person with the same kindness she'd shown Xuě. It was such a contrast to Xuě's past that tears pricked the corners of her eyes. She sniffed. Her cat chuffed, and her stomach gurgled at the aroma of the cooked mutton, onions, and cabbage

She took a bite. The dumpling melted in her mouth. Unfamiliar spices flavored the meat. It had been so long since food had tasted this good. She tried to savor it and eat slowly, but the dumpling disappeared in a few bites, and she licked her fingers.

Bayarmaa returned and offered her another one, her eyes twinkling with laughter.

"*Xièxiè*," Xuě said, gratefully accepting another dumpling.

After everyone ate, the elderly gentleman stood in front of the fireplace and told a story. Aynur stood next to him, translating, but, with the warmth of the hut and a full stomach, Xuě struggled to keep her eyes open. She snuggled next to Bao. He draped an arm across her shoulders. His fingers drew circles on her upper arm. She relaxed, linking her fingers together on the other side of his waist. Her eyelids drooped, and her head fell forward. She jerked awake, trying to blink back the sleep.

Sitting up straighter, she focused on Aynur and the story-teller, but the words faded, and the two men wavered in front of her, morphing into one person before splitting into two again.

Bao shook her shoulder. "Come. Let us find a place to sleep. They've put down sheepskins and felt blankets for us. We should be warmer tonight."

Xuě stretched and stood. Bao clasped her hand, and she walked with him over to the left side of the fireplace to one of the beds on the floor their hosts had prepared for them. The soft sheepskins and pile of blankets called to her.

Again, she was struck by the kindness of these people. Despite their circumstances, they'd let them into their home. At one time, her village had hosted strangers, too. They extended a welcome, food, and a place to sleep for the few travelers who passed through their remote village. Each family took turns housing and feeding any travelers that arrived. Then Mao's soldiers came and took everything, claiming it belonged to the government. The few travelers who crossed the mountains after that stole food. Her village no longer welcomed them. They chased them off. At least, they hadn't resorted to eating them.

She shuddered.

"What?" Bao asked, a look of concern on his face.

"It's nothing."

"Are you sure?"

"*Shi*," she said, banishing the memories. Nothing could bring her parents and those happy times back, but if she made it to India, she could ensure a better future.

She sat on the makeshift bed and ran her hands along the luxurious sheepskin. Soft and warm, it beckoned to her weary body. She slid under the felt blanket and sighed. It felt so wonderful she never wanted to leave.

Bao slipped in next to her and curled around her. Lovely heat seeped into her from behind and engulfed her. Soon, her husband's breathing deepened, and he slept. Unable to keep her own eyes open, she allowed them to close and surrendered to her body's needs.

Soft lips trailed kisses down Xuě's neck, pulling her from sleep. A spiral of desire seeped, inch by inch, into every pore of her body. She shivered, and her nipples peaked and ached for Bao's touch.

Someone turned over, and blankets rustled. Xuě froze and pushed Bao's hand away. It was one thing to make love at night in the presence of the other shifters, but to do it with humans, strangers, even . . . she didn't know if she could do it.

Blinking, she stared into the darkness and looked around the quiet tent. Other than deep breathing, no sound disturbed the night. But what if someone was awake like them? What if someone heard them?

She waited a moment, studying the others. The women had settled on the other side of the fireplace with the young children. The men slept on the other side next to the shrine. Their hosts had set the shifters up closer to the men.

No one moved, and she relaxed back into her husband. Perhaps if they were really quiet . . . Even the thought sent spirals of heat coursing through her body. It had been days since they'd made love. She needed this.

As if he read her mind, he slid his hands under her shirt and cupped her breasts. She arched into his palms, thrusting her hips back against the hard ridge of his *jījī*, and bit her lip to stop the moan that rose from deep within her. He nipped the side of her neck, and she gasped. Her *yukihyō* purred.

Again, she froze. Did anyone hear that? But nothing moved.

He eased her onto her back and kissed her. A groan rose in the back of her throat, and she silenced it. The scent of their desire swirled around her, increasing the ache to have him inside of her. She opened her legs, offering herself to him. He slipped in between them and ground his hips against her *àikòu*. Electricity jolted through her. She ran her hands down his back and grasped his bare ass, pulling him closer.

Xuě thrust her *bàoyú* against his bulging *jījī*. She wiggled under him, stripping off her pants. He seemed to sense her urgency. With one quick stroke, he buried himself inside of her, holding still, his muscles tense.

She bucked under him, urging him to move. Instead, he stayed put until she thought she'd scream in frustration. When she couldn't take it any longer, he pulled out and plunged into her. With each pass, he rubbed against her *àikòu*.

Desire wound around her tighter and tighter. She strained against him, every part of her seeking release. Her cat yowled as it crashed over her.

Her eyes flew open, and she convulsed around him. Gritting her teeth, she swallowed the cry that threatened to burst forth. He pumped again and grunted, coming inside of her, before collapsing on top of her. She wrapped her arms around him and kissed his cheek, his weight a comfort in the glow of completion.

He rolled off of her, drew her into his arms, and nuzzled her neck. She rested her head against his chest. A satisfied smile curled her lips. Contentment flowed over her.

In the darkness, an unintelligible whisper and a sigh pierced the silence. The unmistakable smell of musk and desire filled the air. Heat rose, burning Xuě's cheeks.

Someone had heard them, and they weren't the only ones.

Xuě woke to the smell of food cooking. She couldn't place the scent. Bao still slept next to her. She slipped out of his embrace, pulled her pants on, and approached Bayarmaa who stood by the stove with a young woman who looked to be her daughter and a little older than Xuě.

The younger woman stirred a large pot of something. When she saw Xuě, she smiled and said something to Bayarmaa. Bayarmaa picked up a bowl and gave it to her daughter, who ladled a thick, porridge-like liquid into the bowl. She handed it to Xuĕ.

"*Xièxiè*," Xuĕ said.

The young woman smiled, giving her a spoon.

Xuĕ scooped up a spoonful and blew on the steaming porridge. White and thick, it contained cubes of meat and something she couldn't identify. The woman watched her expectantly. Xuĕ sipped at the thick, slightly salty liquid in her spoon. She smiled at the woman and Bayarmaa and took another bite to show that she liked it.

They nodded and chatted happily to each other.

Aynur walked over to her. "Do you like the chi feng?"

"I . . . it's interesting and . . . filling." She spooned some more. "I'm not sure what this," she held up a white cubed piece, "is, but it's . . . tangy."

He laughed. "*Shi*, it's actually goat cheese."

"Goat cheese?"

Her stomach curdled a bit at the thought. Her family didn't eat cheese. No one in her village ever had. She didn't particularly like it, but she'd never say anything that would offend their hosts.

"*Shi*. They milk the goats and make cheese, butter, and curd. Chi feng is a type of milk tea, a staple for breakfast. It has millet, cheese, and lamb jerky. Chingis and his family were very excited to have us stay last night."

"They're wonderful people."

He nodded. "They are. We can't stay. I'll have to lead you to the next village. The army will be out looking for their missing squads."

The blood drained from Xuĕ's head. Ghostly echoes of gunshots rang in her ears, and she swayed. Their gazes met. Concern etched lines at the corners of his eyes and mouth.

"Will this village be safe?"

"It snowed last night. Our tracks have been wiped out. We will continue across the steppes away from the village toward Lhasa, the capital. We must avoid the Chinese highways as much as possible." He glanced at the sky. "We only have a few hours before the next storm hits. If troops do come, that storm will cover our tracks."

She hoped so. These lovely people didn't deserve what Mao and his army would do to them. "Have they ever followed you onto the steppes?"

"No. Tibetan Resistance has kept them busy, but now . . . I don't know. They might. Usually, at this village, I'd hand you off to Bantowa who'd lead you around Lhasa and by the animal tracks through Nathula Pass into India. But he isn't here," he frowned, "and we can't go back right now. I'll have to lead you until he comes."

She was glad their guide hadn't showed up. After Zuhre's warning, she didn't trust Bantowa, no matter Aynur's assurances.

"Do you know the way across the steppes?"

"I—"

Her stomach dropped. She clasped her hands in front of her. How many people would die because of Mao's desire to have them?

"Aynur," Zuhre called.

"Excuse me," he said and crossed to his partner.

Xuě sighed.

"Are you all right?"

She turned. Bao stood in behind of her, his expression solemn.

"I don't know. Something is wrong . . . and not just with the PLA." She starred blindly at her hands. What if they had a traitor in their midst and the PLA found them? This village . . . "How many more?"

He grasped her shoulders and pulled her into an embrace. She leaned against him, wrapping her arms around his waist.

"They'll be fine."

Fine. Nothing would ever be fine. Not until they left China behind for a new life . . . if they made it out.

# Chapter Seventeen

Four village women gathered within the Chingis' tent. In their arms, they carried sheepskin-lined jackets and hats. Xuě longed to slip her arms into the sleeves and snuggle into the warmth it promised.

Aynur stood in front of the women. Shaking his head, he said something Xuě didn't understand.

The women smiled and pushed the jackets at him.

He sighed, nodded, and said, "The people of the village want to give us these gifts of thanks for the *chiru*. We cannot refuse their generosity. Nor can we be caught. If we are . . . "

He didn't need to finish his sentence. If they were caught, the soldiers would know this village had helped them. Xuě's insides knotted. They couldn't be captured. Even if they didn't know what they were, the soldiers wouldn't care.

One of the women with gaunt cheeks but sparkling black eyes crossed to Xuě and handed her a jacket and hat. The woman turned to Bao and gave him a larger set. Excitement filled Xuě. Years had passed since she'd worn anything so cozy. Donning the jacket, she sighed with pleasure. How she'd pack it and Bao's in her backpack when they shifted, she'd figure out later. At that moment, the luxury of wearing something that kept the cold from freezing her skin overrode everything else. She closed her eyes and savored the feeling.

"It's time to leave."

Aynur's voice penetrated her thoughts. She opened her eyes and took a deep breath. After one night, she'd miss the Chingis family, the heat of the tent, and their generosity.

Xuě walked over to Bayarmaa. "*Xièxiè*," she said and bowed.

The woman smiled and nodded vigorously, bowing in return. Then she handed Xuě another backpack. Bayarmaa motioned to the jacket and to the bag and pushed it into Xuě's arms. Xuě tried to refuse, but the woman persisted with such kindness and determination that Xuě gave in. Now, both she and Bao would be able to carry their jackets.

A grin spread across Xuě's face.

"We must go." Bao touched her arm.

With a sigh, she slipped the pack over her shoulders and followed him into the frigid air.

In the early morning light, the entire village stood outside of their tents to wave goodbye. The sutra streamers flapped gaily in the brisk wind. The sight warmed her heart. Even in the face of hardship and Mao's army, this group of people smiled, laughed, and was willing to share what little they had. Even the wind howling down from the tops of the mountains, freezing whatever it touched, didn't deter the villagers from seeing them off.

Xuě's spirits lifted, and she pulled her new jacket closer around her. She glanced once behind her as the group headed out of the village toward mountains whose tops disappeared into the gathering clouds. The jacket sleeves reached below her hands, protecting them from the bitter cold. The hat kept her ears warm. She'd be forever grateful to the people who had given so much to strangers who only brought danger.

The village fell behind as she strode across the steppes. Her breath created white clouds in the air, and snow shushed under her feet. The scent of a wild yak herd nearby tickled her nose, but they had no time for hunting.

Bao stepped up next to her and smiled. "How are you this morning?"

"Better. Staying with Bayarmaa and her family helped. They were so kind."

He nodded and reached down, entwining his fingers with hers for a brief moment.

Her steps lightened, and happiness lit her entire body. Hope burgeoned within her. They'd survive another day.

"How old were you when you went to your family?" she asked.

A few moments passed in silence, and then he said, "I was nine . . . I think." He shrugged. "I'm unsure of my age, but I know I spent at least two *nián* with the monks."

She smothered a gasp. Two full years before he found a family. "So long?"

"*Shi*, but I don't mind. The monks were kind. They opened my mind to many things and taught me to read and write. When my parents finally adopted me, I was both sad and happy to go."

"Sad?"

"I learned much from the monks. How to quiet my mind and focus, to meditate. But it was lonely."

"You didn't become a monk."

"No. I thought about it, but not everyone's cut out to be one." He turned and stared at her until she met his gaze. So serious and full of . . . Xuě didn't dare to believe what shone in his eyes. She glanced away. "I'd met this girl with silver eyes who'd haunted me from the moment I saw her."

Warmth blossomed in her and just a bit of fear. What if she didn't live up to his dreams?

"But you couldn't know we'd meet again."

"No, but I hoped and prayed for it. To be a monk, you must be willing to release all worldly attachments. To serve others above myself? I could do that, but to give up the girl whose soul spoke to mine? Even my young self knew I couldn't do that. Leaving meant I had a chance. If it was meant to be, it would happen."

"I can see why your village liked you. You're wise and kind. You're like a monk."

"In some ways, but I'm more grounded in this plane. I have fears and doubts that wouldn't bother most monks. And I have wants and desires I've no wish to release." His thumb traced a circle on the back of her hand, sending a tendril of desire snaking through her.

Heat rushed up to her cheeks. Had anyone heard him? Ahead of them, the shifters had paired off, except Aynur, who strode ahead. The quiet murmur of low-pitched conversations hovered on the air. She glanced over her shoulder. Zuhre walked a few paces behind them. She smiled at her friend. The woman nodded and returned the smile.

"Would you like to join us?"

Zuhre shook her head. "It's nice. This time of . . . quiet. I'm liking the . . . how do you say—*tinçlik* . . . peace."

Xuě had to agree. There'd been so few moments of peace. She was enjoying it, too.

Another snowstorm pummeled the steppes. Outside the manmade cave they'd taken refuge in, the wind howled and whipped wave after wave of thickly falling snow past the opening. Aynur had led them along an animal track up a hill and into a cave just as the storm's fury increased to whiteout conditions. A day didn't go by without one. As the storms hid their movement from the PLA, Xuě welcomed them, as long as they hit after they reached their destination.

She leaned against the wall and inhaled the lingering scent of long gone men. The shelter was empty except for a pile of dried yak dung stacked against one of the walls. According to Aynur, the resistance used the cave, and this was one of the stops along the way. Xuě no longer cared. It offered refuge from the weather outside and a place to hide from prying eyes.

Her legs shook with fatigue. The long days taxed everyone, even Aynur's endless supply of energy seemed to be fading. How long could they keep this pace? It'd been days since the last sighting of a PLA patrol, but no one believed they were safe. The remoteness and storms of the steppes sheltered them for the time being. But for how much longer?

Much to Xuě's delight, the elusive Bantowa still hadn't manifested himself. *May he never do so.*

Bao's musky scent surrounded her before a hand touched her shoulder. She leaned into him and his warmth. He pulled her into an embrace, and she rested her head against his chest. A sigh escaped her as she relaxed and wrapped her arms around him.

"How are you doing?"

"I'm tired, but good," she said, snuggling closer.

His arms tightened around her. His very presence brought her a certain amount of peace, and some of her concerns receded.

"Here."

Xuě looked up. Zuhre held out some jerky. With a smile, Xuě took the food from the other woman. Her stomach growled, and heat burned up her neck and cheeks. "*Xièxiè.*"

Understanding lit Zuhre's tired face. "We all hungry. It's *xíng*. It's a long day." She paused and rested her hand on Xuě's arm. "I fight to keep going. Everyone does."

The wolf shifter turned away, but Xuě stopped her. "Zuhre . . ."

The woman faced her, curiosity in her eyes.

"How do you do this? How do you live with the not knowing?"

The other woman shrugged. "We help people. That makes me . . . happy." She motioned with her hand. "Come. Sit at the fire with us. You feel better."

Beyond Zuhre, the rest of the group gathered around a cheery fire. It tempted her. Being surrounded by other shifters had changed Xuě's views on life. She hoped when they settled in India they'd continue to be friends.

Stepping out of Bao's embrace, she crossed to the others.

The conversation stopped. Everyone turned to her. Pinpricks of heat flushed her body. Pema scooted over and patted the seat next to her.

"*Xièxiè,*" Xuě said and slipped in beside her.

Bao sat next to her.

"We'll push on to the next village after night falls," Aynur said. "It'll be another long trek. We'll travel as our animals through the night as we can cover ground quicker that way. The Chinese highway is not far from here. We'll have to cross it as the village is on the other side. If Bantowa is still missing, Zuhre, Nur, and I will continue on with you to the border."

Hope rose within Xuě that Bantowa would continue to be missing.

Pema stretched out her legs and grimaced. "These roads have changed Tibet. They've made it easier to travel, but more and more Han Chinese are coming here. The Chinese government is taking our lands, taking the nomads' children, and resettling them in the cities. They've chased the Dalai Lama out. If we don't stop them, it won't be long before the Tibetan people, our culture and way of life, are no more." She fisted her hands. "I can't let that happen."

"You're not alone," the alpha said.

Pema grunted and bowed her head, her shoulders tense. "I know, but they just keep coming, and so many Tibetans are content to let it be."

Silence filled the cave. Xuě struggled to find words of comfort, but she was fleeing Mao's government because she saw no other way. They couldn't stay in China and be safe, nor could they stay in Tibet.

In her village, everyone had believed China's takeover of Tibet to be right, that they were freeing the Tibetans from a tyrannical religious government that kept the population poor and dependent. Xuě had, too. She hadn't questioned it, not even after the government had taken her village's livestock and the famine crept in. This was another crime to lay at Mao's feet.

Aynur stood, drawing Xuě's attention. "Everyone should try to get some rest. We leave at dark."

No one moved.

Xuě lungs burned, and she inhaled as she realized she'd been holding her breath. Traveling as her cat was easier, but the backpack rubbed at her shoulders. Someday, they'd have a home to live in. No more traveling unless they wanted to. Only hunting when needed. And sleeping through the night without fear. No more fatigue to dog her steps, even after what little sleep she managed at night. But, each day, no matter how hard, meant they closed in on the Indian border and out of Mao's grasp.

She leaned against Bao, resting her head on his shoulder. He draped his arm over her shoulders. The tension released, and she relaxed against him. Silence engulfed the group with only the crackle of the fire breaking it.

The silence stretched and spread. Outside, the howling wind stilled, and a calm settled over her. Despite the distance they still had to travel, for the first time since they'd fled her village, she felt inexplicably safe.

"I'm going to get some sleep," Bao said and lay down.

Sleep sounded perfect. With her new jacket and Bao's arm wrapped around her, she closed her eyes.

As she drifted off, Aynur's voice wafted through the cave. "We'll wake you when it's time."

# Chapter Eighteen

In the middle of the night, Aynur halted. He shifted and faced the group. "The highway is just over that rise. Nur and I will scout ahead to make sure the way is clear. We'll be back soon."

Xuě crouched, watching the wolves grow smaller as they loped away. Pema paced back and forth, her impatience infecting the group. Soon, Akilina and Zuhre joined Pema. Xuě didn't want to waste the energy. They had many more *gōnglǐ* to travel before the night was over.

Several minutes later, the two *láng* returned. Aynur stopped in front of them and turned toward the highway. Xuě fell into line with the other shifters.

They followed him, but when they actually crossed the highway, Xuě couldn't tell. The storm had covered it in snow so that not a speck of it showed.

They approached another Tibetan village as night gave way to dawn. In the distance, a herd of *chiru* milled in a large group. Her cat twitched and, despite the fatigue, wanted to chase after them, but Aynur stopped and shifted. His nostrils flared, and he smiled.

"We have some time to hunt if anyone is interested."

Her *yukihyō* roused at his words. Adrenalin pumped through her veins. Another hunt.

This one followed the same method as the day before. Their teamwork brought the hunt to a quick close. Soon, Xuě and Chang were carrying a *chiru* between them as a gift to the village with Zuhre and Nur walking behind them. Xuě's stomach growled at the scent of fresh meat, but they'd reach the village soon. She hoped they'd be as generous as the last nomads.

"I can take your end," Huan offered.

Xuě smiled at him. "*Xièxiè*. I can carry it a bit farther."

"She could carry it a lot farther," Bao said. "When I first met her, she brought down a full grown *pán yáng* and dragged it for at least two *gōnglǐ* in the mountains."

Huan's eyebrows rose. "Two *gōnglǐ*. That's a long distance."

Blood rushed into Xuě's cheeks at Bao's praise, and they prickled with heat. She bowed her head to hide the blush. "One does what one must."

"Well, even if you can, I'd like to help carry it in," the bear shifter said.

"If I need you, I'll let you know." The snow sucked at her feet with each step. Handing the *chiru* off would be a welcome relief, but she wanted to show them that she could be useful and not a drain on them.

Huan moved up the line next to Chang. The two chatted, or more like Huan talked. Chang walked in silence.

Although she knew little about the two bear shifters and their backgrounds, of the two, Huan talked . . . a lot, and Chang said very little. Perhaps she spoke so little because Huan did enough for the two of them.

A smile crept across Xuě's lips, and she swallowed a chuckle.

Pema dropped back and walked next to her. "You've really carried a full grown *pán yang* that far?"

Xuě nodded. "I have. Many times."

"Did no one help you hunt?" the wolf shifter asked.

"Snow leopards hunt alone. It's how we're made. This hunting in groups is . . . different, but, no, even if I had wanted them to, it wouldn't have happened."

"Why?"

The other woman's questions brought back the loneliness and isolation of her life with her parents.

Xuě frowned. "My village feared me or hated me. I never knew which."

Pema's eyes widened. "What horrible people! I'm sorry I asked."

Xuě shrugged and blew out a breath, trying to release the emotions that threatened to spill over into tears. "It's *xing*. You didn't know."

Silence fell between them.

The weight of the carcass grew heavier, and Xuě adjusted her hold on it.

"I can take over for you if you want. You have nothing to prove," the other woman said.

Xuě looked at her. Their gazes met. "Don't I?"

Pema averted her gaze.

Even amongst other shifters, Xuě couldn't escape the judgment. Some part of her sensed they viewed her as less capable, even though it was her and Bao who brought the *chiru* down each hunt after the *láng* chased them to them. Other than helping to carry or dress the kill, neither Chang nor Huan had truly done anything with the hunts.

Perhaps it didn't matter and meant nothing, but why would she be seen as less capable?

They walked into the small encampment. Aynur led them to one of the tents where he "knocked" on the closed flap. An older man opened it, his welcoming smile drawing deep grooves in his weathered face, his tongue slipping out quickly before disappearing. He said something in Tibetan to Aynur and motioned for them to follow him.

Once again, Aynur responded and motioned for Xuě and Chang to bring the kill forward.

The older man grinned and called to a few people inside the tent. Two young men stepped forward and accepted the *chiru* with broad smiles. Xuě handed the animal off with relief and followed the others inside.

The tent resembled the first one they'd stayed in, and the family's friendliness energized Xuě. The warm meal and soft bedding ensured a good sleep.

As night fell, the shifters left, both Xuě's steps and soul lightened. Once out of sight of the village, they packed up their clothes. The others shifted into their animal forms. Xuě wait- ed until she helped Bao with his pack, adjusting it for comfort. Then it was her turn to strip, roll her warm coat into the smallest ball possible, and stuff it into her new rucksack. Bao would help position hers.

When everyone was ready, Aynur led them west across the steppes to the next village. This process repeated itself over and over. Each day bled into the next as they raced across the steppes. Days turned into weeks, and still no sight of any PLA patrols or Bantowa.

The vast land spread out into the horizon, broken up by valleys and mountains. Xuĕ often wondered how he navigated what seemed like an unchanging landscape of snow, but every day they slept on the floor of another family's tent, or occasionally another manmade cave. They hunted as they neared the next stopover, if they came upon game, and would give their kill to the village who hosted them or eat at night in the cave in their animal forms as there was no time to dress and cook the kill. Each family shared their food, their stories, and their tents with happy smiles. This generosity kept her moving forward, despite the fatigue.

With every day that passed, her hopes buoyed higher and higher. Surely, they'd reach India before Mao's forces caught them, even if China controlled Tibet.

Faint light on the horizon announced the dawn. In the distance, a village materialized. First, a dark blotch against the white snow. Soon, the festive sutra streamers that decorated all of the tents they'd encountered so far revealed themselves in the pale light. The closer they drew to the village, the faster her heart beat. Her *yukihyō* balked until each step became a battle between her and her cat.

Finally, Aynur stopped, and Xuĕ padded up next to the others. Her *yukihyō* chuffed a warning.

She swiveled her ears back and forth and surveyed the area, searching for any sign of danger. Nothing. Aynur paced back and forth. Tension pulsed in the air. Usually, he shifted and led them into the village. However, instead of shifting, he jogged down the line of shifters. When his gaze met hers, it commanded her to follow him. She dropped into the line of shifters and headed back the way they'd come. Despite the long night of travel, he kept up a brisk pace.

The silence intensified, and an eerie stillness settled over the steppe. Xuě's muscles tensed. A boom rattled the ground, shattering the stillness. A large puff of snow exploded several feet in front of them. For a second, she froze before she sprinted ahead. Her pack banged against her stomach. The sound of her heartbeat echoed in her ears as she zigzagged across the snow behind the others. Where could they go? A long expanse of flat ground stretched out before them. Although uneven, there was nothing deep enough to hide in.

All of a sudden, Aynur stopped and faced the village. Xuě rushed past him and skidded to a halt. Bao slid into her, and she jumped to the side, her tail poofed. She couldn't stay there, but she couldn't lose him, or she'd never escape. Searching the horizon for an indentation . . . anything to slip into and disappear, she shook her head. A line of Tibetan warriors on horses galloped toward them. She closed her eyes. Surely, she was imagining them, but they advanced on the shifters at a rapid pace.

Her *yukihyō* froze, and she crouched as low to the ground as possible. Xuě struggled against overwhelming fear and her cat's instincts.

*Please. We can't stay like this. We'll die.*

Her cat receded, allowing her to take control. Spinning toward the village, she froze yet again. Two PLA trucks trundled out from behind the tents. *Where had they come from?*

She glanced over her shoulder at the advancing warriors. Her gaze met Bao's. His eyes reflected the terror that rolled through her. Aynur howled and bolted to the left. The other shifters dashed after him. Her cat shuddered, refusing to move.

Something bumped her from behind, breaking her out of the paralysis that gripped her. Adrenaline spiked, and she leapt forward. Her legs pumped under her as she raced to catch up to the others.

But they had nowhere to hide. Their only hope lay in the

Tibetan warriors.

The retort of guns filled the air. Her pelt twitched in response. This couldn't be it. They'd come so far. Another week would see them across the border. They couldn't be caught or killed now when she could almost see India. Everything around her seemed to slow down as if time stopped. The sound of guns and the cry of men faded into the distance. She pushed harder and gained on Huan and Chang, passing them as they lumbered after the *láng*. Her paws skimmed over the snow, and she caught up to the *láng*. Bao panted behind her. The air vibrated around her from the ongoing battle.

She raced onward, her breath burning in her throat. The plain sped by under her paws. Up ahead, the snow dipped. Aynur sprinted toward that depression in the steppe. Her legs churning under her, she kept pace. Her muscles burned, but she pushed through the pain. A few feet from the indentation, the *láng* disappeared into the snow. Underneath her, the snow crumbled away, and she slid down a slope into a roughly hewn tunnel just wide enough for a few people to stand abreast. It continued several feet before bending off to the right. Eyes wide, she leapt the last bit down and to the side to avoid hitting the others. Turning, she jumped out of the way as the rest skidded down the incline behind her.

As the last of the shifters reached the bottom, she searched for Bao. He trotted up next to her, and her tense muscles eased ever so slightly. He'd made it uninjured. Their gazes met, and she bowed her head. Even though fear had consumed her, she'd broken free of the paralysis and escaped. Something had changed. Perhaps she'd found her inner courage.

He rubbed his head against her. Her cat leaned into him. He chuffed and licked the side of her face.

Muted war cries echoed overhead. The ceiling rattled with the boom of larger artillery. She pressed against Bao.

The snap and flash of light behind her signaled that someone was shifting.

"Everyone shift," Aynur said.

Light and pops filled the tunnel as the rest of them followed suit.

"Zuhre, pass out the rifles. Those who know how to use them should carry them. I hadn't planned on us using this tunnel as we're so close to a village, but we have no choice."

Nur stepped forward as did Pema and Bao. Zuhre gave each of them a rifle and handed the last one to Aynur.

Xuě's heartbeat accelerated, and she caught her breath. Bao knew how to use a gun? Was he the one who'd shot Gang? Where and how had he learned this? That Pema and Nur could shoot guns came as no surprise, but her husband? Who was this man she'd married?

"Although I knew of this tunnel, I've never been in it. We're safe for the moment, but we can't stay here. Our tracks will lead the PLA to us should they win. We can't let them find us."

"Where does it lead?" Huan asked.

Aynur hesitated. "I'm not sure. It could lead us directly into the village."

Murmurs rose around her and bounced off the walls.

"If it does, what happens if they find the other entrance?" Pema asked. "We could be trapped."

"We have little choice," Aynur said. "If we go up there, we'll be in the middle of a firefight. If we follow the tunnel, we have a chance to escape." He studied the group in front of him. "Nur and Pema, take the back. Walk side by side. Bao, up front with me. The rest follow in single file."

The hairs on her arms stood on end. She rubbed her coat-covered arms. Her *yukihyō* balked about going deeper into the tunnel, but she followed Bao up to the front of the line where Aynur and Zuhre talked in Uyghur. They stopped speaking when Bao and Xuě reached them.

Zuhre smiled, but it didn't hide the concern in her eyes. "You might be safer in middle." She motioned back toward the other shifters.

Heat flushed through Xuě and singed her cheeks. She swallowed the angry words that threatened to burst through her lips. Zuhre meant well, but it stung that more than Pema considered her a liability to the group. A *maruta*, useless. If Zuhre thought this way, what must the others think? Even Bao?

The urge to bow her head and concede rose within her, but she refused to cower in the middle. She would hold her own.

Thrusting her shoulders back, she lifted her chin and said, "I wish to be close to Bao. I understand, but I," she swallowed to moisten her suddenly dry mouth, "I'm not helpless."

"I didn't say you're—"

Aynur interrupted Zuhre in Uyghur. Her eyes widened, and she stared down at the ground for a moment before turning back to Xuě.

"I sorry. I'll be right behind you . . . if that okay," Zuhre said.

Xuě met Aynur's gaze. He nodded. She would've thanked him, but he spun on his heel and took off in a ground-eating pace into the darkness, a rifle over his shoulder and a flashlight in one hand. Bao kept up with him. Xuě took off after them.

Silence engulfed them, their footfalls barely disturbing the dusty ground. They'd traveled maybe half a *gōnglǐ* when the faint sounds of voices wafted through the tunnel ahead of them. Aynur halted, and the tunnel went black. Her eyes adjusted to the sudden darkness. Several hundred feet ahead of them, a faint hint of light flickered. The shifters bunched up behind Xuě. A thick cloud of tension hung in the air.

"Stay here. Bao and I will scout up ahead. If you hear gunfire or we don't return, shift and be prepared to fight," Aynur whispered.

Xuě's stomach dropped. Fight. Her *yukihyō* chuffed and urged her to turn and run, but to where? The way behind offered no more escape than the way ahead. She soothed her cat as best she could.

Before Bao could move off, she grabbed his arm. "Be careful and come back to me."

He brushed a kiss across her lips. "I will. I promise."

More promises he couldn't keep, but she clung to them and offered up a silent plea to her parents and his. *Keep him safe.*

Zuhre slipped her hand into Xuě's and squeezed, reminding her she wasn't alone. They were in this together. All of them.

Xuě drew in a deep breath and squared her shoulders, readying herself to face whatever would come.

# Chapter Nineteen

Several seconds passed. Bao and Aynur's shadows grew more distinct the closer they drew to the light. Their shadows created monsters on the walls before they paused at the end of the tunnel. Aynur's lighter hair glinted in the pale light. Xuě tensed, but nothing happened. Even with her enhanced sight and hearing, their conversation and movements remained a mystery. Then Aynur disappeared around a bend. Bao hesitated a few beats before following.

Moments dragged by, no sounds, and neither of them returned. The pall of tension hanging over the small group ratcheted higher as everyone waited in silence.

"We can't stay here," someone whispered. "We need to see if they're okay."

"No," Zuhre said. "We wait. It hasn't been long enough."

But it felt like they'd been waiting for *xiǎoshí*, even if only ten minutes had passed. Surely more than ten minutes had passed.

"We must shift. It's taking too long," Akilina said.

Zuhre rustled next to Xuě. "It too soon. Be patient."

But Xuě's cat chuffed and twitched. Akilina was right. The men were in danger.

"I'm shifting," Xuě said. "Something's wrong."

Zuhre touched her arm. "Xuě—"

"No, something's wrong. I can feel it. Everything in me says I must go."

Even as she said this, a shot rang out, and someone yelled. Xuě's heart thundered a loud tattoo in her ears, sweat slicked her palms, and her cat quivered and froze. *No, we must find Bao. We can't freeze now. Come on. We can do this. We must do this.* Her cat whimpered. Without another word, she dropped her pack and slipped out of her clothes. She stuffed

171

them in her pack and shifted.

Unsure of when, or if, they'd make it back, she grabbed the pack with her mouth and sprinted down the dark tunnel. As she approached the bend where the light met the dark, she slowed to a trot, stopped, and dropped her pack to the side. The tunnel veered right. The last few feet, she crawled belly to the floor and peeked around the corner. It opened into a medium-sized cave. The jagged, pale gray walls looked manmade like the rest of the tunnel. Smoky torches dotted the walls at regular intervals, illuminating the interior. Four PLA soldiers stood over an unconscious Bao. The metallic odor of blood tickled her nose. Heat prickled along her skin, and she gritted her teeth and panted. Her *yukihyō* struggled with her to run the other way, but Xuě refused. She wouldn't lose her last family member to them. These men wouldn't hurt her husband any more than they already had. But where was Aynur?

She searched the cave. Over at the other side, a soldier smacked Aynur across the face. His words carried back to Xuě. A few feet from him, more soldiers guarded some prisoners, mainly women and children. By their sheepskin coats, hats, and boots, they looked to be Tibetan, perhaps from the village.

She curled her lip. Cowards. How easy for them to overpower the weak.

"Where are they? We know you're not alone." The man spat in Aynur's face. Aynur stared over his shoulder, unresponsive. His gaze connected with hers for a brief moment before moving away. "You tell me, or your friend over there dies."

"I don't know who you're talking about," Aynur said. "We travel alone."

"You must think I'm a dumb animal like you. I bet they're in that tunnel." The man turned to his subordinates guarding Bao. "Fan, Yun, search the tunnel. Bring the others here."

"*Shi, xiānshēng,*" they said in unison.

Xuě inched farther into the dark. If she could get them far enough into the tunnel, they could bring them down. But what would happen to Aynur and Bao? Would they send other men in or would they kill them?

Her *yukihyō* twitched, balking. *These men aren't like us. They're not like yukihyō. We do this or die. They are maruta. Maruta.* Her cat chuffed and stopped retreating.

The soldiers stomped toward the tunnel, their footsteps pounding louder than the *tanguus* played during the lion dance. Xuě hunkered down, her muscles tightening in preparation to attack. The soldiers turned the corner and stepped into the darkness. Zuhre rushed past her, her naked body a burnished gold as the light hit it, and cried, "Aynur—" She pushed past the startled soldiers and disappeared around the corner.

"Zuhre, what are you—"

A slap echoed in the cave, cutting off Aynur's words.

"Grab her," someone yelled, but snaps, pops, and cracks interrupted his orders, followed by a growl and screaming.

The soldiers' faces blanched, and they backed away toward the cave, rifles at the ready. Xuě pounced, and the soldier crumbled beneath her. *He's a pán yáng.* Her claws dug into his throat, and she ripped it out. His cries subsided into a gurgle. She shuddered and closed her eyes for a brief moment. It barely registered when Akilina in her large blonde wolf form took the other one down. Blood splattered Xuě's fur. Her *yukihyō* shook and tried to freeze again, but Xuě pushed against it and won. The image of Bao laying helpless on the floor and the terrified women and children huddled defenseless against these monsters permeated every corner of her mind. Not stopping to see if the soldier was dead, she bounded over him and into the cave. One of the soldiers who'd been standing over Bao lay next to him in a pool of blood. The other one watched wide-eyed with a look of terror on his face. He swung his rifle around as if unsure where to point it and what to do next.

Zuhre had raced onto the next one. Akilina sprinted past her, her bloodied muzzle open, exposing sharp canines. The bellow of a *xióng* shook the cave, and Chang charged past Xuě. Snarling and the sound of rending flesh punctuated by yelps and screams filled the air.

Xuě leapt for the soldier who stood over Bao. He spun at

the last moment. Eyes wide, he raised his rifle, but too late. She swiped her paw, claws unsheathed, across his neck. He collapsed to the floor. A small trickle of blood oozed from his neck. Her cat protested, but she couldn't stop yet. She had to keep going, or all of the shifters would die.

Sailing over the soldier's inert body, she joined the fray. Shots rent the air, and bullets ricocheted off the walls. One of the shifters yelped. The children and women wailed.

The cacophony of sound threatened to overpower her, but, within minutes of it starting, the battle ended. Of the soldiers in the cave, only the officer remained standing, and Aynur held him at gunpoint.

The man curled his lip and spat. "Filthy animals. Do you think you can escape? There are more soldiers out there waiting for you. They'll come looking for us, and they'll round you up—"

Zuhre snarled and stepped forward.

Aynur stuck the gun against the man's breastbone. "Careful, or you may end up like the rest of your unit. If she doesn't rip your throat out, I'll pull the trigger."

The man's eyes rounded, and his face drained of color. He swallowed the rest of his words.

Without taking his attention from the man in front of him, Aynur said, "Akilina, check the entrance. Make sure no more soldiers are coming. Sit if you don't see any."

The blonde wolf trotted over to the entrance. After a few minutes, she sat.

With the danger gone for the moment, Xuě padded back to where her unconscious husband lay and nuzzled him. His shallow breathing indicated he still lived. Her cat chuffed, and relief spread through her. She licked his face, and he moaned. Nudging him gently, she sat on her haunches and waited. His eyes opened.

He blinked, struggling to focus on her. Confusion filled his eyes. "Xuě?"

She butted him with her head and chuffed. He cupped her cheek and smiled then winced. Blood trickled down the side of his face from a small cut on his forehead where a bruise was forming. He pushed up onto his side and leaned on his elbow, but fell back into a prone position, groaned, and closed his eyes. His chest rose and fell, but his face paled and pain pulled his features taut. Her chest tightened, and she nudged him again.

Bao lifted his hand and rested it on her front leg. "I'll be fine. I just need a moment."

"Where are Pema, Huan, and Nur?" Aynur said.

A noise behind Xuě brought her to her feet. She spun, crouching in preparation to strike. Instead, Pema and Nur stumbled into the light, weighed down with several backpacks.

Pema dropped her load to the floor. "Right here. We've been guarding the tunnel. So far, no one has come, but we brought as many of the packs as we could carry."

Huan sauntered behind the two with only his pack on his back.

Bao moaned, pulling Xuě's attention away from the bear shifter.

"Good. Nur, bring some rope. We'll tie this," his lip curled up in a snarl, "*man* up. When you're done, gather up the rifles."

Nur placed the packs on the floor and trotted over to Aynur. Removing his own bag, he pulled out the rope and bound the officer's feet and hands together behind his back. The man protested, but Nur ignored him.

"Pema," Aynur said. "Go back to the entrance of the tunnel and keep watch. Everyone else, take turns shifting in the tunnel and return when you're done. We don't need to scare these people any more than we already have. As you're the closest to the tunnel, you can start, Xuě." He glanced over at the women and children huddled in the corner. He said something to them. One of the women nodded and stood up.

Xuě glanced down at Bao.

"Go shift," he said.

She nodded and padded over to the pile of backpacks. Only six were there. Hers had to be where she'd left it. She trotted back into the tunnel past where Pema stood at the entrance and stopped when she turned the corner. The two bodies of the men they'd killed lay in the middle. Both stared at the ceiling, unseeing. Blood pooled under them. She shook from head to toe and closed her eyes for a moment to gather herself. With a deep breath, she jumped over the dead men and walked the few steps to her backpack where it leaned against the jagged wall. Drops of blood stained it.

Another shudder rippled through her. Every time she put it on, those stains would be there. She'd have to carry it, always reminded that she'd killed someone. When they reached India, she'd burn it.

Turning her back on the bodies, she shifted and reached for her clothes. A puff of cold air lifted the hair on the nape of her neck, chasing goose bumps across her skin. It crawled as if someone watched her. She glanced around, searching the dark, but nothing stirred. Her heart galloped in her chest, and she caught her breath. Were the soldiers' spirits lingering?

Unwilling to find out, she threw on her clothes, grabbed her pack, ran past Pema into the cave, and stopped, panting.

Pema's eyes widened. She stepped toward the tunnel, rifle raised. "Did you see someone?"

"No, I—"

Heat rushed up Xuě's cheeks and burned her ears. She averted her gaze. In the face of Pema's question and out in the light with everyone else, Xuě's fears seemed silly. Perhaps she'd imagined it.

The wolf shifter nodded in understanding and smiled. "It's creepy in there. That's why I'm here. I can see down the tunnel, but I'm not standing with," she motioned to the bodies, "*them.*"

"Xuě," Aynur called, "are you done?"

"*Shi.*" Xuě moved away from Pema toward Bao who sat propped up against the wall.

"Zuhre, you're next," Aynur said.

Aynur's mate trotted across the cave and drew even with Xuě.

"Zuhre?"

The *láng* looked at Xuĕ.

"Don't go all the way in," Xuĕ said.

Zuhre cocked her head to the side.

"The soldiers . . . they're . . . and . . ." Xuĕ didn't finish. She found it hard to talk about them.

Understanding lit her golden eyes. The *láng* picked up her pack in her mouth and jogged to just behind Pema and out of sight of the villagers.

Xuĕ returned to Bao. She crouched next to Bao and took his hand in hers. "How are you?"

The corners of his lips turned up in a slight smile. "I have a headache, but I'm alive."

"What happened?" she asked.

"The soldiers were all over in the corner where the women and children are. We didn't see them at first. When Aynur stepped farther into the cave, one of them saw him. I'd already followed him. The soldier fired a shot. He missed, but it ricocheted off a wall and grazed my forehead. Aynur refused to shoot because of the villagers. They separated us and knocked me out. That's all I remember. How did you overpower them?"

"A combination of surprise and luck, I think. And, perhaps, our ancestors are protecting us." She filled him in on the battle.

His eyes widened. "You killed two?"

She nodded. "More. I had to. They were coming for us, *and* they were threatening to kill you." Their gazes met. "I couldn't let that happen."

He cupped her face with his hand. "You're very brave."

"No," she said, shaking her head and breaking the connection. "I did what had to be done."

"*Xièxiè.*" He brushed his lips over hers.

A tremor shook her body before she could suppress it. Overruling her cat to kill had been easier. Was she becoming like them?

Her gaze drifted to one of the soldiers she'd killed. If it weren't for the pool of blood and sightless eyes, he could be sleeping. No one had moved him. Of course, no one had moved any of the dead yet. Her skin crawled, and she averted her eyes.

Bao touched her chin and brought it up so that their gazes met. "Are you okay?" he asked.

"I—I don't know. Killing them was easier this time. That frightens me."

"You did what was necessary."

"That could become an easy excuse."

"Did you enjoy it?" He caressed her cheek, his gaze searching hers.

She pulled away from him, her lip curling up, and shook her head. Her stomach clenched. "No." The scenes replayed themselves in her mind, and she quivered. "No. In order to do it, I couldn't think. I saw the soldier standing over you, his rifle raised, and I . . . " The words stuck in her throat. A tear trickled down her cheek, and she shook uncontrollably.

He drew her into his arms. "Sh . . . Sh . . . Everything's *xing*. We are safe."

*But for how long?* She didn't say the words aloud, but it was only a matter of time before they were caught. It could be only a few hours before the PLA came into the tunnel and captured them. Even now, the distant sounds of battle penetrated the cave.

"Bao, I—" The words stuck in her throat. Did she love him? How could she love someone she barely knew?

Too soon. It was too soon.

# Chapter Twenty

By the time everyone had shifted, Aynur had organized the village women and children. He'd offered them some of the rifles they'd captured from the soldiers. A number of them accepted. He'd also made all of the shifters take one. Xuě reluctantly agreed. She'd never handled a gun, let alone shot one. A number of times, Bao had to remind her to either point it at the ground or over her shoulder. Every time she adjusted it, her muscles tensed. What if she dropped it and it went off? Someone was going to die because she killed them by accident.

Finally, she walked over to Aynur who stood talking to Nur and handed him the rifle. "This is a bad idea."

"You need—"

She shook her head before he could finish his sentence. "Give it to someone else. Leave it with these people. Whatever you do with it, I shouldn't have it. I'm more dangerous to us than to the enemy. Until I can learn what to do with one, I don't want to touch them. And there's no time to teach me right now. I'll rely on my snow leopard. At least with her, I know what to do. Besides, I don't know how I'm going to carry it in my cat form."

He stared at her for a moment before nodding. He handed it to Nur. "Give it to Gan. She is in charge of the villagers."

Huan and Chang came over and joined them. Bao slipped in next to Xuě, grabbed her hand and gave it a quick squeeze. She glanced up at him. Although still pale, some color had returned to his cheeks.

Huan held out his rifle. "She's right. I'm not a good shot. I feel more comfortable as my *xióng* than shooting them. Chang was always better at this than me." He gave Aynur his gun.

Aynur passed it on to Nur and studied the shifters who

gathered closer. At the entrance, Zuhre stood guard, a rifle at the ready.

"Is anyone else uncomfortable carrying one?" he asked.

Akilina stepped forward and offered hers to him without a word. He nodded and took it from her.

"Is that everyone?"

No one said anything.

"Okay. We'll leave the rest with the villagers."

He turned to where most of the women and children waited and said something in what Xuě now recognized as Tibetan. A middle-aged woman separated herself from them and approached the shifters, her heavy coat nearly a replica to the ones the shifters wore. Long, black hair spilled out from under her hat and down her back. She carried a rifle over her right shoulder.

"This is Gan." Aynur motioned to the woman, who smiled and nodded. "She has offered to guide us out of here if we choose. We are on the other side of the village. But we have a choice. We can either stay and help them fight off the PLA, or leave."

Bao tightened his grip on Xuě's hand. "What about these women and children? The PLA know of this tunnel. They'll come back here for them. We can't leave these people alone."

"How does everyone else feel about this?" Aynur asked.

"Bao's right," Akilina said. "We can't leave them to die."

Aynur looked from one face to the next. "We could be captured."

"I'll die before I'm captured," Xuě murmured, "but I won't leave these people. If the PLA beat the warriors, they are as good as dead. I can't do that again. It would be my fault."

Her quiet words brought an echo of "me, too" from the group.

"Then we stay and fight," he said. He addressed Gan in Tibetan. She smiled and hurried back over to where the other villagers were.

A pit opened up in Xuě's stomach. Her cat shrunk back and urged her to shift and run, but she couldn't leave them.

They had the ability to possibly save these people, unlike her parents.

"Are you truly prepared to fight?" Bao asked her.

She reached up and pushed a strand of hair out of her face. Her hand shook. "No, but—" The words stuck in her throat.

"We can't leave them," Bao finished for her.

Their gazes met, the silver in his eyes dulled to pewter. His haunted expression mirrored everyone else's around them.

Beyond them, the village women had organized and had moved some of the dead soldiers to the tunnel.

Bao stood and swayed.

"Will you be able to fight?" she asked him.

"I'll find a way."

Aynur walked past them toward them women.

"Aynur."

He stopped at the sound of his name, turning his golden gaze on her.

"What will happen to these women and children without their husbands and fathers?"

He frowned and shook his head.

"They'll be okay."

She jumped at the sound of Pema's voice just behind her and turned toward her. "How do you know?"

Pema shrugged. "The Tibetan Resistance will see to it that they are taken care of. Tibetans on the plateau take care of each other. Where do you think the warriors came from?"

"We will do what we can to save them. There isn't much more we can do."

Aynur's words flowed over Xuě. A weight pressed down on her, and she struggled to push aside the feeling of helplessness. To give up now would hand an easy victory to the PLA. Never again would she let that happen.

"Where did this fierce Xuě come from?" Bao asked.

Heat prickled in her cheeks. "I'm not fierce. I'm done."

Pema draped her arm across Xuě's shoulders. Their gazes met. Respect blossomed in Pema's eyes.

"I thought you were . . ."

"Weak," Xuě said. "*Shi*, I know. All of you did. My animal isn't a *láng* or a *xióng* or a leopard or any other fierce carnivore. She's a snow leopard. A beautiful, shy cat that hates these fights with humans. Every time I have to kill a soldier, she freezes and urges me to flee. I have to overcome that instinct." She stared down at her clasped hands. "She's not the only one who hates this, who's terrified and wants to run. I don't want to fight, or kill, these men, but," she looked up and stared at the women and children across the room, "I don't want to die. Nor am I willing to let them die." She motioned to the villagers. "Not if I can do something about it. What little I can do."

"Your cat really freezes when confronted?" Pema asked.

"*Shi*, even when I'm in human form," Xuě said. "Not by other animals, but when humans approach and threaten us? *Shi*."

Pema stepped away from Xuě and studied Bao. "You don't seem to do that. Why?"

Bao dabbed at his forehead with the sleeve of his shirt. "I use my training with the Buddhist monks to help me overcome those instincts. They're still there, within me, but I don't believe they're as strong as what you experience anymore, Xuě."

Xuě cocked her head. Had he truly overcome them? "Is that what happened when the cannibal attacked?"

He bowed his head. "He was unexpected. I wasn't prepared."

"I didn't know," Pema said, her expression serious. "I . . . I'm sorry that I thought you were just a coward."

"But I *am* a coward," Xuě insisted.

Pema clasped Xuě's hands. "No. You're not a coward at all. You're very brave. Both of you. I'm glad you're with us."

Heat suffused Xuě's cheeks once again, but, this time, she smiled. "*Xièxiè*. Me, too."

"Pema, Xuě, Bao," Aynur said. "We need your help over here." He motioned to an area. "Pema, I need you to help the Tibetan women carry the bodies over to the tunnel. They've already stacked a few on the others." Aynur turned to Xuě and

Bao. "I'm going to have you two go back down the tunnel to watch for the PLA."

"And if they show up, what do we do?" Bao asked.

Xuě's heartbeat ratcheted up, and she licked her suddenly dry lips. Being in that tunnel with the dead soldiers . . . A shiver cascaded down her spine. "Can't we just keep watch at the entrance of the tunnel?"

Aynur shook his head. "They'll see someone standing in the light, but they won't see you in the dark. If someone comes, you can run back and warn us."

What good would that do? Did he still see her as a weak link in a fight? Was it because she didn't want to carry a weapon? Of course, she wouldn't be able to carry one anyway because she'd be in cat form.

Still, she'd be in the tunnel with all of those dead soldiers. She'd have to jump over them to escape the live ones . . . if they came down into that part of the tunnel. While it was long, it wasn't that long. With bullets ricocheting off the granite walls and the confines of the space, they'd be easy targets.

"No, I want to help, but I think this is a bad idea."

Bao rested a hand on her shoulder. "She's right. Sending us down there when we know we'll have to fight could be a problem. With only two of us, and no weapons, we can only hold them off a short time and will most likely die. The bodies of the dead soldiers will create a wall. It may frighten the soldiers."

"That's my plan, but we need to have someone at the other end who can warn us." Aynur glanced from one to the other.

Bao slid his hand down to hers and held it. "There's only one way to go once you get in the tunnel. Whoever you send down will die before they can get back to warn you. Let us protect the entrance. They'll only be able to walk two at a time, side by side. We can easily pick them off."

"Or . . . " Xuě paused. Should she tell them her idea? It disrespected the dead. Would their spirits haunt her for this?

"What?" The tone of Aynur's voice cut through her misgivings.

"I," the words threatened to dry up again, but she pushed on, "what if, rather than piling the dead up, we left them through the tunnel in different places?"

Something resembling admiration gleamed in his golden eyes, and he smiled. "When they come across them, at least at first, they'll make noise. We'll know if they're coming." He inclined his head toward her. "Smart."

She dropped her gaze to the dusty floor and shrugged. "I only know I wouldn't want to come upon a dead body in a dark tunnel. They may not care."

"Oh, no, they'll care," Aynur said. "These aren't your typical soldiers who died of a gunshot. These were killed by animals. They aren't the same at all, and it will frighten them. We'll do it your way, but we'll need your help, too. Follow me."

He spun on his heel and strode to where Pema and Gan stood at the entrance to the tunnel. Xuě and Bao trailed behind him. By the time they reached the trio, Gan was nodding at Aynur.

Aynur turned to them as soon as the two walked up. "You and Bao can take the first body to about halfway down the tunnel. We'll start there. We want them to be surprised. Let them be in the dark long enough to make them comfortable. Pema, you and Nur will take the next one and leave it a few yards away from where Bao and Xuě left theirs. I think two, maybe three, should be enough, don't you?"

The others nodded, but Xuě's stomach tied up in knots. When she'd thought of the idea, she hadn't considered how they'd carry it out. Now, she'd be dragging a dead body behind her. She shivered.

"Maybe this isn't such a good idea," Xuě said. "I mean, it doesn't seem right to treat the dead so poorly."

Pema snorted. "They don't care about our dead. Besides, they're Mao lovers."

"I—"

"We can't afford to worry about them. We must take care of ourselves." Aynur stared intently into her eyes.

She nodded and bowed her head. "All . . . right . . ."

Perhaps she and Bao could do a prayer over the bodies even if they couldn't bury them.

"Bao?" Her gaze met her husband's. She shook her shoulders to dislodge the tension and discomfort at the thought of carrying one of the soldiers down the tunnel.

He took her hand. "I'll be with you."

She searched his face for any sign of disquiet, but, if he felt any, he hid it well. "This doesn't bother you?"

"Of course. I'd rather not be here at all. I'd rather be in my village with my parents and you, surrounded by friends, but we're not."

She turned her attention to their clasped hands. Tears stung her eyes, and she swallowed. "No, we're not and never will be again." Drawing in a deep breath, she steadied herself, stepped toward the pile of bodies, and paused.

Where did they start? Her cat balked at picking up a body. So did Xuě. She curled her lip and hesitated.

"Which body do we take?"

"I—" Bao's hand hovered over the pile. He closed his eyes, bowing his head. His lips moved, and the words that poured from his lips caressed her ears. "*May you be well and happy; if not, may you have a peaceful death and a good rebirth.*"

They settled over her and evoked a calm.

"What are you doing?" she asked.

He didn't respond for a few moments.

"Bao?"

He turned, his lips downturned. Sadness haunted his eyes. She blinked and reached out to him.

"Are you *xíng*?"

With a nod, he said, "I blessed them. Perhaps they will find more peace in death than in life."

Xuě doubted this, not with them disturbing their bodies. Now, they were going to use the dead bodies like things. And all because of her idea. Either way, she would be in the tunnel. At least, this way she wouldn't be there as long.

"We can go first, if you want," Pema said.

"No, we can do it, right, Xuě?" Bao squeezed her hand.

Unable to do more than nod, she leapt over the pile and helped her husband take a body off the top. She grabbed the soldier's feet and led the way down the tunnel. Every cell in her body screamed in protest. Her *yukihyō* cowered. If only she could join it and be free of this horrifying chore.

Instead, she powered on into the darkness. It closed around them, and she gulped air to try to calm her shaking. Absolute silence fell between them, and the tunnel stretched before them as if it would never end. Their footfalls barely disturbed the dust on the uneven floor. With each passing moment, she increased her pace until they ran. In her mind, she envisioned the large *pán yáng* the two of them had carried the first day they'd met. She couldn't think of their burden as a man. Everything about what they were doing made her skin crawl.

Finally, faint light broke the absolute darkness, outlining the tunnel's opening into the larger cave section. She slowed and stopped about 15 *mǐ* away from it. Bending her knees, she gently placed the body on the ground and rubbed her hands on her pants, as if that would take it away. The open steppe, even with the battle raging, beckoned. Her *yukihyō* fought with her to shift and run, but that way meant certain capture and possibly death.

No, their current course of action offered a chance of survival. Turning back toward Bao, she averted her gaze from the body. A loud click echoed in the cave behind her, and she jumped. She glanced over her shoulder.

Nothing. The hair on the nape of her neck rose. Not needing any other encouragement, she took off back the way they'd come.

About halfway through, they ran into Pema and Nur. They'd placed a head on top of the body. One of the shifters had decapitated this particular soldier. Xuě stared over Nur's shoulder, her stomach threatening to lose its contents, and pressed close to the granite wall to avoid touching the dead body. Pema led the way, carrying the feet. She paused as they drew even.

"You've already placed yours?" Pema asked in a tone only

loud enough for the shifters to hear.

"*Shi*," Xuě panted. Her heart raced, and not just from their sprint. The sooner she got out of the tunnel, the better.

"That was quick. Is everything okay?"

The odor of dead human and drying blood tickled Xuě's nose. She turned her head away, willing herself not to breathe too deeply. Her stomach flip-flopped.

"We thought we heard a noise in the cave at the other end," Bao whispered. "Perhaps only a few more steps that way," he motioned away from them, "would be good enough for this body."

"Okay," Pema said.

Nur and Pema continued a few more feet before laying the body down. Xuě and Bao waited for them. They could go back together, and Xuě wasn't going back in that tunnel unless they had no other way to escape.

A frigid blast of air rushed past them accompanied by a moaning sound.

Xuě didn't need any more encouragement. She sprinted toward the light and sailed over the pile of dead bodies with the pounding of the others' footsteps on her heels.

She skidded to a halt. Gan stared at her, wide-eyed. Xuě gasped for air, bent over, and leaned on her knees to catch her breath. If Aynur wanted a third body placed in there, he'd have to find someone else. Gan peered over the pile of bodies, rifle at her shoulder. But no one followed them. Of course, no living creature followed them. As for the dead . . .

The woman turned to Xuě with a quizzical look on her face. She said something to Pema who responded. Gan shook her head, grinned, and replied.

The wolf shifter blushed, and her gaze met Xuě's before she said, "Gan says that's just the wind. If it blows from a certain direction, it enters the tunnel and howls like a *preta*. When it does that, it signals a storm is coming."

Gan spoke again. Pema nodded before translating for the others.

"She said these men will receive a proper burial once all

of this is over. They don't want ghosts haunting their village."

Now that she'd left the tunnel, some of the tension left Xuě's body. Did she believe that howling was the wind? She shuddered. Not really, not when combined with the sounds, but at least they'd get a burial, which was more than many of the others had received.

Aynur approached. "Are all three placed?"

Pema shook her head. "There are two. Bao and Xuě heard a noise at the other end. It might be better to leave it as is."

The alpha consulted Gan. He nodded. "All right. Nur, you stay here and watch for any activity." He handed him a rifle.

Nur blanched but didn't contradict him. Xuě stifled the impulse to clap her hands.

"Bao, Xuě, there's a storm coming in. Since the two of you can see in snowstorms better than the rest of us, I need you to shift and scout out the area when the snow starts falling . . . if they haven't found us yet. Until then, you can rest." His attention moved onto Pema. "Go relieve Akilina from her post at the entrance. Be sure to take a rifle with you."

Without a word, Pema jogged off across the cave. Xuě picked up her pack and hurried over to the other side, as far away from the dead bodies as possible, and sat. She leaned against the granite wall. It poked into her back, even through her heavy coat. She adjusted a few times until she found a comfortable spot and closed her eyes. Her stomach grumbled, but she ignored it. Even if she had food, she wouldn't eat it. No matter how many times she rubbed them on her pants, the feel of dead body remained on her hands.

Bao dropped down next to her. She cracked her eyes open. He'd rested his arms on top of his knees. They sat in silence. His presence brought her comfort. She relaxed against the wall and stared off into space. The noise from the others in the cave swirled around her in a comforting hum.

"How much farther do you think we have to go once we survive this?"

He smiled. "You think we'll survive this?"

"I have to, or I'll give up." She studied him. "Don't you believe it?"

He shrugged. "I pray to Buddha to protect us then do what I can to see that we are. But do I believe we'll see India? Anymore? I don't know." Again, he shrugged.

"You can't give up hope—"

"I haven't given up hope. I question if we can escape Mao."

Xuě clenched her hands, her breath caught in her throat, and fear seeped into her. If Bao didn't believe . . . No, she wouldn't fail her parents, or them. Nor would she let Mao win. They'd cross the border into India and be free.

# Chapter Twenty-One

The day wore on, and the storm announced its arrival with a roar. It pushed large snowflakes into the cave and obliterated the daylight from the small opening at the entrance. An eerie howling pulsed through the tunnel. It vacillated between high and low tones, as if something moaned and screamed in agony. With the onslaught of the storm, the sounds of battle abated along with the likelihood of anyone other than the Tibetan Resistance or the remaining villagers finding their hiding place.

Xuě shivered, and her cat cowered. *Was it the wind or ghosts?*

A shudder wracked her body, and she screwed her eyes shut, covering her ears.

The comforting scent of Bao wrapped around her before a hand touched her. She cracked open her eyes. A frown etched a deep groove across his brow. He leaned in close, brushing his lips against her forehead.

"Can I help you?"

Her teeth chattered, and she nodded, unable to speak.

He slipped down next to her and opened his arms. She pressed closer to him, and he wrapped an arm around her. Resting a hand and her head on his chest, she focused on the steady rhythm of his heartbeat. Her breathing returned to normal, and the tightness that had wound itself around her insides eased.

The fury of the storm continued to rage outside, but the wind died down to occasional gusts. At which point, it whipped through the tunnel, or in through the entrance, the torches flickered, and shadows gyrated along the craggy granite walls. Ghostly howls accompanied these gusts. With each howl, she clutched at Bao, holding her breath and releasing it in a gasp.

"Sh . . . sh . . . we're *xíng*," he whispered into her hair. "We're safe."

But Xuě watched the tunnel entrance for any sign of ghosts. Zuhre relieved Nur, who practically ran from the post. The female wolf shifter clenched her jaw and dropped to the ground. She motioned to Chang, who trotted over. As soon as she reached her, Zuhre pulled the other woman down next to her.

Xuě drew away from Bao, all of her attention on the two women by the tunnel.

"There's something, or someone, in the tunnel."

A terrified yell rumbled down the passage and burst into the cave. Xuě jumped. Bao's arm tightened around her. Eyes wide, she stood, every part of her urging her to run, but her husband grabbed her hand. Their gazes met. He shook his head.

They couldn't run. They had to stay. If they didn't, the women and children would die. She wouldn't let that happen.

Straightening, she nodded at her husband. Admiration gleamed in his eyes, and warmth suffused her body.

Aynur raced over to where Zuhre crouched. They spoke rapidly in Uyghur. He turned to the other shifters and said, "Snuff out the torches. We can see in the dark. They can't. Those of you not using the rifles, shift when done." He ran over to the Tibetan group. His quiet words reached Xuě. "Gan, keep the women and children over in the corner."

Gan shook her head. She said something in Tibetan.

Aynur frowned and looked as if to argue, but Gan motioned to some women behind her. They gathered around the wolf shifter and their leader. He nodded.

Soon, dark twilight engulfed the cave. Flashes of light and popping sounds filled the cave. A few children whimpered, but the women quickly shushed them. The sharp tang of their fear swirled in the air.

Her *yukihyō* quivered, nearly as frightened as the children, but she overrode the fear and crept over to join the other shifters who gathered near the entrance of the tunnel.

Fear wound tighter and tighter around Xuě.

Heavy footsteps drew closer. Voices echoed down the passage, the words jumbled together. Were they Tibetan or PLA?

Another cry erupted from the tunnel.

She tensed and crouched next to Bao. They waited behind Zuhre, Nur, Aynur, Pema, and the five Tibetan women who wielded rifles.

Minutes ticked by. The shuffling of footsteps stopped just beyond the pile of dead bodies. A light hit the wall above the pile as a gust of wind surged through the tunnel. Its wail crescendoed into a roar and rushed over Xuě with a gust, sending a chill down her spine. She fought the urge to cower. The wind disappeared as quickly as it came, leaving behind a preternatural chill.

The light moved down the wall, illuminating the dead.

"The troop is dead, *shàngwèi*," someone whispered.

Whispering did them little good.

"All of them?" someone else asked.

"*Shi*, I think so."

"Do you think they are in there?"

"We must go in to find out."

"How do we get in?"

"Push the pile over."

"But, *xiānshēng*—"

"Now."

There was a pause. The pile didn't move. Xuě hunkered down, ready to attack. Then the top body fell off with a sickening plop. The second joined the first, revealing a pasty face framed with short, straight black hair of a young man, his eyes wide and mouth turned down. He didn't see them in the dark.

Light flashed from the barrel of a rifle. The soldier fell backward with a cry.

"Attack!" someone yelled from the passage.

Two more soldiers appeared and were taken out, but more followed. The pile toppled as men poured through the mouth into the line of fire. Cries and screams mixed with the report of gunfire. Soldier after soldier fell on top of the pile. They couldn't see their enemies in the dark.

Xuě crouched behind the others. Why would the officer send his men to certain death? Was he trying to distract them?

Something wasn't right here.

She leaned into Bao. He turned to her. She motioned with her head to follow her. They crossed to the cave entrance where Chang stood guard. Outside, the storm raged, white blanketing the world, but, in the distance, dark shapes staggered toward them.

Narrowing her eyes, she backed away. They needed to alert Aynur.

Behind them, the cave quieted.

"Is that all of them?" Aynur asked.

"*Shi*," Pema said. "Even the," she spat in the dirt beside her feet, "major."

Chang stood. "No. They're coming from the front."

"Grab their guns and ammo. Bao, Xuě, Chang, move away from the entrance."

Aynur's voice broke Xuě's paralysis. She darted to one side of the entrance, trying to get far enough away to give the shifters and villagers armed with guns, but staying close enough to help if needed.

Bao hunkered down next to her, rifle at ready. The anxiety in his body transferred itself to her. If he was nervous, this didn't bode well. She panted and shivered. He pet her head, whispering soothing words in her ear.

The alpha stationed himself on the other side of the opening. Gan knelt just below him, and Nur squatted at his feet. Pema, Zuhre, and another Tibetan woman copied their formation. All of them trained their rifles out at the storm.

"Don't shoot unless I tell you to. These could be Tibetan Resistance," Aynur said. He turned to Gan and spoke to her. She responded and nodded. "Gan knows most of the members of the resistance in this area. If these are them, we hold our fire. If they aren't . . . "

Silence descended. The seconds ticked by. Tension mounted. Xuě crouched, her muscles shaking and hackles raised. A gust of wind sent snow devils swirling into the cave. The scent of blood chased the snowflakes.

How close were they now? Surely, it wouldn't be much longer.

Gan set down her gun and ran out of the cave, shouting and sobbing at the same time.

Aynur and Pema relaxed and smiled.

"What?" Bao asked.

"It's the resistance," Pema said. The stress lines around her eyes smoothed. She placed the rifle against the wall and leaned against it, bowing her head. Fatigue emanated from her.

Pema's reaction seeped into Xuě. They could shift and relax without fear. Perhaps they could sleep for a few hours. She yawned as if the thought of sleep gave her body permission to acknowledge the exhaustion that dogged her.

She stood and stretched, chuffing at Bao and rubbing against him. He stood, and they crossed to where they'd left their packs. Settling down, she rested her head on her front paws and yawned. Her eyelids drifted closed.

A commotion jolted her awake. The women and children who'd huddled in the back had realized the men limping into the cave were friends. They rushed forward to greet them. Xuě fell asleep to the sound of happy cries mixed with tears.

When Xuě woke, the soft sound of relaxed breathing filled the cave. Bao's warm body pressed against her side. She blinked sleepy eyes and raised her head, swiveling her ears back and forth. Aynur and Zuhre slept next to each other. Pema had found a spot with Akilina a few feet away from Xuě and Bao. Chang and Huan had retained their human forms. Huan was curled around Chang. The Tibetans kept to their corner, the men absorbed into the women's and children's camp.

A Tibetan women guarded the entrance, her silhouette outlined against the snow covered steppes and a dark, crystal clear night sky. Another woman armed with a rifle stood by the passage. A single torch flickered next to the woman guarding the tunnel.

The scent of unwashed, wounded bodies assaulted her nose. Her cat rumbled in protest. She rose and padded over to the entrance. Inhaling the clean, crisp air, she purred with pleasure.

The guard turned to her, eyes wide and tense. The acrid smell of her fear swirled around Xuě. Xuě nodded to the woman and sat opposite of her, wrapping her tail around her feet and staring out into the silent night. After a bit, the woman relaxed, her breathing returned to normal, and her fear dissipated. Her attention went back to her duty.

Soft footsteps rustled behind them. Xuě cocked one ear back. By the weight and gait, it was Pema.

"Can't sleep?" the wolf shifter asked and sat next to her, looping her arms around her knees and slipping her hands inside the long sleeves of her coat.

Xuě shook her head.

"I can't either. You want to shift."

It wasn't a question. Xuě nodded. She'd spent so much time in her *yukihyō* form that she itched to be human for a while, but the popping and flashes of light could wake the others. With the other shifters, transforming from animal to human or vice versus was part of life. She'd grown accustomed to doing it out in the open with them. But with regular people? Her entire life up until they'd joined Aynur and his band she'd hid her abilities from the villagers and anyone not like her. The group had hidden them from their Tibetan hosts as well. Now that they were in such close quarters, what would they do?

Pema said something in Tibetan to the woman. The woman replied with a nervous smiled, handing Pema the rifle. She stood and disappeared into the cave.

"You could always shift in the tunnel."

Xuě hissed a negative.

Pema laughed. "I don't blame you. Maybe you can check

outside? There might be a place where no one would see you."

But would Aynur be okay with it?

Xuě glanced back toward the sleeping shifters. She could scout out the surroundings, find a place to conceal her shifting, and return before anyone knew what she'd done. The idea was tempting.

The silent world outside beckoned. The chill night air would bite at her skin, and the snow would sting the soles of her feet, but it'd be worth it. She chuffed a thank you, quickly retrieved her pack, leaving it next to Pema in case she couldn't find a spot, and stepped out into the night.

Lifting her face, she closed her eyes and breathed in the fresh air. It filled her lungs and energized her sleepy cat. Being with people who understood her had satisfied a need she'd never realized she'd had, but she'd missed the peace being alone brought her, too.

She paused at the entrance and looked around. Which way should she go? Directly ahead lay a vast empty steppe—no village in sight. She frowned. If that were the case, where had the men come from? She shook her head. The answers would have to come later when she could ask Aynur. Right now, she had to find a place to shift . . . if there was one. She turned her attention back to the land around her.

To the left and right, the ground sloped up ten or so feet, but the slope was gradual. Perhaps she only needed to walk a short distance to shift.

She turned left and trotted up the incline. At the top, the steppe spread out in front of her. Snow blanketed everything and twinkled in the starlight.

Off in the distance, maybe a half *gōnglǐ* away, the village sat. A light flickered. Was it the enemy? Or had the resistance forces become separated with a portion of them ending up in the cave? Was there a sentry on guard?

Her tail twitched, and she crouched, watching for any other sign of life other than the light, but, after a while when nothing moved, she retreated down the hill, her feet dragging. Shifting might not be a possibility. At least, not outside. The flash of light could attract attention. They didn't need another battle. They *never* needed another battle.

The entrance loomed ahead of her, the aroma of unwashed and wounded bodies tickled her nose, and she hesitated. The sheer number of people pressed down on her. If only she could shift . . .

Her *yukihyō* growled in protest.

*It's not you. It's all of this. I'm feeling . . . trapped. If only this were over . . .*

A chuff of agreement answered her thoughts. The race across China and Tibet to India was wearing on her cat, too.

She stopped just beyond the entrance and sat. Soon, she'd have to go in, but, for a few more minutes, she'd soak up the tranquility of the empty land.

"Xuě," Pema whispered.

Xuě stood and walked the last few steps to join her friend.

"No place, huh?"

Xuě shook her head and plopped down next to Pema inside the cave, crossing her paws and resting her head on them. At some point, she'd have to shift to tell Aynur of her findings. He needed to be made aware of the danger. Which meant, of course, confessing about her excursion. Although he hadn't forbidden anyone going outside, he'd probably be mad. Her impulses once again could've put the others in danger.

Why had she done it?

"Hey, what if I got a blanket. Maybe you could shift under that."

Pema's voice interrupted her downward spiraling thoughts. Xuě lifted her head. Energy surged through her. But would the flares singe the blanket?

"Or I could hold it up to block your shifting from the villagers."

Had Pema read her mind?

She stood and head butted Pema, who laughed.

"*xíng*, where's your blanket?"

Xuě pushed her backpack toward the other woman. Pema opened the bag and pulled out the blanket.

"Here, you stand in this corner." She set Xuě's bag in the corner and held up the large piece of cloth.

She shifted and dressed. Stretching, she luxuriated in the feeling of her human body. Both forms had a good side, but, until this flight, she'd never spent this much time as her cat. When she'd escape to her cave, she'd shift back to her human form and sit outside, absorbing the silence, especially after the famine started. Before the famine, some of the villagers talked to her. Slowly, they stopped, even turning their backs when she drew near. At the end, other than her parents, the only person who had anything to do with her was Shi Sheng. He helped her bring the game into the village. The last time, he'd glared at her and called her an animal. Unable to speak, she'd blinked away the tears. She'd never expected friendship from him, but hadn't he respected her?

That day, he revealed he hadn't. No more than the Japanese. A *maruta*.

She shoved the memory away, but the more time she spent in her animal form, the less human she felt, the more his statement resonated in her.

Which was she?

Picking up her pack, she returned to where Bao lay and settled down next to him. He stirred and opened sleepy eyes. A sweet smile spread across his face. He lifted his blanket and opened his arms.

"Come here."

Without a word, she joined him. His lips trailed kisses along her neck. A shiver rippled across her skin, awakening all of her nerve endings.

"The dead—"

"Shh . . . we are living. Let's celebrate that." He kissed her jawbone and nipped her earlobe.

She quivered, and desire pulsed in her *bàoyú*. Running her hands under his shirt, she caressed his bare skin.

A tremor shook his body. Hers responded, arching toward his touch.

On the other side of the cave, a child whimpered. She

stilled, but, then, his lips closed over a nipple and all thoughts fled. Electricity snapped through her veins, and she gave herself over to Bao's ministrations.

# Chapter Twenty-Two

The following morning, Xuě approached Aynur, her steps hesitant. Her heartbeat accelerated. He stood next to Zuhre, his head inclined as they spoke softly in Uyghur. She waited for him to acknowledge her.

A few minutes passed. Zuhre nudged him, and he looked up, his golden gaze keen.

"Good morning," he said.

She smiled. "Good morning."

Glancing away, she fidgeted with the frayed seam of her shirt.

"What is it?"

"I—"

The words stuck in her throat. She peeked up at him. Only curiosity and patience filled his expression.

Again, she averted her gaze and, swallowing, took a deep breath before trying again. "I went outside last night—" She paused.

Silence greeted her. Dare she look at him? She couldn't. Instead, she stared at her fingers working at the seam of her shirt. Fibers of the fabric had come loose, sticking out and separating. They'd need to be trimmed and patched.

"Xuě?"

Aynur's voice commanded her to look at him. Their gazes met. His expression hadn't changed.

With another deep breath, she barreled on. "I went out to see if I could find a place to shift. I . . . I didn't want to disturb or scare anyone. Instead, I saw a light in the village." He opened his mouth, but she rushed on. "I only went up the incline and looked over the edge."

When she finished, she stared down at her feet, her shoulders slumped.

"You saw light?" he asked. "In the village?"

She nodded, keeping her focus on the ground.

He didn't say anything for several seconds. Her muscles tightened, ready to spring away if necessary. But her cat chuffed. There was no scent of anger or disappointment in the air around them. Perhaps she'd misjudged him?

Gathering her courage, she raised her chin and met his gaze.

He smiled. "This is good information. Well, we'll have to find out who's in the village. *Xièxiè* for telling me." With that, he returned to his conversation with Zuhre.

Xuě retreated to sit next to Bao.

"What was that all about?" her husband asked.

"I—"

Before she could tell him, Aynur came over.

"Be ready to go when I tell you," Aynur said, looking out into a world of white. Another storm had descended on the steppes, bringing with it more snow. "This storm will be the perfect cover for you and Bao to scout the village to see who was behind the lights last night."

Was he sending her and Bao to the village to punish her? Or did this mean he finally accepted her as an equal? That he saw her more than just a *maruta?*

Bao frowned. "What's he talking about?"

"I went outside last night, looking for a place to shift, and saw lights on in the village."

"So, now, we get to find out who."

It wasn't a question. She nodded.

Most likely, if no one came, the PLA had won. She didn't say it aloud. She didn't need to.

How many dead would they stumble across in the snow? She shuddered. Sometimes, her animal's abilities were a curse. Her *yukihyō* chuffed in protest.

*I'm sorry.*

"Hey, we'll be all right." His voice rumbled in her ear.

She snorted. "You don't believe that."

"I," he blew out a breath, "I do . . . sometimes. Sometimes,

I don't. Right now, with this storm and the quiet, India seems very close. Maybe another week? We could slip away without them finding us. We could leave now—all of us—if it weren't for the women, children, and the injured men. If it's PLA at the village, they could have prisoners. We'll need to free them. But, right now, I'm feeling like our chances are good. Ask me tomorrow, or after we return from our time out there," he motioned to the entrance, "and my answer could change."

She nodded. Her belief in their chances of escape went up and down, too. And going out in the snow? Her cat balked, echoing her own misgivings.

"You told Pema that you're able to keep your animal calm even when we must fight. Teach me how. Maybe she, and I, won't be so scared when we have to go today."

His chest rose and fell. For a moment, he said nothing.

"Okay. It is something the Buddhist monks taught me to do. It has helped me many times over the years."

He sat up straighter and removed his arm from her shoulders. She slid a little farther from him to give him room.

"Now, do as I do."

Crossing his legs, he closed his eyes and rested his hands palm down on his thighs.

"I can't if I can't see you."

He chuckled. "Let me know when you've copied me."

Xuě straightened, closed her eyes, and crossed her legs. "Okay."

"Focus on your breath. See it leave your body. Be with it all the way out of your body and watch it dissolve into the space around you. Sit in that space in between breaths. Let the inhale come naturally. Do this with each breath."

It sounded easy, but soon her thoughts and emotions were swirling around as violently as the snow outside. She was doing this wrong. Her body tensed, and she breathed in ragged pants. Her cat paced in agitation.

"I can't focus on my breath," she said. "Too many thoughts."

"It's okay. Notice them, but don't judge them. Let them be, and turn your focus back to your breath. This happens to most of us, even monks."

"Really?" Surely, monks didn't suffer from such a cacophony of thoughts as she did.

"They do. Let's try this again. Draw in a deep breath. Slowly . . . Let it fill all the way to the very edge of your stomach and release it."

Xuě inhaled slowly and allowed herself to exhale in an even manner. She did this several times. Her heartbeat settled, and the thoughts that had seethed in her mind quieted a bit. Instead of racing around, they flitted in and out. Her *yukihyō* chuffed and calmed.

"How are you now?" Bao said, his voice coming from faraway.

"Much better."

"That was step one. Would you like to try step two?"

She nodded.

"This is where you learn to work with your animal."

Xuě frowned. Didn't she already work with her animal?

"Xuě? Bao?" Aynur's voice interrupted them. "It's time. We can't wait any longer."

A vise clamped around her stomach, and her breath stuttered in her throat. She wiped her damp palms on her pants. Her cat whimpered.

"Breathe," Bao whispered in her ear.

That one word calmed the shaking inside, and she drew in a gulp of air, releasing it slowly.

He squeezed her hand. She forced a smile that she didn't feel.

"We'll be all right," he said.

She nodded. Hollow words, but she kept her silence, allowing him to think they comforted her.

Standing, she picked up her backpack.

"Wait," Aynur said. "You know where the village is, but not the size. According to Gan, there are 18 tents. The attack started on the side furthest from the cave. If there are any survivors, they'll most likely be closer to us than the other way."

Xuě turned to go.

"One more thing."

Xuě glanced over her shoulder at Aynur.

Concern gleamed in his eyes. "Be careful, you two."

With a nod, she retreated to the corner out of sight of the villagers and Tibetan resistance where Nur stood guard, and shifted. Although the cave was still dark, with everyone awake, she no longer worried about shifting. And, in the day, the dead didn't seem as scary. A shudder rippled across her fur at the smell and nearness of the dead bodies piled in the opening of the tunnel.

That wasn't entirely true.

Bao head butted her. She turned away from the bodies, lifted her pack with her mouth, and carried it back to where they'd been sitting. She set it down against the wall. Her husband placed his bag next to hers and licked the side of her face. She rubbed against him and chuffed.

After a deep, calming breath, she followed him out of the cave but took the lead. The wind had died down, settling into an eerie stillness, but the heavens answered with a steady, heavy snowfall, cloaking everything in shadows.

She kept close to Bao, his left shoulder lightly brushing against her back hip fur. Nothing moved. Snow piled up on her back. With a shake, she dislodged some of it.

With each step, she swiveled her ears back and forth, searching for any sound of life. The soft shush of snow falling and silence greeted her. Tension crept up her muscles. The day before, gunfire had rocked the steppes. Now, nothing. Where had everyone gone? Were they all dead?

In the distance, the shadowy outlines of the tents rose. The festive sutra streamers muted by the storm. Still, nothing stirred. Not even a sentry. Her cat balked.

*We can do this,* Xuě repeated over and over in her head, pushing ahead.

Despite the mantra, the farther into the snowbound landscape they went and the closer they came to the tents, the more intense the scent of human death grew. Her cat trembled and panted. She would've halted and turned back if her husband hadn't continued to plow forward, pulling ahead of her. How could he be so unaffected by this?

*Deep breath. We're xíng.*

Bao stopped a good distance from the village, dropped into a crouched position, and looked back at her. She settled down next to him. His tail twitched. His cat liked this no more than hers did. They crept closer. They approached from the opposite side of where the battle had been fought.

The tents toward the back of the village, and nearer to them, suffered minor damage. Bullet holes peppered some of them. The ones at the front of the village had taken the brunt of the conflict with devastating results. A few lay in complete ruin, their walls shredded, their supports bare to the elements, like bones of a dead animal. In one, the sutra streamers dragged against the ground, draped over the fireplace in the center. A dead PLA soldier leaned against it, his unseeing eyes staring out at the world, his body abandoned by his compatriots.

The smell of death hung heavy in the air. Her stomach curdled. Again, her *yukihyō* resisted moving forward.

How many of the bodies covered with snow strewn around the village were abandoned PLA? How many were villagers?

One of the PLA trucks sat empty, buried under a thick layer of snow. The other was nowhere to be seen. Could that truck have held the troops who'd attacked them in the tunnel yesterday?

Xuě stopped. The hair on the ruff of her neck stood. Bao crept a few more feet ahead and halted.

Where were the men?

A moan sifted through the hush. Xuě's gaze met Bao's. She cocked her ears. He inched forward, but she backed away.

Something was wrong.

He glanced back at her. She shook her head and continued to retreat farther into the storm.

"Zhōngwèi, we've found another rebel."

"He survived the night?" another voice asked.

"*Shi.*"

The falling snow muffled the words but not enough that

she couldn't understand them. Bao froze before joining Xuě where she crouched a short distance from him.

"Kill him," the man said.

Her heart leaped and beat loud in her ears. The poor women and children in the cave. Heat prickled along her nerve endings, and she narrowed her eyes. She stifled a growl that threatened to erupt.

"But, *xiānshēng*—"

"Kill him."

For a moment, nothing disturbed the quiet, then a shot rang out. Xuě jumped, and her cat urged her to run, but she steeled herself instead. They needed to know how many PLA survived. How many they'd have to fight.

*Work with me*, she pleaded with her cat. It trembled, but settled a bit.

"Get the other soldiers and bring them to this tent. When the snow stops, we'll go to the cave."

"*Shi, xiānshēng.*"

She crept forward and peeked around the edge of the tent. Bao pressed up against her back hip. She glanced at him before turning her attention back to the tent. A soldier stepped out, huddled into his coat, and hurried toward another tent, disappearing inside. Several minutes passed. When he emerged, he limped. The clothes hung on his frame.

She sniffed the air and hunkered down farther into the snow, her ears flattened to her head.

Was it the same man?

Her cat said no.

He glanced around him. Xuě shrank back, but he didn't react to her. Instead, he slunk off to another tent. A few minutes later, a couple more men appeared from the same tent in PLA uniforms carrying rifles. They, too, glanced around them before heading off in another direction.

They didn't look Chinese. Could they be Tibetan resistance?

Inside the tent next to her, someone said, "Why must we find these animals anyway?"

"It doesn't matter," the voice she'd identified as the lieutenant said. "You do as you're told. Besides, it shouldn't be long now before we catch them. With the villagers dead, we'll corner them in the cave and cage them like the animals they are. They won't escape us. We'll return home heroes, and Mao will reward us."

"Do you think the other troop has them now? Why haven't they contacted us?" another one asked.

"I'm tired of your questions." The harshness of the officer's tone chafed against Xuě's nerves. "The next person who asks me anything will be shot. You obey orders, nothing else. Understand?"

A chorus of voices responded. She frowned. How many were in the tent? Five? Ten?

She inhaled, trying to discern the number. The pungent scent of blood, unwashed bodies, fear, anger, excitement, and the sharp metallic tang of ammunition and guns nearly overpowered her. Focusing on each odor took some concentration, but, with the help of her cat, she determined there were ten within the tent.

Xuě backed away from it and collided with Bao. She nodded to him, and they retreated to a partially destroyed tent several feet away from the one full of PLA soldiers.

The three soldiers who'd disappeared into the village, returned with three more. They entered the tent with the officer. Yelling erupted from inside. A shot punctuated the shouting. Silence fell for a second. Then someone else yelled followed by more shots. A hole appeared in the side of the tent.

She flinched with each report of the guns. Eyes wide, she turned to Bao. Every muscle in her body tensed, preparing to bolt. They had to warn the others. He nodded. Spinning, she froze.

The storm had obliterated their footprints.

Bao bumped her shoulder, nodded at her, and trotted toward the back of the village. Her tightly wound muscles loosened. It had been a straight line from cave to the village. They could find their way back.

*Deep breath*. This was good. If the storm had covered their trail in such a short time, it would hide it when the PLA came looking.

She loped alongside Bao, once again grateful for the storm. Perhaps the spirits were protecting them with all of this snow. A shiver coursed down her spine, and she shook it off. Perhaps it was better not to think about the spirits at all.

The sounds of conversation reached her before she approached the entrance of the cave. With a quick look behind her to ensure no one trailed them, she turned right, following Bao down the incline, and halted in the entrance.

Chang crouched a few feet back from the entrance, a rifle in one hand. Relief spread across her face. "Good to see you two made it back."

She nodded, and warmth spread through her. Although she'd lost her parents, this journey had brought her friends. She ducked her head, trotting farther into the cave, and her *yukihyō* chuffed.

Shaking off the snow, she searched for Aynur. He stood by the children in the back corner talking with Zuhre.

They had to warn everyone. The PLA was coming. People were going to die . . . again.

Bao had already picked up his backpack when she joined him to shift. Cold air trailed its fingers across her skin. Goose bumps pimpled her flesh, and her hair stood. She trembled and yanked her clothes on.

"What did you find?"

Xuě spun. Aynur stood behind them.

"When the snow stops, they're coming for us," Bao said.

"Let them come," Pema said. "We'll be ready for them."

"I—"

How could anyone be ready to kill another person? Both her cat and her human side shuddered.

Bao slipped his arm around her shoulders, and she smiled at him as the tension in her body eased.

"How many are there?" Aynur asked.

"We're not sure," Bao said.

The wolf shifter frowned. "How can you not be sure?"

"One of the trucks is gone. We don't know where it is, but we overheard the PLA talking about looking for the tunnel entrance. It's possible they're the ones who came at us yesterday. Much of the village is destroyed. We heard moaning. I was going to check it out, but—" Bao paused and glanced at Xuě.

Pema drew closer. "What happened?"

"I refused to go. I . . . I was scared." Xuě stared down at her clenched hands.

Bao squeezed her shoulders. "She was right to be afraid. Seconds later, we heard more voices. It was a PLA lieutenant and a soldier. He had the soldier shoot the wounded man."

Pema gasped. She said something Xuě didn't understand, but it sounded like a curse word. Aynur scowled.

"He sent the soldier out to gather up the rest of his troops. Even with the solider gone, there were at least five different voices in one of the tents. Fighting erupted, whether it was amongst themselves or not, I'm not sure, but that's when shots were fired and we left," Bao said.

"What do you mean you're 'not sure'?" Aynur asked

"Not all of them spoke, though. I detected ten men in the tent."

Bao raised his eyebrows at her.

She tapped her nose. "I was closer than you. They were stinky. Anyway, the soldier the lieutenant sent out to gather up the rest of his troop entered a nearby tent. The man who came out wasn't the same one who went in," she said. "He was shorter and limped."

"And the group he brought back seemed different than the PLA soldiers we've seen."

Their gazes met. Her cat stirred, as if to say, "I told you so."

"You saw that, too? I wasn't sure."

Bao nodded. "*Shi.*"

Pema grinned. "So, they thought they had killed all of the Tibetan resistance, but they hadn't."

"We don't know," Bao said.

"And there's still that missing truck." Aynur fell silent. His mouth tightened. "Someone will have to go through the tunnel to see if the truck is at the end."

Xuě took a step back. Perhaps he'd send someone else.

The corner of his mouth tipped up. "Don't worry. You've done enough this morning."

He glanced around, catching the attention of the other shifters and Gan, who joined them. He spoke briefly to the Tibetan woman. She said something and motioned to a few of the women in the other corner. A brief conversation took place. With a nod, she turned to Aynur and spoke some more.

Next to Xuě, Pema let out a deep breath. Before she could say anything, Aynur addressed the group.

"Gan and these two women have offered to check on the truck. You can go rest."

Rest. Rest came in small bursts with one eye open and haunted dreams.

Xuě retreated to the area where they'd left their bags and stood looking down at their stuff. A small tremor started in her stomach and spread to the rest of her body. What happened if more PLA came before they could leave this cave? What if they didn't win the next battle? What if—?

"Hey."

Bao's voice interrupted her thoughts. She inhaled, but the shaking continued.

"Are you *xíng*?" he asked, touching her shoulder.

She shrugged and leaned into him. What was "*xíng*" anymore?

He slipped his arms around her and drew her closer. "Do you want to try the second step I was going to teach you before we left this morning?"

"I don't know if I can focus right now." A tear slipped down her cheek. She closed her eyes and took a shuddering breath.

His arms tightened, and his lips brushed the top of her head. She turned and buried her head against his chest. Sobs shook her body. She struggled to bring them under control. Her *yukihyō* chuffed her support, but nothing stemmed the tide of the sorrow and fear that rolled over her. She gasped deep gulps of air and clung to her husband.

# Chapter Twenty-Three

"Gan told Aynur the other truck was parked at the entrance of the tunnel," Pema said to the gathered shifters, her eyes sparkled with excitement. "We did it."

"For now, but for how much longer?" Huan's deep voice rumbled through the group.

The same thought had gone through Xuě's head, too. How many more battles could they survive?

"As many as we need," Bao whispered in her ear.

She cocked her head at him. Had she said her thoughts aloud?

A smile lit his eyes. "I'm beginning to be able to read your expressions. And," he paused, his silver gaze boring into her soul, "I know how you think."

"You do?"

"*Shi*, my beautiful wife, I do."

She raised an eyebrow at him. "What am I thinking now?"

He cleared his throat and coughed. "I—"

"You don't know *every*thing about me." She grinned.

"Well, but I'm learning."

True, he was. The worry and fear eased a bit. That he cared enough to know her as he did sent a warm tingling rushing through her. She hoped she'd grow into being the wife he deserved.

She squeezed his hand. "*Xièxiè.*"

"Always."

*Always.* When her parents had insisted she marry this man, she'd feared what would become of her. Looking back, if she hadn't married him, her life would no longer be hers. She'd be in Mao's clutches or dead. She had so much to be grateful to him for. How could she repay him?

With wonder, she reached up and cupped his cheek. His

eyes widened, and joy lit his face.

"Xuě, I—"

"Everyone, we'll leave tonight if the Tibetans have control of the village. Gan has asked us to do so. She fears more soldiers are coming. If the PLA are gone, they will move their tents to another location tomorrow. They don't want to stay in this place." Aynur's voice stopped all conversation.

A groan slipped through Xuě's lips, but she didn't blame them. Another night in a cave full of dead people sent shivers running through her.

"What will they do with the trucks?" Akilina asked.

"They plan to leave them. They want nothing to do with anything PLA, except perhaps their rifles. The trucks would bring them more trouble. They've lost enough."

Xuě nodded. These people had lost enough, all to protect them. Well, perhaps not only for that. They fought for their freedom, just as the shifters ran to stay free.

"I think we should take one," the pale wolf shifter said. "We drive it as far as we can. When we draw close to a village, you or Pema can go ahead and let them know we're allies and not enemies."

Aynur shook his head. "We'd be too easy to track, too easy to see and hear."

"But we could move faster and get some rest," Chang said. "Even if we only used it for one day. We drive it until it runs out of gas and leave it there."

"No, too many things could go wrong."

Zuhre put her hand on her mate's arm. "It's good. They not expect us to do this. They look for people . . . animals, not truck. Truck has radio maybe? We hear their—I don't know word—what they going to do. We make our own—" She said something in Uyghur.

Bao said, "Plan."

"*Shi, xièxiè*. Plan. It could be good, no?"

"I—"

"Please, Aynur. We," she motioned to the shifters around her, "need break. *I* need break."

He looked around the group. Xuě held her breath. What would he decide? Bao squeezed her hand.

"All right, but we must find a way that lets the resistance know we aren't the enemy."

Pema stepped forward. "If we hang a blue prayer flag on it, the Tibetans will know we're friendly."

"And the PLA will know we're not them."

"What if we travel at night?" Xuě asked.

Aynur smiled at her. "*Shi*. That makes sense. We leave tonight anyway. We travel through the night. If we come upon another village, we can stop at a distance, let them know we are friends, and continue on." His mouth turned down. "But does anyone know how to drive one? I don't, nor does Zuhre and Nur."

Bao let go of her hand. "I do."

Xuě pulled away from her husband. How? Only the military had these trucks. And he knew how to shoot their rifles. Could he be betraying them? Leaving clues for the PLA to find them? Is this why they barely stayed ahead of Mao's soldiers?

One moment, she thanked her parents for choosing him for her husband, and, the next, she wondered who he was and if she could trust him.

From everyone else's expressions, she wasn't the only one who questioned his loyalties.

"I—" Bao ran his hand through his hair. "A little over a year ago, I joined the PLA."

Xuě gasped and drew farther away from him.

He stared straight ahead, his face a stoic mask. "They came to our village looking for recruits. This was before the famine truly set in. Some young men in our village signed up. I was one of them. They trained me to drive the Yellow River trucks as well as shooting the rifles. But what I witnessed and, with starvation setting in on the villages, including mine, I had to get out. Not only would they discover my abilities, but my parents needed me."

Aynur stared at him, his gaze as keen as a finely honed knife. "How did you escape?"

"After a few months, I pretended a head injury. I forgot things, made mistakes."

"You're lucky they didn't kill you," Huan said.

"My friends urged them to let me return to my parents. I was their only son." Bao looked at Xuě, catching and holding her attention. "I was lucky, but I believe fate saved me. I was meant for something different."

Heat swept up Xuě's neck. Her cheeks tingled. She averted her gaze and focused on her tightly clasped hands. How had she doubted him? Time and again he'd put himself in danger to protect her. And she'd done the same for him. When would she learn to trust him?

But what did she really know about him? He said he knew her, knew how she thought, but he remained a mystery to her.

Aynur nodded as if satisfied with Bao's answer. He turned to the rest of the group. "Does anyone else know how to drive these trucks?"

Head bowed, Huan said, "I do. Many young men of my city were pressed into service. Well, most of them joined willingly, including me. I believed I could hide my secret. No one would ever know."

The shifters murmured in agreement. How did he hide it living in a city? In Xuě's village, everyone knew. In the city, certainly someone would notice. How had he met Chang? She looked around the group. How much did she really know about these people? They were friends and yet strangers.

"I was lucky. My mother's brother was a commanding officer. He didn't know of my," he waved his hand in front of himself, "shifting ability, but he gave me light duties. One of them was driving the truck, probably because of my mother. My mother loved her brother, but never trusted Mao and fiercely guarded my secret from everyone, including my father. She begged her brother to get me out. She must've worn him down because he released me from service with some excuse."

"You can take turns driving, then," the alpha said. "In the meantime, we'll rest. We need to fill our canteens before we leave, and a few of us must go to check out the village. Do I have any volunteers?"

Pema stepped forward. "I'll do it."

"You can't go alone." Aynur looked around the group.

"I'll go with her," Akilina said. The fair-haired woman smiled. "It'd be nice to get out of this cave for a while."

And put herself in danger, but, *shi*, Xuě itched to leave this cave and the dead bodies behind.

"We'll wait until dark falls."

The two women nodded, and the group broke up into smaller segments. Xuě returned to her spot by their back-packs. Bao had never told her about his time with the PLA. Not that they'd had much time to talk, nor had she thought to ask such questions. Her waking moments had been consumed with survival or grief. A number of the young men in her village had left to become soldiers. That Bao had struck her as out of character. This quiet man brought peace to her. How could he have spent any time in Mao's Army?

"Hey," Bao said, bumping her shoulder. "What are you thinking?"

She raised her gaze to meet his. "That I don't know who you are."

He smiled and held her hand. "We're still learning."

"*Shi.*" She stared at their clasped hands.

"What do you want to know?"

"I—" So many questions threatened to spill forth, but they'd come out as gibberish and too quickly for him to an-swer. "When did you join the PLA? I'd never picture you as a soldier."

He chuckled. "I'm not. It's why I did my best to get out, but this was at the beginning of the famine, before people started starving, before I saw Mao and his movement for what it is."

"A lot of our young men went to the army. They left a few behind. I never understood why."

"One of our duties was to collect the food from the local communes. More than once, I overheard the director of the commune speaking to a chairman of a collective about totals. Anyone could see the totals they gave us took almost all of their food. The commanders didn't care, nor did the managers. Many of my comrades were too blinded with fervor to see it. I wasn't. You saw what they did to your village. Our commanders frequently ordered us to beat farm workers if what we were given was under the totals." A haunted look flickered in his eyes. He gazed off into the distance, his face a mask of dismay. "There was no concern for the people. I faked injury after injury until they sent me home."

"Did you ever say anything?" Xuě asked.

He shook his head. "You heard what happened in that tent. A soldier is no more important to them than the farm workers. We can easily be replaced."

"Can I join you?"

Xuě looked up. Huan towered above them. She smiled and waved her hand to the ground next to them.

The burly bear shifter settled in front of them. "*Xièxiè* for confessing."

Bao shrugged. "It made sense. The truck will get us to India faster, even if it runs out of gas after a few hours. It can cover in a few hours what would take us most of the night. Besides, we need to trust each other. If someone lies, how can you believe what they say?"

Something flitted in the back of Huan's eyes before disappearing. Xuě narrowed her eyes.

The bear shifter nodded. "Your confession gave me the courage to admit it. I'm not proud of my choice to be a member of the PLA."

Xuě leaned toward Huan, studying him. His expression gave nothing away. Perhaps she'd imagined it. "How were you to know? None of us did . . . until it was too late. And still many believe in Mao and his plan for China."

Huan bowed his head. His voice came out in a low whisper. "I did at one time. China would be a great world leader. I believed every word Mao said. We lived in the city of Lognan in Gansu. I stayed in the army for a year."

She drew back. "A year?" That was a long time.

"My mother had always been against me joining. I rebelled

and joined anyway." A light flush crept up his pale cheeks. "All of my friends had gone. I felt I could be an asset, although no one would ever know of my animal. My mother made sure I'd never tell anyone. Being in the army provided food for my family. We weren't questioned about our party loyalty. But the longer I stayed in, the more I saw, the less I wanted to be there."

"What changed your mind?" Bao asked.

"It was really hard to hide my bear. It suffered, and so did I. Lognan is in the mountains. The BaVong River runs through it. It was easy to go into the mountains and shift. I could avoid the patrols and sneak off at night. In the army, our every move was watched, regimented more than in school. My mother wanted me home. She feared my secret would be exposed, especially when my comrades found out how good I was at wrestling."

Xuě raised an eyebrow. "Wrestling?"

"*Shi*. We wrestled with each other for fun. No matter how big or strong the other opponent seemed, I could always beat them." He smiled, pride shining in his eyes. "But my ability drew the interest of the higher ups." He let out a deep breath with a sigh.

Xuě stared at him. "Did you ever shift by accident?"

"No. Word came that my mother was gravely ill. She begged my uncle to release me from my service term. He did. She wasn't. My uncle had sent her letters about what I was doing. She feared what they'd discover, and she was right. A month after I got out, the PLA came to our house, looking for me. I was out, but my mother knew something was wrong just by the way the officer treated her. When I came home that evening, she gave me what little food they had and told me to go. I left after the sun set." He turned haunted eyes on them. "I don't know what happened to my parents, whether they live or . . ."

He didn't need to finish his sentence. The PLA cut down any they believed to be enemies of the state.

"I'm sorry." Xuě touched his arm. It seemed that all of

them had lost their families.

He nodded, but said nothing.

Wrapping her arm around Bao, she snuggled against him. He put his arm across her shoulders and kissed her forehead.

"Huan? Bao?" Aynur's voice broke the silence that had fallen between them. "Could you come over here, please?"

Both men stood, leaving Xuě alone. She rubbed her arms, the chill seeping in with the departure of Bao's warmth. So much pain, so much loss for all of them. How would they ever overcome it?

The sounds of the Tibetans laughing quietly in the corner and the children playing soothed her aching spirit. Although she couldn't understand them, even in the face of danger and loss, these people found joy in what little they had. They had each other. Pema stood amongst them. For once, the young woman looked her age and carefree.

At the entrance, Akilina crouched with her back to the cave. Zuhre and Nur sat next to each other, leaning against a wall, their faces in repose as they caught up on some sleep. Chang lay on her side by herself a few feet from Xuě, her eyes closed, her chest rising and falling in a steady rhythm.

The shifters were all she had now. More than she'd ever had. In her village, it had only been her parents.

Her parents . . .

Tears stung her eyes. A tightness pulled at her chest, and she caught her breath. She blinked back the tears and lifted her chin. They had died to save her. She'd do everything she could to make sure they hadn't died in vain.

# Chapter Twenty-Four

Night descended. Torches flickered on the walls, giving the illusion of twilight when Zuhre and Nur returned from their scouting of the village.

Xuě sat up straight, pulling away from the wall. Next to her, Bao roused from his nap, blinking sleepily at her in question. She motioned toward the two wolves who headed for the back of the cave near the tunnel where they'd shift. He pushed himself up with a grunt.

"What do you think they found?" he said.

She shrugged. "I don't know, but I hope it's good news. We could use some of that."

The sooner they left this cavern of death, the better.

"*Shi*, we could."

The pair crossed to Aynur and spoke in low tones. Aynur's face lit up, and his smile eased the knot that was growing in Xuě's stomach.

"The resistance has won. The village is ours." He turned to Gan who'd come up beside him, her face a mask of worry, and told her the news.

The cave erupted in cheers.

Xuě grinned. Bao grabbed her and kissed her. All the fear and anger coalesced into a hunger for this stunning man next to her, but he drew back. Desire swirled in his eyes along with relief. The need to feel his *jījī* inside of her roared to life. The smell of pheromones and need eddied around them.

She curled her hands into a fist, resisting the temptation the man before her presented. Her *yukihyō* mewed and twitched her tail. Xuě agreed with her cat, but common sense told her it'd have to wait.

"Bao," Aynur said, "we need to find out which truck has the most gas. You and Huan can go check them out."

"We could drive the one from the other end of the tunnel to the village where we can meet up," Huan said. "Then we can siphon the gas from one to the other if we have something to do that with." He looked at Bao.

Bao cocked his head to the side, a thoughtful expression on his face. "They might have something in the trucks for that. We used to carry extra gas with us. I'd imagine they'd do the same out on the steppes."

"You'll have to go through the tunnel." Xuě shuddered.

He frowned before smiling. "But it'll get us out of here and farther away than if we don't."

He was right. Despite being full of the living, an aura of death hung over the entire cavern.

"All right then," Aynur's voice broke through the excited chatter, "everyone gather up your things. We'll leave as soon as possible." He glanced at Bao and Huan. "We'll meet you at the village."

She touched Bao's arm. He paused, a questioning look on his face. Leaning close, she kissed his cheek and whispered, "Be careful."

He hugged her and brushed his lips across her forehead. "I will."

Bao picked up his backpack and followed Huan. They jumped over the bodies and disappeared. The wind gusted past the entrance, pushing loose snow in front of it, and howled through the passage.

Xuě shivered and secured her pack on her back, glad she didn't have to go with him. That tunnel with its howls and moans would remain with her for a long time.

Pema walked up next to her and smiled. "You ready?"

Xuě returned the smile with one of her own. "I can't wait to leave this place."

"You're not alone. I think everyone feels that way," Pema said.

"I know I do," Chang said. "This place is creepy."

Xuě had to agree. Would the resistance abandon this cave? If she were one of them, she wouldn't ever be able to return here. Would the dead haunt them?

"Aynur?"

He turned at her call.

"Do you think we could say a prayer over the soldiers who've left?" Xuě asked.

He frowned. "What?"

She hesitated. Would he laugh at her reasons? "The soldiers over there." She pointed to the pile of dead soldiers. If she spoke of their death that close to them, they might attach themselves to her. "I don't want their spirits to follow us."

His face was inscrutable, and he narrowed his eyes.

She shifted her weight from foot to foot waiting for his answer.

"I'll ask the villagers if they'd be okay with that," he said.

Glancing down at her hands, she inhaled to calm her racing heartbeat. "*Xièxiè.*"

A few minutes later, he said, "The Tibetans will say prayers for all the dead before they move the village. They don't want the unsettled ghosts following them either."

"Can I do my own?"

"Don't you trust them?" His golden gaze pinned her to her spot.

"*Shi*, but I . . . " Her attention drifted to the pile of dead. She swallowed and shook loose the shiver that seemed stuck between her shoulder blades. It cascaded down her spine. Would he laugh at her if she told him the truth? "I'd liked to do my own. For me."

He inclined his head. "We leave for the village in a few minutes."

She dragged her gaze back to him. "What if they can't start the truck?"

"They'll let us know."

He was right. For a split second, she hoped the truck wouldn't start and Bao would return to help her with the prayers. Facing that pile alone filled her with dread. Would her prayers be enough? Would they soothe the spirits, sending them on their way?

Aynur strode off and joined Zuhre who slipped her arms around him. A weary smile lit his face, and he pulled his mate close.

Xuě averted her gaze, and the yearning for Bao's calming presence intensified.

Wiping her damp hands on her pants, she licked her suddenly dry lips. *You can do this.* She clenched and unclenched her hands, took a deep breath, settled her pack more firmly upon her back, and stepped toward the passageway.

"What are you doing?"

Pema's voice halted her slow progression.

Heat rose into Xuě's cheeks. "I," she glanced at her friend and looked away, "I was going to say a prayer over the bodies."

"Why?" Scorn emanated from the feisty shifter.

Refusing to make eye contact with her, Xuě said, "Because I'd rather not have them follow me, and it'll help me deal with my part in the killing."

Silence followed her words. It sat between them like a heavy shroud.

Xuě turned her face away so Pema couldn't see her reaction. What did this strong woman think of her now? Did she still see her as useless? Like a *maruta*? While she struggled to overcome her fears, hadn't she proved herself to the group yet? Would Pema see her desire to pray over the dead as a sign of weakness? Because she wasn't going to leave without doing it, and she hoped Pema would continue to be her friend despite that. Lifting her chin, she stepped forward and away from the wolf shifter.

"Mind if I join you?" Pema asked from behind her.

Relief spread through her, and Xuě stopped. "I'd like that."

Pema moved up beside her. Chang and Akilina stood next to her.

"Did you say you're going to pray over them?" Chang asked.

Xuě studied Chang's face. The bear shifter betrayed no hint of her thoughts.

"*Shi.* I can't leave them without prayers."

"I," Chang glanced sideways at Akilina who stood impassively beside her, "want to do that, too."

Akilina bowed her head for a moment. Her ice blue gaze met Xuě's. "I'd also feel better if I helped."

"We only have a few minutes," Xuě said. "We'll have to make them short."

"Then let's do this." The wolf shifter strode toward the passageway. When no one moved to follow, she turned, put her hands on her hips, and raised her eyebrows. "Are you coming?"

Xuě grinned. It was just like Pema to galvanize them into action. The grin withered, though, as she approached the pile. She bowed her head, wishing she had something physical to offer them beyond the few phrases of prayer she remembered from her childhood.

*"May your spirit be at peace*
*And hurry to the next life . . . "*

She faltered, but Pema took up the prayer.

*"May your next life bring you happiness*
*Away from the pain of this one . . . "*

Pema's voice faded away only to be replaced by Chang's.

*"May your spirit be free of sorrow*
*And never be separated from the sacred happiness . . . "*

Chang grew silent, only for Akilina to finish the prayer.

*"May you be at rest and full of loving kindness*
*And find your way to the peace of Buddha's garden."*

"So be it," Xuě said.

"So be it," the others chorused.

A gust of wind howled through the passage, swirled around the bodies, and rushed back the way it came, wailing as it went. The hair on Xuě's body stood on end, and she gasped.

"Did anyone else . . . " Xuě couldn't finish the question.

Wide-eyed and pale, Pema said, "I think we should leave."

Xuě raced back to the other side of the cave where Aynur waited with Nur and Zuhre.

"Are you done?" Aynur asked.

"*Shi*," Xuě said.

"Do you feel better now?"

Her cheeks burned. What could she say? "I guess."

His gaze scanned the others who stood silently with her. "I saw the three of you were with her."

Akilina and Chang avoided meeting his gaze, but Pema raised her chin.

"We were."

"And?"

"There's nothing to tell," Pema said. "We should leave."

The corner of his mouth quirked up. "*Xíng*. Let's go."

The shifters fell into line and trotted out into the moonless night. Their breath hung in front of them, and Xuě snuggled deeper into her coat, grateful for the warmth it provided.

Zuhre slipped into line next to Xuě. "Everything good?"

Xuě met her concerned regard. Should she tell her? Pema had denied everything. To say something would admit Pema lied.

Uncertain of how to respond, Xuě said, "*Shi*. I'm just ready to leave. This cave isn't a place I want to be anymore."

When they'd first arrived, it'd seemed like a safe haven, and, now, it'd become a tomb.

The sooner they left it far behind, the better.

"I'm glad to leave, too."

Silence fell between them. Zuhre's quiet presence brought Xuě comfort, but so did all of the others. Being among people whose experiences mirrored hers, or were close to hers, and could understand her gave her a sense of belonging that her life in the village had lacked.

Not for the first time, she hoped they would stay together if they crossed the border into India and escaped Mao's reach.

Her feet sunk into the deep snow. Were the PLA to come now, they'd easily follow them back to the cave. But the night was quiet and peaceful with the occasional gust of wind. Every so often, it swirled loose snow past them.

The village rose in front of them, a dark shadow with pinpoints of light against the white empty land. In the distance, a truck rumbled, announcing its approach. She turned toward the sound. Twin lights bounced up and down. A quiet cheer rose amongst them.

Bao and Huan had been successful. This night, they'd be riding instead of walking.

The last time she'd ridden in the back of a truck was when she met her husband. She closed her eyes, trying to stem the unwanted memories of that time. This ride would be different, although not so much different. That first one brought her to freedom. This one would, too.

Xuě walked toward the village behind Chang. Zuhre had dropped in behind her. No one spoke. Aynur skirted the edge and met up with a sentry who raised his gun and shouted an order.

The alpha stopped and called out to him in Tibetan.

The soldier lowered his gun and smiled. Their conversation continued. Xuě, and the rest of the group, waited quietly until they'd finished.

Aynur turned back to them and motioned them forward just as the truck drew up to the front of the village and stopped next to the other one. Several Tibetans emerged from the tents, guns drawn. Upon seeing the shifters with the sentry, they came forward.

Pema called to someone who rushed over to her when he saw her. They hugged.

"Hey, everyone, this is my cousin, Jinpa."

Just as she said this, the lights of the truck switched off, and Bao jumped out from the driver's side. Huan opened the other door and grinned.

Relief spread through Xuě, and the tightness binding her shoulders loosened.

Pema's happiness was infectious, and Xuě laughed. She hurried over to Bao. He smiled down at her, grabbing her hand, and faced the group.

"It took us a bit to get it running, so I've left it on for now," Bao said over the roar of the engine. "There are twenty gas cans in the back. Half of them are empty If the same is true with the other one, we might be able to make it to India."

Xuě cheered along with the rest.

"We also found blankets, *bakkwa*, and sacks of rice in the back," Huan said.

"Maybe we should leave some of those with the Tibetans as a *xièxiè*," Chang suggested.

"We'll ask," Aynur said.

"They'd be grateful for them." Pema broke away from her cousin. "Jinpa told me that the PLA did their best to destroy everything these people had."

Anger swelled inside of Xuě, and she clenched her hands. These people had done little but offer to help them, and the PLA would kill them for it. She shook her head. Why was she surprised by this? Wrong or right, the soldiers followed their orders.

"Let's load up the truck and hand out the blankets," Aynur said.

Without a word, Xuě followed the others to the back of the truck. A large khaki green fabric stretched over poles that arched over the bed of the truck to form a protected "room" of sorts. A few bullet holes marred the otherwise taut material. Black exhaust billowed out of the tailpipe, and the sharp tang of chemicals filled the air. She coughed and grimaced with distaste. Covering her nose, she jumped up into the truck and grabbed some blankets.

Once they were moving, if the wind blew the right direction, they'd be spared the stench.

Huan pulled two empty gas cans out from under the built-in benches and handed them to her. "Let's move these empty gas cans to the other truck."

Xuě passed the cans to Akilina who stood on the ground outside. "Take these to the other truck. I'll follow you with a couple more. We can bring the full ones back here."

Akilina took the cans and climbed into the other truck. Xuě turned around in time to grab two more from Huan. She jumped down to the ground and crossed the few feet to the other truck. Akilina stood in the opening with full cans. Xuě put hers down and grabbed the ones from the other woman. The full cans were heavy, but not as heavy as a full grown *pán yáng.*

"Let me take those," Bao said.

With a grateful smile, Xuě handed them off to her husband who lifted them into the other truck. She took the empty ones Huan passed down and carried them over to where Akilina waited with full cans. Pema joined them. A few minutes later, they'd transferred everything to their truck, and all of the shifters gathered at the back of the trucks ready to leave.

"There's quite a bit of rice and *bakkwa*," Xuě said to Aynur. "How much should we keep? How much should we give to the resistance? And the blankets?"

"I think we should give most of the food to them and only keep one blanket for each of us. They have children to care for," Pema said. "We can always hunt or shift."

"Pema's right," Zuhre said. "We don't need . . . all the food. They helped us. We must give them . . . as much as we can."

"We'll only keep what we need for emergencies. We'll give them all but one bag of rice and a week's worth of the *bakkwa*." Aynur's deep voice stopped anymore discussion.

Xuě agreed with him. Without the resistance and these families, the shifters wouldn't have made it this far. They could show their gratitude by leaving most of the food with the Tibetans.

Aynur called the Tibetan soldiers over. The food supplies and blankets quickly changed hands. The soldiers smiled and nodded before returning to the tents.

"Do you know when they will move their village, Pema?" Xuě asked.

"Jinpa said tomorrow. The soldiers are going to help the village find a new place to set up their tents." Pema climbed into the back of the truck.

Xuě followed her. She settled on a built in bench next to the Tibetan. "Did he know about your village?"

The wolf shifter bowed her head for a moment. When she looked back up, fire flashed in her eyes. "No. He is angry as I am. I will come back and help them fight once it is safe."

The others filtered into the back. Aynur knocked on the

back of the cab, and the truck jolted forward. Xuě lurched sideways nearly landing on the floor. She grabbed ahold of the bench and hung on as the truck bounced over the steppes. Perhaps crossing the steppes on foot would be better than this bone-rattling ride.

Xuě cracked her eyes open and squinted. Beams of sunlight shone through the holes in the fabric. One of them struck her full in the face. She winced, moving slightly to the right to avoid being blinded, and stretched. A groan slithered past her lips. Every bone and muscle in her body protested. Her butt was sore, and she really needed to stand.

Around her, others stirred as the jolting of the truck decreased and it rolled to a stop.

"Good morning." Bao's husky voice drew Xuě's attention to the back. He stood outlined in the opening against the backdrop of the bright blue sky and the white snow.

Huan stepped up behind him.

She smiled. "*Nǐ hǎo.*"

A tired smile tipped up the corners of Bao's mouth. Dark circles smudged the skin under his eyes. Fine lines of strain bracketed his mouth.

"We've stopped. We've reached some mountains and have no way to go around them. We'll need to take the road . . . if there is one." He paused. "We can't get through these mountains without them, and the flats seem to be behind us now. I don't know if we should be traveling during the day instead of the night. We'd be like a *pán yáng* with its foot stuck in a crack."

Pema straightened next to Xuě. "But the resistance could attack this truck during the day. It'd be an easy target."

"They could attack it even if we're moving," Aynur said. "Huan and Bao need rest, but I see now we didn't think this through. Maybe we need to leave this truck behind and continue on foot."

"I . . . I could learn to drive it." Xuě looked up at Bao. His eyes widened, but he smiled in approval. She turned back to Aynur. "If one of them would teach me. I could drive during the day, and one of them at night." She'd never driven a truck before. The thought sent fear skittering across her skin, but it'd mean they'd reach the border sooner.

"We traveled as much distance last night as we do on foot in five days," Bao said. "If we have enough gas, we could reach the border within three or four days."

Aynur's sharp gaze studied him, suspicion lighting the depths of his eyes. "How do you know this?"

"I spoke to one of the rebels. He knows Chinese. He gave me this," Bao pulled out a round device with foreign markings on it, "and said that, if I keep the arrow pointed to here and drive that way, the border of India and Tibet is about 800 more *gōnglǐ*. It's also a safe place to cross. The resistance uses it. The PLA doesn't know about it . . . yet. There is also a highway, but it leads to Lhasa and the Nathula Pass."

"Lhasa is held by the Chinese," Pema said. "We must avoid it if we wish to make it to India."

Bao shook his head. "We won't be going to India. The rebel said the Nathula Pass is closed. If we wish to go to India, we'd have to cross north and west of here. It's too dangerous. We must go to Nepal instead."

Nepal . . . They'd only discussed India, but Nepal? Xuě shivered. Did it matter? At this point, they needed to get out of China's reach. Nearly any other country would be safer. And the faster they could get there, the sooner they'd be free.

Hope lit a fire inside Xuě. "Teach me how to drive. If I drive during the day, we'll reach the border sooner. We'll be free."

"I will teach you," Huan offered. "Bao did most of the driving last night."

"All right," Aynur said. "Before we go farther, I need to stretch my legs, and we should eat."

Giddiness bubbled up, and the urge to dance around and holler like a crazy woman brought her to her feet. This whole nightmare could be over in a few more days.

# Chapter Twenty-Five

The truck stalled again, and Xuě bit back the urge to scream and cry. How could this be so hard? She wanted to pound on something or tear the steering wheel out.

"You need to let your foot off the clutch more slowly and apply the gas at the same time." The soothing tones of Huan's voice only exacerbated her already frayed nerves. "If you release the clutch too quickly, the engine will stall."

Yes, she was figuring that out, but the truck had been built for a much larger person, and her toes barely touched the tip of the clutch. All of which made it harder for her to work the clutch. Inching her butt forward on the seat until her elbows practically rested on the steering wheel, Xuě pressed down on the clutch with her left foot, kept her right foot on the brake, slipped the stick shift into neutral, and turned the engine on again.

She blew a breath out and tried again. The truck jumped forward, but didn't die. She pressed down on the accelerator, and the engine revved up.

"*Xíng*," Huan yelled over the engine noise, "now shift down into second."

Xuě let her foot off the gas a little, pushed in the clutch, and shifted into the next gear. A loud grinding sound set her teeth on edge, but she found the gear and pressed on the accelerator, and the truck lurched forward again. The engine wound up again.

"Shift up and to the right," Huan yelled.

She repeated the process again. This time, the shift was smoother, and the truck bounced from the uneven ground and no longer jerked to a stop from her shifting. Success! She grinned at her teacher before turning back to her task.

The truck flew over the ground as fast as she could run at

top speed. The giant tires crunched in the snow. It bounced over another hole and slid sideways.

Panicking, Xuě pulled her foot off the gas, terrified they'd tip over, hoping the truck would stop before it did. The truck slowed and lurched to a halt. Huan yelped, screams erupted from the back, and Xuě came close to body slamming the steering wheel.

The blood drained from her head, and she swayed. She could've killed everyone. Maybe she shouldn't drive. She yanked her hands from the steering wheel as if it burned her and turned to Huan. He'd slid off the seat and sat in a ball on the floor board.

"Are you hurt?" she asked.

Pale-faced, he said, "No, I'm *xíng*, but you can't drive that fast over the snow. I should've told you. You were doing so well I didn't think . . . "

"I . . ." What could she say? She stared out at the empty land ahead of them. "It's *xíng*. I think I shouldn't drive."

"No, no, you were doing a good job, but you need to drive slower."

She nodded, but didn't believe him. If she'd been doing a good job, they wouldn't have almost flipped over.

"Try again," Huan said, "but, this time, drive slow. Snow is very slippery, and the ground is uneven."

"No. I—"

"Xuě, you can do this. Wait here, and I'll check on the others."

He left before she could say anything.

Tremors wracked her entire body, and heat prickles danced along her skin. Bile rose in her throat. She bent over, clutching her stomach as it threatened to expel what little contents it had.

She didn't have time for this.

"Everyone's good if a little shaken up."

Huan's voice broke through the haze that had engulfed her. She didn't look at him. Tears stung her eyes. If he saw her crying . . . Heat rushed to her cheeks, and she bowed her head.

A hand squeezed her shoulder.

"You can do this."

A tear slid down her cheek, and she swiped it away.

"Why don't I drive? You can take your turn in a little bit, okay?"

Lifting her chin, she straightened her shoulders. "No, you're right, I can do it. I'll just drive slower."

"Really, it's *xíng*." He opened his door, a concerned frown on his face.

"Huan! Wait . . . if I don't do it now, I probably won't do it. I'd like to be able to help you and Bao." She smiled at him.

"Are you sure?"

"*Shi.*"

But she wasn't sure at all. Uncertainty clawed at her, and her *yukihyō* didn't like the truck. The noise, the speed, the bone jarring jolts as it zoomed over the uneven ground. Given a choice, she'd rather be outside, the earth racing under her paws, the wind ruffling her fur, but there was no time. She had to focus on escaping.

She shook her head to dispel such thoughts. This truck would get them to the border in a few more days where they'd be free to start a new life and leave the fear behind.

Hope stirred within her, and she reached for the keys.

The sun had a few hours before it'd reach its zenith when a red light blinked on the panel in front of her.

Her attention still on the snow-covered ground in front her, Xuě asked, "What does the red light mean?"

Huan leaned toward her. "We're running low on gas. We should stop and put more in the tank."

"Okay." She shifted down, the gears grinding a bit, and stopped.

"I'll get the cans and fill it up. Why don't you let me drive for a few hours, so you can rest."

She smiled her thanks and lifted her hands off the steering wheel. They'd cramped from the hours she'd gripped it. She rolled her shoulders, stretched her arms, and turned her head from side to side to release the pent up tension.

Bao had driven through the night over snow and hazardous terrain, only stopping at dawn. Only two hours of it, and her body ached as if they raced across the 45 or so *gōnglǐ* they'd managed to cover in that time.

It humbled her that he chose to marry her. Once they reached Nepal, she'd show him how much she appreciated him.

Someone knocked on her window. She jumped, her *yuki-hyō* tensed to flee, but it was only Huan. He opened the door. Beyond him, the other shifters were out in the snow. Some stretched, some walked around, and some stood talking to each other. Off in the distance a herd of *chiru* watched them.

"Aynur thinks we should stop for a few minutes to allow everyone some time out of the truck," he said.

She hopped down to the ground, her legs threatening to collapse under her, and joined the others, looking for her husband, but he wasn't there.

"He's in there," Zuhre pointing to the back of the truck, "sleeping."

"*Xièxiè*," Xuě said. "I would join him, but I want to keep Huan company and switch with him when he's tired."

"It is . . . hard?" Zuhre asked.

"Not so much hard, but it is new and it frightens me sometimes. I nearly crashed the truck. My cat likes it even less."

"Then why do it?"

Xuě turned to Pema. "Because we'll reach Nepal sooner with three drivers." She raised her chin. "And I am tired of always being afraid."

Zuhre touched her arm. "Fear is not . . . bad. It keep you . . . safe."

"But it also can be bad." Xuě looked down at her hands,. Memories of the times she'd froze or done something stupid that would've resulted in the shifters getting caught rushed through her mind.

"There's good fear and bad. I know. I have fear, too." A haunted look flickered in Zuhre's eyes. They cleared, and she smiled at Xuě. The wolf shifter waved her hand. "All of us do. It's . . . how do you say?"

"Normal?" Pema offered.

"*Shi*. It's normal." Zuhre's accent made the word nearly unintelligible.

"I get scared, too, but I get angry when something scares me. Fear makes me feel helpless. I don't like feeling helpless." The Tibetan growled under her breath and glanced away.

"Is that how you felt after finding your village?" The words slipped out before Xuě could stop them.

Pema's eyes widened, and her face paled.

"I'm sorry. I didn't mean—"

"No. It's exactly that. I'd never felt so helpless in my life as that moment." Her gaze connected with Xuě's. "Then rage pushed out the fear. I vowed they would pay. All of them, especially that Mao lover Gang." She spit in the snow.

Both Xuě and her cat shuddered. The leopard had tried to kill her, would have killed her if someone hadn't shot him. Had Bao saved her?

Her gaze drifted to the truck where he slept.

"It's time to leave." Aynur's voice carried across the snow.

Xuě stepped toward the truck, but Zuhre stopped her.

"You're doing well. You'll be good."

Warmth spread through Xuě, and she smiled at her friend.

"*Shi*," Pema said, "*xièxiè*."

Xuě raised her eyebrows in question at the Tibetan.

"For conquering your fears. It's not an easy thing to do." Pema placed a hand on her shoulder. "I'm glad you're on our side, my friend."

"So I am . . . am I," Zuhre said.

Xuě walked next to the two women, her steps light. Friend. They considered her their friend. She raised her face to the sun and inhaled a deep breath, allowing that feeling to sink in. Never during her life in the village had she thought she'd ever have any friends. Now, she had eight, if she included her husband.

She straightened, a sense of purpose and belonging filling her, and strode to where the others waited with Aynur.

"Which one of you is driving?" the alpha asked.

"I am," Huan said.

Aynur studied Huan. "You need to rest, but we need to keep moving. Stop and switch places in a few hours with Xuě. When Bao wakes, come back and sleep." He turned to her. "Are you okay with this?"

"*Shi.*" Despite her inexperience driving, Aynur trusted her. This strengthened her resolve to do everything she could to prove she deserved that trust.

"Good." His gaze encompassed the entire group. "Everybody in."

Xuě circled the back of the truck and peeked inside. Her husband slept with his head against his pack, his eyes closed. Determined to do her part to get them to Nepal before Mao and his army could capture them, she trotted up to the passenger side door and climbed in.

Huan smiled at her. "Ready?"

She nodded.

He turned the key, and the truck rumbled to life. Soon, they sped across the tundra, their compass fixed squarely in the direction of the Nepal border.

# Chapter Twenty-Six

*Two days later*

Something poked her shoulder hard. Bao's scent tickled her nose over the smell of diesel. Xuě blinked, opening her eyes, and frowned. They kept two people in the front to help each other stay awake, and she'd fallen asleep. Her *yukihyō* grumbled at being woken, but it had to be her turn to drive.

She straightened and blinked again, trying to clear her eyes of the last vestiges of slumber.

"Look," Bao yelled over the roar of the engine, pointing in front of them.

An orange-pinkish sky highlighted a mountain range. It towered over the steppes. She widened her eyes. Were those the Himalayas?

Her gaze met Bao's.

He grinned and nodded.

Excitement coursed through her.

"How far?" she asked.

"Maybe sometime tomorrow." He shifted gears, slowing the truck, and shut it off. "We should fill the tank before it gets dark."

He opened the door, but she grabbed his arm to stop him. Her gaze collided with his. She reached for him. Their lips met. Fire raced along her veins, and he pulled her closer.

The gear shaft pushed into her ribs, and she leaned back, breaking the kiss.

Desire simmered in his silver eyes. She squirmed on her seat as heat pooled in her *yīndào*.

"Hey." Aynur's voice pierced the passionate haze that had engulfed her. "Why'd we stop?"

Heat zinged to her cheeks, and she ducked her head to

237

hide her reaction. Had he seen their kiss?

Bao slid off his seat to the ground and pointed ahead of them. "We're close to the Himalayas, and I thought we could fill up the tank before night falls."

Xuě slipped out of the truck and joined the men on the other side.

"How long before we reach them?" Aynur asked.

"Probably a day and a half if the gas and truck hold up," Bao said.

"All right." Aynur studied the darkening tundra. "Since we're stopped, we'll stay to hunt. The *bakkwa* is nearly gone and the rice is getting low. Besides, I grow tired of both. It would be good to eat fresh meat again."

Her *yukihyō* chuffed at the mention of hunting and fresh meat. Her mouth watered at the thought. They wouldn't be able to cook it, though. She frowned. Raw meat, but it was better than no food. She'd had many days without food. If only they'd been able to stop in villages, but they'd avoided them since the battle. Staying in a village chanced another firefight and more needless deaths.

"I'll check to see who wants to hunt," Aynur said.

"I'd like to," she said.

Aynur shook his head. "We need you to save your energy for driving."

Her cat growled.

She clasped her hands in front of her and stared at them. "I know, but . . . I *need* to shift, to feel the freedom of my animal form. This truck is very . . . confining. Driving wears on me and my cat. She would like to come out and hunt."

"As would mine," Bao said.

The other shifters climbed out of the back and joined them at the front.

"And mine," Akilina said as she walked up to them.

"Does everyone want to hunt?" Aynur asked.

A chorus of agreement answered him.

"Then we hunt as a team in our usual formation." Aynur pointed at Bao, Xuě, Huan, and Chang. "The four of you will follow behind us. Pema, Nur, Akilina, Zuhre, and I will separate off the weakest member of the herd and chase it toward you. We'll howl to let you know we're coming. You can bring it down."

The excitement of the possibility of hunting faded. Group hunting worked, but her *yukihyō* longed for the days of the solitary hunt.

*It's fresh meat and better than nothing.* Inwardly, she sighed.

She caught Bao's penetrating gaze on her. He inclined his head, understanding in his eyes. She gave him a half-smile, turned to the truck, and opened the driver side door. Without looking at the others, she removed her shoes and stood on top of them to keep her bare feet from the snow. Her coat quickly followed, and she laid it across the driver's seat. On top of that, she placed her folded pants, and finally her shirt. The frigid air chafed at her skin, and goose flesh rippled across it. Her nipples peaked, and she shivered.

Stepping off her shoes onto the snow, she shivered again. The cold bit at her feet, but she ignored the discomfort and set her shoes on the floorboards. She pushed at the door, but couldn't shut it.

"I'm changing here, too," Bao whispered in her ear. He dropped a kiss on her bare shoulder.

A different kind of shiver coursed through her body, her *yukihyō* purred, and tendrils of desire flared to life.

He stepped back, giving her room. She slipped by him and shifted. Her cat twitched her tail and chuffed when his stood next to her. He head butted her and trotted over to the others.

With another tail twitch, she followed him. It could be days before she felt him inside of her again. She wanted him now.

Aynur lifted his head and sniffed. Xuě did the same. The faint scent of *chiru* teased her senses. She turned to pinpoint the direction of the herd. It was to the south of them.

Her desire changed to anticipation of the hunt.

Muscles tense, she waited for Aynur to lead. He trotted south. The other *láng* joined him. She, Bao, Huan, and Chang remained at the truck until the *láng* were shadows moving across the steppes before they followed them.

The snow shushed under her paws as she kept pace with the others. Her cat reveled in the feel of it.

The *láng* were pulling away, so she increased her pace. A large dark, seething mass appeared on the horizon.

*Chiru*!

Terrified bleating ripped through the quiet dusk. The ground vibrated under Xuě's feet as the herd thundered closer. Xuě crouched, prepared to dart out of the way, but the *chiru* swerved east. A lone *chiru* charged toward them, its white legs churning in a blur against the snow. The five wolf shifters streaked across the steppes behind it.

She pressed herself as close to the ground as possible to blend in. The *chiru* veered to the left at the last second. Xuě pounced, claws fully extended, but she grazed the antelope's haunch. It screamed. Bao gave chase with Xuě and the two *xióng* close behind. He leaped forward and landed on its back, bringing it to the ground.

It flailed its legs, trying to get free, its cries frantic.

Huan lumbered to its head and silenced it.

A good-sized animal, all of the shifters would eat well that night.

Two points of light illuminated the snow ahead of them. A band of stars stretched across the sky above them. Xuě wanted to talk to Bao, but the roar of the truck engine made that impossible without yelling.

The hunt and fresh kill had revitalized Xuě. They'd stopped bothering her. Once they reached the Himalayas, Aynur believed the PLA would give up and let them go. Xuě questioned whether this was true, but each *gōnglǐ* closer to Nepal brought them closer to freedom and out of Mao's reach. They'd traveled for more than two days without seeing a sign of them. Would they make it?

Xuě didn't know, but hope burgeoned within her stronger than the fear of what could await them in Nepal. The truck jolted over a deeper hole, and she bounced on the seat. Her foot came off the pedal for a second, and they slowed down. She gripped the steering wheel tighter and sat farther up on the seat, her entire foot fully on the pedal again.

"Do you want to switch?" Bao yelled over the engine noise.

"No. I'd like to drive for a bit longer."

"Okay. Just let me know when you're ready."

"I will."

Driving required her to focus. If she sat next to him in the dark, the fears and worries would overtake the excitement and hope. With everything inside of her, she wanted to keep them at bay. When they overwhelmed her, she made bad decisions. Too many bad decisions that could get them into trouble. Of course, out here where only the Tibetans and animals lived, perhaps they'd be safe.

But she couldn't trust that. The attack on the village had showed her that nowhere within Mao's reach was safe. Maybe not even Nepal.

What if Mao could reach them there?

No, she couldn't think that way. She had to focus on the now. And, right now, they were almost to Nepal, almost free. Tomorrow would come, and, if the PLA blocked their way yet again, they'd escape.

*We'll be free. We have to be free.*

The truck bounced over another hole, pulling her out of her thoughts. She inhaled and pushed the thoughts away.

A long, dark shadow rose from the steppes in front of them. A light flared as they neared. It was a village.

She glanced at Bao. Since they had started traveling by truck, they'd steered clear of the villages. Was it too late?

Shifting down, she slowed the truck and gently braked until they rolled to a stop. She turned off the lights.

"What are you doing?" Bao asked.

"Don't you see the village?"

"*Shi*, just go around it."

"Are you sure? The light . . . I'm afraid they'll think we're the PLA and attack," she said.

"Let me drive. We'll—"

"No, it's okay. I can drive around the village, but I'm worried. A light came on. I don't want them to think we're the PLA."

"We're too far away for that. They can't hear us yet."

"How do you know? Maybe they have a shifter like us."

Bao sighed. "Xuě, you worry too much. We need—"

His words were cut short by a rap on Xuě's window. Aynur frowned at them.

She rolled it down. Cold air filled the cab.

"Why are we stopped?" Aynur asked.

"There's a village up ahead. A light came on. I thought they heard us and . . . we've been trying to avoid villages." Even as Xuě repeated what she'd told Bao, her reasoning sounded stupid. She should've veered to the right or left and gone around it.

The alpha turned and looked ahead of them. The village had gone dark.

"We're at least three *gōnglǐ* away. A little far for humans to hear us yet. Perhaps something else woke them. Start the truck. Let's see if the light comes back on," Aynur said.

Xuě did as instructed, but didn't switch on the lights. Within a few minutes, a light flickered in one of the tents. Eyes wide, she met Bao's concerned gaze and turned the engine off.

"What now?" she asked.

"Keep the truck off and wait here. I'll get Pema, and we'll go to the village."

Zuhre's face appeared over his shoulder. "What's going on?"

He said something in Uyghur. Zuhre's eyes widened. She responded. He shook his head. They argued back and forth until Zuhre bowed her head. When her gaze met Xuě's, frustration glimmered in them.

Whatever they'd said to each other, Zuhre didn't agree, but she left. Pema appeared a few minutes later. The two *láng* shifted and loped off in the direction of the village.

Without the heat of the running motor, the air temperature dropped. Even with the heavy coat, Xuě's hands grew cold. She rubbed them together in an attempt to warm them.

"Come here. We can share body heat." Bao's voice promised much more than just shared body heat.

Desire zipped through her veins and pooled in her *bàoyú*. Their gazes met, and she caught her breath. Passion had molded his features into sharp angles. It wrapped around her and drew her in.

"What about the others?" she asked.

"They're in the back."

"But—"

Bao silenced her with a kiss. He pulled back and opened his coat. His pants outlined the hard length of his *jījī*. It beckoned to her. Her *yukihyō* meowed and growled, urging her to mate with him.

Climbing over the stick shift, she pushed up her coat and settled on his lap. His *jījī* pressed against her *àikòu*. She slid her fingers through his hair and brought her lips down to meet his. He groaned into her mouth, and she ground against him, a moan rising in her own throat.

He broke away to feather kisses down her chin and neck up to her earlobe where he caught it between his teeth and gently bit down.

"Bao. . . Please. . ."

"Not yet. I want to touch you."

He cupped her breasts through her shirt. Her nipples peaked, aching for more. Her cat yowled in protest when he took his hands away, but he undid the buttons and slipped his hands inside. He pinched and tweaked them. A protest rose and died in the back of her throat as her desire built higher and higher.

Hot lips closed over a nipple. Her body jerked, and her *bàoyú* clenched. She dropped her head back and bucked against him. He bit down lightly on her nipple and slipped a hand between them, rubbing her *àikòu*.

It wasn't enough. She needed him inside of her. Now.

He opened her pants and shoved a hand in them. One finger slid inside of her.

Her eyes opened in surprise and a wave of sensations crashed over her like a sudden thunderstorm. Her body shook with the intensity of it.

"So beautiful," he whispered before he kissed her, capturing the moan that slipped through her lips.

The waves of the orgasm subsided, and she collapsed against him, her body tingly and replete. Her eyes drifted closed. She kissed his neck and chin, smiling.

"Turn around," he ordered, his voice nearly a growl. "I want to be in you."

Her *yukihyō* purred, and fire shot through her nerve endings, awakening her desire once more.

She wiggled, bumped her head on the ceiling, but managed to face the dashboard. Her pants had dropped down to her knees in the struggle. A moan erupted behind her followed by the touch of a warm hand on her bottom. He caressed her butt then grabbed her hips and lifted her.

"Open your legs."

His gravelly voice sent tingles shooting to her *bàoyú*. Without a word, she spread her legs. He pulled her down and filled her. He lifted her up and brought her back down as he plunged deeper into her. The head of his *jūjī* rubbed against something inside of her *bàoyú*. She caught her breath as another orgasm built inside of her, this one more powerful than the last.

He pumped faster and faster into her. Each thrust stoked the fire higher and higher until it became a blazing inferno that consumed her. The heat burned her inside and out as he came in her. A scream threatened to burst forth. She bit her lip trying to suppress it. It came out in a hissing breath. Her body convulsed around him, and she felt like she was coming apart in a million tiny pieces.

Panting, she fell back into him, her entire body as pliable as tanned *pán yáng* hide.

It had been so long. She'd missed the feel of him inside of

her, how this act made them one.

He kissed the top of her head and pushed on her hips. "We can't stay like this."

"I know," she said and slid to the side.

She wriggled and pulled at her pants, yanking them up. Her bottom brushed against his lap, and she gasped. He was hard again. Another wave of desire tightened her nipples and stole her breath.

"We can't even if I want to," he said and groaned. "Move now or I will love you again."

Xuě climbed back over the gear shift and sat. Steam had fogged the windows. If Pema and Aynur came back now, they'd know. A different kind of heat rushed to her cheeks, and she cracked the window, letting in the frigid night air. It sent goosebumps rushing across her bare skin. She looked down. She'd forgotten her shirt was open. Another blush burned her cheeks as she quickly buttoned it up and closed her coat over her rapidly chilling body.

Rolling the window back up, she folded her arms and tucked her hands into the long sleeves of her coat. The fluffy sheepskin engulfed them in warmth. She sighed and snuggled down deeper into the warmth.

"Xuě?"

She turned to her husband. A heart melting smile tipped the corners of his mouth. His molten gaze pierced through her.

"I—"

Her *yukihyō* chuffed a warning and tensed. Xuě held up her hand, silencing him. Cocking her head, she rolled the window down a crack. The shushing sound of padded feet on the snow set her heartbeat racing. Was it Aynur and Pema? Or a shifter in Mao's army?

# Chapter Twenty-Seven

Xuě raised her head and inhaled. *Láng.* Another inhale. Three *láng*, and the tension in her shoulders released a bit. They were returning and hopefully with good news.

Light flashed in front of them accompanied by the telltale sounds of popping bones. A few minutes later, Aynur showed up at her window with Pema and another person at his side.

Bushy brown hair framed a wide face. Thick eyelashes drew attention to his golden-brown eyes. Pock marks left deep divots in his skin. His tawny gaze swept over her, and he smiled, revealing straight, white teeth. Taller than Aynur and broad of shoulder, the man set Xuě on edge. Her cat hissed and growled.

She inhaled again. Something sinister lurked under that smiling exterior.

Why had Aynur brought him here?

"Xuě, Bao, this is Bantowa. He's the guide I've been looking for. He'll take you the rest of the way."

Xuě glanced at Bao. He didn't show any signs that there was anything wrong. But he was a man. Bantowa probably only preyed on women. She searched for Pema. What did she think of this Bantowa?

The outspoken woman stared at her, frowning, and shook her head. Why didn't Pema speak up?

"Bantowa has told us there are more shifters still trying to escape. We need to help them. You'll make it out safely with him."

How did Bantowa know? Who told him? The resistance?

Then Aynur's words sank in, and her stomach clenched. She brought her attention back to him. She'd forgotten Aynur saying that, once they'd found Bantowa, he and his pack would leave them. "You're not coming with us."

"No," Aynur said.

*Zuhre!*

Tears stung her eyes, and she blinked them away. Of all the shifters besides Bao, she'd grown closest to Zuhre.

"I . . . I thought, since the PLA has been so close to catching us, you'd change your mind and come with us." The words came out almost as a plea. She bowed her head and breathed deeply like Bao had taught her, trying to control the rioting emotions that threatened to overtake her.

"We were going to, but with Bantowa here," Aynur inclined his head toward their new guide, "I know you'll be safe."

Xuě wanted to blurt out, "No, we won't," but she flicked her gaze to Bantowa. His smile deepened, and two grooves cut his cheeks on either side of his lips. A knowing glint flickered in his eyes. She suppressed a shudder and narrowed her eyes at him. Her *yukihyō* urged her to run, but Xuě straightened her shoulders. She hadn't come this far to be stopped by another shifter, especially one like him.

This man couldn't be trusted, but what could she do? Aynur trusted him, which seemed odd to her, even with their previous association. Maybe he was so focused on saving more shifters he couldn't see the danger that lurked in front of him. Perhaps she was wrong.

Somehow, she doubted it.

"We must help the other shifters fleeing Mao if we can. This may be our last time before we have to leave, too." Aynur's words interrupted her thoughts. "Zuhre, Nur, and I will stay here in the village."

"Should we drive you there?" she asked.

"No. It'll wake the villagers. Do what we planned and go around it. I'll get Zuhre and Nur."

He left her staring at Bantowa. At least, she wasn't alone.

"Can you drive?" Bao asked him.

A guarded look entered Bantowa's eyes. "No, but I can ride up front with you."

"Only if you can drive," Xuě said.

Bantowa frowned at her.

Bao bumped her arm. Their gazes met, his held a question. What could she say in front of the new guide?

When she didn't respond, Bao said, "We drive in shifts."

Bantowa frowned. "I'll get sick in the back. I need to sit up front."

"It will take us longer," Xuě said. "This is easier and better to have the drivers up front."

It was a little lie. He didn't need to know they stopped every few hours and everyone got out to stretch, except at night when they kept moving, stopping only to change drivers. But they did keep the drivers up front. She didn't lie.

Besides, she didn't want to be alone with him.

Bantowa's frown deepened into a scowl. "I'll talk to Aynur. I must sit in front." He strode off.

"What is the matter?" Bao asked.

Xuě studied the steering wheel.

"Look at me." Bao's voice was soft but commanding.

She raised her gaze to meet his. "I don't like him. He makes me uncomfortable. My cat doesn't either."

He raised an eyebrow. "I—"

"I don't either," Pema said. "I tried to talk to Aynur about it, but he wouldn't listen to me. He says Bantowa's the only one who knows the paths through the mountains. I think we can find someone else. I *know* we can find someone else."

"Aynur might not like—"

"What might I not like?"

Aynur's voice cut into their conversation. Bantowa, Zuhre, and Nur stood behind him.

Heat rushed into Xuě's cheeks, and her instinct to flee stirred.

"We want to keep traveling with you, Zuhre, and Nur in our group. We don't need Bantowa," Pema said with a bit of a snarl.

Bantowa's face flushed dark red, and a muscle popped in his check.

"Pema." A warning sounded in that one word.

"If you aren't coming with us, you're no longer our leader,"

Pema said. "Perhaps the rest of us should vote on it."

Xuě gasped. How would Aynur react to Pema questioning his authority?

His eyes narrowed. "You're being foolish. Bantowa is an experienced guide. He knows these mountains better than anyone. He's the only choice we have."

Pema raised her chin and straightened her shoulders. "We're almost to the Himalayas. We can probably find someone who can guide us through to India."

Xuě opened her mouth to correct Pema—they were going to Nepal, but the wolf shifter shot her a warning look that silenced her. Pema was right. They should let Bantowa think they were going to India.

Bantowa stepped closer, crowding her. "This is the last village before you reach the mountains. You won't find another one."

The smaller woman straightened her shoulders and raised her chin. "Then, we'll go it alone if we can't find one here."

"Or you could use me."

While there was nothing overtly wrong with the words he spoke, unease skittered down Xuě's spine.

Pema crossed her arms. "No."

"You must ask the others first, Pema," Aynur said.

He was right. This decision belonged to everyone. Even if Xuě agreed with Pema, all of them needed to vote on it.

"I'll get them."

The wolf shifter trotted off to the back of the truck. It rocked a little as the others jumped down. They didn't appear for a few more minutes.

Xuě hopped down to the ground, forcing Bantowa to back up. He smiled at her, and she swallowed the bile that rose in her throat.

"Where are you going?" Bao asked.

She motioned to the shifters gathering a short distance from them. "To join the others." She shut the door.

Bantowa stepped closer to her.

"Excuse me," she said, but he didn't move.

"You're a snow leopard, right?" Some emotion slithered across his face.

Her *yukihyō* quivered and chuffed a warning, but she clenched her jaw, refusing to back down even as everything in her urged her to run. "*Shi*." She averted her gaze, unwilling to look into his eyes again. Darkness and something disturbing lurked in them. "Please move."

"*Shi*, move." Bao stepped up next to her. "My *wife* wishes to pass."

The guide backed up. His entire demeanor changed at Bao's words. She glanced up at the abrupt change in his body language. His gaze flicked back and forth between them. Understanding dawned. He backed up even farther, his eyes widening.

Icy tendrils slithered down Xuě's back. His reaction confirmed her instincts. He worked for the PLA. There was no other explanation.

Without acknowledging him, she strode past him. A foul aura encapsulated him. No matter he tried to hide it from the men, it oozed out of him like the smell of day-old carrion in the summer.

Bantowa stepped in behind them.

When they reached the group several strides away, everyone fell silent. The women bunched together, starring warily at Bantowa.

Huan stepped forward, smiled, and nodded. "*Nǐ hǎo*. I'm Chee Huan."

Bantowa bowed slightly. "Bantowa."

"I'm Akilina." She offered her hand, but didn't state her last name. Bantowa held it a little too long. She frowned and crossed back to Pema, shooting Chang a look.

Chang nodded, but kept her hands deep within the long sleeves of her coat. "Chang."

Like Akilina, she hadn't told him her last name, but Xuě didn't know it either. None of them knew each other's last names. It hadn't mattered. Why had Huan given it?

"How can I convince you to allow me to guide you to safety?" Bantowa asked.

Pema stood in front of the other women, her arms crossed. "You can't."

"Pema—" Aynur had joined them.

"No, I don't trust this," she waved in the general direction of Bantowa, "person. If everyone decides to go with him, I will not."

"I thought you were . . . coming with us," Zuhre said.

"I'll come back and find you. If we get a Tibetan guide, they'll need me to talk to him."

"You won't find one," Bantowa said. "Since Mao has brought war to Tibet, he has closed all of the borders. Only I know how to get through them."

Xuě narrowed her eyes at him. "He lies," she whispered in Bao's ear.

Bao's eyes widened, and he squeezed her hand.

"If we don't find a guide, we should use Bantowa," Huan said.

"No," all of the women chorused, even Zuhre who stood behind Aynur.

"I've led many groups over the mountains to safety. They're dangerous, even for shifters. I know the quickest, easiest route to go. I know the weather, caves to rest in. It'd be foolish to attempt this without an experienced guide."

Everything Bantowa said was true, but everything about him made both her and her cat uneasy. This man brought trouble.

"It's late, and we have a long day tomorrow," Aynur said. "Zuhre, Nur, let's go to the village." He nodded to the others. "As I'm no longer your leader, I'll leave the decision up to you."

The three turned. Zuhre looked over her shoulder at them, her gaze connecting with Xuě.

"Wait!" Xuě ran over to Zuhre, who'd stopped, and hugged her. "I'll miss you."

Zuhre's arms wrapped around her. "Me, too. You've become a friend." She motioned to the rest of their company. "All of you."

The women gathered around and exchanged hugs with the wolf shifter.

"I must go," Zuhre glanced at Aynur who waited with a frown and leaned, speaking in a very low tone, "but be . . . careful of Bantowa. I do not . . . how do you say—" she puckered her lips.

"Trust?" Xuě asked.

"*Shi*, trust him. He reminds me of . . . my ex. He'll turn on you."

Pema growled. "We know, but the men are blinded by him."

Akilina and Chang frowned and glanced sideways at the man who waited with Bao and Huan.

A pit opened in Xuě's stomach, and she shivered. Her cat cringed. If the others agreed, would she go with them? Would she have a choice? No, she'd rather go alone over the Himalayas than follow him. Even if she never made it to Nepal, she could live in those mountains with the aid of her *yukihyō*.

The Tibetan wolf shifter's shoulders drooped. "I don't like him and I want to go with you, but Aynur . . . there are others to save."

"You think so?" Pema asked. "I wouldn't be so sure. I think he lies about everything."

"Aynur goes back to help others. I'll go with him. We'll talk . . . but he's stubborn like a *luòtuó* when he makes a . . ." Zuhre fumbled for the word.

"Decision?" Xuě asked, stifling laughter. Did Aynur know his mate thought of him as a two-humped beast of burden?

"*Shi*, decision. Perhaps we'll catch up to you?"

"I hope so. I'm certain he lies."

Next to Xuě, Pema nodded. "I am, too. Make Aynur change his mind."

"I'll try, but . . ." Zuhre shrugged.

"Zuhre, are you coming?"

The wolf shifter turned toward Aynur. "*Evet.*" She faced Xuě. "Watch for Bantowa. I think he'll . . . follow you . . . make trouble."

A chill raced down Xuě's spine. "I will." She gave her friend one last hug. "Be safe."

Zuhre raised her gaze. Tears shimmered in her eyes. "I'll miss you."

"I'll miss you, too," Xuě said.

Akilina pulled the woman into another hug. "We *all* will."

With a sniffle, Zuhre disengaged herself, gave them a sad smile, and walked over to Aynur and Nur. The trio turned and trotted off toward the village.

Tears stung Xuě's eyes as she watched her friend go. The first friend she'd ever made. Would she see Zuhre again? She hoped so.

"Xuě?" Bao's call brought her back to the present.

Xuě plodded over to where the men waited with Bantowa. The other women moved just as slowly as Xuě. They stopped a few feet away from the men.

"What do you think?" Huan asked. "I say we bring Bantowa with us."

"I don't know," Bao said.

Xuě glared at Bao. After what had happened by the truck with the man talking about taking them through Lhasa and Nathula, he didn't know?

"I say no," Akilina said.

Pema huffed and shook her head. "Well, you know my answer."

Chang stepped between Akilina and Pema. "I don't want him either."

Xuě's gaze met Bao's. His face gave away none of his thoughts. Perhaps she was mistaken. Her *yukihyō* hissed. No, her cat and her instincts never guided her wrong. "I . . . I must say no, too."

Huan waved his arms. "You're being foolish."

Pema growled and glared at the bear shifter. "I don't trust him."

"You can't listen to the women. They're ruled by their emotions," Bantowa said.

Xuě hissed, Pema stepped forward her fists raised, Akilina

snarled, and Chang growled.

Bantowa's eyes widened, and he backed away, hands up. "I wasn't serious. You women must calm down." He turned to the men with a smile. "See, they can't take joke."

"I'm not following," Pema waved her hand at Bantowa, "this." She spit on the ground and said something in Tibetan. "You can go on without me if you do."

Bantowa narrowed his eyes at her before his face cleared and he shrugged. "I don't *have* to be your guide. I do this as a favor to Aynur."

*Sure he did.* He didn't even really know Aynur. How could Aynur leave them to be guided by this . . . man? Everything about him set off warning signals. Unless Aynur brought them this far making them think they were safe only to turn them over at the end. But why do that when he could've handed them over numerous times? He fought beside them, nearly died instead of betraying them. No. The alpha must be blinded by something.

"Don't be surprised if the mountains kill you without my guidance." Bantowa smiled at Bao and Huan. "Do you wish to go with these women or me?"

Xuě searched Bao's face. Surely, he wouldn't choose this man over her.

"I go with my wife."

At Bao's words, Xuě released the breath she'd been holding.

Bao walked over and took her hand, squeezing it. His expression sent warmth spiraling through her.

Bantowa sneered. "A man ruled by his woman, I see."

Bao frowned. "A man considers many things when making a decision, not the least of which is how someone treats others. These women aren't only friends, but they've saved me more than once. I wouldn't abandon them for a man who speaks out of ignorance and disrespects them."

The wolf shifter drew himself up to his full height and narrowed his eyes. He towered a full head over Xuě. Her *yukihyō* shrank away, but she squared her shoulders and refused to cower. She gritted her teeth and glared at him, daring him to try something.

"You'll regret this decision. I can get you through the Nathula Pass just beyond Lhasa safely." He spun on his heel and stalked off into the night.

The group's mood lightened as he disappeared, but unease gripped Xuě. No matter what Bantowa claimed, his nature wouldn't allow him to guide others over the mountains for nothing. He got something from it. She'd seen enough men like him in the village to believe that. The more she thought about it, the more she questioned whether those shifters had escaped. The fact he claimed he could get them through a pass the PLA had closed confirmed that he was lying. And his reaction to finding out that she was married to Bao solidified her feelings about him. The only way he'd know about her and Bao would be from the PLA. Bantowa couldn't come with them. He worked for Mao. She was certain.

She searched their surroundings for him. He loped across the snow toward the village.

They needed to warn Aynur and the others, but how?

"You ready to leave?" Huan asked.

Reluctantly, Xuě turned to the others. "We can't leave yet. We need to get Aynur and his pack back."

"Why?"

Pema's attention lingered on Bantowa's dwindling figure. "Because he lied about the pass, Huan. Did you forget what Bao said? Not only does the PLA holds both Lhasa and that pass, but the pass is closed. He said he'd lead us through it. If he lied to us, he lied about the other shifters. We can't leave without warning them."

Huan frowned. "I thought perhaps he knew of a way to get by the PLA undetected."

"If there was, the Tibetan Resistance would know of it. That's why they told me of this other route," Bao said. "A route they haven't shared with Bantowa."

Huan paled. "How do you know they haven't shared it? Why would this village recommend him then? What if it's a trap?"

"Can we really leave Aynur and the others to be captured after all they've done for us?"

Akilina's question weighed heavy on the frigid air.

"We must get them to come with us, but how?" Xuě asked.

"We tell the truth, but we must sneak into the village," Pema said. "There are Tibetans that have welcomed Mao's regime." Anger and shame burned in her eyes. "It's not in our nature or upbringing to fight, but if we don't, our way of life, my people, will disappear, our land will be destroyed. Mao claims that Tibet belongs to China because of Kublai Khan and the Yuan dynasty." She snorted. "If that's so, why aren't they invading the Soviet Union?"

No one answered her. No one needed to. The Soviet Union could fight back and probably win. Mao wouldn't risk that.

"So, what do we do?" Xuě asked.

Huan shrugged. "I say we leave them. They've chosen to go. Aynur wants us to continue on. Let's go." He strode off toward the truck and climbed into the driver's seat.

Xuě turned suspicious eyes on the bear shifter. He'd avoided fighting the PLA soldiers, and he pushed to take Bantowa as their guide and now this? Was Huan a Mao spy? She'd believe that more than Aynur.

She glanced at Pema. Their gazes met, and understanding passed between them. Pema would be watching Huan, too. Would the others?

Akilina frowned. "I'm not leaving them. Chang?"

Chang shook her head. Confusion shone in her eyes as she stared at the truck. "I . . . don't know. I mean, no. We have to rescue them," her expression hardened, "but we can't tell Huan."

"I thought you and Huan were . . ."

Pema's voice trailed off at Chang's scowl.

"No. He'd like that and tried, but no. He often sits and sleeps next to me. We talk, but he tells me little about his life prior to here. I don't share mine either. I don't want to encourage him. But, no, we met right before we joined you and

Aynur. Huan claimed to be running like me. I thought it safer to travel with a man." The bear shifter growled and clenched her hands into fists. "I should never have let him come with me." She glanced down, her face now a stoic mask. "You can't trust men, except Bao and perhaps Aynur, although he was quick to leave us with that *man*."

Yes, Aynur had left them with a stranger—one none of the women trusted. He didn't seem to care how they'd felt about the would-be guide either. After they'd raced across the Qaidam Basin and the steppes, evading the PLA, he just left them with that Bantowa to "save" other shifters. Why abandon them now? And how did he think he could escape the PLA again?

But if Aynur was a PLA operative, why work so hard to get them across the steppes? Why not turn them over earlier?

It made no sense. Certainly, Xuě couldn't believe Zuhre was. She refused to believe it. Not after all they'd shared.

As for Nur, he'd said little to any of them. He could be, but . . .

"So, what are we doing? How do we save them?"

Akilina's voice broke into Xuě's thoughts.

"You truly think Huan is PLA?" Bao asked.

Chang nodded. Xuě wasn't sure, but agreed Huan needed to be watched.

"It'd explain how easily we were tracked," Pema muttered.

"Are you coming?" Huan yelled.

Xuě looked at everyone. They had to do something quick or it'd be too late. "What if a couple of us pretend to climb into the back and go to the village for the others? Huan wouldn't know."

"How will they catch up to us?" Bao asked.

"I don't know. We'll find a way," Pema said.

"But—"

"No," Pema interrupted Xuě, "it should be Akilina and I. We'll join you in the back. When we draw even with the village—as close as we can get, make an excuse for Huan to slow down. Perhaps say you just want to make sure Aynur and his pack haven't changed their minds. When you do, Akilina and

I will jump out. *Láng* can travel farther and faster than *xióng* and snow leopards. Besides, I'm sick of sitting in the back of this truck, inhaling its fumes." She looked to the blonde wolf shifter. "What do you say, Akilina?"

The woman nodded. "I'll come." She stared intently at the others. "It shouldn't take us long to find them. We can follow you."

Chang snorted. "Anyone can follow us in this truck, but once we get to the Himalayas . . . Find us quickly."

"Let's join Huan before he gets suspicious," Bao said. He turned and walked toward the truck.

Xuě jogged to catch him. The others followed close behind.

"I'll join him up front so you can rest," he said to her. "This will give us at least four or five hours before he realizes the others are gone."

"That long?" She looked up at him. "They may not be able to catch up. We can travel far in four hours."

They reached the truck, and Xuě veered to the back with the other women. The truck roared to life as the four women stopped behind it and climbed in.

It seemed the truck had just hit top speed when it slowed. Pema and Akilina stood, their backpacks on.

Xuě grabbed Pema's hand as she passed and yelled over the engine noise, "Be careful."

The other woman squeezed her hand. "And you."

She caught Akilina's gaze. "You, too."

Akilina inclined her head, her piercing blue eyes full of determination. "We'll bring them back."

The two women jumped out of the truck and waited until it jerked forward, leaving them behind, before they shifted and loped off toward the village.

Xuě stood in the doorway, holding on to the bar that served as a doorframe, and watched them until they disappeared into the darkness. The truck bounced over a hole, slamming the door shut on her fingers. She yelped and let go just as her feet left the floor. She came down in a bone-jarring thump, and her knees connected with the wood. Pain radiated up her legs.

Her cat chuffed. She blinked several times.

Chang pulled her up on the bench, her dark brown eyes staring at her with concern. "Are you *xíng*?"

Xuě inhaled a deep breath. "*Shì.*" She shook her hand, opening and closing it in an attempt to ease the pain, and clung to the bench with the other one.

Slowly, it ebbed away only for her knees to throb. She straightened one leg and then the other. Other than the aching, nothing was broken. They would be bruised, though. Hopefully, they would travel by truck for a few more days, and her knees would heal before she had to run.

Every hole the truck sped over, she jounced up and around. Next to her, Chang clung as desperately to the bench as Xuě did. If they hadn't, she and Chang would've been flung around the inside of the vehicle.

Why was Huan driving so fast? They could easily crash.

She glanced over at Chang. The woman's eyes were wide with fear. The same fear that welled inside of Xuě.

The truck skidded to the side and jolted to a halt. The engine sputtered and died. Xuě slammed into Chang, and they tumbled to the floor.

Something was wrong. Something was very wrong.

Gingerly, Xuě stood, her legs shaking. She turned and helped Chang to her feet.

"What are you doing?" Bao's voice penetrated the back of the truck.

"Get out!" Huan snarled.

"Huan?"

"I said get out, or I'll shoot you? Get the women."

"I'm going to shift," Chang said in a bare whisper. "When I do, scream. I want him to think I'm on his side."

Xuě nodded.

Chang shifted next to her in flashes and pops. The *xióng* snarled at her, and Xuě screamed.

"Xuě!"

Bao frantic cry nearly undid her, but she had to trust Chang.

Someone grunted. It sounded like Bao.

"Move, snow leopard, before I put a hole in you," Huan said.

Footsteps approached the back of the truck and stopped at the door. The door flung open. Bao stepped back, eyes wide, and shuffled sideways. Before Huan could respond, Chang roared and launched herself at him. With a swipe, she knocked the gun out of his hands. Huan collapsed under her weight.

"Hold, Chang," Bao cried. He pointed the gun at Huan. "Why? Why would you do this?"

"Because they have my parents. They told me that if I didn't bring more shifters to them, they'd die in prison. I have no choice."

"Once you bring us in, they'll die anyway. Mao and his government don't want anyone knowing about it, including our families," Bao said. "We'd be back in that place. All of us."

"I have to chance it."

Chang stuck her muzzle in Huan's face and growled. Spittle dropped on his face. He recoiled.

"Chang, please . . ."

"Bao!" Aynur's voice split the air. "What's going on?"

A wave of relief washed over Xuě. Chang looked up from Huan, who struggled and shoved her off of him. He leaped up and ran toward the front of the truck.

Bao raised the rifle, but before he could pull the trigger, a shot rang in the air, and blood spread across Huan's back. The bear shifter collapsed face first to the ground.

Who had shot Huan? Xuě scanned the area.

Several feet away, Aynur stood, the rifle still at his shoulder, smoke curling upward from its barrel. The alpha walked over to the downed shifter, rifle ready, and nudged him with his foot. Huan didn't move. Aynur flipped him over. "He's dead."

Relief warred with sadness in Xuě. She bowed her head. Even if she'd suspected him, she hadn't wanted to believe it. Huan had been kind to her. He'd taught her to drive the truck. They'd laughed together, but it'd all been an act.

Would Huan have done this if it weren't for Mao? At one time, she would've said no. Now, she wasn't sure.

"You can shift now, Chang," Xuĕ said. She placed a hand on the bear shifter's shoulder. "*Xièxiè*. You saved our lives."

Chang leaped into the back of the truck and returned a few minutes later just as Zuhre, Pema, Nur, and Akilina appeared in the distance.

"How did you know about Huan?" Bao asked.

"Pema and Akilina told us. The women were right. All of them. We stopped at the edge of the village because Zuhre refused to go in. She insisted we go around the outside and scout it out first. If it weren't for Zuhre, we would've been captured. We saw Bantowa come in. He was met by a PLA officer, who wanted to know where the other shifters were. Bantowa asked about us. The officer yelled at him, called him a filthy animal, and ordered his men to get their gear together. We started to leave when we saw two trucks at the back of the village. I stabbed holes in their tires, but I don't know how long that will keep them from following us and they will know we're in one. We must abandon it." Aynur snarled. "I should've known better. But— He's never acted this way before. He's guided quite a few shifters safely to India. But there was something off about him this time. I didn't want to see the truth."

"But you wanted to save others," Zuhre said. "You only heard that you could help others. You thought we were . . . safe. That they could make it out."

"That's no excuse, Zuhre. When all of you," he motioned to Xuĕ and the other female shifters, "refused to go with him, I should've listened to you. And I should've known we had a spy in our midst. We've brought many through the Qaidam Basin and onto the steppes and never been trailed like this. Nearly caught four times. I should've known."

"*Shi*, but they had Gang." Pema spit. "You couldn't know Huan was a spy. He killed PLA soldiers alongside of us. There were many times he could've turned on us, but he didn't. Why did he? Why did he wait so long?"

"The PLA has his parents. They promised not to kill them

if he brought other shifters in. Perhaps he knew this was his last chance," Xuě said.

"He thought that?" Pema's bark of laughter was ugly. "Either he was naïve or an idiot."

"No," Chang said. "I think he was denying the truth. We all know his parents are dead. Just like mine and most likely everyone else's here."

"We need to go. The longer we wait here, the closer the PLA gets to capturing us."

Aynur was right. They had to keep moving.

"What about Huan?" Xuě asked.

"Leave him. We don't have time for a traitor." With that, Pema turned her back on the dead shifter and climbed into the truck.

"Pema," Aynur said, "we're not taking the truck."

"I think we should," Bao said. "The five of you have already traveled quite a distance. If the trucks are disabled, we can drive it through the rest of the night and abandon it in the morning."

Aynur stared at Bao for a second before turning to the others. "Does everyone agree?"

There was a chorus of assents.

Xuě sighed in gratitude. After landing on her knees, she didn't know how far or fast she could've gone. She would've slowed them down. Hopefully, by morning, they'd be less sore.

From the front of the truck, Bao beckoned to her.

Without another word, Xuě joined him with a slight limp.

He narrowed his eyes. "Are you okay?"

"*Shi.*"

She wouldn't tell him about her knees unless she had to. He'd worry when there was nothing he could do.

"Why don't I drive first? We'll trade off in a few hours," he said.

Xuě looked at her husband. "Are you sure?"

He nodded. "I can't imagine you got any rest in the back with the way Huan was driving. This will give you a little bit of time. You can sleep. There's no need to help keep me awake.

After what just happened, I'm not tired."

"*Xing.*"

Neither was she.

Could she rest after everything she'd just seen? She didn't know. Some part of her cheered they'd found the spy and eliminated him, but another part mourned for a person she'd thought was her friend . . . until he'd turned on them. She shuddered.

With a quick glance behind her to ensure Huan was truly dead, and a silent prayer for his soul, she limped around the front of the truck and climbed in. Curling into a ball, she leaned her head against the back of the seat and closed her eyes.

The truck engine roared to life, drowning out everything else.

# Chapter Twenty-Eight

The truck rolled to a stop, waking Xuě from an uneasy sleep. She yawned and stretched. Her muscles protested, as did her knees. Cracking her eyes open, she met Bao's gaze.

He smiled. "I need to stretch my legs. Do you mind taking over?"

She shook her head, sat up, and gently probed the bruised areas. They stung, but not as bad as she thought they would.

Darkness blanketed the land still. They probably had a few more hours of night before they'd have to abandon the truck. Hopefully, she'd be able to keep up.

"Do you want to step outside with me?"

His smile warmed her, and she pushed her door open and jumped down to the ground. The jolt nearly brought her to her knees and forced a groan out of her, but she pushed through it and joined the others on the other side of the truck.

"Do you think we'll find a guide?" Chang asked.

"We'll be okay," Pema said. "If we use the device the Tibetan Resistance gave us, it'll keep us headed in the right direction. We still have it, don't we, Bao? Xuě?"

Xuě stopped next to them. The more she moved, the less her legs complained. "*Shi*. It's in the cab."

"But once we get into the mountains . . ."

"We can find a guide. If we don't, we'll find the trail the resistance uses." Determination rang in Pema's voice. "And if we don't, we'll make our way over on our own. Others have. We can, too."

"All right, it's time to get back into the truck. There are only a few more hours of night. We could use the distance between us and that village."

At Aynur's words, all conversation stopped. The group returned to the truck. Xuě entered the driver's side and waited.

Someone knocked on the back to signal they were ready, and she started the engine. Despite her aching knees, she eased the truck into first gear and drove into the night.

At some point, the level ground gave way to an incline. The engine rumbled and worked harder. The snow turned to a mixture of dirt and snow.

She shifted down and decreased her speed, straining to see beyond the lights of the truck. Muttering to herself, she turned the headlights off and it was so much easier. Why had they been driving with the lights on all of this time? They weren't human.

Mountains rose on either side of her. The compass had taken them straight into a ravine. On their right, a river flowed. The land sloped upward at a steady grade. Xuě kept the truck in a lower gear to keep the engine from bogging down. When the land leveled out again, she shifted gears and increased their speed.

The terrain alternated between flat and a gradual climb until she slowed the truck as dawn kissed the sky pink. Allowing it to roll to a halt, eyes wide, she stared ahead.

In front of the truck, the Himalayas towered over the steppes. Icy snow with small tan rocks peeking through covered the steep incline only a few steps away from the front of the truck. It would be slow going. Too slow. The PLA would catch them easily. They needed a different place to ascend.

Shivering, she jumped down to the ground and gently shut the door. She squatted and stood a few times, testing her knees. They barely twinged now.

Turning, she studied the truck tracks. They continued until out of sight as far as the eye could see—an easy trail to follow for anyone interested. They couldn't go that way anyway. Their only escape was through the mountains.

Her *yukihyō* twitched its tail and chuffed, anxious to be in her native habitat again. It urged her to shift and take off, but Xuě refused. They'd come this far together. They'd cross the border as a group.

If they wanted to escape, they'd have to leave this area

quickly. They could hope for a storm or for the wind to cover their tracks, but the weather was growing warmer. Snow seemed unlikely.

She leaned back against the truck and gazed at the dark clouds that shrouded the peaks. Snow, but not close enough.

Off to the right, the mountains curved around and blocked her view. To the left would lead them toward Nathula Pass and India. Nothing marred the barren landscape, not a tree, not a herd of *chiru*, not a village.

No village meant no guide. They'd have to traverse the mountains on their own. Could they do it? Did they have a choice?

She opened the door. "Bao?"

Her husband stirred and blinked sleepy eyes at her.

"It's time," she said.

His eyes widened, and he sat up.

"I'll get the others." She turned and walked to the back.

The sounds of the group moving around permeated the canvas. The door opened, and Pema jumped down first, followed by the others.

Xuě smiled. "We're here."

Aynur studied the tracks, frowning. "We should've come by foot."

Pema crossed her arms and scowled at him. "We'd be far behind and the PLA would've caught us by now. However we traveled, they'd be able to follow us. But we are at the mountains, and we can disappear into them."

Xuě gasped. Aynur had been there leader until he'd left for the village. Perhaps Pema no longer felt he deserved to be their leader anymore?

Aynur narrowed his eyes and growled.

Zuhre touched his arm. "She's right, Aynur. We're here. We have no time to . . . worry about the," she waved her hand at the truck. "We must . . . go."

The *láng* nodded, but scowled at Pema, who didn't back down.

They didn't have time for this in fighting. The sooner they

disappeared into the mountains, the better.

"I say we head that way." Xuě pointed to her right. "We can walk diagonally up the mountains or until we hit a river and follow that up. It'd probably be best to travel in animal form."

Aynur's golden gaze pierced through her before he looked to the left and then the right, studying the mountains. With a nod, he said, "Perhaps you and Bao should lead. Your animals are more at home in this type of territory than ours."

Lead? Xuě glanced at Bao, catching his attention. He smiled.

"If everyone is okay with me leading . . ." Xuě looked from one shifter to the next.

No one dissented.

"*Xíng*, um, let's get our stuff, shift, and go then."

Xuě straightened her shoulders, walked to the cab, and retrieved her backpack. She'd gone from being sent to the back to leading. How had that happened?

Pride swelled, and a little fear. What if she led them wrong? No. She'd have to do her best.

Xuě padded around a rock and stopped. Tail twitching, she crouched and surveyed the small valley that spread out below them.

The game trail led farther up the mountain, but, in the distance, smoke curled out of ten to twenty stone houses built into the hillside. Their flat roofs and two to three stories surprised Xuě. Each story was built a bit higher up the hill, almost as if a part of the mountains. Below them, a herd of sheep milled around a shepherd and what looked like a large dog. A river had carved out a winding path. Foot trails, both human and animal, passed through the village. Some heading up into the mountains, others led down to the river, and one went right in front of the huts.

As they'd been traveling for a few hours, creating several false trails in hopes they'd lose those who might follow, it had taken them longer to cover as much ground as they could have. The mid-morning sun shone down on the bustling village. Its white houses stood out against the green of the valley. Who knew how many people lived there or where they were. These were mountain people, hardier than even the Tibetans who lived on the steppes, she imagined.

Fear and hope trickled through her.

They'd have to shift.

She turned and chuffed at Bao. He padded up next to her. The others had stopped just beyond the rock. Trotting to an overhang that had a rock blocking the view of the village, she shifted and quickly donned her clothes and returned to where the others waited.

"There's a village in the valley. We could avoid it, but we might be able to find someone who could guide us through the mountains," she told the others.

Even though she was leading them through these mountains, this decision belonged to everyone, and she still felt uncomfortable telling the others what to do.

Snaps, pops, and flashes filled the air. Soon, the shifters stood in their human forms on the path.

"I knew we'd find people in these mountains," Pema said. "We'll find a guide here."

"Do we take the chance, though? They could be friendly with the PLA."

Aynur's statement brought a scowl to Pema's face. The female wolf shifter obviously hadn't forgiven him for leaving them with Bantowa. Xuě frowned. Pema would have to get over that. To cross the mountains and reach Nepal safely, all of them had to work together.

"I think we take the chance. This could be the route the resistance uses," Chang said. "If there are a lot of people fleeing Tibet, the villagers must see groups like us all of the time."

Xuě raised her eyebrows. Like them? She doubted it. Groups of Tibetans or perhaps Chinese, but their group came from different parts of China and maybe beyond. How often did they see people with different ethnicities traveling together? And would that make them suspicious? Would the villagers report them to the PLA?

"What if we send Pema down with you, Aynur?" Akilina asked. "The two of you speak Tibetan. You could ask about a guide and see how they react to you."

Uncertainty filled Xuě. "Does anyone else want to take the lead?"

Bao touched his fingers to Xuě's. His touch calmed her. "I think we need to get closer before we decide. We follow the trail we're on now as humans. If someone spots us, they're less likely to be suspicious of us as we are now than as a *xióng*, some *láng*, and snow leopards traveling together."

"I'll go first," Pema said. "If we run into someone, they could think I'm your guide."

Aynur narrowed his eyes, his mouth turned down. He'd suggested Xuě lead earlier that day. If Pema was less combative with him, would he be okay with her offer?

Zuhre placed a hand on her mate's arm. Their gazes connected, and he nodded.

"*Shi*, Pema should lead," he said.

Surprise flared in Pema's eyes, but distrust and anger still lurked in her gaze. Without a word, Pema turned and started down the trail. The group followed her. Xuě stayed toward the back. Bao fell in beside her.

Xuě released the breath she'd been holding. Perhaps the two could settle their differences now. They'd been at odds since Aynur and his group had rejoined them. Pema's apparent suspicion and fury interfered with their ability to work together, but Aynur hadn't been much better. Their constant sniping when in human form had set everyone else on edge. The Tibetan's feelings were understandable, but they didn't have time for it. And Aynur . . . well, Xuě wondered how Bantowa had fooled him, and she questioned his judgment as a result.

But people made mistakes. If the others hadn't been there to stop her a few times, her actions would've resulted in them being captured.

Heat prickled in her cheeks. Memories of those times upset her. How could she have been so stupid?

"Hey." Bao's voice drew her out of her thoughts. "Is something wrong? Do you not want Pema to lead?"

Xuě shook the memories away and attempted to smile. "No. I'd rather someone led us into the village. I," she stared off into the distance unseeing, "I don't know if I should lead again, though."

He caressed her cheek, and their gazes met.

"You did well. Better than that. You made smart decisions and listened to everyone."

"But I—"

Pride and a fierce intensity flared in his silver eyes. "No, you're more capable than you see yourself to be. Stop putting yourself down."

She couldn't look at him. His belief in her humbled her. It also scared her. What if she didn't deserve it? What if she was really just a *maruta*? Her *yukihyō* chuffed in disagreement and twitched her tail.

"What do you think we'll find in Nepal?" Xuě asked. "I'd grown used to thinking that we'd be in India. Do you think we'll be safe there?"

Bao slipped his hand into hers, curling his fingers around hers. A jolt of desire and a warmth, not just physical, shot up her arm and infused her entire body. The fear of never being accepted, of being alone, and hated lessened a bit more.

# Chapter Twenty-Nine

Pema halted about half a *gōnglǐ* from the village amid an outcropping of large boulders. "This should be a safe place to wait until Aynur and I return or signal for you to join us."

"If you see us captured, run," Aynur said.

Xuĕ bit her tongue and caught Zuhre's gaze before looking around the group. No one uttered a protest, but a mutual understanding passed between them. If Pema and Aynur were caught, they'd rescue them. They'd come too far and risked too much to not cross the border and escape together.

The two set off, disappearing around the corner of one of the boulders.

Without a word, Xuĕ crouched next to the boulder closest to the village, peered around it, and watched the two wolf shifters approach the huts. Bao's scent engulfed her as he settled down next to her.

A few minutes later, a dog barked, and a man tending some sheep spotted them. The man waved and smiled, calling to the pair. A young boy waded through the sheep to stand next to the man.

The man spoke again. Pema and Aynur drew closer to the person until they stood in front of him. His tongue flicked out and over his lips, and the man nodded and pointed to a hut.

Pema and Aynur said something to him, turned, and continued into the village, stopping to greet other villagers.

The man looked toward the mountains away from the village, his attention on the sheep milling around him. He herded them up a path leading higher into the mountains, with the boy prodding the stragglers forward.

Her cat twitched its tail, impatient to keep moving. Xuĕ agreed with it. If the village proved unsafe, they'd have to wait until night to skirt it. However, from a distance, everything appeared normal, and Xuě's spirits rose. Soon, they'd have a guide and be on their way.

"Do you mind if I get a look?" Chang asked.

"No."

Xuě scooted back and gave her place to Chang.

"*Xièxiè*," the bear shifter said.

Xuě stood and stretched her legs. "There isn't much to see."

"I know, but it gives me something to do."

How long would the others take? Hopefully, not long.

Xuě turned to the group. Zuhre and Akilina leaned against a rock to the side of the trail, talking quietly. Bao had joined Nur above the outcropping where they could watch the trail below undetected should someone, or something, come from the direction of the steppes.

Crossing to the two wolf shifters, Xuě looked down at them. "May I join you?"

Zuhre scooted over. "Please. We have little time to talk. We're always . . . running. It's nice to sit and enjoy my friends."

The day brightened a bit at Zuhre's words.

"You did well leading us," Akilina said.

Embarrassed heat flooded Xuě's cheeks, and she averted her gaze to her hands. "*Xièxiè*. I—"

What could she say? She'd been proud when Aynur told her to lead and everyone had agreed, but she also questioned her ability to do so. And the responsibility scared her. If something had befallen them, it would've been her fault.

Zuhre touched her arm, drawing Xuě's attention up. Kindness filled her friend's golden gaze.

"Akilina and I talked about this. You were . . . how do you say—"

"Thoughtful," the blonde wolf shifter said.

"*Shi*, thoughtful and you showed us . . . courage." The woman bowed her head, her long brown braid slipped over her shoulder and curled in her lap, before bringing her gaze back up to stare intently into Xuě's eyes. "I think you surprised Aynur, too." She laughed quietly. "He likes to think he can know a person at first meeting, but he's not always right."

No, he certainly wasn't. Bantowa proved that, but Xuě didn't want to talk about herself. They had some time. Perhaps she could get to know them better.

"How did you meet, Aynur?" Xuě asked Zuhre.

A shadow crossed over the woman's face. "It's a long story and full of . . . unhappy memories. I—"

Xuě touched Zuhre's hand. "Then let us talk of something else."

Zuhre smiled, although sadness still lurked in her eyes.

"My family and I lived outside of Baotou in Inner Mongolia Autonomous Region near the *Da Xing'an Ling* mountains. When I was young, after the monks placed me with a family," Akilina said, "I used to join the other children, when we weren't tending our animals, and play among the ruins of the Great Wall."

Xuě gasped. "You've seen the Great Wall?"

"*Shi*. It was long in parts, but not that high. We'd climb it and jump off, pretend we were part of Genghis Khan's army." Akilina chuckled.

"Did no one mind you were a shifter?" Xuě asked.

"Oh, no. The monks who delivered me to the village blessed it before they left. The monks didn't know of my abilities, but the villagers, and my parents, didn't know this. They saw me and my *láng* as almost sacred. Only when the famine hit and the game moved farther north to avoid being hunted did my life change. And, then, the villagers turned to eating their own and my parents died . . ."

Silence fell. A lone tear trickled down Akilina's face. She looked up. Her gaze, intense and full of anger, caught Xuě's.

"I was lucky. I know this. Even though I looked like no one in my village, I was accepted. But I couldn't stay after that. People changed, and I had a bad feeling that, if I stayed, I wouldn't survive."

Zuhre reached over and rested her hand on Akilina's. The other woman nodded wearily.

"I had traveled alone for many miles, wandering, when I came upon a PLA troop. They were celebrating." The blonde wolf shifter snarled. "They'd captured a shape shifter like us at a village. A *xióng*. She was chained in a cage. The soldiers were poking at her with a pointed stick. The officer in charge laughed, saying it was no better than an animal like her deserved. I wanted to go in there and rip all of their throats out, but . . ." She bowed her head, her body shaking. When she looked back up, rage blazed in her eyes. "There were too many of them." Her gaze grew distant. "I followed them for a few days before giving up. That's when I headed west to leave China. North to Mongolia was out of the question. The border was closed. I had hoped to get to India, but Nepal will work."

"How did you . . . find out about Aynur and us?"

"I didn't. You found me."

"Like Bao and I."

Akilina raised her eyebrows at Xuě.

"We were coming down the mountains into the large desert when Aynur, Zuhre, and Nur found us."

"I—"

"That bear shifter was me."

Xuě swung around to where Chang stood and looked back at Akilina who shook her head.

"I—I didn't know. You didn't shift the whole time I followed you."

"I refused. They would've treated me worse in human form. They might've even tried to . . ." Chang didn't finish the sentence. She didn't need to.

Zuhre leaned forward. "How did you . . . how do you say . . . get away?"

"One night in the early morning hours when only a few were awake, one of the soldiers guarding me told another at shift change that if I were in 'human form', he'd let me out and screw me. Then he could tell all of his friends he'd fucked a *xióng*. I waited until the other left before I shifted and told him that if he let me out and off my chain, I'd let him." Chang bared her teeth.

Eyes wide, Xuě asked, "He let you out?"

"And off the chain. I knocked him out, stole his clothes,

and escaped into the night."

"When did you meet up with Huan?" Xuě asked.

Chang scowled. "Not long after. There were whisperings in the troop that they were looking for a shifter who led others like ourselves out of China. I thought I was so smart. I should've known I was being used as bait, and Huan was a spy."

"You didn't question his appearance?" Akilina's voice cut through the silence that followed Chang's confession.

Chang recoiled. "He was another shifter. Even if he pestered me and tried to woo me, I couldn't believe one of us would support Mao."

"Did anyone know about your animal?" Xuě asked.

"Only my master, but he never said a word. My master's wife might've known, but she never admitted it." Chang scowled. "They were rice farmers who owned a lot of land before the government took it from them and moved us to Sichuan."

"Are they . . . " Zuhre didn't finish the sentence.

The bear shifter bowed her head. "I don't know. They came in the middle of the night, tore open the door, and dragged me outside. I shifted and attacked the nearest soldier, but I was surrounded. I—" All color leached from her face. "The sound of my master's wife's screams haunts my dreams. If they are alive . . ."

Xuě touched Chang's arm. The woman flinched.

"Did they have other children?" Xuě asked

"Only one son, but they told me from the time they brought me into their home that I was to marry their son." A tear trickled down Chang's face. Her anguished gaze pierced Xuě. "They were kind to me. I was lucky."

"Do you know where their son is?" Akilina asked.

"No. He'd joined the army not long after we moved. There was nothing for us in Sichuan . . . Nothing."

Xuě studied Chang's face. Was she lying? Chang had stood with the women against Bantowa and stopped Huan, but . . . She didn't know these people very well, not even Bao. She'd thought Huan was on their side, but he'd proved otherwise. What if Chang was another spy?

"Pema has given the signal to join them," Bao said. He leaped down from his perch next to Nur.

Xuě stood and pulled her pack on. Her thoughts swirled in her head, and her heart beat an uneven tattoo. Her cat tensed, prepared to flee.

These people she'd considered friends could be enemies. Why would they travel together this far only to betray them? Huan had killed for them before turning on them. Any one of these people could do that, too.

*Even Bao*, a voice whispered inside her head.

She banished the voice. Bao wouldn't do that. He'd proven himself time and again.

Using the technique Bao had taught her, she inhaled and focused on her breathing until the panic abated enough for rational thought to take hold. Not everyone was like Huan. These people had fought beside her, defended her, comforted her. They'd become her friends, but . . . so had Huan. She'd watch them until they crossed the border to freedom.

# Chapter Thirty

Glee shone in Pema's eyes when the group stopped in front of her. "Everyone, this is Choden. He has agreed to take us through the mountains." Her expression said, "See, I told you so."

The man smiled at them, his teeth stark white against his dark tanned skin. Deep wrinkles bracketed kind, twinkling eyes. His tongue peeked out between his lips in greeting as he faced them before he chattered at Pema, who laughed.

A pungent, redolent odor wafted off the man, one Xuě couldn't quite place, and it tickled her senses. He smelled unlike any other human she'd met. She narrowed her eyes in concentration. Where had she smelled this before? Her cat twitched her tail, but the answer escaped her. Did no one else notice it?

A quick scan of the group revealed not one reaction that would indicate someone had.

"He's happy to be of service. There is a Tibetan settlement in Nepal in the Himalayas that he thinks we'll be happy in." The stress lines around Aynur's eyes had lessened. Relief tinged his words.

Chodan said something else. Pema gasped, and Aynur's eyes widened. Xuě tensed, prepared for bad news. Her cat chuffed.

"The village knows what we are. They're happy to keep us out of Mao's hands. We're not the first to come through here, looking for help," Pema said.

*How could they know?* Images of the battle on the steppes rose like a specter in Xuě's mind, erasing all other thoughts. Concern for these strangers battled with her desire to escape Mao and his forces. "What happens if the PLA follows us here?"

"We've thought of that and asked them. They can claim they didn't see us," Aynur said.

Bao wrapped his arm around Xuĕ. "She's right. It'll be hard to deny our presence in the village if our scent leads directly to here."

The other shifters murmured in agreement.

Pema pointed to the mountain and the path behind them. "Look."

Had the PLA caught up to them? Xuĕ fought the urge to freeze and turned. The tension that had a tight grip on her body eased, and relief swept over her at the sight that greeted her. Sheep covered not only the area the shifters had just traversed into the village, but also up onto the animal trail they'd been on.

"They will cover our scent with the sheep's as they have done in the past," Aynur said. "We're far enough ahead of the PLA there's a good possibility the native animals of the Himalayas will obscure our scent, too. With the other false trails we've left behind, they'll find it hard to follow us."

Choden said something, and Aynur rested his hand on his shoulder and spoke at some length. The other man nodded and grinned. He motioned to the village behind him, but Aynur shook his head.

"Perhaps we should ask everyone else whether they want to stay or not," Pema said.

Aynur glared at her but inclined his head. "He has offered us a place to stay for the night. I don't think it's a good idea."

"I don't either. We're close to freedom, the PLA may not be that far behind us, and I'd like to put more distance between us and them." Bao squeezed Xuĕ's shoulder and looked down at her. "What do you think?"

Xuĕ glanced at Pema and Aynur. Tendrils of animosity swirled around the two of them. Was Pema still smarting from Aynur abandoning them to Bantowa? She sighed and leaned against her husband. "I agree with Bao and Aynur."

"Me, too," Zuhre said. "The farther, the better."

"I agree, as well. We can't get too far away from the PLA

soon enough." Akilina's blue eyes shone with determination.

"Me, too," Chang and Nur said in unison. Chang glanced at Nur who smiled at her. She bowed her head, her cheeks tinged pink.

Silence followed their interchange. Xuě glanced up at Bao, who raised his eyebrows at her. Did Chang and Nur like each other? How had she missed that?

Pema shrugged. "So do I."

Pema's words brought Xuě's attention back to the conversation.

Aynur cocked his head. "Why did you ask, then?"

The female wolf shifter lifted her chin and glared at Aynur. "Because we need to decide as a group."

The alpha wolf shifter snarled at Pema. "This is wasting time—"

Tension crackled in the air. Zuhre touched her mate's arm. He glanced down at her. She said something in Uyghur, and his expression softened.

He turned to Pema. "You're right. I'm no longer the leader here. I gave that up before the last village. I must remember that."

Pema inclined her head, but said nothing. The anger emanating off her lessened by a small amount.

Choden spoke to Pema and Aynur and trotted back to the village, disappearing into the second story of a hut.

"Do you want to tell them or should I?" Aynur asked.

Pema cocked her head to the side and stared at him for a second, as if weighing his words. "It doesn't matter, but thank you for asking."

"Are you sure?" the alpha asked.

"*Shi.*"

Xuě blew out a breath. Perhaps now they would get along.

"Choden has gone to get supplies and prepare for the trip," Aynur said. "It will take a few minutes. We are welcome to—"

A tiny, white-haired woman approached the group, a smile on her lined face, causing Aynur to turn his attention to her. She motioned to the group to follow, saying something to

Pema and Aynur in Tibetan.

Pema grinned. "This is Amala. She's offering us food."

Xuě's stomach grumbled, and embarrassed heat burned her cheeks.

Bao chuckled. "I'm hungry, too."

"I think *all* of us are hungry," Akilina said with a laugh. "I'm surprised no one heard *my* stomach. It was very loud."

Warmth seeped through Xuě. Had this happened in her village, no one other than her parents would've eased her discomfort. As much as her parents had loved her, they had never truly understood her. How could they? They weren't half animal, but they'd done their best. Now, these people around her were fast becoming like family to her. What would happen when they reached Nepal?

Bao squeezed her hand. "Are you coming?"

Drawn from her thoughts, Xuě followed the other shifters into the village.

Every house faced south. Three and four stories tall, the houses were white washed stone with black wood trimmed windows. So many windows. A blue, red, and white striped valance covered the top of each window.

Amala entered the first story. The other shifters followed her in. By the time Xuě walked into the dim interior of the house, the woman had disappeared, and the others were climbing a rope ladder to the second story. With manure littering the hard packed dirt floor, it was apparent the family lived in the stories above their sheep. Thick one foot walls would keep the worst of the cold out and the animals protected while the heat from the animals would rise into the living quarters.

Xuě squinted at the overwhelming pungent animal odor. Underlying the animal scent was another one. One she didn't recognize, but her cat chirped. Her stomach growled again, distracting her, and she hurried up the ladder after Bao.

The ladder ended in the kitchen where the shifters gathered around a yak dung fire with a large pot boiling over it. Some of the smoke slipped out of the small hole above the pot, but much of it hung in the air around them. Strands of cheese curd dangled from the ceiling. A common sight in a lot of the Tibetan tents Xuě'd stayed in. However, the tent walls had been black. Someone had painted these stone walls sunshine yellow. A strip of maroon circled the top of the wall and separated the bright yellow walls from the cream ceiling.

To the right, four beds about a foot off the ground lined the walls.

Amala stood next to the pot ladling out chi feng into a bowl to the grateful shifters. As much as they ate chi feng, one would think Xuě'd developed a taste for cheese curd by now, but she hadn't. Not that she disliked the salty protein, but she'd rather eat meat, given a choice. Of course, she'd never tell her hosts that. Food was food, and cooked food was a luxury they hadn't had for days.

When Amala handed her a bowl, Xuě said, "*Tujay-chay.*" The woman's eyes twinkled at Xuě's mangled attempt at saying "thank you" in Tibetan she'd learned from Pema.

The backdoor of the kitchen opened into a courtyard behind the second story where they sat on the ground and ate in silence. Xuě dug into her food. The chi feng disappeared quickly, assuaging only a small portion of her hunger. She stood and returned to Amala, holding the bowl out and motioning with her hand that she would clean it if the woman showed her where. The older Tibetan nodded, the skin around her eyes crinkling when she smiled, and ladled more into Xuě's bowl.

Surprised, Xuě started to protest, but stopped. To refuse would insult this lovely woman. Joining the others in the courtyard, she sat next to Bao. The bowl of hot chi feng steamed in the chill air, warming her hands.

"You asked for more?" Pema's tone held censure.

"No," Xuě said. "I tried to ask her where to clean the bowl. She misunderstood and filled it again."

Understanding lit Pema's face, and she laughed. "Did you hold it out to her?"

"*Shi*, but I motioned with my hand as if washing. I won't do that again."

"Well, if you want to clean your dish, next time, say *bsang*. She'll understand," Aynur said.

"I will."

Xuě held her bowl out to the group. "Would anyone else like some more? I don't feel right being the only one who got extra."

Only Pema leaned forward and held her bowl out. Xuě poured half into it.

The other woman grinned. "*Xiéxiè*." She lifted the bowl to her lips and drank the liquid.

"What's on the third story? Does anyone know?" Chang asked.

To the right of the courtyard and over the living quarters of the second story rose a third one. The mountain served as its back wall and portions of its floor where it extended beyond the second story's ceiling.

Pema nodded, but didn't answer until she'd set her bowl on the ground next to her crossed legs. "Every Tibetan house has a prayer room or area. If it's this large, it will be on the top floor so that no one is higher than the altar to Buddha."

Chang raised an eyebrow but remained silent. Xuě understood. The government discouraged religion of any kind. With little time spent at the monastery and her parents forced to hide their beliefs, she'd grown up without it. The thought of any entity, real or imaginary, being raised above another struck her as odd. It was part of the reason she struggled with Mao and his regime prior to the famine and massacre of her village. They claimed that everyone was equal, but she hadn't seen this in practice. Depending on who you were and who you were connected to determined how you were treated, even in her small village.

Aynur stood. "If everyone is done, we should thank Amala for the food and wait outside for Choden."

Xuě got to her feet. "I'd like to wash my bowl. Amala was kind enough to feed us. She shouldn't have to clean up after us, too."

"If we have time," he said.

Without another word, Xuě walked into the house. Amala stuck her tongue out at Xuě.

Xuě did the same and said, "*Bsang?*" She motioned with her hand to demonstrate cleaning.

The woman's eyes lit up, and she pointed to a large basin attached to one wall. Next to the basin was a small table with a towel on it. Xuě crossed, quickly washed her dish, and dried it with the towel. The other shifters copied her, stacking their bowls in hers on the table.

"*Tujay-chay,*" Amala said.

Xuě inclined her head. "*Tujay-chay.*"

The words seemed inadequate to express her thanks for the woman's hospitality and generosity. All of the Tibetans they'd encountered had treated them the same way. Xuě vowed to be more like them when she and Bao settled in one place.

"Xuě, are you coming? The others are already outside," Bao said. He stood on the top rung of the ladder.

"*Shi.*"

With a final smile to Amala, Xuě hurried after Bao to join the others. The shifters had gathered around Choden. He spoke to Pema and Aynur, pointing toward the mountains to the west of them. Pema spoke rapidly to their guide. He frowned and responded.

She turned to face the shifters. "Choden says it'll take us about a week, depending on weather, to reach our destination. There is a storm coming, but we'll reach the first cave before it hits if we leave now."

Pema said something to Choden. The old man smiled and trotted up the path out of the village. A young boy called and waved to them, the sheep around him baaing. Choden approached the young boy, who spoke at length. The older man nodded, frowning. He motioned to Pema who stepped closer. She glanced back toward the way they'd entered the village and scowled.

Uneasiness settled in the pit of Xuě's stomach. Something had happened.

"A group of soldiers has been sighted," she said.

"How far away?" Chang asked.

*And how had they found them so quickly?*

"We still have several *gōnglǐ* on them, but we need to move out now before we put this village in danger and are captured."

Pema spoke to Choden. He nodded and said something to the boy. A young man jogged up from the village. They broke the herd into two. The young man led his group in the direction the shifters had come; the boy prodded the rest of the sheep into the village.

"What are they doing?" Akilina asked.

Pema glanced her way. "They're using the sheep to disguise our scent and trail. Once the younger boy has gone through the village, he'll follow us up the path far enough to throw the soldiers off our trail."

"What if the troop discovers they helped us?" Xuě couldn't stop the question from escaping. Images of the cave rose in her mind. She shuddered.

Pema turned to Choden. Xuě could only assume she relayed her question because the villager said something with a smile so chilling Xuě shivered.

"They will take care of them if they have to. They try to not draw attention to themselves, but they won't allow other shifters to be taken by Mao and his army," Pema said.

"Do they know about . . . Bantowa?" Zuhre nearly spat out the name.

Pema narrowed her eyes, her nostrils flaring. "*Shi.* Even if they don't find us, he may not survive. Any shifter that betrays another shifter doesn't deserve to live." She looked around the group. "Any more questions?" No one said anything. "Good." She addressed Choden.

Choden inclined his head and spun on his heels to jog up the path leading deeper into the Himalayas.

The shifters fell into line, some next to someone, some single file. Xuě padded behind the others with Bao at her side. Aynur brought up the rear. Only the soft padding of their footsteps and the sound of their breathing disturbed the silence.

Xuě mulled over the conversation at the edge of the village.

Pema had said something about the villagers not allowing Mao to take other shifters. Were they shifters, too? If so, they had to have come by it naturally because the older villagers couldn't have been a result of the medical experimentations of the Japanese. It would explain the odd scent and Choden's strength and agility, but what was their animal?

She'd never thought that shifting could be something created by nature. It had always seemed to be a curse, even when her *yukihyō* had helped her. What would it've been like to grow up in a village full of other shifters? To be accepted and the norm? How would her life have been then? Certainly better than what hers had been.

Her cat growled in protest.

*I'm sorry. I'm grateful for you, but I've struggled to fit in and being different keeps me from doing that. Except now.*

A purr rumbled through her, easing the tension that had engulfed them.

With a deep breath, Xuě turned her attention away from her past.

The farther away from the village they climbed, the more dangerous the trail grew. The grayish brown patches of dirt that had lined it near the village disappeared under larger and larger patches of snow until every patch of brown disappeared under a blanket of white. Snow covered the tops of large boulders; the air grew thinner. The hillside rose in a steep incline to their right and fell just as steeply to their left. Still, the old man continued up, his pace never slowing regardless of how steep or hazardous it became.

Xuě's breathing grew ragged. The air burned her lungs. She struggled to keep up, refusing to say anything. She wouldn't be the weak link.

Next to her, Bao's breath came in great puffs. His steps lagged. Chang had dropped back with them, and the others were pulling away from them. She wasn't alone.

"Choden," Aynur called, his voice echoing up the path.

Choden glanced over his shoulder and frowned. He stopped, waiting for Aynur to reach him. Understanding dawned on the older gentleman's face. He said a few words to Aynur.

Aynur faced the group. "Choden has agreed to slow down. We'll stop for a few minutes to rest, but we can't stay long. We've traveled a few *gōnglǐ* already, but he fears it's not enough."

He removed his canteen, took a drink, and passed it to Pema. She smiled her thanks and drank.

Taking a cue from their alpha, Zuhre and Nur followed suit.

The canteens slowly made their way around the group, finally reaching Xuě. With a grateful smile, she accepted the canteen from Chang. The cool water soothed her raw throat. Done, she passed it to Bao. He nodded his thanks.

Aynur joined them at the back again and collected his canteen. He gestured to their guide. The older man turned and started up the path again at a slow jog.

Gritting her teeth, Xuě followed. Although a better pace than earlier, it'd wear her down.

"How are you doing?"

Bao's hushed question sent warmth spiraling through Xuě.

"I'll be *xíng*. I grew soft riding in the truck. It's good to be outside again."

A chuckle erupted behind them. "You'll change your mind by the end of the day."

Xuě snorted. "I'm sure it'll be sooner than that, but, if we are to escape, I have to be *xíng*."

She glanced at Bao. Admiration shone in his eyes. Desire swirled between them.

"You . . ."

Aynur cleared his throat.

Heat prickles rushed up her throat and to her face. Xuě averted her eyes and focused on the path in front of them. She'd forgotten Aynur was there.

Bao squeezed her fingers, and she smiled. Even though the PLA chased them, hope rose within her.

The journey wasn't over, but the end neared. Soon, they'd be free.

# Chapter Thirty-One

The line stopped in front of Xuě. She swayed. Bao steadied her, but he stumbled when Aynur bumped into him.

"Sorry," the wolf shifter mumbled.

"Why are we stopping?" Bao asked. The weariness in his voice echoed Xuě's.

Too tired to answer, Xuě shook her head. She trudged up to where the group stood in a circle.

Pema was talking, but Xuě couldn't focus on her. When the wolf shifter grew silent as if waiting for an answer, Xuě looked up. No one responded. Had anyone heard her?

The long day had taken its toll on everyone. Chang leaned against a boulder, her eyes closed and head bowed. Lines bracketed Zuhre's usually smiling mouth, her shoulders drooping. Akilina sat on a snow-covered rock, leaning over her knees, her long, blonde braids nearly brushing the ground. Nur squatted beside Akilina, his hand resting on her shoulder. Even Pema looked haggard.

"Did anyone hear me?" Pema asked. "Choden needs us to stay here for a few minutes. He says he needs to check the cave before we stay there for the night."

Pema's words filter through the fog of fatigue that held onto Xuě's brain. Why would he need to check a cave? Perhaps for snow leopards? She'd noticed some snow leopard scents on the way up. Her cat had chuffed to let her know, but they were a few days old. What other animals lived in caves up here?

Before she could work through any possible answers, Choden reappeared and motioned for them to follow.

With a groan, Xuě forced her muscles to obey her commands and staggered after him.

Their guide turned off the path onto a smaller one, forcing them to walk single file. Several minutes later, the scent hit her, stronger than before. It was the same scent as in the village, but the sheep and human scents had masked it. Her cat balked and froze. Bao bumped into her, and she tripped, falling face first into the snow. She rolled over onto her back, staring at the dark clouds overhead. It felt good to lie down. Perhaps they'd consider leaving her there.

"Hey . . . we aren't there yet. You need to get up." Worry shadowed Bao's silver gaze.

"I know. There's something about this cave—something unsettling."

"You smell it, too."

She nodded. "My cat refused to move."

"Smart cat." Aynur's face appeared next to Bao's. A smile glinted in his golden eyes. "My *láng* isn't thrilled either, but we're safe. Choden and his village are yeti shifters. You may have noticed that he doesn't tire, despite his age. They have no love of Mao and what is happening in Tibet. It's why he agreed to guide us over the mountains."

This explained why she hadn't recognized their scent. They didn't have yetis in the mountains where she grew up.

The stench of the yeti would explain why it had been a few *gōnglǐ* since she'd scented another snow leopard. Such a large and dangerous predator would keep the reclusive cats away. Given a choice, she'd steer clear of them as well, but their guide had been nothing but kind. Had the villagers intended to harm the group of shifters, they could've done it earlier.

*We are safe. They won't hurt us.*

A single snowflake drifted out of the sky and landed on the tip of her nose. They needed to join the others before the storm hit and they couldn't.

Her cat trembled and chuffed but allowed Xuě to climb to her feet. She dusted herself off.

"We have no choice. We must do this." Bao asked.

She smiled. "*Shi.* My cat just needed some reassuring."

He entwined his fingers with hers and squeezed. "We will make it."

"I know."

Although she didn't know. She just had to believe.

"Let's get moving," Aynur said.

With a nod, she followed the others' tracks to a large boulder. Their tracks disappeared behind it. It hid the entrance of the cave. Her *yukihyō* hissed at the redolent odor of yeti. It permeated everything, but a cheery fire burned in a pit and calmed the fearful cat. Shadows danced along the walls that loomed close but domed above them into darkness. Animal bones lay strewn against the rough, rock walls. Although none looked to belong to snow leopards, *láng*, or *xióng*, Xuě chose not to study them too closely. Who knew what yetis ate.

The others sat in a circle, their backs straight, shoulders tense. No one spoke.

Chang spun and jumped up at the sound of Xuě, Bao, and Aynur's approach. "I . . . I didn't realize it was you. I thought it might be . . ."

Xuě waved her back. "It's okay. I get it."

No matter that Aynur claimed they were safe, Xuě doubted she'd get any rest here.

"Why did Choden have us wait on the trail?" Xuě asked.

Pema stared at her, opened her mouth, shut it, and finally spoke. "I heard Aynur tell you that Choden and his village are yeti shifters, am I right?" Xuě nodded. "Good. The wild yetis and yeti shifters share this cave. According to Choden, the two groups have an agreement of sorts. They leave each other alone. As the shifters rarely go deep into the wild yetis' domain, they live in peace. Choden offering to guide us through these mountains not only saved our lives, but could put that agreement in danger. We must do our best to avoid them. He wanted to be sure this cave was uninhabited before leading us here."

"Will we be safe here?" Akilina's gaze darted around the large cave.

Pema turned to Choden and said a few words. The old man nodded and responded at length.

"*Shi*. He has left out some signs that let the wild yetis know the cave is occupied. We will need to move on in the morning."

Outside the wind picked up, howling past the entrance and pushing snow in front of it. Snow that would cover their tracks and, hopefully, wouldn't drive any wild yetis into their hide-out.

Zuhre scooted over, making room for the three stragglers. Although Xuě would like to sit next to her friend, she gave that spot to Aynur. Just as Xuě wanted Bao next to her, she imagined Zuhre would find reassurance in Aynur's nearness.

The creepiness of the cave rivaled that of the one with all the dead soldiers.

*Only seven more days.*

Choden opened his pack and passed out some cheese curds and *bakkwa*. The group ate in silence.

Somewhere out in the darkness, a spine chilling roar rent the air.

Xuě jumped and stared at the entrance, holding her breath. Nothing appeared. Still, she couldn't stop the shivering and leaned into Bao. He wrapped his arm around her shoulders and pulled her close, murmuring soft words of comfort in her ear.

A small sliver of early dawn light slipped between the mouth of the cave and the large boulder that hid it when Xuě awoke the next morning. The storm had passed, and they'd survived. Her cat itched to leave. So did Xuě, but everyone else slept, except their guide. He was missing. Perhaps he'd gone out scouting.

She inched away from Bao and crept to the entrance to look out over the frozen landscape.

One pair of footsteps led away from the cave, but the storm had obliterated yesterday's tracks as they'd hoped would happen.

Where had Choden gone? Would he lead them back to the trail? Or was there another trail leading from the cave directly to Nepal?

A shushing sound behind her heralded she had company. Akilina's scent tickled her nose.

"It's beautiful, yet terrifying, isn't it?"

Xuě turned to the woman next to her. "*Shi*, but I'm not so scared of the mountains as I am of the yeti."

Akilina tucked a long braid into her coat. Dark shadows bruised the skin under her eyes. Judging from her appearance, she'd slept about as well as Xuě had. "That's the terrifying part. That roar last night—"

"It sounded very close, didn't it. I thought one would appear in the cave and tear us apart."

"I'm glad it didn't."

Xuě chuckled at the wolf shifter's understatement. "Me, too."

The other woman grinned.

"You're not alone. I don't think any of us wanted to meet a wild yeti." Pema's voice startled Xuě.

Xuě glanced at the wolf shifter who stood just behind them. "Are we leaving soon?" Xuě asked her.

"*Shi*. Choden is checking the area, making sure it's clear. He should be back in a few minutes."

"How do you know?" Akilina asked.

Pema rubbed her eyes and yawned. "He told me before he left. The roar concerned him as well last night."

Akilina snorted. "It concerned me, too. I stared at the entrance for a long time, thinking we'd be battling a yeti before dawn broke."

Xuě leaned against the boulder, tempted to sit as they'd be leaving when Choden returned. They'd be on their feet the rest of the day. "Can he communicate with them? The wild yeti?"

The Tibetan frowned. "I don't know. I think so. He didn't really say, but, if they have an agreement, it must be that they can."

It made perfect sense, but Xuě had never met a yeti until Choden and his village, and they weren't the same as yetis in the wild who didn't shift. Did they speak words? Or were they like regular snow leopards? Did they communicate with one another through markings, either scent or scraping the ground with their hind legs, and vocalizations? Were they more like humans? This cave had a fire pit. Did the wild yeti build fires? Or was it only the shifters?

More than ever, Xuě wished she knew Tibetan so she could ask Choden these questions.

A gust of wind whooshed through the gap. She shivered. Behind them, the others stirred. She pushed away from the boulder.

"I think I'm going to rest with Bao while I can. It's going to be a long day."

The two other shifters nodded, and Xuě joined Bao next to the cold fire pit. Zuhre handed her a piece of *bakkwa*.

"*Xièxiè*," Xuě said and took a bite. Her cat growled in appreciation. Perhaps they could hunt a *pán yáng* before they reached Nepal.

The other woman smiled, but said nothing.

"How are you thins morning?"

"*Xíng*. I am tired, but . . . happy—I think that is the word."

"Will you and Aynur settle in Nepal?" Xuě asked and took another bite of the jerky.

Zuhre glanced at her mate. He sat next to Nur. He looked up, caught Zuhre staring at him, and smiled. The smile lit his entire face, his golden eyes glowing in the dim light of the cave. His look spoke of not just love but adoration and commitment. For a moment, Xuě envied that, wanted that with Bao. No, she was grateful for what they had. It was enough.

Some silent communication passed between Zuhre and Aynur. The fatigue seemed to melt away, and all of the lines on her face smoothed. She glowed with contentment when she faced Xuě. "I don't know. I go wherever he goes."

"You love him." It wasn't a question.

"I do. He," she motioned to her chest, "made me better after my family sent me away. I was in . . . pieces. He put me back together. I belong with him."

"Would you like to stay?"

Xuě didn't know why she was pushing Zuhre for an answer. She wanted her to say "*shi*". For once, she wanted to feel safe and live among friends.

The other woman shrugged. "If he stays, *shi*." Zuhre's eyes widened. "Oh . . . you want me to stay."

Xuĕ bowed her head. "You're my friend."

"*Shi*, but," Zuhre shot a look toward Bao. Xuĕ's husband was engrossed in a conversation with Nur, "wherever he goes, I go," she inclined her head toward Aynur.

"I—"

Would she blindly follow Bao wherever he went? Did Zuhre discuss those decisions with her mate? Xuĕ would want some say in what she and Bao did, where they lived, how they lived. Bao wouldn't make all of the decisions without her, though. Perhaps she would've before this journey, but not now. Such a decision affected both their lives.

"Xuĕ?"

Zuhre's voice drew her out of her thoughts. Their gazes met.

"Choden's here. We leave as soon as everyone's ready."

Pema's announcement saved Xuĕ from having to give Zuhre an answer. Relieved, she finished the jerky and picked up her backpack. She wasn't ready to answer that question.

"Let's go," Bao whispered in her ear.

Xuĕ shivered as heat zipped through her. Even his most innocent of words could make her want him.

# Chapter Thirty-Two

Rather than return to the trail they'd come up the day before, Choden veered right out of the cave and followed a narrow animal track that traversed across a steep slope. Last night's storm had dumped five maybe six feet of snow, making travel dangerous. To the left, the mountains rose into white, puffy clouds. Snow perched precariously on the incline above them. To the right, it dropped away for several hundred feet. Any loud sounds could dislodge the snow and end in disaster.

Despite the speed with which he moved, Choden's steps barely registered on the trail ahead of them. Xuě kept her footfalls as light-footed as his, placing her feet in Pema's tracks, the snow barely shushing under her feet.

Around midday, they stopped for a short break, passing around the canteens. No one seemed inclined to talk. Whether out of fear of wild yeti or fatigue, Xuě didn't know, but the group gathered in tense silence, waiting for Choden to continue.

Even with the slower pace, Xuě's legs and feet ached by the time their guide finally motioned for them to stop. Like the day before, he went on ahead, leaving them alone.

Soon, night would swallow the remaining sunlight, and darkness would descend. Normally, she found comfort in the darkness, but the terrifying roar of the night before had rattled her. She no longer feared Bantowa and Mao's army. No, the thought of meeting a wild yeti face to face sent both her cat and human self into a panic.

*Breathe*, she reminded herself and drew in a lungful of air. She released it slowly as Bao had directed her many days past. She repeated the process until her heartbeat eased to a more normal rate. Fear would do her no good.

But time stretched out, and her control over her fear diminished with each second that ticked past.

No sooner had the last daylight gave way to star shine than their guide reappeared, a smile on his face.

"He says we're to follow him. The cave is unoccupied," Pema said in low tones.

Xuě released the breath she was holding along with a good bit of tension.

Behind her, Bao chuckled.

She looked back at him and raised an eyebrow. "You can't tell me you aren't relieved."

He shrugged.

"I know I am," Akilina said.

"Let's go. It's not much farther." The impatience in Pema's voice gave it an edge.

Xuě bit her lip and strode quickly after the wolf shifter.

A few minutes later, they arrived at the cave. The smell of yeti reached her even several feet away from the entrance. Choden slipped between two rocks and disappeared. Pema followed him. When Xuě moved to go in, her cat balked. Breathing in, she pushed past the instinct to run and joined Pema and Choden.

Darkness engulfed her for a second before her eyes adjusted. The narrow entrance hid the size of the cavern that went back several feet. Animal bones lay in piles along the walls, their whiteness bright against the rusty red walls. Unlike the one they'd stayed in the night before, this one lacked a fire pit. But without dried dung, or any other type of fuel, it didn't matter.

Murmurs rustling behind her announced the others had all entered.

"No fire tonight," Pema stated the obvious.

"Can we shift? We will be warmer as our animals," Akilina said.

Pema spoke to Choden. He shook his head and spoke at length.

The wolf shifter turned to them. "He thinks it's better if we keep to our human forms. Wild yetis have no interest in our animal forms, but Choden doesn't want to encourage other animals to start using these caves, which are mainly occupied by yetis. While we don't smell exactly like humans, we don't smell like full animals either."

"The stench of yeti is so strong, I could barely get my *xióng* to enter. I doubt one night would make a difference," Chang said.

Pema shrugged. "He's our guide. He knows his way over these mountains. We should honor his wishes."

"What does he think about hunting?" Aynur asked. "We need fresh meat if we're going to continue at this pace. We could leave part of our kill in the cave for the next yeti to find."

Pema raised an eyebrow. "You can ask him."

He inclined his head. "You've taken the lead on this. I didn't want to intrude."

She narrowed her eyes. The expression on her face said she questioned his motives. After a moment, she nodded. "*Xíng*. I'll ask him."

Choden's head bobbed up and down, and a smile accompanied his response.

"As you could hear, he thinks this is a good idea. He believes they'll see it as a peace offering and sign of respect," Pema said. "Early morning is the best time to hunt."

Xuě's stomach grumbled at the thought of meat. Her *yuki-hyō* meowed in anticipation, but they'd have to wait until morning.

"Here." Zuhre handed her a piece of *bakkwa*. "It's very little, but it . . . should help?"

"*Shi. Xièxiè*. I know we must conserve food, but—"

"We also need to keep our energy up," Aynur said. "Let's pass around the *bakkwa*. Everyone take a piece. Tomorrow, we shift and hunt first thing in the morning." He looked to Pema. "We can shift to hunt, right?"

"*Shi*," she said.

"What about eating?" Bao asked. "If we can't cook the meat, we'll have to eat it raw. I'd rather be in cat form to do that than as a human."

Xuě frowned. She hadn't thought beyond eating fresh meat. Yes, she'd rather be in cat form if they had to eat it raw.

"We'll have to do it outside and drag the animal in. Is everyone okay with that?" Pema asked.

Xuě would agree to almost anything for a solid meal. Her cat twitched its tail in anticipation of a hunt. But would it be another group hunt? The terrain would make that difficult. And would Choden shift, too? Would she finally get to see a real yeti?

Part of her was excited at the possibility, but another part shuddered. This journey had turned into something she never could've imagined. It had tested her, pushed her, forced her to grow, and brought something into her life she never thought she would have: friends. And it had brought her Bao.

She glanced up, her gaze catching his, and smiled. Despite all they'd been through, or perhaps because of it, her life was richer for his presence.

Bao wrapped his arm around her, sharing his warmth. "We should rest."

They retrieved their blankets from their backpacks. Xuě spread hers on the ground where they laid down. He tucked his arm around them before spooning her.

The other shifters settled down, and only the soft sound of breathing broke the silence of the night.

Despite the fear, the hardships, and the tragedies she'd faced, hope burned bright. Contentment blanketed her for the first time in a long time.

"I think you and Bao should lead the hunt. Although you're not familiar with these mountains, you hunt in this type of terrain all of the time. Choden will lead us to where we will most likely find some bharal or a musk deer. You can either chase it toward us or . . ." Pema stopped talking.

There weren't a lot of other options, except to take it down themselves. Her cat twitched with excitement. It'd been a long time since she'd gone on a solo hunt. While this wasn't truly solo, it was close. So close.

Exhilaration buzzed through her.

"Not all of us need to go," Aynur said. "Zuhre, Nur, and I can stay behind. I think too many of us could cause problems."

Chang stepped forward. "I think it'd be better for me to stay behind as well."

"*Xíng*, so, it's me, Bao, Akilina, and Xuě." Pema looked at those around her. "Is everyone *xíng* with this?"

Everyone agreed.

"What would you like to do, Bao?" Xuě asked.

"We can work in tandem. If you can, chase it to me and I'll take it down."

Xuě frowned. It'd work, but the thrill of completing the hunt appealed to her *yukihyō*. However, this was about survival. The time would come when she could hunt alone again . . . she hoped.

Choden spoke to Pema.

"We need to get moving. The sooner we catch something, the sooner we can eat." Pema licked her lips.

Xuě laughed. Her stomach gurgled. *Shi*, time to hunt.

Stepping outside, she stripped, stuffed her clothes in her bag and shifted. Within minutes, Bao, Akilina, and Pema stood next to her in their animal forms. Choden maintained his human form. Xuě rubbed her head against Bao, and he chuffed.

Before she could do more, the yeti shifter turned and trotted up the path. Her paws barely disturbed the snow as she followed close behind. When they stopped, the cave had disappeared. Down below them, a small herd of about ten bharal used their hooves to dig at the snow and eat the hardy grass underneath. A large ram guarded his ewes and juvenile offspring.

She dropped to a crouch, her tail twitched. Choden backed away, blending into the landscape. Bao brushed past her, moving further up the path. Their gazes connected in silent understanding. He would come at them from a different angle, creating confusion and giving them a better opportunity of catching one of them.

Sidling up to a boulder, she peered down at their prey. One of the ewes took a step, favoring a back leg. A gash darkened its slate blue pelt. Something had attacked it, but the ewe had managed to escape. If Xuě could get close enough, this one would be their meal.

With each step, she moved in on the ewe. The ram's head swung around in her direction. Xuě froze. But the ram turned away from her, his attention drawn by something else. Ahead of her, Bao inched down, circling around to come at them from the bottom. The bharal herd lifted their heads as one and bolted.

Xuě sprang forward, her cat's instincts taking over as she bounded down the mountain, the injured ewe in sight.

It struggled to keep up with the rest of the herd, but Bao cut it off. It bleated and darted back the other way into Xuě's path. At the sight of her, the ewe veered once again, but its injured leg gave way, and it stumbled.

Xuě pounced and swiped its legs out from under it. It bleated in terror as she landed on top of it. Its heart beat a rapid, terrified tattoo, and it struggled to stand under her. Leaning in, and avoiding its long horns, she sank her teeth into the back of its neck. The bone crunched under the pressure, and its neck broke. It stilled, its body twitching as life left it.

The scent of blood filled her senses, and she licked her lips. Battling the urge to eat, she climbed off and crouched next to it for a moment, panting. Adrenaline and elation pumped through her. It had been too long since she'd hunted like this. It was rarely this easy, but, with Bao's help, they'd return with their meal sooner than anticipated. Now to get it back to the cave.

She stood, clamped onto its neck, and dragged the large ewe up the mountain toward the path.

Bao trotted over to her and head butted her, purring. She glanced at him and kept moving. Once they reached the path, she'd let him take the kill. At the moment, her cat refused to let it go. It didn't want to share.

By the time she reached the path where Akilina, Choden, and Pema waited, the weight of the ewe seemed to have doubled. She set it down, panting.

Admiration shone in Choden's eyes, and he spoke rapidly. Pema nodded and grinned. Choden said something else and turned back down the path toward the cave.

Bao licked the side of her face. Their gazes met. He chuffed, and she head butted him. He touched the bharal with his paw, as if asking if he could drag it for a while. She chuffed. He picked up the kill and dragged it down the trail after their guide.

Akilina and Pema waited for Xuě to fall in behind him before they followed her.

Warmth spread through her at this sign of respect, lightening her spirits. She padded after her husband head held high.

The shifters alternated carrying the ewe. When they approached the cave, the others stepped back, and Bao nudged Xuě forward to drag it the rest of the way.

She widened her eyes. This told the others that the kill belonged to her. For anyone else, this might not matter, but, for Xuě, she often considered herself more of a burden than a help no matter how hard she tried. Humbled by their actions, she bent down and dragged it the rest of the way.

When they reached the cave, the others stood outside, smiling.

A flash of light and the sound of cracking announced a shift.

Pema reached for her clothes and quickly donned them. "You should've seen these two hunt. *Shi*, we saw them on the steppes, but it's nothing like watching them do it in the mountains. It was amazing."

"Did you help?" Zuhre asked.

Pema laughed and shook her head. "Oh, no. We would've been in the way. My animal is surefooted, but not like them. Truly, Xuě must've leapt 7 *mi* to bring this bharal down."

Uncomfortable with the praise, Xuě bowed her head and

licked one of her paws. However, her cat had grown impatient and growled.

Aynur chuckled. "Xuě is right. We should eat, but," he smiled at her, "you should go first."

Her *yukihyō* preened, but Xuě stepped back. All of this made her feel accepted and wanted, but she'd done no more than any of these others would've done. And the excessive praise, when she'd simply used her cat's abilities to hunt, seemed overkill. She didn't deserve to be treated differently than anyone else simply because she'd brought down a bharal, something she'd been doing since a child. It was somewhat insulting, as if they saw her as less than them. All of them were equal here. Her cat just happened to be built for this territory.

"Xuě?" Aynur said.

She shook her head and sat still, refusing to eat yet.

Zuhre moved to her and crouched next to Xuě, searching her face. "You should eat."

Again, Xuě shook her head.

"What's wrong?" her friend asked, then her eyes widened. "Oh—" The wolf shifter averted her gaze, pink tinting her cheeks. "We . . . I'm sorry."

Pema rushed forward, remorse in her eyes. "I didn't mean . . ." She bowed her head. "I've never seen someone hunt like that before. It really was amazing. Until I met you and Bao, I only ever caught glimpses of snow leopards. I knew very little about them. But to watch the two of you hunt in the mountains was incredible. Please, we didn't meant to make you feel less than us." She glanced up, catching Xuě's gaze. "I know I've seen you as weaker than us, but I didn't understand your animal."

"She is right," Aynur said. "You're a valued part of our group. You've saved my life more than once."

Shame filled Xuě. Her insecurities had blinded her to the kindness and admiration of her friends. She'd have to work hard to make it up to them and not allow it to happen again.

Head butting Zuhre and purring, she bent and tore into the bharal. Bao joined her. Aware of the need to save some for the wild yeti, she ate just enough to slack her hunger and keep her cat happy.

Backing away, she signaled for one of the others to take her place and crossed to her pack. She stretched, shifted, and dressed quickly, snuggling into the warmth of her coat.

Her belly full, she waited for the others to finish so they could leave.

# Chapter Thirty-Three

A soft shuffling sound woke Xuě. Her cat on high alert, she tensed under the blanket. Behind her, Bao stirred, his arm tightened around her. An unnatural stillness settled over the occupants of the cave. The even breathing of sleep changed to a silent watchfulness.

Careful to not make a sound, she turned her head toward the entrance.

No one sat just within the opening, ensuring nothing caught them unawares, as they'd done from the time she'd joined Aynur and his pack. Whose turn was it? Had anyone been assigned?

She searched the prone figures on the floor. Besides her and Bao, only six other shifters filled the space. That brought their total to eight when it equaled nine.

Who was missing?

Choden. Why? Could he be the one at the entrance?

Xuě sat up. Bao grabbed her arm, but she shook it off. Even with her cat balking, she refused to lie there in fear. Fear had gripped her for so long and so many times she'd almost brought disaster upon them.

Not this time.

Rising, she crept outside and stopped, transfixed by the sight of a large creature covered in white, shaggy fur squatting with its long arms resting on its knees just beyond the cave. Without her cat's abilities, she would've never seen it. The yeti turned and pierced her with its dark brown gaze. The pungent smell of yeti mixed with human nearly overwhelmed her senses.

All her hair stood on end. Her breath caught, and she fought the urge to run. Using the technique Bao had taught her, she attempted to calm the panic clawing at her. Several deep breaths later, she had stilled the frantic need to run.

"Choden?" His name slipped past her lips in a high-pitched whisper.

The yeti smiled, revealing a mouth full of large canines. He motioned for her to join him. This was Choden, their guide, not a wild yeti. He wouldn't hurt her . . . would he?

Her *yukihyō* yowled, but Xuě pushed forward until she stood next to him. As a human, he stood no taller than her, but, in his yeti form, even sitting on his haunches, he dwarfed her. He could easily break her in two. If he'd wanted to, he would've done it sooner. Unless he was waiting for an opportunity to get each of them alone.

She glanced up at him, but he looked off in the distance. She followed his gaze. A light flickered in the darkness, moving steadily upward. Her heartbeat pounded in her ears.

Someone was tracking them. If it were a villager, they wouldn't need light. Nor would Bantowa. Was he leading the PLA? But how?

A chill ran down her spine. Did they have another traitor? "Xuě?"

Bao's voice brought Xuě out of her thoughts. She turned. The other shifters stood behind him.

"Come," she said, "you need to see this."

She didn't wait to see if they came or not. Instead, she resumed tracking the movement of the light. It moved up another mountain across from them. They'd be safe unless—she glanced at the other shifters—they had another traitor.

Could that be it? If so, which of them would do it? Surely not Aynur, Zuhre, or Nur, although Nur rarely spoke, he'd helped the alpha and his mate several times, and, according to Aynur, the PLA had never come this close to capturing them this many times. Neither Akilina nor Pema seemed like they would do anything to betray the others. That left Chang. But the bear shifter had stopped Huan from turning them in on the steppes. She would've killed Huan if Bao hadn't stopped her. Was it all an act?

A terrifying roar split the air next to her, rattling every

bone in her body. Her cat cowered, urging her to run, but Bao clasped her to him. A quiver rippled through him, mirroring the one that rushed through her.

The roar echoed down the mountains. The light paused, flickered once, and snuffed out. Their guide nodded and disappeared into the cave. A few minutes later, he joined them again in human form and spoke to Pema and Aynur at length.

Pema frowned and said something back to him. Choden shrugged and shook his head.

"What did he say?" Chang asked.

"That is his son guiding another party into the mountains. They planned for this before Choden left with us. It's the PLA and," Pema spit, "Bantowa." She snarled.

Bao's arm tightened around her. "He's not bringing them to us is he?"

"No. Part of what Choden has been doing is communicating with the wild yeti. His son is leading them to a place known to," she glanced at their guide, "incite the wild yeti. They don't like humans in their mountains. A troop like the one his son is leading will anger them." She smirked. "It won't end well for the troop or Bantowa."

What a horrifying death. Xuě couldn't relish it like Pema, but the PLA hunted their group and thought of them as filthy animals. If they didn't escape the PLA and Mao, she'd end up like Chang before the bear shifter had escaped. All of them would.

"What about his . . . son? Will he be okay? Won't Bantowa know his," Zuhre waved her hands, "son, and people, is more?"

Pema relayed the question to Choden. The old man's answer brought a smile to the wolf shifter's face.

"It's not the first time PLA troops led by a shifter have disappeared in the Himalayas."

A shiver coursed down Xuě's spine, grateful she and Pema were friends.

"It's either them or us," Bao whispered in her ear.

Looking up at him, she couldn't deny that fact, but she struggled with the senseless loss of life. All for what? A few medically altered humans? With all of the people dying from the famine, didn't Mao have more important things to worry about?

She gritted her teeth and swallowed the growl that threatened to erupt. Every time she thought of that man, anger crashed through her. In his quest for the "perfect" state, he'd killed thousands, maybe even millions, of people, including her parents. The anguish of her loss rolled over her like an avalanche. She blinked back the tears that burned her eyes.

Damn him! Damn him to the eighteen layers *Diyu*!

If these soldiers would follow him without question, then they—

No, she wouldn't think that way, wouldn't let that happen. She couldn't become like him and his followers. She'd do what she must, but she'd never revel in the death of a person, even one that was her enemy. The moment she did, they won. She'd never let them win.

"Well, I'm not going to be able to sleep. What do we do now?" Akilina asked.

"We could hunt and get an early start." Xuě glanced down at her feet. The snow had melted on her shoes, soaking through to her skin. She shivered. "I know I won't be able to sleep either. I'm ready to go if anyone wants to join me."

"If Choden is okay with it, hunting now and leaving early works for me," Pema said. "It's only an hour or so until dawn. A good time to hunt." She turned to their guide.

A few minutes later, Xuě and Bao had shifted and were following Choden into the mountains with Pema and Zuhre for company. The hunt took longer, and the sun kissed the jagged peaks by the time the group returned with a juvenile bharal. Not the big kill she'd hoped for, but enough to tide them over and leave some for the wild yeti as a "thank you".

After seeing Choden in his yeti form that morning, his size and strength, those canines giant compared to any she'd ever seen, she understood the primal fear that gripped her even at the smell. If she could avoid facing a wild one, and an angry one at that, she would.

They ate in silence, and Choden dragged the carcass into the cave. He returned and headed up the mountain. Xuě padded behind Pema in her cat form. No one had shifted after eating. Their guide had agreed they needed more distance between them and Bantowa. Once they reached their next location, they could shift.

Xuě sat with her knees drawn tight against her chest, her blanket wrapped around her. The dark red dirt from the past couple of nights had worked its way into the material. Even shaking it out didn't do any good. Usually, she sat with the blanket between her and the dirt to protect her coat, but not tonight. With no fire for the second night, the frigid, thin air hovered around them like a ghost waiting to suck their souls out of their bodies. Although she didn't want to damage her coat, staying warm superseded that.

Even with her hat on and the Tibetan coat, the cold seeped into her. If only she could shift. Her cat could handle these temperatures.

She rubbed her hands together and hunkered deeper into her coat.

Bao dropped down next to her.

"Cold?" Bao asked.

She glanced at him. "Aren't you?"

He draped his blanket over the two of them, creating a sheltering cocoon. "*Shi.* I wonder what it'll be like on the Nepal side."

Assuming they made it to Nepal.

"How many more days do we have to the border?" Chang asked.

"Choden said about a week," Aynur said. "This is our third day in, so four more days. Of course, that could change."

Xuě moved closer to Bao, nestling closer for warmth. "He's been gone a while. Do you think he's okay?"

The group fell silent. Choden had left to check on his son.

It had taken them all day to get to this cave. How quickly could he travel? She knew nothing of yetis and their abilities, other than the myths and what she'd seen that morning.

"Should we take turns on watch until he arrives?" Xuě asked.

Nur rose from his place next to Akilina. "I will take the first one."

Akilina touched his hand. "I'll join you."

A blush spread across his cheeks. Xuě raised her eyebrows. How had she not seen this developing? Nur spoke so little, though. He tended to follow Aynur's orders without comment. Perhaps this relationship with Akilina was changing him.

Aynur handed him a rifle, and the wolf shifter got comfortable just inside the mouth of the cave with Akilina at his side.

"Who'll go next?" Aynur asked.

"I can," Chang said.

Bao tightened the blankets around them. "And I will take the next one after Chang."

"No." Zuhre leaned forward and touched his arm. "You and Xuě hunt each morning. You need more . . . rest. We're glad for this. I go after Chang."

Bao tensed beside her. "*Xíng*, but I don't mind. All of us need to rest."

"She's right. You and Xuě have been hunting. We can cover this." Pema's tone ended the conversation.

Bao's chest expanded as he breathed in deeply, a sure sign of agitation.

Xuě hugged him. "Let's try to sleep. Morning will come soon enough."

The tension in his body released, and he kissed the top of her head. "*Shi*."

She spread her blanket on the floor, and they lay down. He pulled his blanket over them and spooned her, helping to offset the cold rock floor. He slipped his hand between the buttons of her coat and cupped her breast. A different kind of heat swept over her, and she wiggled against him. He nuzzled the back of her neck and pinched her nipple. Her *bàoyú* clenched in response. She grabbed his hand and placed it on her waist. Perhaps later when the others slept, or, at least, pretended to sleep, but not then.

Right at that moment, she wished for privacy. Not only so they could make love, but she had so many things she wanted to say to him without the others around. Since joining Aynur and his pack, they'd had no time alone. They'd faced so much together, but, rarely, did they have time to spend to get to know each other. He'd proven himself to be a man of courage and honor, but what did he like? Besides pleasing her.

The thought of their physical relationship sent electrical pulses ricocheting through her. She squirmed, and he pressed his hard *jījī* against her. His breath tickled her neck before he kissed it. She shivered. He slid his hand into her jacket.

Zuhre murmured something to Aynur, and Chang stood, crossing to Nur and Akilina. Bao's hand stilled, and he pulled her closer, gently nuzzling her ear.

"Later," he whispered.

Her *yukihyō* chuffed in agreement.

A few minutes later, Bao's body relaxed, and his breathing settled into sleep rhythm.

But Xuě couldn't sleep, her thoughts a chaotic whirl.

With their days consumed by fleeing Mao's forces and their nights spent in slumber, all of her emotions were tangled in a jumble of fear, anger, and survival. Even now, they waited for Choden to return. If he didn't, they'd be left to traverse a landscape full of unknown perils and unfriendly wild yetis.

She slipped her hand into her pocket, rubbing her fingers across the cool surface of the compass she'd taken from the truck. Resolve filled her. Even without Choden, they'd push on. They'd reach Nepal.

Closing her eyes, she shut down, focused on her breathing, and allowed fatigue to draw her into slumber.

"Choden."

Zuhre's whispered exclamation drew Xuĕ out of her nightmare where dead soldiers chased her and her parents pointed accusing fingers at her.

The guide collapsed to his knees, gasping. Pema rushed over to him. He tried to speak, but the wolf shifter silenced him. Whatever she said to him, brought him back to his feet. He shook his head. At his words, Pema cussed, and she hit the cave wall.

"What is it?" Akilina demanded

"Bantowa escaped, and Choden's son, Tashi, was injured in the battle, as were some of the wild yeti. All of the soldiers are dead. But they don't know where Bantowa is," Pema said. "If he gets back down the mountain and tells the PLA—"

"*Siki*," Aynur swore. "We must find him." He looked around the cave before turning back to Choden who had slumped to the ground again. In a soft tone, he spoke to the old man. "His son is safe with the wild yeti, but Bantowa is out there somewhere. Will he come after us? Or will he bring in more PLA?"

Xuĕ's heart contracted. "And if he does, what will happen to the village?"

Anger pulsed through Xuĕ. They had to find and stop Bantowa. Even in her mind, she snarled at the thought of him. Drawing in a deep breath, she bowed her head. Steely determination fused with her anger.

She raised her head. "We can track him. How far to the place he was last seen?"

"Several *gōnglĭ*, but, you're right, we can't leave *him* out there." Pema strode to the cave entrance, rage radiating off her. "He can find us by following Choden's tracks." She narrowed her eyes. "But we can find him, too." Spinning, she kneeled next to their guide and spoke softly to him.

Tears shone in his eyes, and he grabbed her hand. If only Xuĕ could understand Tibetan.

"Choden is exhausted. Someone must stay behind with him. Anyone?" Pema asked, her gaze settling on Xuĕ.

Xuĕ bristled and opened her mouth, but Bao said, "My

wife and I are built for this terrain. You would leave one of us behind?"

Pema averted her eyes.

"I will stay," Zuhre said.

Pema stood. "No, I will. Only Aynur and I speak Tibetan. It should be one of us." She turned to Xuě. "I'm sorry. I wasn't thinking."

The apology did little to assuage the hurt of Pema's assumption. Despite all Xuě had done to prove her worth, the wolf shifter still viewed her as a weak link.

Maybe she was. She raised her chin. No, she wasn't. Not anymore.

"We need to leave," Chang said from outside the cave.

Aynur shook his head. "Not without a plan." His gaze traveled over the group. "Choden didn't come up the trail. He went cross country."

Which meant their guide knew these mountains better than he let on. Not that it mattered. They were dependent upon him to get them to Nepal. The more familiar he was, the better.

"We can move faster in animal form, but we may want to split into groups with some of us in human form with rifles." Aynur picked up his gun and slung it over his back. "Do you mind if I partner with you, Chang?"

The bear shifter inclined her head.

"Good. We'll take the trail. He may have found it and could be following it up."

"No," Akilina said, "he's going to get more troops. It's the only possible answer. He can't capture all of us by himself."

"Then he would go back to the village—"

"No," Xuě cut Aynur off. He scowled at her, but she continued. "The villagers knew what Tashi was doing. If he returns to the village alone, they will kill him."

"What if Bantowa suspects the villagers?"

Chang's question hung in the air.

Aynur swung around to stare at her. "Why would he?"

The bear shifter shrugged. "Didn't all of us recognize the

villagers as shifters?"

"I wasn't sure," Xuě said. "I couldn't place the scent."

"But Bantowa is familiar with the Himalayas, or so he claims. Would he recognize them for what they were?"

Chang's words sent a shiver down Xuě's spine.

*Shi*, he would. Or he should. Unless he'd lied about his familiarity with the Himalayas. A possibility, but being of Indian descent, he would've had to have crossed the mountains to get into Tibet, hadn't he?

"The villagers will be watching for Tashi—"

"But they won't be for a *láng*," Akilina said, interrupting Xuě.

"We can't reach the village before he does," Aynur said.

Chang crossed her arms, tapping her foot. "And we'll never reach the village, or find him, if we don't leave. All of this discussion wastes time. We just need to decide what we're going to do and go."

No one responded. Chang was right. They didn't have time for planning. They needed to act before it was too late.

"Pema stays here. The rest of us break up into three groups. Zuhre, Chang, and I will go back the way Choden came to the wild yeti spot. Nur and Akilina, you take the trails back down to the village as far as you need to. Bao and Xuě, go ahead of Nur and Akilina but stay off the path and out of sight. Should you come upon Bantowa, one of you come back and warn the others. Or, if you can, get rid of him."

Revulsion crawled over Xuě, but Bantowa would turn them over to Mao. Catching him gave him the opportunity to escape and bring more PLA after them. The only way they'd be safe from him was death, either theirs or his. She hadn't made it this far to fail.

The group split, and Bao and Xuě trotted off down the mountain. Her cat relished the feel of the snow under her paws and the prospect of the hunt, but tension also gripped her. They weren't hunting bharal or *pán yáng*, or even deer they'd seen on the mountain above or below them during the day. They were hunting another shifter, a dangerous shifter. One who had escaped wild yetis. This hunt required all of her skill and no hesitation.

Could she do it?

# Chapter Thirty-Four

Hours passed in silence. As cats, and without their packs, they traveled faster and covered as much terrain as they had in human form in about half the time. Nur and Akilina were far behind them. Whether Aynur had meant for that to happen or not, it had. The other two shifters couldn't help them if Xuě and her husband needed it. They'd have to ensure they didn't. If all else failed, they'd run.

Bao slowed in front of her. She drew even with him. Below them, in the distance, was the cave where they'd stayed the previous night. Nothing stirred around it. It appeared abandoned, but her pelt rippled in warning. Something was in there.

Was it a wild yeti? Or Bantowa?

Her cat tensed to flee.

*We're safe. We'll stay safe, but we can't leave until we know.*

Her cat shuddered and twitched before settling.

Next to her, Bao crouched, blending into the landscape. Xuě crept to the nearest boulder only a few feet ahead of him and peered around it. Lifting her head, she sniffed the air, but the redolent odor of wild yeti masked everything. That benefited and hindered them. She glanced back at Bao. His tail twitched, and he sidled up to her, the boulder between him and the cave.

A slight sound drew her attention downhill. A large wolf stepped out of the cave and onto the path. Smaller than a full grown male *pán yáng*, but not the same. Not the same at all. Snow leopards avoided *láng* and other apex predators. In normal circumstances, they shared their ranges without any problems. Not this time.

*láng* lived in packs, but this one was alone. The *láng* lifted its head, sniffed, and scanned the area. Xuě jerked back, tucking behind the boulder. Cocking her ears, she listened for any telltale movement. Nothing.

Why had he come after them alone? He couldn't capture them by himself. Not all of them. Why was he doing this?

She peeked out around the boulder again. He hadn't moved, but stood staring up the path. Taking a few, hesitant steps, he drew closer to where Xuě and Bao hid and paused. He cocked his ears and searched his surroundings. She ducked behind the rock and inched deeper into its shadow until she bumped into her husband. Their gazes met. Bao nodded and crept around the rear side of the rock. She backed up some more, her focus on the trail below them. Muscles bunched in preparation for a pounce, she waited.

Minutes passed. The trail below her remained empty. Had Bantowa left?

She slunk forward, every sense trained on the path. At the edge of the boulder, she sneaked a look and met Bantowa's gaze. Triumph flared in his eyes, and he spun, sprinting down the mountain. A growl erupted from her. He wouldn't escape.

Bao streaked past her. His powerful strides eating up the distance between him and the wolf shifter. Was Bantowa slowing down on purpose? Right as Bao reached him, Bantowa faced him, snarling and snapping. Bao swiped a paw across the wolf's face, and the wolf yelped, jumping back. Her husband pounced. The two animals rolled down the path, stopping in front of the cave. Snarls, growls, and high-pitched barks shattered the quiet. They bounded apart. Blood trickled from Bao's shoulder, but deep gouges extended the length of the *láng's* stomach. They circled each other, Bao's tail twitching.

Fear and anger coursed through Xuě, galvanizing her into action. She ran above the trail, leaping down from the top of the cave, coming at Bantowa from behind. The *láng* swung around and charged at her. A growl rolled through her, and she leaped out of the way of his snapping teeth, lashing out, and slashed his side with her claws. He yowled and sprang sideways, skidding across the ground to the rim of the path. Bao attacked, smacking him across his face. Bantowa reared back. Red droplets splattered the snow. His claws scrabbled for purchase, but the snow gave way under his weight. His eyes widened, and terror washed over his face. He slid backward over the ledge and vanished. His howl grew fainter and fainter until only an echo remained.

Above them, the mountain rumbled. The ground trembled under her feet.

An avalanche.

She whipped around and raced through the boulders and into the cave with Bao on her heels. They skidded inside right before a huge sheet of snow crashed over where they'd been standing. It undulated down the mountain with a thunderous roar.

Xuě huddled next to Bao in the cave, watching massive amounts of snow roll past. As it rushed farther down the mountain, the sound became an echo. But the shaking of the ground transferred itself to her body, and she couldn't control the tremors that raced through her, chased by relief for the gravity of what they'd barely escaped.

They'd killed Bantowa together and nearly died. A pile of snow partially blocked the entrance, but they were still alive.

Still alive.

Awe rose within her, filling her and rippling across her pelt. How many times had they escaped death on their trek? Five? Six? How many more times would they have to cheat death before they escaped?

Hopefully none.

A shudder wracked her body, starting at the base of her skull and extending to the tip of her tail. She gulped deep breaths, struggling to bring her emotions under control.

Bao headbutted her and licked her face. His concerned gaze drew her in. She leaned into him, his calm presence comforting her.

Suddenly, the desire to make love to him, to reaffirm life, roared through her. Her cat meowed and chuffed.

*It's too cold. We need to return and tell everyone what happened.*

Despite her thoughts, the desire grew in intensity. She steeled herself against the urges coursing through her. Not only would the dirt stain her skin red, but she'd freeze.

As if to confirm that last bit, she sighed, and her breath created white puffs that hovered in the air in front of them.

*Definitely too cold.*

She rubbed against her husband and padded toward the entrance. He bumped her and licked her face. Their gazes met, his full of promises that warmed her insides and sent tingles rushing through her. Her cat meowed, refusing to leave. The scent of his pheromones overruled her reluctance, but it was too cold to shift.

*As a cat?*

Her cat purred. Bao rubbed against her. She rubbed against him and let her *yukihyō* take over.

Later, she climbed over the snow and out into the late afternoon.

No longer worried about being tracked, Xuě trotted up the trail at a ground eating pace shoulder to shoulder with her husband. Her spirits soared.

Four more days. Four more days and they'd reach Nepal.

A few hours later, they ran into Nur and Akilina. Unable to shift, she couldn't share the news, but the wolf shifters smiled at the sight of them. Xuě rubbed up against Akilina and started back up the trail.

"Xuě?"

Akilina's voice stopped her. She turned back.

"Did you find Bantowa?"

Xuě nodded.

"Is he—"

Xuě nodded.

Nur raised his eyebrows. "How?" His voice rose in disbelief.

Another shifter who viewed her as a liability. When would that change?

"*Shi!*" Akilina spun and strode up the path. "We must tell the others."

Nur shook his head. "But two snow leopards against a wolf?"

"They may be elusive animals, but they are cats with claws. Sharp claws. Against a pack, alone, a snow leopard would struggle, but one of them against one wolf? And two? The *láng* doesn't stand a chance. Think about it. A snow leopard can take down a bharal all by itself. It takes a pack of *láng* to do it as easily as they do."

Nur shook his head. "It's still a stretch."

The blonde wolf shifter stopped, hands on hips. "Really? If you had to face a cat with sharp claws who could jump 7 plus *mǐ* alone, who do you think would win?" She poked him in the chest.

Nur rubbed at the spot and frowned. "I—" He turned. His gaze met Xuě's. She glared at him. His eyes widened. "*Shi*, you're right. Why have any of us thought Xuě, or Bao, are not as strong?"

"Because we didn't understand them."

"I don't know. They struggled against humans."

"They did? Which one of us saved Aynur."

"Well, we weren't there."

Akilina raised her hands in exasperation and continued up the path, shaking her head. "Fine. And in the cave? Who knew Aynur and Bao were in trouble?"

"Yeah, but that's not strength. That's—"

Uncomfortable heat prickled along Xuě's pelt as embarrassment and anger replaced the elation of defeating an enemy. To be talked about as if they couldn't understand them . . . She twitched her tail and pushed ahead of them. If a snow leopard could stomp, she would've. Of course, they didn't stomp. Her footsteps made nary a sound. It didn't stop the maelstrom of emotions swirling inside of her. Listening to them had stirred up all of the insecurities she'd battled since her parents had adopted her and she'd discovered how different she was from everyone else. Always found lacking no matter what she did. When would all of them recognize her worth? Who had brought them a bharal this morning? Certainly not Nur.

She wasn't a *maruta* and never had been. Nor would she ever allow herself to think that way again. Anyone who viewed her that way could catch their own food.

Bao caught up to her and bumped her shoulder. Their gazes met. He rolled his eyes. Laughter bubbled through her. Silly of them. The *láng* had been surprisingly easy to kill. He hadn't tried to escape, but rather he'd turned to fight them.

The question of why he'd come after them alone rose up again.

Nur's voice carried to them, even though Xuě tried to ignore him. "We were stupid to ever think these two were weak links."

"You thought they were. *I* never did."

"Sure—"

"I didn't. That was Pema. Pema sees anyone who shows the slightest hesitation as weak. I don't. Everyone has their strengths. We're lucky to have them with us."

Tired of listening to them bicker, Xuě picked up her pace and increased the distance between herself and Akilina and Nur. The need to shift and talk pushed her forward.

The sooner they joined Pema and Choden, the better.

Exhaustion dogged her steps by the time they reached the cave. Stars twinkled in a moonless sky. Her stomach growled, but the body's yearning for sleep overshadowed the hunger gnawing at her. She wanted to drop down on the floor of the cave and close her eyes.

Pema waited at the entrance of the cave. As soon as she saw them, she strode toward them. "Xuě! Bao! Where's Nur and Akilina?"

Xuě sat and blinked at her. She had to shift before she could answer any questions.

"Oh, come inside. You can't shift out here."

Xuě hesitated at the mouth of the cave. She searched for Choden. Would he be okay with her shifting inside? Their gazes met. The old man flicked his tongue out in greeting and nodded his head.

She padded over to her backpack and retreated farther into the darkness. She shifted and dressed quickly, nestling into the warmth of her coat.

"Aynur and the others haven't returned yet?" she asked Pema.

"No."

Bao trotted past them into the depths, shifted, dressed, and returned to her side. Lines of worry and fatigue bracketed his mouth. She wanted to reach out and smooth them away. Instead, she linked her fingers through his. He looked down at her and smiled, squeezing her fingers.

Pema paced back and forth in front of them. "What happened?" She didn't even stop when she asked the question. Her impatience was palpable.

Bao looked at Xuě and inclined his head.

"Bantowa is dead," Xuě said.

The wolf shifter stilled. The tension flowed out of her. "He's gone?"

"*Shi.*"

"How? Where did you find him?"

Xuě glanced at Bao. He motioned for her to continue. "He discovered the cave we stayed in last night."

Pema started. "Already?"

"*Shi.* He'd shifted and tracked us in *láng* form. We fought. He slipped off the trail. His howl set off an avalanche." Pema gasped. "Bao and I got in the cave before it hit. Bantowa didn't."

Eyes wide and grinning, Pema jumped up. "*Shi!* One less Mao puppet."

Xuě flinched. Bantowa had been a threat to them. While his death removed one more barrier to escaping, she couldn't rejoice in his death.

Bao rubbed her arm. "How're you doing?"

She met his concerned gaze. "I'm—" How was she doing? She drew in a deep breath and stilled her mind as Bao had taught her, or tried. Scenes of the past couple of weeks kept crowding in. Her parents' faces, the gun shots, the first man she'd killed, Gang, the death screams, the battle, Bantowa's death, and the avalanche. The enormity of what they'd faced swept over her like a flash flood.

Her legs threatened to buckle, and she leaned against the wall. The room spun, and darkness crowded in at the edge of her vision. Little white dots floated in front of her.

Perhaps she should sit.

"Hey."

Bao's voice came from far away.

She swayed and slid down the wall. Resting her forehead on her bent knees, she focused on taking deep breaths and keeping the darkness at bay.

Bao crouched and rubbed her back. "*Liàn rén.*"

His whispered endearment startled and pleased her. She raised her head.

He caressed her cheek. "Do you need anything?"

Unable to speak, she shook her head.

"Are you sure?"

All of a sudden, the grief she'd buried since losing her parents engulfed her. Tears burned her eyes. A sob stuck in her throat. She tried to stop the rioting emotions, but they spilled out. Heat flushed her body, and the cold froze the salty droplets on her cheeks. She swiped at them.

He pulled her into his arms. "It's okay. Let it out. I'm here. I'll always be here."

But could he always be there? He could've died any number of times during their trek. It could've been him who'd slipped over the side and been buried by the avalanche instead of Bantowa. Tomorrow, something could trigger an avalanche while they were on the trail and sweep him away from her. Even if she crossed the border of Nepal, he might not. And, if he didn't, could she go on?

The thought of losing him shot a searing pain through her chest, and she gasped. Another sob wracked her. She couldn't lose him, not her Bao, not her *liàn rén*.

She clung to him and buried her face against his chest. This man was her life. She wouldn't let him die.

He nuzzled her hair. "You are my *xīngān*. I won't let anything happen to you."

His heart and soul. She was his heart and soul.

Love meant very little in marriage and was rare. People didn't marry for love, and she'd never expected it. Marriage was for children and bringing families together, but, somehow, he loved her.

And she loved him.

*She* loved *him*.

The wonder of the realization stalled any words she might have said. Instead, she drew his face down and kissed him with all of the passion that thrummed through her. His mouth opened, and she slipped her tongue inside. A moan escaped her. She wanted more, needed to be closer.

Someone coughed, breaking the spell.

Embarrassed heat burned her cheeks, and she pulled back.

Love glowed in his beautiful, silver eyes. He gently kissed her forehead and drew her back into his arms. She breathed in his scent, and contentment settled over her. The worries melted away replaced by determination.

Nothing would stop them from creating a new life together in Nepal. Nothing.

# Chapter Thirty-Five

"Pema says Bantowa is dead," Aynur said the following morning.

Bao's arm tightened around her. "*Shi.*"

"Why would he come after us alone?"

Xuě had wondered the same thing. "I don't know."

"Why would a shifter side with Mao?" Pema asked. "He was a *chǔnlǘ.*"

Zuhre leaned over to Xuě. "What does . . . *chǔnlǘ* mean?"

Xuě raised her eyebrows. "It's stupid donkey, idiot."

Her eyes widened. "Ah . . . Pema is . . ."

"Fierce." Xuě considered saying "volatile", but the wolf shifter had become a friend. Her loyalty and nerves of steel more than made up for any volatile emotions. She never rushed in without thought, but her temper flared to life with little provocation.

Zuhre smiled. "*Shi*, fierce is a good word for her."

"What happened with the wild yeti?"

A frown clouded her friend's expression. "They were not . . . friendly, but Tashi stopped them from . . ." She looked to Aynur who sat on the other side of the cave next to Nur.

As if sensing his mate's gaze on him, he halted in mid-sentence and glanced at Zuhre. A corner of his mouth tilted up in a half smile. She motioned to him. He rose and joined them. Sliding his hand down Zuhre's back, he kissed her temple.

"You needed me?"

"Xuě asked about Tashi."

He pressed his lips together and frowned. With a sigh, he said, "Tashi is okay, but the wild yeti aren't happy we're here. They won't attack us, but," he looked around at the others, "we need to get to Nepal. They blame us for the soldiers and the injured yeti. Today will be our last day of rest. I would have us push on, but Choden needs to recover, and so do we."

"They'd be right," Bao said. "The soldiers followed us. Without us . . ."

"But we didn't lead the soldiers to the yeti."

Akilina's comment resonated with Xuě. Yes, the soldiers were tracking them, but the village led them to the wild yeti who attacked. Still, Bao was right, they did bear some responsibility. Maybe not all, but some.

"Will the injured be okay? Should we try to help them?" Xuě asked.

"No. They wouldn't welcome it. Better for us to do as we've been doing." Aynur turned to Xuě and Bao. "Do you think you can hunt tomorrow morning?"

"Perhaps we can hunt tonight and in the morning? Leave a bigger peace offering?" Xuě glanced at Bao. What did he think?

"I think that's a good idea. We can eat more and leave an entire animal to the yetis," Bao said.

"I don't think Choden is up to it," Pema said.

Choden slept on the floor. He'd outpaced them easily the first three days. The stress of his son being injured and the cross country trek must've worn him out, but he refused to return home until he'd led them to the Tibetan refugee camp in Nepal.

"Do we need him?" Xuě asked.

"I," the wolf shifter looked at the sleeping yeti shifter, "I don't know."

"Xuě and I can find our way back here," Bao said. "We can head up the track. If there aren't any bharal or deer within a few gōnglǐ, we'll return."

No one offered to join them, not that it mattered. Xuě relished more alone time with Bao, even if in cat form and unable to talk.

Bao stood. Xuě followed him deeper into the cave. They shifted and padded out into the light. As if he could read her mind, they swung right, taking them deeper into the Himalayas.

A *gōnglǐ* slipped by. They closed in on the second one when she spotted a herd of bharal grazing below them. Bao crouched next to her. He must've seen them at the same time. She hunkered down. One large male, four females, and a few juvenile. The sheep dug into the snow, searching for the grass underneath.

Bao continued straight ahead. Veering left, Xuě crept straight down toward the herd. She placed each step carefully to prevent dislodging any loose pebbles and alerting the prey below.

Step by step, she drew closer to them. One grazed a little closer to her than the others. She zeroed in on it. Her muscles bunching under her, she launched herself forward at full speed. The herd bolted downhill. Bao came sprinting down from the other direction. They swerved back toward Xuě. One fell behind as the others raced down the mountain. It zigzagged in front of Xuě, its scent exciting her *yukihyō*.

Gathering her legs under her, she pounced. She dug claws into its back. It stumbled under the impact, and the two rolled further down the hill. The bharal shook her off and clambered away toward a ledge. But she'd slowed it down, and Bao was upon it. It leapt. Bao lunged after it, sinking his claws into its back and latching onto the nape of its neck. His weight didn't stop the forward momentum. Her husband and the bharal disappeared.

Xuě's heart lodged itself in her throat. She charged to the edge, skidding to a halt. Below her, the two twisted and turned in a freefall. They bounced off the side. Bao managed to stay on top of the animal. They hit the incline with a bone jarring impact. The bharal took the brunt of the fall, but they landed in a chute and continued to roll further down the slope, over and over. The sheep got to its feet, trying to break free, but Bao clung to it, dragging it down. The bharal's legs buckled. Their struggle sent them tumbling farther down, finally slamming into a dark boulder a few hundred feet below. Neither moved.

*Bao!*

Xuě meowed in distress and paced along the ledge, looking

for a way down to him. She jumped to a narrow outcropping. Snow slipped under her paws, and she scrambled to stay on it before inching down to a skinny ledge. Gathering her muscles under her, she leapt to a rock about the size of an offering bowl. After every jump, she paused to glance at where the two had come to rest, searching for any sign of life. The longer the two lay unmoving, the more frantic she grew.

Breathing deeply, she brought her panic under control. She focused on the descent. If she fell, she'd be of no help to Bao. From one rock to an outcropping to a sliver of a ledge, she slowly made her way down. When she landed that last leap, she hit at a full-on run. The ground flew under her feet as she raced to where her husband and the sheep lay.

Its head at an odd angle, the bharal was dead, but Bao's chest rose and fell.

He was alive.

She licked his face and chuffed. Inhaling, she searched for injuries. Nothing that she could sense or smell. She meowed and licked his face again. He didn't respond.

This couldn't happen. He'd promised to never leave her. He couldn't—he couldn't die. Not now. Not. Now. Not ever.

Panic seized her, and she pushed at him.

*Up! Damn it! Up!*

She pushed him so hard he slid a little across the ground. He moaned. Encouraged, she head butted and groomed him.

*Bao . . .*

His paw twitched, and his eyes fluttered open. Joy shot through her. He shook his head and blinked. On wobbly legs, he managed to stand, but quickly sat back down. He sat there for several minutes, breathing deeply and staring straight ahead of him. Xuě meowed at him and rubbed against him gently. He leaned into her. Sitting, she let him rest against her and waited for him to make the next move.

Minutes passed before he stood. He walked around as if testing his body, checking for injuries. When he came back to her, he bumped her and turned to look up at the cliff.

They wouldn't be able to carry the bharal up that.

The cliff extended for a hundred or so feet either way. Beyond it, the incline rose sharply on both sides. Dragging this carcass back to the cave seemed impossible, but she would do it.

Determination flowed through her. She bent to grab the neck of the bharal with her mouth and bumped heads with Bao. Putting her paw on the sheep, she pushed down when he tried to lift it. He looked at her, and she shook her head. He bent down again. She growled at him. Eyes wide, he backed away. With a nod, she grabbed the animal by its neck and dragged it across the snow covered ground. It slid with relative ease once she got up to speed.

On the way up the hill, she rested every 7 *mi* or so. Each time she set it down, Bao tried to help. She growled at him, and he'd back away. He'd nearly died to catch this. She wasn't taking any chances. He needed the rest.

By the time she deposited the carcass on the trail, her muscles shook from the strain. Relief washed over her. Although a long ways out, the rest was easy compared to what they'd just done. This time, when Bao reached for his kill, she let him take it.

They started down the trail. Unease inched up her spine. Nothing stirred, only snow and rocks as far as the eye could see. Bao slowed his pace. Soon, they stopped. She glanced over her shoulder.

Nothing.

She searched the mountain above them. Something moved. Something large and white.

Her cat froze.

A chill wind swept down the hill redolent with the scent of yeti. It roared, and her fur stood up. They couldn't escape it if they dragged the dead bharal. Perhaps they would give their peace offering tonight instead of in the morning.

The yeti bounded down the hillside toward them. Bao placed himself between her and it. She twitched her tail, but now wasn't the time to argue.

They backed away, leaving the hard won kill to the beast.

It sprang onto the path and cocked its head at them. It bent down, ripped a hind leg off the sheep as if tearing a piece of paper, blood spraying all over the snow, and tossed it at them.

Xuě jumped back, unsure what the yeti was doing. It ripped another hind leg off and threw that at them, too. Then, it bent down, tossed the sheep up on its shoulder, and nimbly ran down the hill. Blood dripped down its back.

The speed and ease in which it traversed the steep slope left her breathless. They couldn't have fought it, even rested.

A shiver coursed through her. Bao chuffed. Their gazes met, his reflecting the astonishment she felt.

What had just happened? Had they met a wild yeti?

Glad to have escaped a battle of any kind, she grabbed a leg. Bao picked up the other one, and they headed back to the cave. Her thoughts swirled in her head, trying to make sense of the past hour or so.

Would the others believe their story? Did she? If she hadn't felt the shifting of the snow under her paws and the sharp tang of blood on her tongue, she'd think she was hallucinating.

Hysterical laughter bubbled up and erupted as a weird meow. Bao glanced at her, but she kept her focus on the trail in front of them. In cat form, she couldn't tell him what was going on in her head. Honestly, she didn't know if she'd be able to tell him at that moment anyway. It all seemed a little too much like a fairytale parents told their children to keep them inside.

Without the whole body to drag, the trip to the cave passed quickly and without incident. Bao slipped through the entrance before her, dropped the haunch a few feet in, and padded over to their backpacks where he shifted and dressed.

Oh, to have a fire and eat cooked meat again. But not tonight. Maybe not until they crossed into Nepal.

She placed her portion on the ground next to Bao's, trotted deep into the cave to shift and dress. As soon as she came back to the front where everyone congregated, Aynur hurried up to them.

"What happened?"

Should they tell everyone about Bao's fall? She glanced at Bao, leaving the decision up to him.

"We met up with a yeti on the way back," her husband said.

Everyone's eyes widened. A few gasped.

"It roared at us." Xuě shuddered at the memory. "We decided we'd let it have it."

"How'd you end up with these?" Akilina motioned to the legs. "Did you try to stop it?"

Xuě snorted a laugh. "Only if we'd wanted to die."

"Yeah. The yeti tore them off and tossed them to us."

"Why?" Chang asked.

Pema rose from where she sat by Choden. "It was a gift. Choden says the wild yeti thought you were offering your kill to them. In return, it thanked you by returning the best and meatiest parts."

Xuě met Bao's gaze. Maybe.

"Wild yeti don't usually take kill from other animals."

Not willing to argue and hungry, Xuě shrugged. "Perhaps we'll hunt in the morning." She glanced at Bao, but he didn't say anything.

"No," Aynur said, "this is enough for now. Is everyone hungry?"

Xuě's stomach gurgled. Everyone laughed.

Aynur's eyes lit with laughter, and he grinned. "I'll take that as a 'shì'. You and Bao should eat first."

Turning away to hide the blush that stained her cheeks, she grabbed her bag, stripped, and shifted.

The scent of the blood excited her cat, but her mind shied away. She should be grateful the yeti hadn't taken it all, that they'd been able to bring something back, that Bao hadn't died in the hunt. And she was, but . . . Maybe tomorrow they'd be able to cook meat and eat as humans. Maybe. She shook the thoughts away, bent down, and ate.

Bao brushed against her, joining her. Jagged streaks of longing sped through her. With her hunger abating, she itched to run her fingers through his hair, touch every part of him, and ensure everything was truly in one piece and whole. Once she determined that, she wanted to show him how much she cared for him.

But night would have to fall for that to happen. Even then, the cold and being surrounded by others limited what they could do.

With the sharp edge of her hunger gone, she stepped away from the haunch to give others their share. Back to the dark corner, she shifted and dressed. She settled on the ground and wrapped her blanket over her shoulders. The light of the day was giving way to the cold, dark blanket of night. It beckoned to her.

Unable to sit still, she crossed to the entrance and stared out as day faded. Only the barest sliver of sunlight crowned the not-so-distant peaks before snuffing out. Stars winked and twinkled.

Bao's scent surrounded her, and his arm settled at her waist. "Are you *xíng*?"

She glanced up at him, his face in the shadows, but not hidden from her cat eyes. "I—I almost lost you out there." She slid her arms around him and held him tightly. "You can't do that again."

He rested his chin on top of her head and inhaled. "I promised I would never leave you. I won't."

"You promise?" Even as she asked the question, she knew such a promise meant nothing.

"How could I leave you now when I've spent my whole life waiting for you?" He nuzzled her ear, his warm breath sending fire through her veins. "But you must promise never to leave me, too."

"Never. I will never leave you, *xīngān*."

He stilled at her words. His arms tightened around her, and he pulled her closer, nipping her ear. A shiver shimmied through her, awakening every part of her body. His hands cupped her breasts, and she pushed back against him, biting her lip to stop the moan that rose in her throat.

"I want you."

Turning in his arms, she drew him to her and kissed him.

Electricity jolted through her as their lips met. His *jī/jī* pressed against the apex of her thighs. She pressed closer, losing herself in his caresses.

# Chapter Thirty-Six

"I heard you say you almost . . . lost Bao?" Zuhre strode beside her at the back of the line the next morning. The sun kissed the horizon a pale pink. A lone bird circled, catching an updraft. "I didn't mean to, but . . . I . . ." Pink tinged her cheeks.

Xuě glanced up the line to where Bao was talking to Akilina. "*Shi.*" They had agreed not to say anything, but Zuhre asked. What could she say?

Zuhre's eyes widened. "How? Was it against the yeti?"

"No. He went over a ledge during the hunt."

The wolf shifter gasped.

Xuě touched her arm. "Please don't say anything. Bao doesn't want the others to know, to worry. He's fine." Her heart stuttered at the memory of his brush with death.

Choden shouted. He'd stopped. Pema stood next to him. Both were staring at the path ahead. Zuhre and Xuě caught up to the front. Red blood dotted the snow. They'd reached the spot where the wild yeti had stolen their kill.

Their guide spoke rapidly to Pema and Aynur.

Bao stepped forward. "This is where we ran into the wild yeti."

"We thought . . ." Pema bit her lip.

"You didn't believe us," Xuě said. "You can see where we stopped dragging it farther up." She pointed where they'd left the bharal and backed away from the yeti.

The others studied the mountains as if searching for the elusive animal.

"It's gone," Bao said. "It ran off down that way." He motioned off to their left.

"Down the hill," Aynur muttered, frowning, "toward the battle site." He said something to Choden. The old man's frown lifted, and he smiled, responding. "Choden was concerned about the wild yeti taking your kill—what that could mean for us, but, now, he understands. He thinks our 'gifts' to them are softening their anger."

Xuě hoped so. The way that yeti had torn the haunches off the bharal and tossed the rest on its shoulder before it ran down the mountain had convinced her that she'd be happy to never encounter another one. Ever.

Choden started up the trail again. Zuhre and Xuě stayed in the back.

"Bao almost died and you met a wild yeti?"

"*Shi.*"

Zuhre shook her head. "That is . . . scary."

"*Shi.*" In her mind's eye, the yeti loomed above them once again. The memory of its thick, shaggy, white coat, long, powerful arms, dark, intelligent eyes, and mouth full of large canines sent a shiver through her.

"I'm sorry we didn't . . . believe you."

Xuě touched her friend's arm and smiled. "It's *xing*. Choden said they didn't do that. I was too tired to argue."

They drew even to where she'd dragged the carcass up onto the track. A long path of dark rust-colored dirt marked the climb out and camouflaged the trail of blood. The snow on the path hadn't. The groups' footprints had obliterated any others.

She zeroed in on the spot where Bao and the sheep had come to rest. A shudder rippled through her, and she closed her eyes for a brief moment. Her breath stuttered in her throat. From this angle, the distance from where they'd leapt off the edge to the bottom looked even farther. Jagged, red cliffs ended in a chute of snow. The chute let out into another shorter cliff, but a boulder split it in half. Thankfully, they'd hit the boulder instead of going over.

"Xuě?"

Zuhre's concerned voice drew her out of her memories. Their gazes met.

"Bao—?" Her gaze followed the rust-colored path. "Down

334

there?"

"*Shi*, down there. The bharal leapt from that ledge. Bao followed it over, and I—" Xuě couldn't finish the sentence. It replayed in her mind, and all of her emotions rushed over her in an avalanche.

She looked away, searching for Bao up ahead, assuring herself he was alive and okay. He passed by it as if nothing had happened yesterday. Was he unaffected?

Breathing deeply, she blinked away the tears that threatened.

"Oh, Xuě." She touched her shoulder. "He is . . . lucky."

Unable to speak past the lump of tears in her throat, Xuě could only nod.

*Shi, he was lucky, but so am I.*

She allowed Zuhre to speak uninterrupted, all of Xuě's words trapped by the near tragedy of yesterday's hunt. It reopened the wounds from her parents' deaths, ones she hadn't finished grieving. Ones she might never finish grieving. He'd woven himself into her life, entangled her wants and needs with his into a tapestry that, without him, would fray and unravel. If Bao died, it'd break her.

Tears slipped down her cheeks. She'd nearly lost him twice, once to the soldier she'd killed, and once to the hunt. Yesterday struck her harder because she'd accepted the depth of her feelings for him.

Or maybe she was fooling herself.

"Xuě." Zuhre's voice coaxed her from her downward spiral. She raised her gaze from the snow covered path to meet Zuhre's. "I know."

Those two words of shared understanding eased the noose of the pain and fear that had gripped her since Bao's fall. She dragged in a deep breath and exhaled. The tension flowed out of her, and her footsteps lightened.

The trail grew steeper. The red rock gave way to dark gray. Even on the highest peaks, the dark gray granite pushed through the snow. The scenery growing more austere and breathtaking the higher they climbed. Wind whipped up around them and the air thinned even more, but Choden's pace never faltered. Xuě required all of her breath just to keep up. The two women fell into a companionable silence. It comforted her. She stole a glance at her friend. Though Bantowa had brought danger, his betrayal had ensured the group stayed together. Now, she'd have a chance to live in a community of not just people, but friends who understood her. A place where she'd be accepted instead of reviled and feared. The possibility floated in front of her like a mirage always out of her grasp.

Around midday, they stopped. Aynur passed a canteen around and some *bakkwa.*

Choden pointed to a mountain in the distance.

Pema's eyes widened. She grinned at the group. "That tall one to the north is Chomolungma, Goddess Mother of the World. She is the tallest mountain of the Himalayas. Many have died trying to reach the top. We won't be going there. We're headed to the south of it. There's a little known pass only animals use. One more night on this side of the mountains. Tomorrow should see us on the other side."

"Is the other side Nepal?" Chang asked. Hope and disbelief rang in her voice.

"*Shi.* We're almost there."

Excitement built and buzzed around Xuě. The news infused her with a zing of energy. Nepal. Another country, a new life, and freedom awaited them. It almost didn't seem possible.

Choden headed up the trail. With Nepal only one more night away, she smiled and stepped into line.

The narrow ravine they'd been traversing for the past hour curved around, and the sheer, high cliffs marching alongside the animal track fell away on either side, opening into a valley. Below them, a sparkling lake nestled in the center. A beautiful jewel tucked away, forever guarded by the giant sentinels that reached their jagged peaks toward the sky.

Xuĕ gasped and stopped next to Pema. All conversation ceased.

Peace blanketed the land. It spread its tendrils up the slopes to where she stood with the others. She closed her eyes for a moment, allowing it to seep into her. Wonder and joy unfurled within her. There was a fullness of spirit she'd experienced only fleetingly in her life. Turning her face to the sky, she basked in the glory of it.

When she opened her eyes, she almost expected the Jade Emperor's heavenly palace to be floating on a cloud above the lake.

Bao's scent wrapped around her. She turned to him and smiled. Their gazes met. He entwined his fingers with hers. She smiled.

"There's a cave on the other side of the lake," Pema said. Her voice drew Xuĕ back to the reality. "We'll stay there tonight."

"Can we go down to the lake and fill up our canteens?" Aynur asked.

Pema passed the question onto Choden. The old man nodded and spoke rapidly in Tibetan.

"*Shi*, but we can't stay here long. We need to get to the cave before the sun goes down. The temperature around the lake drops after sunset."

They picked their way down the slope between a jumble of round, snow-covered rocks of various sizes to the edge of the lake. Erosion had molded them into perfect spheres. The rocks continued into the lake. The water was so clear that, even as it deepened from pale blue to turquoise and gradually to a navy blue when the depth plummeted, the bottom looked within reach.

Zuhre, Nur, and Aynur knelt by the edge and dunked the canteens into the water.

The lake called to her. Oh, if only they had time to bathe. She'd love to get the film of dirt off her skin, but, at this elevation, the water would be frigid. And with snow on the ground

. . . She shivered.

"Are you cold?" Bao asked.

Smiling, she looked up at him. "*Shi*. Just thinking about a bath."

"In that water?" Laughter danced in Bao's eyes.

"It looks inviting, but I'm sure it's cold," she said.

"My fingers are going numb from filling the canteen. I don't recommend it." Aynur lifted the container, took a drink, and passed it to Chang.

Xuě laughed. "It was a thought. Well, a wish, really. I try not to breathe too deeply."

A chuckle rippled through the group. No one had bathed in days. If anyone tracked them now, they'd only have to follow their nose.

"*Shi*, a wish," Zuhre repeated. "I tell you if you . . . touch the," she motioned to the water, "stinky is better." She handed her canteen to Xuě. "Drink?"

Xuě took the canteen. "*Xièxiè.*"

Bone-chilling water burned an icy path down her throat to her stomach. She shivered. No, she wouldn't be bathing today. Perhaps if they had a fire to sit by afterward. Even then, maybe not.

She passed the canteen to Bao. His hand grazed hers, and a zing of awareness rippled through her. She raised her gaze to his. Heat simmered in the silvery depths of his eyes. Memories of their bath in the cave rushed through her. Tingles erupted across her nerve endings. Mesmerized, she licked her suddenly dry lips, and her nipples peaked. His eyes widened, nostrils flaring.

"Are you going to drink or not?" Pema asked.

"*Shi*." Bao raised the canteen to his lips, breaking the spell. He took a few sips and gave it back to Zuhre.

The wolf shifter topped off the canteen and slung it over her shoulder. Amusement lit her eyes.

Embarrassed heat flooded Xuě and chased away any lingering desire.

"It's time to go," Pema said.

"I walk next to Xuě, okay?" Zuhre asked Bao.

He smiled and moved up the line. Xuě watched him long-ingly. Her family had never discussed sex, not openly. She stole a glance at Zuhre. Would she really want to do it where everyone else could hear?

Zuhre touched her arm. "It is *xíng* to—I don't know how to say it—your husband. It is what we are meant to do."

Xuě's cheeks burned even more with her friend's words. She bit her lip. Had anyone heard? But the others appeared deep in conversations.

"I—" What could she say? How should she respond?

"It is good . . . easier when you like your husband."

Xuě looked at her. "I—*shi*."

The other woman smiled. "I—my first husband—he was," the shadow of unhappy memories darkened her eyes, "not nice. It hurt. With Aynur—"

"I don't want to know."

Zuhre's face paled.

"I'm sorry. I—we never spoke of—" Embarrassment si-lenced her.

"I know." Zuhre patted Xuě's arm. Their gazes met briefly before Xuě looked away, her cheeks aflame. "It is okay to want Bao."

"What about how you were raised?"

"It is because of that that I came to see it this way. He lied about me. I didn't," she motioned with her hands, "but my family believed him. Aynur showed me what it was meant to be. No . . ."

"Shame?"

"*Shi*. No shame. I left all that when I left my . . . village. Those looks you and he give each other made me smile."

Xuě averted her eyes. "I don't know if I can do that."

"It's okay. You don't have to, but he's a good man."

Xuě found Bao in line. Laughter lit his face at something Aynur said. "*Shi*, he is."

Zuhre leaned in. "No shame. Fear of what others think about your . . . sex life shouldn't . . . shame you."

"I—*xièxiè*. You're a good friend." Whether Xuě could let that go remained to be seen. She'd learned to hide every emotion, every reaction for fear of ridicule and rejection.

Zuhre smiled, joy shimmering in her eyes. "*You* are a good friend. Now, you show him how much tonight, *shi?*"

Xuě gasped.

Her friend laughed. "And I will show Aynur."

Xuě didn't want to talk about this anymore. Cheeks burning, she closed the distance between them and the other shifters.

"How do you think Nepal will be?" Xuě asked.

"I've heard tigers and leopards live in the jungles of Nepal," Chang said.

Her cat shuddered. She didn't know if she'd survive in a fight with either of those animals. Nor did she want to find out. They didn't live in the Qílián Shān Mountains where she'd grown up and certainly not where she'd hunted. After her encounter with Gang, she'd be happy to never see another one, shifter or otherwise.

"We don't have to live in the jungles," Bao said. "As snow leopards, we'd do better in the higher elevations. We'd be unlikely to run into them there."

Chang looked back at her. "What if the settlement Choden is taking us to is in the jungle? Will you stay?"

"I—" Xuě glanced at Bao.

He shrugged. "It may not be."

Aynur scowled at the bear shifter. "It might not be an issue anyway. If it's full of shifters, that alone will keep the native predators away. We aren't there yet. I know we won't decide whether we'll stay until we see it."

Chang shrugged. "And we might not want to stay there." The way she said it implied Xuě and Bao might not want to.

Xuě studied the bear shifter, but the woman's expression gave nothing away. "Or the others might not want us there."

No one responded, and a pall descended over the group as the silence stretched out. Why had she allowed herself to be goaded by Chang? And what was with the bear shifter anyway? Maybe Huan's death had affected her more than she let on.

Even with the PLA chasing them and all of the loss, Xuě's life had improved since marrying Bao. She had friends now, a good man, and the possibility of freedom.

If only her parents could've been part of it. But they'd never have survived this race across the country—not in the condition they'd been in. Maybe not even if they'd been healthy. It had taxed her, a shifter. But she would've done everything possible to see them live.

She raised her chin. When they stopped running, when they made it to Nepal and started their new life, she'd build an altar to honor her parents. If she and Bao had children—part of her wanted that—to be normal, but part of her feared what their child's life would be like. Whatever it was like, she would teach them to honor the grandparents who'd sacrificed everything for her and Bao.

"I will be glad to see this journey over," Akilina said.

Murmurs of agreement filled the air.

"When I left home, I only sought to get away from the famine, the death. I didn't know about Mao or that the PLA would hunt us." The blonde-haired wolf shifter looked back at Xuě. "I'm grateful Aynur, Zuhre, and Nur found me. All of you have made my loss easier."

Nur reached over and linked his hand with hers. Something passed between them. Xuě glanced away, her cheeks burning, unwilling to intrude on a private moment.

"You see it, too," Zuhre said and motioned toward Nur and Akilina.

"*Shi.*"

"It is good. Nur needs . . . someone. Akilina is strong and . . . smart."

"Do you," Xuě drew in a deep breath before plunging on, "do you still believe in your religion?"

Zuhre eyes widened. "I . . . no." She opened her mouth, but shut it without saying anything.

"What?" Xuě asked

Their gazes connected.

"Do you have a . . . ?"

"Faith?"

Zuhre nodded. "*Shi.*"

"I did, but we haven't worshipped in years. We had to hide our altar. I," Xuě stared at Bao's back unseeing for a moment, "I don't know what I believe anymore." She turned to her friend. "And you?"

"When I became a *láng*, I became a jinn, a . . . I don't know how you say it."

"Spirit?"

"Spirit . . . no. It's a . . ."

"Demon," Bao said.

"That's it. Demon." Zuhre's shoulders dropped. "Only demons can shapeshift. To them, I'm evil, a demon. Even if my . . . no longer husband had never said I'd cheated, once my *láng* came out, my family would've—" She slashed her hands down. She turned her face away from Xuě. "Sometimes, I think they're right."

Xuě gasped. The people of her village had always treated her as separate, but had they viewed her as evil? Her parents hadn't. Shapeshifters in Buddhist tradition could be good or bad and were rarely one or the other. Regular people were capable of being both good and evil, too. But that fact hadn't kept the villagers from fearing her. A shapeshifter could do more damage than a regular person, or so they thought. All one had to do was look at Mao to know that to be false.

"Zuhre, you're not evil. *They* were evil."

"I—" Tears created icy tracks down Zuhre's cheeks.

"When was the last time you turned into a demon?" Xuě asked.

Zuhre's eyes widened. "I—"

"The same number of times I have, or Bao," Xuě motioned to her husband and expanded the gesture to the rest of the group, "or any of us."

The wolf shifter didn't say anything.

"Do you think I'm a demon? That I'm evil?"

Zuhre shook her head. "No."

"Aynur?" Xuě asked.

"No."

"Bao?"

"No." Zuhre's gaze connected with hers, a tremulous smile broke through the tears. "I . . . *xièxiè*. I thought I was done with all of those . . . feelings. Sometimes, I—" She shrugged.

"Me, too." Xuě touched her friend's hand.

Zuhre squeezed it.

Even though Xuě had convinced her friend that religious belief was wrong, her own old doubts and fears rose within her, threatening to smother her newfound confidence.

For Zuhre's insecurities mirrored her own. She glanced at the group that strode ahead of them. Did the other shifters feel the same way? With their backs to her, she couldn't tell. Perhaps she wasn't alone. Perhaps every one of them questioned if they were more beast than human, and wicked because of it. Or was it only the medically created that wondered about this? Did Choden and his village see themselves as evil? Or did they accept who and what they were without question? Perhaps living within a village where everyone shifted prevented such thoughts.

Her *yukihyō* chuffed in protest.

*I'm sorry.*

It twitched its tail. How could she fault it for being upset with her?

Being a shapeshifter didn't make her evil. Evil depended upon much more than that, didn't it? Killing someone for pleasure like Gang . . . that person would be evil. She'd killed more than one person, too, but that had been to survive and no different than anyone else, human or otherwise, would've done. Evil was that cannibal they'd encountered. Or Mao.

Mao.

Anger roared through her, and she clenched her hands at the thought of the Chairman. With all of his laws that had caused the famine and ordering people killed—that was evil.

Surely, that word didn't encompass her just because of her

abilities. The same abilities she'd used to help her village.

No, she wasn't evil. Nor were any of her friends. Everyone had the capacity for it, just as they did for goodness. Shifter, or not, mattered little.

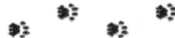

The following morning a few hours after they'd left the cave by the lake, they crested the pass. Choden stopped, bringing the group to a halt. The land of another country unfurled before them.

Nepal.

Far below the gray scree, lush green beckoned. Even amongst the more barren areas, green grass peeked out from under snow and in between the rocks. A river wound its way through the mountains.

They were free.

All the fear and worry of the past several weeks fell away. Excitement warred with trepidation within Xuě as she took in the sight. Her heart pounded, and she couldn't prevent a grin from spreading across her face. Every fiber in her wanted to scream and shout for joy, but snow lay piled high on the mountain above them. The threat of an avalanche was ever present. Instead, she turned to Zuhre and hugged her.

Her friend hesitated before returning the hug and laughing quietly. She released the wolf shifter only to have Bao pull her into his arms.

"We did it," he said.

"We did it," she whispered back.

Elation shining in his eyes, he kissed her. Excitement and joy exploded into passion. It zinged through her, her heartbeat raced as if she chased a *pán yáng*, and she clenched her *bàoyú*, wishing they could celebrate in private.

Now wasn't the time, but soon.

He was panting when he stepped away from her, promises of pleasure swirled in his beautiful silver gaze.

She cupped his cheek. His eyes closed, and he turned his

face into her hand, kissing her palm. Tingles spread up her hand through her arm to the rest of her body.

She smiled.

Stepping away, she turned and faced Nepal, their new home. Bao drew her back against his chest and wrapped his arms around her.

The entire group stared in silence at the land below them. Slowly, the excitement dissipated a bit, and tears pricked her eyes as a riot of emotions surged up and mingled with everything else.

They'd made it. They were safe—all of them, but they'd lost so much in the process . . . their families, their homes, their country. So much gone to gain their freedom.

If only her parents could've shared this moment with them . . .

She blinked away more tears and raised her chin. She still had Bao. The man who'd saved her life in so many ways. The man who held her heart. The man who'd helped her find her courage. She clasped his arms closer to her, leaned back, and kissed his chin.

He looked down at her, his face awash with hope. It seeped into her, chasing the sadness away.

Their future awaited them, and it promised to be more than she ever imagined.

# Chapter Thirty-Seven

"We should be in the village by this evening."

Pema's voice interrupted Xuě's thoughts.

The village. Her chest tightened, and a shiver of anxiety rippled through her.

"It's a shifter village," Bao said, seeming to read her mind.

A shifter village.

She released the breath she'd been unconsciously holding. Yes, she could do this. The journey had changed her, challenged and strengthened her. It had shown her she could overcome almost anything with the right people. Not only had she gained confidence, but she had friends.

Her gaze fell on Zuhre, Pema, and Akilina. All of them so different but friends none the less. But Chang . . . Even after Huan's death, she kept to herself. Perhaps if she made more of an effort. If anyone knew the isolation of loneliness, it was Xuě.

Moving up the line, she drew next to the bear shifter. "*Nǐ hǎo.*"

Chang glanced at her and nodded.

An awkward silence stretched between them.

Xuě opened her mouth but closed it quickly. What should she say?

"Are you looking forward to reaching the village?"

The other woman shrugged.

Xuě frowned. "You aren't excited at all for this to be over?"

Chang flicked a glance at her and nodded, her face an impassive mask.

"I am. I'm looking forward to sleeping in the same place every night and a bath."

The bear shifter shrugged. "I like traveling. It's safer that way, harder for you to be caught."

Her heart skipped a beat. "You think Mao will find us?"

"Maybe." Chang clenched her hand, the only sign of possibly deeper emotions. "A day's journey from the border of Tibet doesn't feel far enough to be safe."

If it were the border of Tibet and China, that'd be different, but the Himalayas stood between the two countries. The trail they'd taken resembled more of a track and sometimes nothing at all. Without Choden, they could've wandered through the mountains for months, maybe years. Combine that with the wild yetis and other dangers, the distance grew much larger.

No. Mao would have to work too hard to capture them. And he'd have to find them. With Bantowa and the rest of his troop dead, the PLA would be lucky to find the yeti shifters. If he'd been able to track the shifters who'd come before them, he'd have found their village by now.

Xuě nearly ran into Aynur, who'd stopped in front of them.

He crossed his arms over his chest. "It's over, Chang."

"It's not over."

Xuě touched the other woman's arm and gasped at the animosity in her eyes. It took her a minute to respond. "*Shi*, it is. We're in Nepal."

An ugly laugh slipped past Chang's lips. "All of you are stupid to believe you can escape Mao." Her lip curled in a snarl. "Do you really think a border can stop him? He'll find us. All of us."

Xuě recoiled, eyes wide. "I—"

"Why are you here? Walking next to me?" Chang snarled.

"I thought," Xuě swallowed, licking her dry lips, "I thought we were friends."

The woman snorted.

"Chang—"

The bear shifter turned and shoved Xuě. She fell against a rock.

"Chang?"

"*Leave me alone.*" She swung at Xuě.

Struggling to breathe through the pain, Xuě flinched, and

her *yukihyō* froze for an instant. Then she leapt to the side, but the blow never connected.

Aynur stood behind Chang, restraining her. "Chang—"

The bear shifter yanked free. A crazed look in her eyes, she bared her teeth at them. "We might make it to the village, we might even live there for a while, but we'll never be free. He'll find us, and, when he does, we'll all be dead." She muttered to herself unintelligibly and pushed past them.

Heart racing, Xuě stared at Chang's back, stunned by her words and actions. Bao's scent swirled around her a second before he slipped an arm around her. Some of the tension tightening her muscles eased, and she relaxed against him.

"She's only saying what the rest of us feel," Pema said. "About Mao." The woman stared at the mountains behind them, fear flickered in her eyes for a second before disappearing. "He won't venture into Nepal, though."

"Get out of my way, old man, or I'll kill you," Chang yelled.

Xuě spun. Everyone froze. What was Chang doing?

The bear shifter towered over Choden, who stood in the middle of the path. She raised her fist when Choden didn't move. Snarling, she swung. He ducked and slapped her. She crashed to the ground and covered her face, her shoulders shaking as sobs wracked her body. Sympathy softened his expression. Pema said something to him in Tibetan. He pointed at Chang.

Pema crouched next to the bear shifter. "What's wrong?"

"Go away. Leave me. I'll only bring trouble."

"You're—"

"No, I'm better off dead." The woman hugged her knees, resting her head on them, and rocked back and forth.

Aynur squatted next to her. "We're not leaving anyone."

Chang raised her head, fear and loathing contorted her features into an ugly mask. "You don't understand. You don't *know* me." She laughed. The pain in that laugh wrapped around Xuě and squeezed, cutting deep. "Huan was my 'brother'. His parents were mine. He told the PLA about me and let me be captured when they came for our parents. They died because of him." She looked up at them unseeing. "They *died* because of him." Her gaze hardened, and she growled. "I would've been an experiment because of him. An experiment." She panted. "We were to marry. I couldn't when he returned. He wasn't the man I knew. The man I'd trusted."

"You *lied* to us," Pema said.

"I know. I thought you'd think I was helping him, and I was ashamed. Ashamed of him, ashamed that I'd fallen for his lies. How could he do it?" She bowed her head. "He told me when he found me after I escaped that he'd changed his mind, that Mao was evil. He wanted us to escape, to be together. It wasn't until Bantowa that I realized he'd lied." Tears streamed down her face. "And I killed him . . . I . . . killed . . . him . . . My brother . . . "

Xuě studied Chang. Could they believe the bear shifter? Had her circumstances really overcome her and she'd gone mad for a moment? Or was she pretending? And what could the bear shifter do now that they'd reached Nepal? Could she lead Mao to them?

Her gaze connected with Bao's. The expression in his eyes echoed the uncertainty surging through Xuě. He shook his head.

"We need to make a decision. Do we abandoned her here? Or do we take her with us?" Aynur asked.

Pema looked up. "If we leave her, she could follow us. If she comes with us, we can watch her."

"We bring her," Xuě said.

Hope shone in Chang's eyes. She looked at Xuě. "I'm sorry. I—I—"

Xuě inclined her head in acceptance of the bear shifter's apology.

Choden said something, and Pema stood.

"Come," Pema held her hand out to Chang and helped her up, "we need to leave if we're to make the village by dark."

Choden turned down the mountain, and everyone fell into line with Chang situated between Aynur and Nur. Xuě hung to the back with Bao, Akilina, and Zuhre.

"What do you think?" Akilina asked.

"I don't know. She lied to us about Huan." Xuě's *yukihyō* chuffed. "I want to trust her, but I can't."

"I don't . . . either." Zuhre touched Akilina's arm and stopped them. "My *láng* says we . . . watch her."

"My cat says the same."

The other three nodded. They would watch and wait. Xuě hoped her instincts were wrong, and Chang wouldn't betray them like Huan did.

The hours passed in a blur. Choden jogged down the mountain as if anxious to reach the village. The *gōnglǐ* sped by. Snow-laden hillsides gave way to grass. Until finally, they reached a narrow ravine, and the path switchbacked down a steep incline. Below them, a river had carved out its own path. It crashed over rocks, spraying water high into the air, its thunderous roar loud even from a distance.

Choden veered off onto a smaller trail, loped down the hill, and headed straight for the river. He stopped in front of a precarious looking rope bridge that appeared more broken than solid, turned to Pema, and the shifters who raced after him, and spoke. She nodded. Without hesitation, he grabbed the rope "rails" and stepped onto the first wood slat. The bridge swung under his weight. He paused, allowing it to settle, before he stepped onto the next wooden slat. It rippled under him, but he continued as if it were solid land.

One by one, the shifters crossed after him until only Bao, Zuhre, and Xuě remained. It was Xuě's turn. She stared wide-eyed at the bridge. Four long ropes spanned the river, two shoulder-height and two supporting wooden steps. At every wooden step, shorter ropes ran from the top ropes to the bottom, securing it. But each piece of wood varied in width with a foot or two between them and an opportunity to fall into the churning water below. Some pieces looked ready to disintegrate.

Xuě's *yukihyō* balked.

She closed her eyes for a moment and gathered herself, calming her cat and the fear that rushed through her.

Raising her head, she gripped the ropes and stepped on the first wooden slat. The bridge undulated. She gasped, her gaze going to the roiling water below. Pulling her focus back, she drew in another deep breath, inched her hands forward, and hopped to the next step. The plank creaked, shooting fear through her, and she jumped to the next one, completely letting go of the rope. It cracked, and she lunged for the rope, catching the top one as the step broke under her. Air met her feet, and she hung by one hand, suspended over a mass of white water.

Her heart hammering in her chest, her cat yowling in terror, she scrambled to find purchase on the bottom rope. It swung back and forth. She held onto it with a death grip.

"Xuě'!"

Bao's terrified yell reached her ears, but she couldn't respond. Her throat had closed up with fear.

Eyes wide, she stared down at the water, struggling to curb her panic.

*Deep breath. Deep breath.*

She couldn't stay here. She looked back the way she'd come. The bank was closer, but she'd still have to cross the river . . . somehow. At the other side, Choden, Pema, Akilina, Chang, Aynur, and Nur waited, worry etched across their features. She had to get to them.

If she inched along the rope, she could make it. It'd take longer, but she didn't trust the wooden planks. She slid first one foot and a hand along the rope and then the other pair, waiting for the bridge to stop rocking before she moved again. When she reached a vertical rope, she placed a hand on the other side of the rope, pushed down a little to stabilize it, and moved her foot around it, slowly allowing her weight to shift to that side.

Despite her care, the bridge undulated from side to side. Her back swung toward the water, and her feet nearly slipped off the rope. She wrapped her arm around the top of the rope and hung on for dear life until it quieted. She repeated the process, each time wondering if the next step would plunge her into the water below and determined to make sure that didn't happen.

By the time she reached the other side, every muscle in her body trembled with fatigue, and she collapsed to the ground.

"Are you *xíng*?" Aynur asked and helped her to sit.

Unable to speak, she nodded, resting her head on her knees, gasping. She was alive. Somehow, she'd survived.

*Bao!* She looked up in time to see him begin navigating the bridge. Her heart in her throat, she held her breath as he maneuvered around the broken step with ease. Unlike her, he returned to the wooden planks and crossed without incident. Zuhre quickly followed him.

Shame rose in her. She was a coward, and her fear cost them time. Just when she thought she was overcoming her fears and moving forward, she discovered she was wrong.

Tears pricked at the corner of her eyes, but she swallowed them. Tears didn't solve anything. They didn't have time for tears. They'd only prove how weak she was.

"That was very . . . how do you say . . ."

Zuhre's voice drew her out of her spiraling dark thoughts.

"Cowardly?" Xuě said.

"No." Zuhre grabbed her arm and squeezed lightly until Xuě met her gaze. "No." She turned to Aynur and spoke in Uyghur.

"Brave," Aynur said. "That was very brave."

"*Shi*. Brave. You could've died. You're not a . . ." The wolf shifter paused again, the expression in her eyes fierce.

"Coward," Bao said and crouched next to Xuě. "You're not a coward, Xuě."

Xuě shook her head. A brave person wouldn't have clung to the rope, but would've returned to the steps.

Bao pulled her to him and kissed the top of her head. "A coward would've returned to the other side or stayed where you were, paralyzed. You pushed on, despite what had happened." He lifted her chin and stared into her eyes. "You are very brave. You amaze me."

Embarrassed heat flushed her cheeks, and she stared at her clasped hands in her lap.

"Come," Aynur said. "We need to leave." He gazed at her in concern. "Are you ready?"

"*Shi*." She wasn't, but she wouldn't slow them down any more than she already had.

"Are you sure?" Bao whispered in her ear.

She smiled at him and lied, "*Shi*."

Her husband stood and offered her his hand. She took it and let him pull her up.

Glancing around the group, she flushed. Everyone stared at her.

"What is everyone waiting for?" Xuě asked.

Zuhre shook her head, admiration lighting her eyes. Xuě bent her head and took a deep breath. Perhaps she'd been too hard on herself. Her cat chuffed. Raising her head, she straightened her shoulders, and her gaze met Choden's. He studied her, then nodded. Without a word, he turned and strode up the hill, his pace slower than before, if still *gōnglǐ* eating.

Choden crested a hill and halted. He spoke to Pema. Ahead of them, light pierced the darkness, glowing in welcome from the stone huts. Sheep bleated restlessly, and a yak or two grunted. Smoke wafted from several chimneys. Grass surrounded them as far as the eye could see and shimmered silver in the starlight.

He stood quietly as if waiting for something. Then, a shadow rose from the ground and approached them. A man.

Xuě lifted her head and breathed deeply. A cat shifter of some sort, although not snow leopard nor a regular leopard. She couldn't place the scent. As he approached, Bao stepped forward.

"Fu?" Bao asked.

The man's eyes widened. "Bao?"

"*Shi.*"

They bowed.

Fu grinned. "It has been a long time."

"*Shi.* You made it out of the monastery."

Fu bowed his head, a shadow of sadness drifted across his face. "I barely escaped the PLA."

Bao's shoulders drooped. "And the monastery?"

"I—" Fu shook his head, "I don't know. They came in the night. The monks rushed the remaining shifters out." He glanced down at his hands. "I—"

"It was as the monks wanted," Bao said.

"*Shi*, but—" His golden cat eyes glimmered in the darkness, and he drew in a deep breath, looking around the group. "Are these friends?"

Bao nodded. "*Shi.* And my wife." He drew Xuě to his side. "Xuě, this is Fu. We slept next to each other for the two years I lived at the monastery. He was my best friend. I never thought to see him again." He smiled down at her before meeting Fu's gaze. "Fu, my wife Xuě. She is the one."

A smile lit the man's face. "You found her."

"I did." Bao squeezed her shoulders.

"That's wonderful. I have much to tell you, too." He broke off and studied the group, his gaze stopping briefly at Chang. Fu cocked his head, as if trying to place the bear shifter. But the moment passed. He nodded at Choden, flicking his tongue out in greeting, before turning back to Bao. "You're welcome to stay and make this your home." He gestured toward the other shifters. "All of you. We don't have much . . . yet. A flock of sheep, but we will share what we have."

"We thank you," Bao said. "We won't be a burden."

"I know. Come join us for a meal. We've been expecting you."

Fu spun and trotted down the hill. They followed him in silence. Xuě's muscles burned as the cat shifter jogged up the hill and she tried to keep up. When she thought her legs would refuse to move anymore, he stopped in front of some stone houses. Built into the hillside and facing south, they resembled the yeti village. A few were two stories.

As they approached, doors opened, and people came out. One woman held an infant on her hip, its head resting on her shoulder. It blinked sleepy eyes at them and rubbed one before sticking a hand in its mouth.

Startled, Xuě glanced at Bao.

"Come, let's get everyone situated. If you don't mind splitting up?" Fu said.

A murmur of ascent rose from the tired shifters.

"Good. Do you have a leader?" the cat shifter asked.

"*Shi*," Aynur said. "Pema is our leader."

Pema lifted her chin, her gaze meeting Aynur's, and stepped forward.

"Let's get this done quickly so we can eat and go to bed. It has been a long night waiting for you to arrive," Fu said. "If you don't mind, I'd like Bao and his wife to stay with us."

Pema nodded.

He said something in Tibetan to their guide.

The yeti shifter grinned, then frowned and spoke quickly to Fu. Fu narrowed his eyes at Chang and grimaced. He motioned to two large men who towered over everyone else. They stepped forward, one as fair as Akilina, the other with long, black hair and a swarthy complexion.

"Alexei and Batbayar, Chang will stay with you, but keep a watch on her."

"We will," the darker one said.

The bear shifter's eyes widened, and she paled, but she didn't say anything.

"What is going on?" Aynur asked.

"What do you know of this woman?" Fu replied.

Aynur frowned. "We found her wandering the Qaidam Basin with another shifter. They were looking to escape Mao as well, or so they said. One turned out to be a spy."

"Her partner," Fu said.

"Partner?" Pema looked from Fu to Chang.

"*Shi*. This shifter came to the monastery with a man, also a shifter. They pretended to be fleeing from Mao. One night, they disappeared. A few days later, a PLA troop came to our doorstep demanding all of the shifters be turned over. The monks denied we existed, but she," Fu pointed at Chang, "told the soldiers they were lying. I wasn't sure if it was her, but after what Choden told me, I am."

Chang shook her head, her eyes wide, backing away. "You don't understand. I had no choice. I—"

The fairer of the two lunged for her.

Chang leapt back, glanced wildly around her, and spun, sprinting away. Light flashed, and the retort of a gun echoed in the air. The bear shifter stumbled and fell. She tried to stand, but collapsed. The baby wailed. Its mother soothed it until the cries became hiccups.

Aynur walked over to Chang and flipped her over. The shifters gathered around. Blood trickled from Chang's mouth. She glared at them.

Xuě's heart plummeted. The bear shifter was a traitor. She'd been lying the entire time, and she even killed her partner? Brother? Husband? And how had Akilina seen her in the cage? Was it even the same shifter?

"Why?" Pema asked.

The other woman sneered, a fanatical light in her eyes. "You think I'm the traitor." She laughed and coughed. More blood dribbled down her cheek. "But Mao is our supreme leader, and he will find you. You'll serve the Republic as you were meant to." She coughed again, her eyes widening as she gasped. Death sat on her shoulder. Xuě had seen it many times. "Just kill me."

Aynur raised the rifle and cocked it.

Pema pushed the muzzled to the ground and looked at Chang, her face impassive. "You aren't worth the bullet."

Chang snarled, but respect gleamed in her eyes. "You're the only one . . ." she panted, "worthy . . . of Mao's army."

A gurgling sound rose in Chang's throat, and blood gushed out of her mouth. Her death rattle hovered in the air, and she went limp. Her eyes stared sightlessly at the sky.

Silence held the group hostage for a moment.

Xuě leaned against her husband and shivered. He wrapped his arm around her and kissed her temple. Relief and sadness flowed through her. They no longer had to worry about Chang, but she mourned another death.

So much death.

"We'll take care of her, Fu, say the necessary prayers," the large, swarthy shifter said.

"*Xièxiè*, Batbayar." With a haunted expression, Fu said, "Let us go inside."

The group wandered back to the houses.

"It's for the best. We are safe now."

Pema's voice broke the hushed stillness.

Safe. One could hope they were safe.

"Come," Fu said. "Let me introduce you to my family." He drew the woman with the baby in her arms to his side. "Bao, Xuě, this is my wife Zhào Mei and our son Zhào Kai. Mei, this is my friend Kwan Bao and his wife Xuě."

Mei bowed and smiled shyly. "It's nice to meet you."

Xuě gasped. "Your son?"

Fu grinned proudly and led them into his house. "*Shi*."

"And you're shifters?" Her brain struggled to wrap around the possibilities of children with Bao.

"*Shi*," Fu said.

Xuě met Bao's gaze and put her hand on her stomach. Hope unfurled within her. An answering echo of it shone in Bao's eyes. Could they have children? Would they?

She glanced up at Bao. He smiled, and joy ricocheted through her.

Freedom, a husband, children, friends, acceptance. She'd never dreamed this for her life, she'd only ever thought to survive, but this? This she would grab with two hands and hold on as tight as she could.

# Note from the Author

Three years ago, when my muse first poked me and said, "Hey, you need to write a book about medically created shapeshifters set in China in the early 1960s," I was excited but a bit intimidated. My knowledge of China during this time was minimal, and the research it would require loomed like the fascinating rabbit hole it turned into. I didn't know about the Great Famine or the Uyghur, that the US was supplying the Tibetan Resistance with weapons for a while (and sadly stopped), the closure of the Nathula Pass between India and China, Unit 731, and so much more that never made it into the book. I knew very little about the Cultural Revolution (and still feel like my knowledge of it is slim because there's so *much* to know) and snow leopards (other than how beautiful they are).

It was a steep learning curve, almost overwhelming, and not particularly easy to research either when you're searching for the truth and not the party line and the animal you've chosen is so reclusive. While I've taken liberties with some of it for the sake of the story (shapeshifters, children not going to state schools, etc.), the Great Famine, the Cultural Revolution, Unit 731, the Tibetan Resistance . . . all of this happened. Yes, the Japanese doctors really did call their "patients" *maruta*.

I hope I've done it justice and my respect for the peoples and their cultures shines through the story and the characters.

I've included a short list of some excellent resources about this time, the places, the culture (many of which you can find in your library or online).

# Resource List

## Books:

*Tombstone: The Great Chinese Famine 1958-1962* by Yang
*The Dalai Lama: My Tibet* by Rowell
*Cambridge Illustrated Hist. of China* by Ebrey
*Nepal in Pictures* by Zuchora-Walske
*Cultures and Customs of China* by Gun
*The Party* by McGregor
*People's Republic of China* by Mara
*Cloud-Dwellers of the Himalayas* by Chorlton
*The Cultural Revolution* by Langley
*Culture Atlas of China* by Blunden and Elvin
*Unit 731 : Japan's secret biological warfare in World War II 1st American ed.* by Williams

## Websites:

Uyghur: http://factsanddetails.com/china/cat5/sub89/entry-4408.html#chapter-2
Turkish married name laws—http://www.hurriyetdailynews.com/ruling-allows-turkish-women-to-keep-maiden-name-after-marrying-95698

Sikkim names: https://en.wikipedia.org/wiki/Indian_family_names

Himalaya weather: https://www.himalayanwonders.com/blog/weather-climate-himalayas.html

China's takeover of Tibet —Tibetan history: http://factsanddetails.com/china/cat6/sub32/item228.html

Tibetan yurts: http://kekexili.typepad.com/life_on_the_tibetan_plate/2010/01/tibetan-nomads.html

Sutra streamers: http://chinatibet.people.com.cn/8333353.html

http://www.tibetculturetour.com/tibetan-culture/religious-practice.html

Eighteen Layers of Chinese Hell: https://china-underground.com/2011/04/27/the-eighteen-layers-of-chinese-hell/

Ghosts in China: https://www.ancient.eu/article/892/ghosts-in-ancient-china/

Lhasa: https://www.britannica.com/place/Lhasa-China

Sikkim: https://www.britannica.com/place/Sikkim

Chinese customs/beliefs: https://ninchanese.com/blog/2016/03/10/chinese-customs-beliefs/

Clothing in China during Cultural Revolution: https://chineseposters.net/themes/women-warriors.php

Tibetan Nomadic tents: https://www.tibettravel.org/tibetan-people/tibetan-nomadic-tents.html

Tibetan rugs: https://en.wikipedia.org/wiki/Tibetan_rug

Sherpas: https://www.everyculture.com/wc/Mauritania-to-Nigeria/Sherpas.html

Himalayan Tibetan homes: http://factsanddetails.com/china/cat6/sub35/item213.html

Tibetan translator: https://www.freelang.net/online/tibetan.php?lg=gb

Tibetan phrases: https://www.omniglot.com/language/phrases/tibetan.php

Tibetan settlements in Nepal: http://centraltibetanreliefcommittee.org/doh/tibetan-settlements.html

If you're interested in information on Unit 731, there are numerous YouTube videos. But, I warn you, this is not for the faint of heart or someone with a queasy stomach. The atrocities humans commit on one another are always horrifying. These were particularly so.